FACE THE NIGHT

a novel

ALAN LASTUFKA

SHORTWAVE MEDIA

Oregon

Cover design and interior design by Alan Lastufka.
Cover illustration by Eight Little Pages.

First Edition published March 2022.

10 9 8 7 6 5 4 3 2 1

Library of Congress Control Number: 2021919002

Names: Lastufka, Alan, 1983— author.
Title: Face the Night : a novel / Alan Lastufka.
Description: First Shortwave Media hardcover edition.
Oregon : Shortwave Media, 2022
Identifiers: LCCN 2021919002 | ISBN 9781733691925 (hardcover)
ISBN 9781733691932 (softcover) | ISBN: 9781733691949 (ebook)

ISBN 978-1-7336919-2-5

For Mom and Dad, my first readers.

FACE THE NIGHT

CELLAR, OHIO

APRIL 1987

1

ADRIANA MENTALLY TICKED off all the things she'd let herself forget over the last three years. Like the way his lips held a cigarette, limp, until he laughed and it shot straight up, threatening to burn his cheek. Or his dirty crew socks, always frayed around his long second toe. Or just how much he bled when she stuck him.

The tattoo machine buzzed in her right hand while she wiped the blood from Eric's arm with the oven towel in her left. When it was new, the towel was bright with *Once Upon a Time* embroidered in fancy script above a sunshine-yellow momma duck and her ducklings. But the years had eaten away at the lettering, so it now read *O ce pon Tim* .

Adriana desperately wanted to live in one of those *O ce pon Tim* stories. She slung the towel back over her shoulder and glanced at her crowded kitchen and living room. Eric's friends had taken over the whole place tonight. She suppressed a sigh, loosened her clenched jaw, and got back to work on his arm.

The laughing, rotting skull tattoo she'd sketched for him wouldn't have been her first choice. It had been years since she'd last inked Eric, but tonight they fell back into the familiar routine the way once- or twice-upon-a-time couples often do. Regression was quick and easy.

"How much longer?" he said.

"Just sit still."

She focused on outlining the little strips of torn flesh that hung over the skull's empty eye sockets, ignoring how Eric leered down her tank top whenever she leaned forward to work.

At the fridge, Gabe asked, "Got any more beer?"

Adriana shrugged. "I guess. Help yourself."

"Huh?" Gabe was swaying. Most of Eric's old friends were over the limit already. She'd lost touch with a lot of them over the last few years, but she had hoped some would've grown up by now.

Adriana repeated herself louder, but in a nicer tone, over the buzz of the tattoo machine and the stereo in the living room. Gabe nodded his thanks as he rejoined half a dozen Robert Smith looka-likes dancing around the stereo and singing in spurts to *The Face in the Window*, the new Vestibule album. Vestibule was supposed to be the next Cure, only out of Wisconsin instead of West Sussex. They certainly warmed the black hearts of tonight's crowd.

"Oh, is there more beer?"

Some girl Adriana didn't know poked her head into the kitchen. She'd tagged along with Ian, maybe? Adriana couldn't remember, nor did she care. Everyone Ian dated looked the same—black hair, black eyeliner, black nail polish. The aforementioned black heart.

"In the fridge," Adriana said.

Eric had only been back in town a few days and already her house was being trashed and her refrigerator emptied. If she hadn't needed Eric so badly for tomorrow, Adriana would have kicked him and his mooching stoner friends out hours ago.

"I like your house," the girl said as she walked through the kitchen to the fridge.

"It's a piece of shit," Adriana said. She gestured to the card table standing in for a proper dining table set, the mismatched cups and bowls piled up around the sink, and the rusted screen door open to the dark backyard. She did her best with what she had, but the house hadn't seen any real maintenance in almost two decades.

"No, it's cool. I love the funky wallpaper." She glanced at the orange-and-yellow paper covering the walls: illustrated spatulas, mixing bowls, egg cartons, and other kitchen essentials.

"You don't have to be kind. It's not mine; it's my father's."

"Really?! See, I knew Ian was lying," the girl said and grabbed a beer from the fridge.

"Lying about what?" Adriana asked. She turned off the tattoo machine.

"He said your dad's the mayor. But no way does the mayor, even here in little old Cellar, own a place like this. No offense. I just mean—"

"It's okay. I get it. But Ian didn't lie. My dad is the mayor. He inherited this house a long time ago, and now I get to live here."

"Mr. Mayor is the piece of shit, not this house," Eric said, sneering. He leaned back, flicked his cigarette, and then brushed away whatever ashes didn't land in his empty longneck beer bottle. His mood improved after he twisted his arm for a better look at the new tattoo.

"This is awesome. It's exactly what I pictured in my head. I don't know how you do that."

Ian's new lady friend was impressed too. "Wow. That is scary good. Like something you'd see on a Wes Craven movie poster."

"Thanks." Adriana turned. "What's your name again?"

"Samantha," she said. She blew her long dark hair out of her pale face.

"Samantha, I appreciate it. Now, if I could only get paid to ink people all day. Then I wouldn't have to live in this dump with the *funky* wallpaper. Or deal with all the crap Mr. Mayor gives me about growing up and being responsible."

Samantha laughed. Adriana smiled, with effort, as she eyed Eric. In that instant she saw everything that he was not: stable, smart, fatherly, off the junk.

"Your dad doesn't know jack," he said, watching Samantha as she sauntered back to the living room dance floor. "You're a kick-ass mom, and Dylan is a rad little dude." He leaned forward and whispered, "I know I haven't sent as much from Cleveland as I said I would. You know, for Dylan or whatever. And I know you're not working right now, but you're getting food stamps, right? You two are okay?"

"I do what I can," she said. "But it sucks doing it alone."

He winced. "I know, I know."

"No, you don't!" Adriana snapped, surprising herself. She didn't want to start a fight, not in front of all his friends, and especially not before tomorrow, but some things she just couldn't let go. Her mind picked up where her voice left off.

You don't know about eating cheese sandwiches four days in a row because that's all the budget allows. You don't know about Goodwill baby clothes so stained and dingy from their previous owners that I sometimes spill a little of Dylan's juice on them first, just so I can pretend all the stains are his. You don't know about skipping dinner at the end of the month so Dylan doesn't have to. You aren't here, fucker! So don't tell me "I know!"

It all hit her hard. But she stayed quiet. She was outnumbered and couldn't afford to piss off Eric before tomorrow.

Dylan wandered into the kitchen on his hands and knees, pushing a Hot Wheels ambulance across the linoleum floor.

Adriana looked at her son with concern. Her baby was growing up so fast. His blond hair seemed to be getting darker by the day. His wide brown eyes always gulping in the world around him. He didn't deserve this chaos.

She softened her voice when she spoke again to Eric.

"Look. Thanks for coming back and everything. But tomorrow in court we all have to look like one happy and sane family. Mommy, Daddy, and child. Can you do that for me?"

Her question was drowned out by a vocal surge from the living room. Adriana glanced over as everyone sang along with the Vestibule record. *"Help me to see in the dark, to build a fire from a*

4

spark..."

When she turned back to Eric, he was standing by the open refrigerator, holding his empty beer bottle upside down.

"If you want more," she said, "then go get more."

He smirked. "I can't drive after major surgery. Girl, my arm is *killing* me."

Adriana was not amused. "And you're drunk."

"Hey, will it be a problem tomorrow if I'm arrested for a DUI tonight?" Eric chuckled.

She stood and grabbed her purse off the back of her chair.

"You're taking Dylan, right?" Eric said as he turned to his son. "Little dude, you wanna go to the store with Mommy?"

Eric lifted the boy and handed him to Adriana, who couldn't resist the baby face but glared at the skull-faced father.

"Chill."

"Don't tell me to chill." Adriana took Dylan.

"I'm just saying, don't let your dad get to you. He likes being a dickhead."

"It is his default setting." Adriana agreed. "Anyway, I think Dylan and I will walk. It's only a few blocks." *I could use a break from these people.* "And the weather's nice."

"Oh, that reminds me: WCLR!"

He said the radio station's call letters with such conviction that she jumped. "What about it?"

"Killswitch Kevin. 88.7. I miss him. I really do. The station doesn't reach Cleveland. But that dude is, like..."

"Eric. Focus."

"...a prophet. April showers. 'Adios, muchachos!' He said so this morning. It'll be sunny the next two days. That's gotta be a good sign. Smooth sailing or something."

Rain or shine, it wouldn't matter at tomorrow's court hearing. She appreciated that Eric was an optimistic drunk but didn't think Killswitch Kevin's weather report could help her tomorrow. Nothing else had been "smooth sailing" over the past two weeks.

Thursday the 16th, two weeks ago, was the day that capsized

everything. It didn't start differently than any other, no warnings or talismans, just a trip to the mailbox. Adriana had finally gotten around to emptying the old iron box perched at the top of a pole by the curb. It was the third week of April, which meant a new issue of *Punk World* should be waiting for her, and there it was, folded in half to make room for something else, something that was much heavier. An overstuffed manila envelope was postmarked with the familiar wheat-sheaf processing seal of the local post office, and the return address had made her knees knock: *Cellar Municipal Court.*

In the empty kitchen, she had tossed the envelope onto the card table, where it landed with a thump. She winced and hoped the noise wouldn't wake Dylan from his nap in the next room.

The package was too large for a jury duty summons. It was thick and far more imposing than the *Punk World* issue, wherein the alcohol-soaked anarchists relived their wild touring days or rattled off their shallow political diatribes. She'd heard enough politicking from her father to last two or three lifetimes, so she barely skimmed that section of the magazine anymore.

But thinking of her father, maybe he'd updated his living will again and sent a copy from work, on the taxpayers' dollar, of course, to remind her of all the assets he'd leave to the local Boys' Club and Cellar school district and all the nothing he'd leave her. That was something he would do. She tore the envelope open—

COMPLAINT TO ESTABLISH CUSTODY

Adriana sank against the card table. Her father, the Honorable Bradley R. Krause, Mayor of Cellar, Ohio, Plaintiff, and Default Dickhead, was seeking custody of Dylan Thomas Krause.

After reading the entire complaint twice and still only really understanding half of it, she sat, papers rolled up in her hands, holding the literal weight of it all. She stared at the phone on the kitchen wall. She may not have understood every section and subsection, but she knew that if she wanted to have a shot in hell at keeping Dylan, she'd need Daddy Eric in court with her.

6

She couldn't face her father alone. Worse than alone: he'd have one of his buddy judges preside. It would be two against one unless Eric showed up to even out the fight. Eric, who'd taken off before Dylan was born. Who she hadn't spoken to in years.

Dammit, call him.

I won't call him.

Adriana didn't want to take care of two kids. She had her hands full enough with Dylan. But a broke single mother going up against the town's beloved mayor alone?

The battle in her head had continued for hours. She imagined calling and unloading on Eric, guilt-tripping him to come back. Or sharing a little about Dylan, how he enjoyed drawing too. Or just straight out asking for some goddamn money. No, not that, but maybe inviting him back from Cleveland for a night or long week-end. Or threatening to mail him a garbage bag full of receipts and invoices from the last few years. She didn't actually have all that paperwork, though it would have easily filled *two* big black garbage bags. *Call him.*

Would he even recognize her voice?

She glanced down at the papers again.

COMPLAINT TO ESTABLISH CUSTODY

She picked up the receiver and dialed.

Now Eric was sitting there in her kitchen at the card table, getting inked, getting drunk, and sending her out on a beer run.

Adriana shuffled Dylan from her right arm to her left and gave him his pacifier. He celebrated his third birthday last month but still found comfort with it. Adriana didn't see the harm. The walk to Glendale's Grocery would be short, but he was already tired. As she reached the end of their front yard walkway, she looked back at the small house shrouded in darkness. The living room window was faintly lit; the dancing shadows inside looked like a congregation of ghosts. Through the window she saw Eric's ghost approach Saman-tha's, her raised pale arms drape over his shoulders; two drunken strangers who would try to see in the dark, try to build a fire from that spark, or whatever Vestibule sang earlier.

Until the morning after, anyway.

2

If Adriana had any idea what kind of trouble was headed her way, she would've made Eric get his own damn beer.

Dylan tried his best to hop through the automatic doors as they entered Glendale Grocery in a single leap. But he came up short, stubbed the toe of his little tennis shoe on the welcome mat, and fell hard to his knees. The fall scuffed up his jeans. Not the best way to end their walk, but Adriana scooped him up and was relieved he wasn't bleeding. Or crying.

Inside the store, they were greeted by the familiar smells of the bakery and produce sections and a familiar voice. Killswitch Kevin's evening show on WCLR echoed around the metal rafters and fluorescent lights. "Listen up, kiddies, here's a new one from our favorite Synthpop strangers from the UK. Yeah, I'm talkin' Depeche Mode, and this one's called 'Strangelove.'"

Adriana grabbed a bagel from the bakery to eat while they shopped, since she had skipped dinner while sketching Eric's tattoo. She tore off a bite for Dylan as they headed for the beer cooler. She snagged a six-pack of the cheapest no-name-brand beer the store carried, then started back toward the registers.

"Mommy, look." Dylan swung his arm at an aisle end-cap display of new Transformer toys and started squirming. Adriana let him down, and he raced to the lowest shelf, the one that held the larger models. He attempted to pick up a box that was almost half his size.

"Mommy, can I have this one?" He teetered as he held up some figure called Shockwave. It looked like an expensive ray gun. Adriana took the box and saw the price tag. For $24.99 she could buy a couple cases of beer and have enough left over for lunch at Cody's Diner tomorrow. *How do they get away with charging that much for some plastic?*

"No, honey, we didn't come for toys tonight."

Dylan scrunched his face. The tears she was spared at the automatic doors looked ready to flow now.

Adriana set the box back on the shelf. The heartbreak tasted sour in her mouth. She calculated the math one more time in her head: *If I skip the six-pack—no one else chipped in—and grab the ten bucks from my End of the World emergency envelope... Shit. Still not enough.*

"Maybe we can get some candy from over here instead."

Dylan looked back at the Transformers for a minute, then slowly made his way toward the candy aisle, stopping to peer at some Hot Wheels that hung on a display. He pointed, excited to see the same ambulance he had at home.

"Look, Mommy!"

"Yup. It's just like yours."

Adriana strolled down the aisle to pick out a few snacks. She found Butterfingers, Eric's favorite, or at least it used to be. *Is it still?* And Skittles, Dylan's favorite. She squatted to grab a pack as Dylan tugged at her shoulder bag, clearly over the shopping excursion.

"I know, buddy. You're ready to go home, huh?"

"Yes," Dylan said.

At the register, Adriana counted the money in her wallet twice while juggling her purse and groceries. She scolded herself for wolfing down the bagel. *I could have bought a whole loaf of bread for the same price. And we have snacks at home. Maybe I should put the candy back? No. Yes. No, I already promised Dylan.*

Sometimes she thought her father might be right. Maybe Dylan would be better off with him. She may have run from his house, and rules, the day she turned eighteen, but she'd never gone hungry or wanted for anything, really. Mayor Krause had never been handcuffed by bagel-or-bread debates.

She put a stop to those crazy thoughts. *You'll just have to do better and be smarter, more careful.* Dad's low-rent house and the tattoo work she did on the side were enough to get by on. She just hadn't been pushing herself. When one of her old high school classmates called out of the blue last month and wanted her to ink him again, she'd turned him down. *Why?*

Was I too tired? Was the design too large for the lousy pay? Lousy or not, you can't turn down work anymore, Addie!

Be better.

Be smarter.

Stop fucking up!

"Have a nice night," the cashier said, and handed Adriana her change. She didn't even remember paying, she'd been so lost in her own head.

"Thanks."

She took Dylan's hand and headed for the automatic doors. "No jumping this time, buddy." She felt an odd relief when the whooshing exit opened on the expansive dark carpet of the asphalt parking lot. A lopsided moon hung overhead and a gentle breeze carried a hint of summer's upcoming warmth. *This life could be a good one*, she thought. *I have a little boy who loves me. I have my drawing. And when I really needed him, Eric was there for me. It really isn't—*

"Excuse me, ma'am." A low voice from behind her.

She didn't need some creep to give her hell right now. Not tonight. She ignored him, tightened her grip around Dylan's tiny hand, and picked up her pace. Then the voice turned tough.

"Ma'am, stop, please!"

When she turned, a heavy-set man in a dark blue security vest waved her back into the grocery store.

"Me?" Adriana said.

"Yes. Could you step back in, please?"

"Home, Mommy!"

"Soon, baby, soon."

In the store again, Adriana asked, "What's going on?"

"Right over here, please."

She followed the security guard into a small room near the entrance that housed a table and a bank of video surveillance monitors. The heat radiating off the buzzing electronics was suffocating. Her mouth had gone bone dry.

Most of the monitors were trained on the exits, the liquor department, and the cash registers. But one camera, focused on the candy aisle, wasn't monitoring in real time. Instead, the image was paused on a grainy black-and-white frame starring Adriana and Dylan. The fuzzy black-and-white Dylan was sticking a Hot Wheels box into Adriana's shoulder bag while she reached for a pack of Skittles.

She looked down at her bag. How had she not felt it? *Wait,* she had, but she thought he was tugging at her because he wanted to go.

Above the glowing monitors, she noticed rows of Polaroids. One photo showed a young boy, maybe twelve, holding a two-liter bottle of Coca-Cola. A balding woman, smiling widely, grappled with a heap of sirloin steaks. A high school cheerleader, frozen in time, pulled mascara and lipstick from her V-neck sweater. Each photo included a name and date scrawled in thick black ink. Banned, all of them, for life, according to the Sharpie on each photo.

Adriana reached into her bag and pulled out the Hot Wheels package. *Be better. Be smarter. So much for not fucking up.*

Ambushed by a camera flash, Adriana looked up as the security guard removed the Polaroid and shook it so the colors would dry.

"Ma'am, please wait here. The police have been contacted."

3

"How could you not know you were shoplifting?"

Officer Matthew Hinkley barely glanced up from his desk.

"I didn't know Dylan put the toy in there."

Adriana was tired of explaining this. What was so hard to understand? She replayed the scene over and over in her head. Had she known? *No.* She had felt Dylan tug on her bag, yes. But he had just wanted to go home.

Officer Hinkley, who was not much older than her, scratched his notes on some official-looking questionnaire while she glanced around the police station. Everything looked so normal and yet so out of place. Bulky black phones sat on every desk. Three small radios, just like the one on her kitchen table at home, murmured quietly. Someone was microwaving popcorn in the breakroom. The smell made her hungry again.

The six-pack of beer was sweating and soaking through the paper bag on Officer Hinkley's desk. Adriana was sweating too, right through her T-shirt underneath her hoodie. But innocent people don't sweat. *So why am I drenched?*

Dylan squirmed on her lap. "Mommy, car." He reached for the stolen Hot Wheels on Officer Hinkley's desk.

"Not right now, honey." Adriana shifted Dylan's weight from one leg to the other and looked at the clock on the station's wall. It was an hour past his bedtime, and she knew it would be difficult to wake him for court tomorrow. *Shit, court! Hey, Judge, sorry the kid's so cranky, the police kept us up late after I was arrested. Mother of the Year here, ladies and gentlemen.*

Officer Hinkley grabbed the toy Corvette, inspected it again, then put it aside, finally looking up from his papers.

"Do you shop at Glendale's often?"

"Yes, it's close to my house. Well, my father's house. He lets me stay there and…"

"Have you ever been caught shoplifting before?"

Adriana paused. She noticed he didn't ask if she had ever shoplifted before, only if she'd ever been caught.

"No."

"I know Paul Glendale. He's a bit of a pain when it comes to his store's zero-tolerance policies, but he's not a liar."

"I saw the videotape. I know what it looks like," Adriana said, "but…"

"Your son put the toy in your bag."

"Yes. But…all this fuss for a Hot Wheels? He's just a kid. He doesn't know any better."

"So he just happened to…"

"Well, I certainly didn't tell him to. I may be broke, but I'm not a thief!"

Adriana caught the glance of a few other officers.

Dylan reached for a pen on Officer Hinkley's desk.

"No. No, honey." Adriana pulled him back. The desk was littered in pens and pencils, Styrofoam cups stained with coffee rings that looked older than Hinkley did, and folders of varying colors in three messy stacks. She feared removing a single pen would trigger an avalanche of papers and garbage.

Hinkley looked at her the way everyone looked at her. Bad mom. Bad daughter. Bad seed.

He grabbed a handful of markers and a few sheets of loose paper from his desk drawer and fanned them out in front of Dylan.

"Hey, little guy, can you draw me a car? Just don't put any of those markers in your mommy's bag, okay?"

The comment felt like a dagger plunged between her ribs. Tears welled in Adriana's eyes.

Hinkley look confused. "Hey, I was kidding."

"I know, it's just…" She didn't want to break down, not here, not now. But the dam broke anyway, and she gushed. "My father's suing me for custody of Dylan. My loser ex is back in town staying with me while we deal with all of that. Dylan and I wouldn't have even been in the store tonight except my ex invited a bunch of his friends over and they needed more beer. I've been looking for work for months and haven't had a good night's sleep since…" She inhaled a shaky breath. "And now this—the last goddamned thing I needed before court tomorrow. I can't lose my son. I just can't. He's my world!"

Dylan looked up from his art project, grabbed a second marker, and offered it to his mom, who was now full-on sobbing.

"I swear I didn't know the toy was in my bag. You have to believe me. I'll lose Dylan for sure tomorrow. My father's got plenty of ammunition already."

Hinkley glanced around the station, then closed the file folder in front of him. He looked up and held her glance for a moment before dropping his gaze back to the folder on his desk.

"I believe you. I'm just going to go grab the release forms we need to fill out. Okay?"

"Oh, God, thank you." Adriana blinked away a few tears.

"It's okay, don't worry."

"But this goes on my record, right? Chief Woodhull knows my father. If he finds out…"

"No, no, no. Well, yes, there is a record. But it's not a big deal. It's what's called a slap on the wrist. No fine, no judgment against you, no reason to alert the chief. Just a stern 'don't do it again' kind of thing." He smiled and added, "But, sorry, I can't do anything about

Paul's Polaroid wall of shame. Sit tight. I'll get the forms, and we'll get you out of here."

Hinkley disappeared as Adriana wiped her face with her sleeve. She pulled the cap off the marker Dylan had given her. The solvents in the marker burned her nose, but she loved that burn. She and Dylan regularly spent entire afternoons drawing and coloring with his markers. The Crayolas may not have precision tips or subtlety, but they were cheaper than her professional supplies. She kissed the top of Dylan's head.

She heard a woman's voice: "His hair was dark and kind of curly but short. He seemed to come out of nowhere."

Nearby, a heavy-set older woman sat at a desk speaking to a senior officer. "I was just stopping at the McDonald's to get some dinner. What kind of monster robs you on the way to dinner?"

"And you didn't see if he got into a car or where he might have gone?" the officer said.

"No. He grabbed my bag and I yelled. He pulled out a knife, a switchblade. Like the ones gangs carry around? I was so scared."

Adriana glanced over just in time to catch the expression on the woman's face. Pure terror.

"Anything else? I mean, we really don't have much to go on here." The officer only sounded half-interested.

"He had a sharp nose." The woman said. "A double chin."

"So he was fat."

"Well…"

The officer frowned, and his five-o'clock shadow sagged.

"I think… I think he had thin eyebrows," she continued. "They were dark, I remember, like his hair, and… I'll never forget his face, though. It almost wasn't…human?"

Adriana's marker was already moving. Lines swept across a sheet of paper, forming a nose and double chin. As the woman kept chattering, the officer nodded, "uh-huh, uh-huh," but Adriana didn't hear a word anymore. She was in a zone. Her strokes were automatic, incisive, and damning. The marker sketched deep-set eyes and a cheek scar before rounding out the face with a broad forehead and angry wrinkles. Her complete immersion was shattered by a voice.

"Hey, who's that?"

Adriana startled and dropped the marker. She bent and picked it up, balancing Dylan while doing so, and said, "The woman over there, she was describing the man who attacked her."

Officer Hinkley picked up the drawing. He glanced from the drawing to Adriana, then back to the drawing.

"Hey, Al—I mean Officer Kasich, is this your guy?" Hinkley moved to the older officer's desk.

Kasich frowned again. "Rookie, how many times do I got to tell you? Don't interrupt. You're here to learn. Watch, listen—"

Then the woman screamed. She pointed at the drawing.

"That's him! It's him!"

Kasich grabbed the drawing from Hinkley and eyed it. "Who drew this?"

Hinkley stepped aside to reveal Adriana, who had pulled Dylan close. She felt exposed, like she was caught in a spotlight while trying to escape prison. The woman turned to her, gushing gratitude. "Thank you so much. My mind. I couldn't quite..."

Adriana nodded. "I know. Not a problem. I hope it helps."

Officer Hinkley returned to his desk like a conquering hero and whispered, "How'd you do that?"

Adriana shrugged. "I just draw a lot. It's fun."

"Well, that's some talent you've got there," he said.

"Drawing has always come easy to me. Sometimes it almost feels like I'm just tracing."

"Cheater," he teased.

This time she smiled, although meekly. "Things, pictures, just come into my head."

"Then bingo, huh? Wow. And so fast. I was only gone a minute or two."

She was not used to compliments. Certainly not from the police. She glanced back at the other woman. Officer Kasich was scowling and eyeing Adriana with suspicion. *That* was what she was used to from police.

"Okay, let's get you out of here," Hinkley said. "There's a pay phone in the hallway if you want to call someone to pick you up. Meanwhile, I'll get these forms filled out."

She motioned to the phone on his desk. "Can't I just use this one?"

He hesitated. "I wouldn't mind, but..." And then discreetly gestured at Kasich. "We wouldn't want to tie up *official business.*"

His youth and enthusiasm seemed so out of place here. Adriana said, "I get it," and hoisted Dylan into her arms.

There were two pay phones hanging on a wall near the entrance doors. She picked up the receiver, dropped in a quarter, and started dialing home. Home, where just an hour ago she was hanging out at her kitchen table inking Eric. Where she'd be right now, safe, if his asshole friends hadn't torn through all her beer.

Three digits into her phone number, she hung up. The pay phone on the station's wall spit her quarter into the return slot with a clatter. She couldn't call home; Eric would still be too drunk to drive.

The city bus didn't run this late. She could call a cab and use half the cash in her End of the World emergency envelope. Because this might be the end, right? *Hey, Judge, it's me again, Mother of the Year. Aren't Dylan's drawings beautiful? We spend our evenings together making art at the police station.* Her head was pounding now. A cluster headache throbbed behind her right eye. *Think, dammit. You need to get home.*

Maybe she could turn on the waterworks and Hinkley would offer her a ride? The look he gave her, she thought maybe he lingered just a moment too long. *Or he was deciding whether or not you were lying.* She glanced back to Hinkley at his desk. Kasich was hovering and had picked up the Hot Wheels Corvette.

"This is what you busted her for, Rook?" he asked.

"You know Glendale. He's a pain in the ass about this kind of thing," Hinkley said.

"Still, this can't be more than, what, two or three bucks?"

"Can I have it back, please?"

"Vroom, vroom," Kasich said, chuckling with his whole belly as he tossed the toy back on Hinkley's desk.

Adriana allowed herself a momentary smile, then looked back to the phone. It was Hinkley who'd dragged her across town to the station. So asking him for a ride wouldn't be out of the question. Though she didn't like the idea of her neighbors seeing her dropped off by the police.

Her neighbors. Of course. "Lisa!" she said to the small phone bank.

Lisa had moved in next door to Adriana a few weeks ago. She'd come over once to introduce herself and twice more to use Adriana's phone while she waited for her service to get connected.

Adriana dug around inside her shoulder bag and found the business card Lisa had given her on her last visit. It was folded, and the corners were dented, but the card was still legible. *Dr. Lisa Shah, MD, Clinical Psychiatrist.*

Office hours were over, but Lisa had written her new home number on the back of the card. Adriana picked up the receiver again.

Her fingers hovered over the number keys while the dial tone droned in her ear. This was a big favor to ask, and an embarrassing one. But she didn't really see any other option. It was too dark and too far to walk carrying Dylan. Eric was useless when he was drunk. And a cab was just too expensive.

She slowly dialed Lisa's home number, then fought the urge to hang up after each monotonous ring. Maybe Lisa wouldn't pick up. It was getting late. Maybe she could just carry Dylan the few miles home. After the fifth ring, the line picked up, and Lisa's voice chirped through. "Hello?"

4

ADRIANA SHIVERED as a gust of wind wrapped itself around her. She stood on the sidewalk in front of the police station holding Dylan against her chest in one arm and the paper bag containing Eric's now-warm beer in the other, waiting for Lisa.

The air didn't feel the same. Maybe it never would. Hearing about the mugging at McDonald's had scared her, sure, but this was something else. The empty street just didn't feel empty anymore. Cellar didn't feel safe anymore. She tightened her protective hug and pulled Dylan even closer.

As vehicles passed, Adriana realized she didn't know what type of car Lisa drove. That put her at the mercy of the motorists, and that feeling of exposure heightened when an automobile approached the police station but seemed to be driverless, a headless horseman. The car's lights blinded her until the vehicle turned, and she saw a man behind the steering wheel.

"Mommy, I'm tired."

"I know. Me too. We'll be home soon, honey."

She was blinded again when another car approached and slowed. A woman's arm waved from the driver's-side window. Lisa had arrived.

Juggling beer and boy, Adriana grabbed for the passenger door as Lisa leaned over and pushed it open.

"God, I can't thank you enough for this."

"Please, don't mention it," Lisa said. "Anything I can do to help. We single parents have to stick together. Heaven knows no one else gives a *you-know-what*."

Dylan crawled into the back seat. Adriana sat up front.

As the car moved through Cellar, Lisa's black hair danced in the breeze from her open window.

"I really am sorry, Lisa. This isn't, like, a normal thing for me."

"No, no, sweetie, you don't have to apologize. But I am curious, you said Dylan stuck a toy in your purse?"

"Yeah, a Hot Wheels."

"And you can get arrested for that?"

"I guess so. Banned for life from Glendale's, too."

"That's ridiculous. Dylan was just doing what he had to do to get what he wanted. That's *proactive*," she said with a chuckle. "My word of the week with two of my clients last month. They both knew what to do but were too afraid to do it. I made them promise me they'd be proactive. I replaced the fear and the unknown with a challenge. It worked. Anyway, you should take it as a compliment."

"How so?" Adriana was surprised that anyone would think turning her toddler into a criminal was a compliment to her parenting skills.

"Well, maybe he sees how strong you have to be and he's emulating that."

Proactive. Strong. Adriana hadn't thought of herself that way, but she liked it.

"Or maybe I'm talking out of my butt. We only met just a couple weeks ago."

Dylan laughed from the back seat. "Butt!" Lisa apologized for her choice of words.

"Oh, don't worry about it. You should hear the mouth on his dad. Or me, for that matter," Adriana said with a quick smile.

"Is his dad the guy staying with you two? Not to be nosy. I've just seen him coming and going the last couple of days."

"Yeah. We have a custody hearing tomorrow."

"Oh? Is he fighting you for visitation or something?"

Adriana wondered how much she wanted to get into it again tonight. For the last two weeks, she could think of nothing else. Now, despite all the excitement of the last few hours, she felt tired. Very tired. And angry.

"Sorry, was that too much?" Lisa asked. She turned off the main road toward their neighborhood. "That was too much. Sorry. Professional hazard. I'm trained to ask the follow-up questions. I mean, we psychiatrists all are."

"No, it's okay. And it's not Eric. My father, Dylan's grandpa, doesn't think I'm fit to..." She couldn't say it. Not to her new neighbor. Was she unfit? Truly unfit to love her little boy and keep him safe in a city that no longer seemed friendly? *Change your focus. Proactive. Strong.* "Eric came back to town to help me with the case. United front and all that."

"Ah. I see."

Adriana could feel Lisa's urge to ask more questions but was relieved when she didn't.

Lisa pulled onto their street, and Adriana braced for the dip in the pavement, two uneven surfaces that always rattled the front end of her old Mazda. Her body relaxed when Lisa's car smoothly rolled past the lousy roadwork.

"Men," Lisa said, almost to herself. "They always think they know what's best. They're useless. All of them." She parked between her house and Adriana's but left the engine running. "My ex? He only gave me two things. A beautiful daughter and a month-long concussion. I made sure that was the last thing he ever gave me."

Adriana fidgeted. More evidence that the world was not safe, not even from the people we know. She wasn't sure how to respond. Anxiety rose in her as though the car were filling with water. She wanted to grab her boy and get out. Then Lisa smiled and patted her hand. "If you ever need anything, sweetie, don't hesitate to call me again or just come on over, okay?"

"Thank you." Adriana popped the car door open. "For that and for the ride."

Grappling with Dylan, the six-pack, and her heavy purse, Adriana was halfway up her walk when she heard Lisa again.

"It's a nice little house you have."

Adriana stopped. The party had ended and the house was dark, but she swore she saw shadows still dancing in the front window. She turned back to Lisa who was locking up her car.

"Dad owns it. And I'm behind on the rent."

Lisa nodded. "Seriously, Adriana. I've dealt with men like your father my entire life. But now my house is safe. For me and my daughter. And for you and your boy. Don't hesitate. Promise?"

Adriana wondered if there was still one place in Cellar that could feel safe. She waved to her new friend. "Thanks again, Lisa. *Really.*"

She reached the porch and realized how empty she felt. If only someone—not Eric, no—someone decent and sincere would push open the front door, show genuine concern, and say, "Where have you been? I've been worried sick." Instead, she clumsily set down Eric's beer on the porch so she could fish her house keys out of her bag while Dylan laid his head on her shoulder.

5

Across town, Mayor Bradley Krause marched down an empty corridor at City Hall. His leather heels hammered limestone tiles and echoed like military explosives. *Click-clack boom.* The sound put a broad grin on his face.

Near the building's entrance, he leaned over a counter and peered into the little welcome office where Maggie Woodhull was sitting in front of a tan IBM Wheelwriter. *One of Maggie's expensive toys.* She'd somehow talked him into an obscenely large budget for technological upgrades around City Hall. Bradley didn't understand why they needed electronic typewriters. The manual ones worked just fine for him. It didn't hurt that she'd sealed the deal while under the sheets with him.

"And how are we tonight, Maggie?"

"Better than most, Mr. Mayor."

She smiled and stood, her height easily eclipsing Bradley, who sometimes began his campaign speeches by joking that even though he was the longest running mayor to serve Cellar Township, he may also be the shortest.

Most of the previous mayors had lasted only a single term, just long enough to realize that the responsibilities and demands of the job far exceeded the perks. Bradley was fine with that. He didn't want downtime. He didn't need an overblown salary. He wanted the tough decisions landing on his desk. He wanted to fight and forage for his community. He wanted to seize power and lead. If that came with limestone floors that rang out for him whenever he stalked the hallways, that was fine too.

"Can I leave these with you to file tomorrow? I don't want you racking up too much overtime tonight." Bradley emptied the manila folder he'd been carrying and pushed a small stack of papers across the counter toward Maggie, who grinned when she saw them.

"Running for a fifth term? Impressive. You know you already beat Father Hen's record, may he rest in peace."

"Henderson was the best mayor this town has ever seen, no doubt, present administration included." Bradley winked. "I may have served longer, but Henderson will never be beat."

"Look at you, being so modest. Five bucks, please."

"Hmm?"

"The filing fee. Or do you think *everything* around here is free?"

Bradley barely suppressed a grin as he reached into his suit pockets for his money clip. The payment and filing were mere formalities. They both knew he was running unopposed, just as he had the last few races. Even so, Bradley liked formalities.

"How'd the council meeting go tonight?" Maggie asked. "You ran a bit late."

"Yeah. A knife fight broke out while debating the township's fourth stoplight."

"Oh, my. No blood, I hope."

Bradley's chuckle soured into a frown. "No blood, but then Councilman Card—can you believe this guy? First term and he introduces a crazy shopping mall project, a large sprawling thing like they have in Cleveland."

"A little too big for his britches?"

"You're reading my mind. I don't see it happening. Who wants that kind of headache? All those kids loitering with their skate-boards, skipping school, hopped up on who knows what kind of drugs. It would be a nightmare."

"And a lot of new tax revenue."

"We aren't hurting for it, at least not enough to go draining Silver Lake and paving through our parks. But that's a worry for another night. I have to get home and prepare for court tomorrow."

"How's Addie holding up? The custody filing must have hit her hard."

"Hey, I've given that girl every chance to turn her life around. And if she's not going to do it for herself, then at least do it for Dylan. She wants to be a tattoo artist. What kind of mother is that? Those so-called clients she hangs around with, you just know they're trouble."

"I'm not saying you're wrong, just hope she's okay." Maggie scrawled on a receipt pad.

"It's what is best for everyone involved, whether she'll admit it or not. She'll have visiting privileges, and I'll give Dylan all the oppor-tunities I gave her when she was growing up."

Maggie handed him his receipt. "I like Addie. But it does sound like she could use the help. Hey, I'm... I'm closing up shop here in five minutes. Do you have any plans for dinner?"

He clenched his jaw, and she noticed. The last time they decided to grab a late dinner, their quick bite turned into a three-day weekend at Bradley's cabin, two awkward phone conversations calling in sick on Monday morning, and one promise to never make plans for dinner again.

"Aw, Mags. Even if I thought that was a good idea, I can't tonight. Rain check?"

"Sure thing." Maggie was a professional. She hid her dejection well.

Bradley slipped his receipt into his money clip, then patted her hand. "We're good? You know I appreciate you keeping the office open tonight, right?"

"Get out of here."

"I'm gone."

"And try not to—"

A scream, piercing and cold, shot through the stone hallways.

"What the hell was that?"

"I don't know. I can't tell where it came from," he said.

He stepped back into the hallway.

"Careful, Bradley."

He moved toward the building's entrance and stared through the glass double doors, surveying the dimly lit parking lot. It was empty save for two visitors' vehicles. The doors shuddered from a heavy breeze that attacked then retreated.

There was a second scream, louder this time, as the door to the ladies' room at the end of the hall exploded outward, smacking the limestone wall, and a terrified woman sprinted up the hall toward him.

"Help me! Help!"

As he jogged toward her, Bradley saw that her blouse and hair glistened. She was soaked.

"What's wrong? What happened?" Bradley said.

"There's a man. In the women's restroom! He attacked me. He—he—he tried grabbing me and—"

She fell into the mayor's arms, sputtering, out of breath. Maggie came out of her office and asked, "Are you okay?!"

"Someone grabbed my shoulder. I swung my purse and slipped. I think I hit him, but I don't know. Next thing I know, I'm down on the floor and—"

"You slipped?" Bradley said.

"Yes, there's water everywhere. I came out of the stall and all the faucets were running, the sinks were overflowing."

"Mags, get Jones on the phone, get him down here," Bradley said. He turned back to the woman: "What's your name? Do you work here?"

"Laurie. Laurie Kaplan. I work at the library. I'm just here to drop off some grant papers."

"Mags, you two go to your office. Lock the door."

Bradley waited for Maggie to usher Laurie back to the office, then headed toward the bathroom. As he got closer, he could hear the Niagara of water from within.

From his pants pocket, Bradley pulled out a key chain with a small knife and flipped it open. It wasn't much of a weapon, better for popping the tab on a can of beer, but it was something. *Wish I had my revolver with me today.*

He got close to the door, listened for a moment, then pushed in.

"I've got a knife! Don't do anything stupid!"

The lights were off, and he felt water surge around his black leather shoes, threatening to soak his socks. He flicked on the lights, illuminating the three toilet stalls and the clogged sinks.

He carefully edged his way around the bathroom, clinging to the wall, and turned off the faucets. Both sinks had wads of paper towels gooped up in their drains. The water stilled to a trickle over the edge of the sink basin and onto the floor.

Bradley glanced under the first stall to his left. No feet, just a few pieces of soaked toilet paper stuck to the floor. He stepped up to the stall door, shoes squeaking on the wet tiles. He took in a breath, then plowed the stall door open, his pocketknife leading the charge like a Civil War bayonet.

The stall was empty.

He repeated the same infiltration with the second stall. Also empty. His heart beat harder as he sized up the final stall. He adjusted the grip on his pocketknife and moved to push the swinging stall door open but instead collapsed into the empty stall. A dark figure fell on him from behind.

"I've got a knife!" Bradley cried out, only to lose the weapon when the intruder pounded his wrist against the cold tiles. He threw his elbows, cursed, then panicked when his mouth and nostrils filled with water as his face was pressed against the wet floor. With a savage howl, he jerked loose and felt his enemy slip away. He stood, turned, and—

"Goddammit, Jones, what the hell are you doing!"

The security guard's uniform was dark with water stains. "Mr. Mayor? Holy shit! Maggie said there was some lunatic in here."

Bradley bent at the waist and gulped damp air.

"Are you okay?" Jones said.

Bradley waved him away. "Yeah, I could've"—he playfully put up his fists like a boxer, gulped in another breath—"taken him."

Jones chuckled. He reached his hands into the sink pools and gathered up the wads of paper towels, freeing the sink drains.

"Why the hell would someone do that?"

The radio on Jones's belt cracked to life, another purchase from Maggie's expanded toy budget. "Are you two okay?" the staticky voice asked.

Jones unclipped the radio. "Yeah, Maggie, we're fine. Be there in a moment."

"Did you get him?" Laurie asked as both men made their way back to the front office. Her voice trembled.

"No. There's no one in there," Bradley said, still dabbing at his wet suit with the paper towel.

"How is that possible? We didn't see anyone come out." Maggie spoke quickly. She was scared, and Bradley wished he could comfort her.

"He must have slipped out before anyone knew what was going on," Jones said. "Looks like it might have been a petty vandal trying to cause some water damage. Maybe someone pissed off about his property taxes. You probably scared him, miss, if he didn't know you were in there. If you'll come with me to the security station, miss..."

"That seems like an overreaction to a tax bill," Maggie said.

"We've heard worse threats at council meetings."

"Thank you, Mayor Krause," Laurie said as she gathered the library's grant papers and followed Jones down the hall to the security station at the other end of the building.

Maggie grabbed her office keys, made her way around the service desk, and bolted the entry doors. Bradley stared out at the dim parking lot through the large glass doors again. The lot still looked empty, but it no longer felt empty.

"Hell of a night, huh?" Maggie said.

Bradley physically startled at the sound of her voice, but he didn't think Maggie noticed. He *hoped* Maggie hadn't noticed.

"Must be something in the air."

6

ADRIANA WAS SINKING in cold lake water. Her throat seized under the water, desperate to inhale. The faint slivers of moonlight that once skipped across the lake's surface were now lost to the dark, rusty water.

She was stuck in the dream again. The same dream she'd returned to since childhood.

She willed her body to relax. Her mouth still trembled in the icy water, but she gave up on trying to breathe. There was no need to in the dream.

She floated down to the muddy bottom of the lake. She cleared away some of the algae and found the dark lakebed.

It pulsed. The sediment rising and falling and—

A rotting arm exploded up from the lake floor, causing a plume of black sludge to rise around her. The hand grabbed her. She struggled, tried like hell to break free, even though she hadn't ever been able to before.

As if to prove her point, the rotten arm yanked her down hard. Her shoulder crashed against the lakebed. She flailed in despair but reminded herself it was no use. This thing meant to keep her down here with it.

She had all but relented when she heard Lisa's voice. Not muffled by the lake but loud and close, a ping in her head.

Proactive, my word of the week.

Lisa's words from the car reverberated like a sonic wave. The words she'd used to justify Dylan's actions at Glendale's, to reassure Adriana she was doing right by her son.

He sees how strong you have to be and he's emulating that.

Adriana was tired of being afraid. She fought back. She pried one rotten finger, then a second. A third finger loosened, then dug in hard, tearing the skin on the back of her hand. She howled, but as her mouth opened, it filled with fetid water. She attacked again and the finger broke off, floating free in the water, tethered only by stringy tendons. That weakened the grip of the repulsive hand.

With another jerk, she broke free. She planted her feet in the muddy lake floor and clamped her own hands around the horrible thing's wrist. *Strong...* Lisa's voice again. Adriana pulled so hard, she feared her arms would detach from her shoulders. But she didn't care anymore.

No. You won't hold me down here. Not again. Not this time!

Everything felt heavier and slower underwater, but she held the arm as it writhed under her grip. She lost traction on the slick algae, and her desperate motions caused clouds of muck to rise and choke her nostrils and mouth. And yet she was winning. She had never felt more powerful.

An elbow and bicep rose from the sludge. She'd never seen that before. She gripped harder, yanked, and soon an oily shoulder emerged as wet dirt pulsated and shifted, setting off more explosions of sediment.

Then, when the filth had settled and the water had cleared, she saw it. A face staring up at her. The dead thing's flesh was gray and soggy. Dark veins—road maps—ran beneath the skin, dead-ending in a gash that split its forehead and cheek, making its sunken, empty eye sockets portals for black snakes that slithered out and fled.

Fuck!

She panicked and let go, hurling herself back and away as the arm continued to grab at her. The face tensed as its mouth opened in soundless rage between vibrating lips.

Adriana couldn't bear the dark, empty gaze any longer. She kicked herself away, spun in the water, and then felt the heat of her pillow against her sweating cheek. She looked down at her legs, which continued to kick, desperate to escape the comforter wrapped around them. Her heart raced. She felt the urge to vomit. She sat up fast and leaned back against the headboard, gasping for breath.

An arm brushed against her leg and she yelped. It was Eric, rolling in his sleep. He slept heavy as a sodden log, just as she'd found him when she'd gotten home from the police station.

She looked at the clock on her bedside table. It was 4:03 a.m.

"Goddamnit."

In six hours, she would be in court, exhausted while trying to win the custody hearing.

She slid out of bed and onto the floor in search of a drawing pad. When her fingers found paper and a pen, she sat upright against the bed. She used the faint illumination from the streetlight outside to draw what she had discovered in her dream.

After all these years, I've finally seen it.

The clock on her nightstand jumped to 4:04 a.m. and Adriana rubbed at her eyes.

But why couldn't the damn thing have waited until dawn?

ERIC SHUFFLED into the kitchen and went straight for the fridge. He surveyed his options, then plucked a beer from the six-pack Adriana had purchased last night. He was oblivious to the stolen Hot Wheels episode, the store security tape, Officer Hinkley, and the car ride home with Lisa.

"Hey, babe," he said over the crack of the can's pull tab.

Adriana poured a few extra Cheerios into Dylan's bowl. Dylan sat at the table eating them one at a time with his hands. "Spoon, honey, remember what Mommy said? Use your spoon."

She'd just put the carton of eggs back in the fridge, forgetting Eric would need to eat, so she reached back in and grabbed two extras. It had been a long time since she'd cooked a *family* meal.

Eric sat next to Dylan and drained half his beer in one long tilt.

"Court's in two hours. Little early for that, don't you think?" Adriana said.

"One can takes the edge off. You're not the only one nervous about today."

Eric lifted the can again, but Adriana was still eyeing him. He put his hands up in surrender, stood, and set the half-empty can in the sink.

"There. Nothing to worry about."

"Everything to worry about," she said, mostly to the cold frying pan of bacon in front of her. She turned a knob on the stove and the burner lit after a few clicks of the pilot light.

From behind her, Eric said, "Wow, Addie, this looks wicked!"

She turned to see him pick up her drawing pad from the kitchen counter. He stared at the face she had drawn from her dream. While she'd captured how the eyes were completely obscured by decay, the nose didn't feel right, and that bothered her, because details usually came easy to her. Faces have predetermined proportions; you can quickly block out any face on Earth once you know the rules. But this face didn't follow the rules. The mouth was good, though, more of a contortion, really, that seemed to throb even in her drawing. Exactly as she'd seen it. Probably. It was just a dream, and images from dreams were hard to hold on to in the light of day. *Or in the dark of four a.m.*

"Is this for a tattoo? I've got to have this one too. Almost looks like he'll jump right off the page and bite me!" He chomped at the air, and Dylan laughed. Eric dropped the drawing on the table and slid his arm around Adriana's waist.

"I think it's going to be okay today. There isn't a judge in the world who would take Dylan away from you."

"As long as the judge doesn't smell the beer on your breath. We're not up against just any judge. They all serve His Honor, Mr. Mayor. None of them know me, not really. All they're going to see is an unemployed, unwed, uneducated kid who can't get her life together."

"Mommy?"

Adriana turned fast when she heard concern in Dylan's voice. He was holding the drawing Eric had dropped next to his Cheerios.

"Goddamnit, Eric. A child shouldn't see that thing!"

Eric shrugged and took his beer can from the sink to sneak a quick sip. "Is he normally such a scaredy-cat? You gotta toughen up, buddy."

"Leave him alone. You're the one telling him it's going to jump right off the page," Adriana said. "I know you're not exactly campaigning for Father of the Year here, but how about a little common sense, huh?"

He chuckled. She needed to get them moving. "Dylan, honey, why don't you go get your shoes? We're going bye-bye after breakfast."

Dylan hopped down from his chair and headed down the hall to his bedroom. Eric reached for his can in the sink again, but Adriana pushed it over with her spatula, spilling a good portion of what was left down the drain.

"That's enough for nine in the morning."

"Yes, Mother."

"Fuck you, Eric. You're supposed to be here to help make things easier. Your addictions are not going to help. At least for today, I need you to be better than that."

"I get it, but you're so stressed out—"

"It's not stress, it's panic. I spent half the night at the goddamn police station with Dylan. If Dad finds out—"

"Police? What the hell happened?"

"Dylan put a toy in my bag when I wasn't looking and some security guard banned me for life, called the cops, had Dylan and me sitting down at the station all night. Not that you care. I had to call my neighbor for a ride home because you were so wasted. Do you know how embarrassing that is?"

The bacon started smoking. It had burned to a crisp. Fed up, she spun the burner off, cursed, and threw the frying pan into the sink.

"You can't be mad at me for something I didn't know. Come here." He tried to put his arm around her waist again, but she held out a hand to stop him.

"Right now, I need to restart breakfast so we can get to court on time. Can you shower and get dressed, or do you need Mommy to help you?"

"Jesus Christ."

"And when you're finished getting dressed, help Dylan with his shoes. Twenty minutes. Hop on it, Eric!"

Eric made his way to the hallway. "Does he have, like, court shoes? Church shoes or something? Does he know how to tie laces?"

"Just put him in his Velcros. I don't care." *No*, she thought, *Dylan doesn't have church shoes because I, his heathen mother, have never taken him to church.* Was that wrong? Should he be going? Would he even understand why he was there? She'd never understood, despite being seventeen the last time she'd slipped on her church shoes and gone. So maybe age had nothing to do with it?

If they made it through the court hearing, the sleepless nights, the looks in public... *Please, God, get us through this and I promise I'll take Dylan to church. For most of the big days. Easter and Christmas, at least. Christmas for sure.*

7

"I DO NOT LOOK FORWARD to cases like these." Judge Thornton's face drooped, as if his dark skin had started to melt one hot afternoon in his stuffy little courtroom and then never reformed. He looked from Adriana to Bradley, from father back to daughter.

Adriana hadn't been able to bring herself to look over at Bradley. Regardless, his mere presence crushed her from the other side of the courtroom. She gripped the edge of the wood table she sat behind, holding on for dear life. Dylan squirmed on Eric's lap in the chair next to her.

Whatever the judge said next would determine the rest of their lives, together or apart. Her eyes welled up and she wondered how so much power could be given to just one man.

"This court strives to keep children with their parents whenever possible," Judge Thornton said. "But only when doing so does not harm the child, physically or developmentally. I've now heard both sides of this case and have weighed both positions."

"Please," Adriana whimpered. Her hushed voice carried more than she expected. The hard tile floor and wood-paneled walls seemed to amplify even the smallest noise.

"I've decided that the minor in question, Dylan Thomas Krause, shall remain in the custody of his mother—"

"What?!" Bradley barked from his side of the courtroom.

"Oh, my God!" Adriana cried out as she cupped her hands over her mouth. She replayed the words she'd just heard, *remain in the custody of*, making sure she'd heard them all correctly. She thought she might burst as the pent-up anxiety inside her released.

She turned and took Dylan from Eric. Holding him close, she kissed his forehead over and over. Dylan giggled.

"—on the condition...," Judge Thornton continued. "On the condition that Ms. Krause is able to secure gainful employment in the next thirty days."

The judge turned his full attention to Adriana. She felt sick from the whiplash. She *had* been looking for work. No one was hiring. At least, not for the type of work she could handle.

The few jobs she held as a teenager were nothing more than part-time gigs at her father's office. After sophomore year, she spent the summer learning to type and file as Maggie's assistant. The following summer she helped organize public events around town. Bradley didn't want her wasting entire summers lying around the house, so he'd handed her those jobs.

She made the mistake of glancing over at Bradley. She saw a little smile form on his lips. He wouldn't be handing out any work this summer.

"It's time to grow up," the judge said. His words echoed around the room. "It's time to take charge of your life and provide for that little boy if you want to retain custody."

"Thank you, Your Honor," Eric spoke up, turning and smiling at Adriana.

"Quiet, young man! I already told you that I did not want to hear from you again. Unfortunately, this case does not concern you. If it did, I might recommend Adriana obtain a legal judgment against *you* for support. I might recommend she have your wages garnished. And I might impress upon you the responsibilities of fatherhood. In that regard, the mayor has exceeded any threshold of fatherly or grandfatherly duty."

The judge refocused his attention on Adriana. "If your father didn't provide the place you live, the car you drive, the money you use to feed and clothe Dylan, and...just where would you two be if your father disappeared tomorrow?"

Adriana forced herself to nod in acknowledgment.

"Show me," he continued, the faintest grin momentarily reversing the age and wear on his face. "Show me you care as deeply as you say you do. Put in the effort and the sacrifice for your son. Do that and I'll dismiss this case."

"And if thirty days aren't enough? To find a job, I mean," Adriana said hesitantly.

"Then you'll force my hand. This court only wants what is best for Dylan. If you can provide that, I'd rather he remains with you. But if you can't..."

Adriana nodded again. She understood.

ADRIANA AND ERIC sat on a bench outside the courtroom. Dylan was on the floor next to them playing. The judge had dismissed them, and they were waiting to hear when the follow-up date would be scheduled. The date by which Adriana needed to find a job.

Eric fidgeted with his lighter. The last time she'd seen him play with that lighter was the day before he left for Cleveland. He'd heard about some construction jobs there. Easy to get, a friend from high school woodshop had said.

His hand spun the lighter over and over as he laid out his plan all those years ago: He would go to Cleveland, work for six or seven months, save some money before the baby was born. Then he'd come back to Cellar and try to find something local, but with a fat stack of cash from his work in the city. That had sounded pretty good to Adriana. Smart, even, which was not normally Eric's strong suit.

Twelve months later, he still wasn't back and hadn't sent any money. Then it was fifteen months, with nothing more than promises about upcoming jobs just on the horizon. After Dylan's first birthday, Adrianna had stopped asking when he'd be back, and Eric had stopped calling.

"Eric, why am I the only one being asked to do more?" she said now, looking at him. She kept her voice low. The long corridor at Cellar Municipal Court was humming with other people waiting for their turn in court, for a form to be filed, or for a license to be issued.

"Don't you want more too?" she asked. "Don't you want things to be easier? Happier?"

He stopped fidgeting with the lighter. "What I want is for this shit to be over so I can get back to my life."

"This is your life." Adriana couldn't believe her ears. "This is your son, you selfish asshole!"

The courtroom doors opened again, and Adriana realized the corridor had gone quiet in the wake of her voice.

"Problem?" Bradley had stepped out of the courtroom with his lawyer, Connor Graham, a tall man whose tan leather shoes matched his tan leather briefcase. Adriana couldn't afford a lawyer and had represented herself.

She didn't respond. She didn't know if she could open her mouth again without yelling. She had won for now. But that didn't cool any of the anger that boiled inside her from the sight of him.

Bradley gave them the date and time of their follow-up hearing. Then added, "I'll wait outside while you and Eric finish up here, but I would like to spend a little time with my grandson today."

Adriana tensed, and so did her voice. Measuredly, she said, "We'll be out in a minute."

Bradley and his lawyer made their way down the hall to the north entrance, shoes clacking in and out of sync. Great men. Distinguished men. *Assholes in tailored suits.*

She looked back at Eric.

"This *is* your life, Eric," she said again. "Feel free to start living it."

Then she picked up Dylan, turned, and walked in the opposite direction of her father.

———————

THE MORNING AIR outside the courthouse hit Eric, and he felt his face flush, or maybe it was all the adrenaline. He'd been in a few beefs with barflies and co-workers back in Cleveland, teased as the new guy on the crew. But no one could get him fired up like Adriana. Always pushing. Always on his back. He cupped his hands as he struggled to light a cigarette in the breeze. He sat down on the steps outside the main entrance doors, the cigarette twitching in his unsteady hand as he brought it up to his lips.

The courthouse was the second largest building in town after Ascension Catholic Church. This included the small tree park stretching out across half a city block in front of the building; Eric used to play in the fall leaves here during Pumpkin Fest when he was Dylan's age. Back when no one hassled him about finding a job or taking care of bills.

The walking path led from the steps through the tree park and around the building like a moat. The trees were just starting to bud again, but there were no leaves to play in today. Eric wondered if Adriana ever brought Dylan here to play. He stuffed that thought back down when he noticed Bradley and his lawyer shuffling papers and chatting in the shade of a large tree. "Shit," he groaned.

Bradley wrapped up his business with his lawyer and approached Eric.

"Eric. Where's that handsome baby boy you stuck my daughter with? I assume Addie left?"

Eric nodded and exhaled a thin trail of smoke.

"Spoiled child. Anyway, I heard you were back in town," Bradley said.

"A few days now, sir. Addie said she needed my help."

"She did, for the last three years. But that time has passed, and I'm not sure how much help you will be now."

"Not much, it looks like," Eric confessed as he stubbed out his cigarette on the step and flicked the butt into the grass.

Bradley's eyes followed the arc of the butt, then turned back to Eric. "I heard the tail end of your discussion with Addie. She's always been stubborn. Always ungrateful. Do you know how many meetings I got pulled out of over the years because her teachers would call me, yammering on about her 'headaches'? They didn't know what to do with her, she complained so loud and for so long. That's why I took her out of school years ago. It was easier to home-school than deal with the school nurse!"

"Addie told me. She also told me you wanted to fuck her tutor. That you all went through three or four of them by the time she graduated. And that it was probably the reason her mom left."

Bradley sat down next to Eric on the courthouse steps.

"It's not easy raising a problem child. Especially alone. That's how I know Addie's got a tough job right now with Dylan, and that's why I'm trying to help."

"By taking him away from her?"

"Not taking him away. Being there for him. I want to be a part of my grandson's life. She never lets me see him. She doesn't return my calls, even before all this nasty court business, but she has no problem living rent-free in one of my properties. Or cashing the checks I send at Christmas."

"Rent-free, sir?"

"Well, all right, *virtually* rent-free. I don't charge her market value."

Eric pulled his lighter out of his pocket and started tapping it against his knee. "I wanted to send her some money. But the work in Cleveland isn't always steady. And my buddy Mike flaked out on the apartment almost as soon as I signed the lease. That shit isn't cheap. I just haven't had extra to send."

Eric wanted to work a full eight hours but was usually let go after maybe only four, paid in cash, and there were only so many ways he knew how to fill the time. Beer, usually. Pills on occasion. A syringe and a spoon when the hours felt particularly long.

"So, you'll be heading back soon, then, I suppose?" Bradley said. "I heard you tell the judge you'd try to stick around to help out here, but I don't know too many crews that could spare a man for more than a few days. Even if he's only part-time."

"Yeah, maybe."

"And that tongue-lashing she gave you in there, that was nothing. Spring training. You don't want to be around for the regular season."

"No, maybe not."

"Taking a few days off to come down here must have cut into your hours and wages," Bradley continued. "If you need to get back, I could help you out with a few bucks. Say a few hundred. Maybe more, even, if you wanted to leave by this weekend?"

"I wouldn't want to owe you, sir."

"No, it's not a loan. Let's call it a gift."

"A gift for what?" Eric's antennae went up.

"Look at it this way. I help you get back to Cleveland, back to work. Then maybe you make it a priority to get Dylan something nice for Christmas this year. My daughter sees that you're trying, maybe she'll be less upset all the time. Everybody wins."

Eric thought about it. "Yeah, maybe," he said again.

Bradley slid an envelope out of his breast pocket and handed it to Eric, who started opening the sealed flap.

Bradley waved his hands. "No, no. Don't go looking at that here. Put it away. There's an even grand in there. Something for your time here, and something to help you get back home to Cleveland. Deal?"

Eric paused. *A deal? With Mayor Default Dickhead?* He decided quickly that he didn't care. This was more money than he'd ever held at one time. He folded the envelope and shoved it into his pants pocket and nodded. "Yeah. I can probably be out of here in a few days."

"Friday. You take that, you're out of here by Friday. That's my offer."

The money more than covered the hours he'd missed at work,

and he did need to get back. And he didn't need any more of Adriana's bullshit, always fighting him on everything. He didn't remember her being like that before the baby.

"Deal," Eric said, and lit another cigarette.

Bradley rose and began climbing the steps into the courthouse. "Duty calls. But try to enjoy this beautiful day. The paper said nothing but sunshine this afternoon."

A long, empty afternoon. Adriana off his back. And a newly minted thousand bucks in cash in his pocket. This should be a beautiful day, indeed.

8

BRADLEY FELT CHOKED by his shirt collar but didn't dare tug at it for fear of revealing his agitation. How long did he and Council President Lois King have to wait in this small windowless room at WCLR? The station was home to local radio personality Killswitch Kevin, not one of Bradley's personal favorites, but the younger voters liked him.

The air inside was stale with cigarettes that could not mask the dense aroma of marijuana. The mayor groused that being stoned at work likely soothed the ego of the aging radio host who had bungled his shot at rock 'n' roll stardom with bad songs and a lousy band. *Don't blame the industry, buddy.*

His mood was also tinged with a faint disappointment in yesterday's court hearing. It had not been the clear victory he had imagined, nor was the outcome disastrous. At least it broke in his favor. No way could Adriana find gainful employment in the next thirty days. Even if the employment market were red hot in Cellar, Adriana hadn't held a real job in her life. And Eric's presence had not moved the needle one little bit. Thank God that deadhead would be gone soon.

A voice buzzed his ear, yanking him back to the stinky little waiting room.

"Remember to hit all three points," Lois said. Again.

She was the first woman to serve as council president in Cellar and had the annoying habit of double- and triple-checking everything she said or did. Bradley knew it was because she was under more scrutiny, maybe only *perceived* scrutiny, than her male predecessor. But that didn't make her incessant reminders any less irritating.

"I know." He ticked off each point on his fingers. "Police budget for new vehicles, utility expansions out to Route 12, and the tax increase to add an additional lane a mile past the *oh-vuck*."

"Don't call it a tax increase, call it a small bump in town revenue. And please, despite everyone else saying it, do not refer to the OVUC as *oh-vuck*. It sounds like you're cursing."

Sometimes I am, he thought.

"It's useful to say the full name, Ohio Valley Urgent Care. People hear 'care' and it resonates subconsciously. It also makes them less likely to riot over a tax increase."

"You mean 'a small bump in town revenue'?"

"Yes, exactly!"

Bradley managed half a smile. Lois wasn't so bad unless he was stressed. God, if only he could loosen his tie. And why not? This wasn't television, for Christ's sake. These monthly spots on WCLR's morning talk show—quick, short updates for the citizens of Cellar—were usually a breeze, even if Killswitch sometimes gave him a hard time.

He stood abruptly and forced a smile. He ran his hands down his gray suit jacket and slacks, smoothing out creases and his nerves. It might only be radio this morning, and Bradley barely stood five foot four, but he projected stateliness no matter what the occasion. And yet...

He paced the claustrophobic room and reversed direction with the speed of a ping-pong ball, staring at the red walls covered nearly floor to ceiling with black-and-white headshots of all the greats, none of whom had ever actually stepped foot inside WCLR's little studio.

Bon Jovi, two years ago, was the only time this outback radio station had snagged a big fish. It happened while the band was on tour with its breakout album, the name of which non-fan Mayor Krause could not recall. But the pinup dolls were only passing through when their bus had stopped in town for lunch at Cody's Diner. The eatery's radio was tuned to Killswitch Kevin's morning show. The guys had liked what they heard and decided to stop by the station for an impromptu interview.

After that, Cody's filled their jukebox almost exclusively with Bon Jovi singles and WCLR reran the interview once a day for at least two weeks. "It was truly *Bon Jovial* to meet the band and their hairdresser," the disk jockey joked.

But that highlight was long gone, and so was Bradley's patience. He glanced at his watch again and barked at Lois. "They should have called us if—!"

Rebecca Lemche, WCLR's morning producer, barged in with all the authority and speed of a DEA drug bust. Lois startled and spilled her papers on the floor. Bradley stopped pacing so he wouldn't stomp all over her impeccable work.

"Mayor Krause, nice to see you again," Rebecca said. She held out her hand and he shared his polished politician's handshake, firm but not painful, with his opposite hand landing on Rebecca's upper arm. He held her there for a moment, making eye contact, and then noticed her spiffy pantsuit, which was out of tune with her dyed-purple hair and sleeves hiked high enough to tease the tattoo on her left forearm.

"Oh, my gosh. I'm so sorry to have kept you waiting!" For a beat, she thought the mayor had fixated on her cleavage but realized, no, it was her blue-black tattoo that Adriana had inked just last week. "Your daughter is *so* talented!"

"I've encouraged her to develop a...profession."

Rebecca nodded, then sped forth.

"Anyway, the wait. Sorryyyy. But we've had to bump your spot by about fifteen minutes."

"Bumped?" Bradley tried to sound amused. "Whose tour bus rolled through town this time? Johnny Cash at the Burger King? The Rolling Stones at Terry's Bait Shop?"

Rebecca forced a big smile.

"No, nothing like that. Councilman Card just stopped by. Breaking news, and Kevin wanted to get him on right away. Besides, we don't play those old guys. Johnny Cash? Come on, Mr. Mayor. We've got to update your record collection."

Bradley wasn't smiling anymore. "Councilman Card?"

"Yes, sir. He wanted to announce his run for mayor on Kevin's morning show."

"His what?!"

Rebecca flinched. "Oh, I assumed you knew."

"Son of a—"

"Sorryyyy," Rebecca said, now staring mostly at her clipboard. "I didn't know I'd be the messenger."

Face flushed, Bradley looked accusingly at Lois. She was as baffled and upset as the mayor. He cooled down, believing she wouldn't have kept him in the dark about something like this.

"Back for you in roughly twelve minutes? Gotta rush!"

Rebecca *gone*. Tiny, smelly room *very quiet*.

Lois broke the silence. "What the hell?" She marched to the radio speaker installed near the door and cranked the black knob to turn up the volume. Benjamin Card's smooth, lively voice fell on their ears.

"...to shine the bright light of the eighties on Cellar too. We need to modernize. Other towns out there are passing us by while Mayor Krause sits behind his business-as-usual politics. And I don't just mean the big places like Cleveland or Columbus. I'm talking about Springdale, Everett, Seven Hills; towns the same size as ours..."

"Son of a bitch!" Bradley said.

Lois turned down the volume. "I did not see that coming. I knew he was fired up about his shopping mall project that you pooh-poohed, but I never even considered..."

Bradley walked over to the radio and turned the broadcast back up.

"...modernizing does not mean leaving behind tradition or our family values. It means bringing opportunities here for the families who have lived in Cellar for generations. Better health care. More job opportunities. Less crime..."

"Less crime!" Killswitch Kevin bit on Card's comment and egged him on. "Let's talk about that. Councilman Card, are you referring to our mayor's own daughter, who was arrested for shoplifting from Glendale Grocery just two nights ago?"

"No, no," Card replied. "I heard that was just a big misunderstanding. Her son had put some toy in the shopping cart or her purse that she says she didn't know about. Honest mistake. Could have happened to me or you or any of us out shopping with our children, right? And I know it's extra tough for those single parents out there. Single parents who have no other option but to bring their children along while running errands."

"That motherfucker!" Bradley clicked off the speaker so hard, the volume knob popped off in his hand. He threw it across the room and it ricocheted to the floor like a bullet off a steel plate. He patted down his suit jacket, which suddenly felt way too tight and very warm.

"Why are you angry? He just gave you a hall pass," Lois said.

Bradley couldn't speak. He was livid. Adriana was *his* ace, not Card's. The little weasel had sounded magnanimous, whereas Bradley had shrewdly hoped to win some sympathy from voters by discreetly stabilizing a family matter. Strong. Silent. Capable of managing mayhem and filial obligations. Now the councilman had outplayed him for his own political gain.

Bradley's suit coat continued to tighten around him. He worked harder to breathe, to puff out his chest against it, but he felt like a sausage ready to burst its casing.

What did Card know about being mayor? What did he know

about running a city? He was a newcomer, a first-term council member, a country lawyer who was untested politically. He didn't even have children. *Yet I raised my kid single-handedly after her mother disappeared and got no respect or appreciation from Adriana for that. She can barely feed and clothe Dylan and rarely pays rent, and now...!*

His thoughts were flying offtrack. He needed to calm down and get some clarity.

"Bradley, are you okay?" Lois stared at the mayor as he slapped his pockets and cursed under his breath. He heard nothing but his own inner monologue: *I will not lose this election. I will not let Adriana or Card or anything else steal this election from me.*

Finally, Bradley found the bottle of pills he had been searching for. He coughed out, "Uh, huh. I'm okay."

He turned his back on Lois as he emptied the bottle into his palm. *Oh-vuck. Only one pill left.* He'd forgotten to fill his prescription again. He hated taking the little things and hated that they always needed to be refilled. His doctor called them calcium channel blockers, *what a load of crap,* and yet they managed to steady his racing heart. They also made him tired, and he didn't think a mayor of his stature should ever get tired, certainly not before noon. He swallowed the one pill dry and tossed the empty container in a nearby garbage can.

"Mr. Mayor?"

Almost immediately his chest and jacket felt roomier. His head also cleared, and he bent to fish the empty pill bottle out of the garbage can. *Evidence.* Probably better not to leave it here, where it could be found and betray him.

"Mayor Krause?"

While rummaging around in the trash, he felt a tug at his sleeve. Rebecca stood above him, clipboard at her side and a strange look on her face, an untidy mix of concern and fear.

"Mr. Mayor, we're ready for you."

9

Officer Matthew Hinkley focused on the Hot Wheels Corvette that was still parked on a corner of his desk. That's why he didn't see the threat coming. Such a petty crime didn't necessitate evidence, so he really should get the toy back to Glendale's, but he was distracted with a much more important matter: Was there a way he could call Adriana without coming on too strong? There really was something about her...

That's when it hit, and his soul nearly jumped out of his body. A six-inch stack of file folders exploded across his desk, compliments of veteran police officer Sgt. Al Kasich.

"These here are cold cases from the last twelve months, Rookie."

Matt Hinkley looked up and tried to hide his momentary fright. His assigned mentor loomed over the edge of his desk.

"Okay?" Matt said.

"Not okay. Do you know what a cold case is?"

"Is that like, uh, lunch meat or...?" He usually kept those kinds of comments to himself, but his nerves were still settling and he'd forgotten to filter.

"Oh, I get it!" Kasich said. "Hey, everybody, the kid does standup!" He faked a laugh with his entire body.

Matt felt his face flush as a few of the other veteran officers chuckled. During training, he imagined things would be a bit livelier on the job. Unfortunately, his first couple months of service at the Cellar Police Department resembled an office job more than anything else. The stack of cold case files now strewn across his desk confirmed what he feared: actual police work only happened on television or in the movies.

"Too many stolen bikes and missing cats around town," Kasich said. "And somebody's got to get to the bottom of these crimes. That someone is you." He turned and started back across the bullpen. "I expect an update report on my desk. *Tomorrow.*"

Matt thumbed the edges of the folders and felt defeat. Kasich was only busting his balls because he was new. Kasich probably went through a similar hazing when he was young and eager—*about a million years ago.* Now Sarge was marking his calendar each day with relish as he moved closer and closer to his retirement and pension, a day that could not come soon enough. *No matter what, I will not end my career bitter, or empty, or whatever the hell it is that makes Kasich hate his job.*

His phone rang, refocusing his attention. On the second ring, he grabbed the receiver. "Officer Hinkley here."

"Mr. Hinkley, this is Adriana Krause. From Glendale's a couple nights ago?"

"Adria... Ms. Krause, yes, I was just thinking—"

"You said you believed me?"

"I'm sorry?"

"You said you believed Dylan put that toy in my bag and I didn't know anything about it."

Matt pushed aside some of the cold case files and found the Hot Wheels Corvette once again. "Uh, yes, that's right."

"Then why the hell did you tell the media I'm a thief?"

"What?"

"I just heard Killswitch Kevin on the radio. I was the topic of his morning show. Everyone in Cellar listens to him! My neighbors. My friends. Oh God, my *father!*"

"Hey, slow down, Ms. Krause. I didn't tell anyone your business."

"Then how the hell did Killswitch know?!"

Hinkley paused and retraced his actions that night. He'd had her call for a ride while he filed his report and then… The police blotter. Every incident bigger than a traffic citation was published in the daily newspaper. Standard procedure. It would have been just a single sentence, not a front-page headline, but all the relevant facts were included. He shared this with Adriana. "I bet Kevin read it in the Courant."

"But you said we didn't have to make a fuss."

"I'm not fussing. The police blotter publishes everything. You can read it yourself, Ms.—"

"*Everything* gets published?"

"Only one line in the newspaper. But no fines or community service—and no prison time!" He was joking again and quickly regretted it.

"I'm not going to *prison* for something I didn't do!"

"Look, Ms. Krause, I know you're upset. I'm just saying, it's standard procedure. I was only doing my job."

Silence. Had she hung up? *Please don't hang up.* Then she spoke, softly, something approaching apologetic. "I guess I should be yelling at the newspaper, not at you."

Matt considered his words before replying. He'd been looking for an excuse to call her all morning, but he'd never asked anyone out before. He wasn't sure how. Then his brain lit up.

"I understand that must have been a surprise, hearing it on the radio like that. But I am really happy you called. I was just looking for your number," he half fibbed.

"Oh? Why? Is there something wrong with my case?" She sounded worried.

"No, nothing like that. Sorry I need…uh…we need a favor. Remember the drawing you did? The mugger at McDonald's?"

"Yeah?"

"Well, it helped! We caught him. Kasich caught him, I mean. One of the cashiers at McDonald's recognized the guy from your sketch."

"Really? That's great."

"Yup, he confessed right in the back of the squad car before we even got back to the station."

"Kasich must be good to get a confession that quick."

"Yeah," Matt admitted. "But now we've got a woman who was attacked in a bathroom at City Hall. And she's kind of messed up about it. I showed her your sketch, but it didn't match. So I was thinking maybe it would be possible for you to come in, meet with her, and make a new sketch? Like you did the other night? That blew my mind; you were so quick."

If he could get Adriana back down to the station, he hoped Laurie would agree to give a description. Kasich had taken Laurie's statement, but Matt did sit in on the intake with him, more training. So it was kind of his case too, he reasoned.

"Thanks. Yeah. But I don't know. I usually only draw tattoos. That sketch the other night, it just kind of happened."

"Well, I don't think we hire consultants for stuff like this usually, but…" He lifted his butt off the chair so he could pull out his wallet. He fingered its frayed edges and found two tens. "…there's twenty dollars petty cash in it for you, if that helps? And my gratitude, of course."

"Really?"

"Yeah, if you've got the time. We don't have much to go on, but the other night you were so…intuitive?"

"That's what I do." He heard her smiling now.

"And I bet your dad would be proud! I mean, I'm sure he told you how he rushed into the restroom with his pocketknife. Brave guy."

Adriana said nothing for a moment. Matt worried he had lost her again. *Stupid, stupid, stupid. She's fighting with her dad, remember?*

"Should I come by now?" she said.

10

IT TURNED Adriana's stomach to imagine being attacked at City Hall —in a bathroom, alone, so vulnerable. After her phone call with Officer Hinkley, Adriana couldn't get the images out of her head: overflowing sinks, clear tap water that turned dark and muddy, and toilet stalls filling up with murky lake water. Then a hand, *the* hand, grabbing her and pulling her to the slippery tiled bathroom floor as she thrashed and screamed for help.

All that vanished, though, when she heard Eric's voice.

"Are you taking Dylan with you?"

She looked up from the floor as she reached under her bed for two shoeboxes and a large plastic bag, all of which were filled with a mess of pens and pencils of various widths, colors, and inks. Art supplies were her safe haven. They kept her head and heart steady even while inking a demonic tattoo.

"Of course not. I think he's seen enough of the police station for a toddler."

Eric, framed in the doorway with a cigarette tucked behind his ear, the afternoon sun throwing shadows across his face, looked like an oil painting of a social misfit. She grabbed her graphite pencil set, which was rubber-banded together in the first box. Graphite smudged easily, which made for some beautiful shading. But would that shading come across in a photocopied Wanted poster? Would her sketch even end up on a Wanted poster, or would it be something they just passed around the station? She probably didn't want graphite if dozens of people were going to handle the sketch; it'd be a mess of fingerprints and dirty hands before everyone got a look, even if she sprayed it with a fixative. But she set them aside to bring anyway.

Eric sat on the bed. "Are you sure you can't take him? I've never been alone with him."

"You can leave him in his playpen most of the time. He's fine in there for now. Just turn on some cartoons. There's a whole stack of tapes next to the VCR my father gave him for Christmas. Right now, he's in love with *Ghostbusters*. I think he has a crush on their secretary."

"That's my boy." Eric grinned.

Adriana turned away, unwilling to liken her innocent son to Eric's conquest of Samantha at his welcome-back party. She pulled a few other pencils and a large gummy eraser out of the second shoebox and put them in a ziplock next to her purse. "I shouldn't be gone more than an hour or two."

"I really don't think it's a good idea."

"Do you have somewhere else to be?" She hated when she snapped like that.

"I mean, yeah, kind of."

Adriana stopped sorting through her pencils and glared. "Where? Where do you have to be right now?"

"Nowhere. Fuck it. Never mind."

Where could he possibly have to be? Samantha came to mind again, and Adriana had to wonder if she was jealous. *But of what?*

"Eric, a few hours. Is that really too much to ask after three years?"

"Now it's a few hours? A minute ago, you said one or two. Why would a stupid sketch take so long? You do them all the time."

"But not for the police."

"What's the—?"

"Eric! This is important. A woman was attacked. And the other day I did that sketch and it actually helped. That's why they're calling me back. Besides, didn't the judge tell me I have to find work?" She paused, turning it over in her head. "Maybe if I do well today, I can turn this into a regular gig. Then they'd have to let me keep Dylan. I mean, a job with the police department? It doesn't get more responsible than that. And all I need you to do is park your ass on the couch for a couple of hours and watch Dylan so I can focus. Okay?"

"I guess I can do that. Will you feed him before you go?"

"He just ate, but there's plenty of cereal if he gets hungry later."

"You'd take him if I wasn't here, though, right?"

"Jesus, Eric!" She threw a watercolor sponge at him. He flinched before realizing what it was.

"Okay, okay, I was just askin'!"

Eric fidgeted with the sponge. But Adriana wasn't done. As she packed her supplies, she tried to shape the question so that it wouldn't sound like a parent lecturing a child. He'd returned home really late last night, stumbled into furniture, and left the light on in the bathroom after brushing his teeth. She wasn't sure it was wise leaving him with Dylan today. But the question... When he looked at her—

"What?" he said. She let it fly.

"Did you bring any drugs home with you last night?"

"No!" His protest was a little too quick. Like he'd practiced in case it came up. Or maybe it was merely the kneejerk response any addict had. Eric squirmed. "I mean, yeah, I went to the Scarecrow yesterday. To see Robbie and some friends. We got some shit; I never lied about using, but I didn't bring anything back."

Adriana glanced at the bruising on his arm above the rotting skull she'd inked for him. Okay. He'd gotten high but outside of the house. That was about the best she could expect from him. But she couldn't quite let it go.

"Promise?" she asked.

Eric tossed the sponge back to Adriana. "Yeah, I promise."

Before Dylan was born, she would make him promise all the time. pinkie promise. Little fingers entwined. A cross-your-heart-hope-to-die kind of promise. But she didn't bother this time. And she didn't have time to search the house for his stash.

"I won't be gone long," she said.

He nodded. Sulking. Not looking at her.

11

"THERE IS A DARKNESS IN CELLAR!"

Mayor Bradley Krause's voice roared and echoed in the elementary school gymnasium, amplified by the public address system's loudspeakers. As he spoke, he squeezed the lacquered wooden frame of the podium, a trick he had learned years before from his first campaign manager. It helped anchor him and calm his nerves when speaking to crowds, in this case the parents, teachers, and schoolkids who had packed the space for this early-morning event.

"There is a darkness—and mark my words: it is spreading!"

As he unleashed his verbal hellfire, he looked out over his audience to measure its impact. The students would cower and peer wide-eyed at him, as they did each time he commanded the room at events. Most important, though, was the effect it had on the moms, dads, and school staff, including the custodians. He needed them to carry his message to their neighbors and friends. And after so many years in office, he hoped his constant themes would continue to stir enthusiasm and possibly a flood of moral outrage.

The turnout was better than he had expected. The packed bleachers and standing-room overflow likely surpassed fire code regulations, which gave him a curious thrill, even as he secretly scolded himself for needing a crutch: his grip on the podium was so desperate, his knuckles turned white. It was the meds, he thought. Goddamn meds. He needed to discuss his prescription again with the doctor, one of only two voters in Cellar who knew about the panic attacks he'd battled in recent years.

"And there is only one way to beat back the tide that is engulfing this community. Confront it. Confront it with every ounce of moral authority we can muster. And we must do it *now*, ladies and gentlemen!"

"Damn right! Tell it like it is, Mr. Mayor!" shouted a father who did not flinch from the commotion in the audience as heads turned and muffled whispers rose like steam from the lips of fellow Cellarites.

Bradley knew he could pause here because he'd hired the man to cause a stir on cue. A few canceled traffic tickets were all it cost to kick up some dust and sucker the local news radio crew into wedging their way toward the angry father to secure an interview for later.

Yet despite his command of the moment, the room spun and felt hot and muggy. He cleared his throat and leaned closer to the microphone. In a deep, imperious tone he pronounced, "Do not blame your neighbor for expressing his concern. He must know what I know. Someday your sons and daughters will thank you, as my daughter thanked me many years ago, for standing up and saying 'No. Not here. *Not in Cellar!*'"

As his voice trembled with righteous conviction, Bradley pulled his cramped hand from the podium and swung his arm up to a bright banner that was the backdrop to his speech.

Bradley's KIDS: Keeping Illegal Drugs out of Schools!

Applause exploded in the bleachers. Voices shouted support while students signed their Bradley's KIDS pledge cards and handed them to their parents and teachers. Only one man in the back of the room noticed the good mayor quickly return to the podium and grip it with all the might of a weakened old man hiding an addiction to his anti-anxiety meds.

POLICE CHIEF WOODHULL kept his eyes on Mayor Krause, who was smiling from behind his podium to the gymnasium full of voters and their kids, as he leaned toward Lois King. She stood next to him with her clipboard.

"This same old speech again?" he asked.

"Works every election," she said.

"Even if the program hasn't shown any real results?"

Lois feigned shock. "Chief Woodhull, surely you know the mayor's fight against drugs has helped keep your streets safe."

"And city council has ample data to prove it?"

The council president was coy. "Isn't that why we're expanding our effort, Woody? With your help, of course."

Chief Woodhull grimaced. He didn't like being a hired gun. Whenever His Honor discussed his drug-free program, he was expected to show up in full uniform and, on some occasions, with his department-issued Glock on his hip. *Bad theater*, he thought. His Glock hadn't fired a shot since...

Well, he didn't want to think about it. *Just smile, collect the pledge cards, and wait to get the hell out of here.*

12

"THAT'S NOT much to go on." Adriana tried to hide her disappointment. "Did he maybe have some tattoos or scars or anything more distinct?"

Laurie Kaplan looked apologetic. She also looked exhausted and clearly was not enjoying another visit to the police station, this time in a conference room with a large wooden table between her and Adriana. It was Officer Hinkley's idea to create a triangle, with him at the head of the table, observing, so Laurie did not feel like she was outnumbered and facing an inquisition. He also said he didn't want to disrupt the magic of Adriana's creative process.

Even though the door was closed, muffled sounds from the bullpen: phones, shoutouts, the whirr of a photocopy machine, etc., were distracting. Adriana, drawing pad in her lap, could tell it was difficult for Laurie to concentrate.

"I really didn't get a good look at him. I told the other officer..."

"Al Kasich," Hinkley said.

"Yes, that I wasn't sure this would do any good. The guy was mostly just a shadow, a blur. Everything happened so fast."

Adriana offered, "It was late, right? City Hall was about to close?"

"Right. And I was tired."

"It's okay," Adriana said. "Take your time."

Rain had started to fall on her drive to the station, but it was picking up in intensity now. It panged against the conference room windows overlooking the parking lot and drummed on the roofs of cars.

"I was *really* tired. I haven't been sleeping well, and my doctor gave me these little white pills. They help, but sometimes I find myself dozing off at the library now, especially during the evening shift."

"Were you taking them the other day, the day you were attacked?" Hinkley asked.

"I take them every day. Just last week I fell asleep at my kitchen table while making dinner. All the water boiled out of the pot. It was the smell that woke me. Awful. Burned dry pasta."

Adriana asked, "Do you think you fell asleep in the bathroom the other night?"

"No. And I know I didn't dream up some creep in there with me, if that's what you mean."

Adriana blushed and quickly apologized. "I didn't mean anything. Honestly. I'm just not sure what to ask. This is kind of my first time doing this."

"Well, that instills a lot of confidence."

WOODHULL WALKED INTO THE STATION, surveyed the bullpen, and felt his shoulders loosen; the school visit was over. Kasich grabbed his desk calendar and crossed out another day. Woodhull knew his retirement was close.

"How many days, Al?" he asked while he pulled off his jacket.

"Hundred forty-seven."

"Only five months? It's not too late to change your mind, buddy. Retirement isn't for everyone, you know."

"Chief, I can't wait to permanently hang up my 'Gone Fishing' plaque." Kasich wiped away the grin and lowered his voice. "But our rookie might need more than what I got left to give. He's gone rogue."

Woodhull followed Kasich's nod and saw Adriana and Hinkley sitting with a woman he didn't recognize.

"The kid suddenly drags in the mayor's daughter *with her crayons* to talk to Laurie there, the vic attacked at City Hall."

"Oh. That's her, huh?"

"Yes, sir. And she's in no shape to...well... Professional opinion: don't expect much from the art class."

Woodhull sighed. The department needed new blood, that was for sure, but he doubted he could summon the grit needed to train them all.

"Just monitor the situation for me, okay, Al?"

"You got it, Chief."

ADRIANA'S SHOULDERS SAGGED. This sketch wasn't going as well as the other one. Was she putting too much pressure on herself? Maybe, but what choice did she have? *I have to find work now. This is an amazing opportunity. Give me something...*

"I'm sorry," Laurie said. She must have sensed Adriana's frustration. "I... I was just so scared. More scared than I'd ever felt in any dream or nightmare, you know? Why did no one see him leave?" She wiped her eyes and gazed out the conference room windows at the rain.

Adriana's sketch was little more than faint lines, the scattered idea of a face. She stared down at the dark lines, the shadows, a face hiding, wanting to come out of the shadows. Like the face from her own nightmares.

Then Laurie turned from the window. "I really didn't get a good look at him."

"It's okay," Adriana offered.

"Worth a shot, I thought." Hinkley stood as Laurie gathered her coat and purse.

Adriana waited until he escorted Laurie out before returning to the sketch and running her gummed-up eraser back and forth over what little she had been able to draw.

This was your best shot at a full-time gig, and you screwed it up. This sketch isn't worth ten cents. What's wrong with you?

She scowled as she berated herself for her useless expertise—transforming rambling half-drunk descriptions of tattoos into exacting pieces of fleshy art, no problem. Sketching the very real face of a very real attacker, *and this is what you come up with?!* Her heart sank.

An envelope landed on top of the big table. She turned to see Hinkley standing beside her.

"I'm sorry. She wasn't giving me much, and..."

"It's okay. Security, your father; no one got a look at him. The creep took off fast."

He pushed the envelope closer to her. She reached in and found two ten-dollar bills.

"But the sketch wasn't any good."

Hinkley shrugged. "I knew it was a longshot. Last time it seemed so easy. Like you could see the robber in your mind or something. But hey, don't beat yourself up. I told Woodhull earlier how helpful the other sketch was. He seemed impressed."

"That's good." Adriana looked back out into the bullpen and saw Woodhull conferring with Kasich. *Wait, of course, the first drawing. They'd caught their man. He'd confessed almost instantly. That could be my in. Why was I stressing so much about this drawing when I've already proven myself?* She perked up and turned back to Hinkley. "I'd get better at this kind of thing if I could work at it full-time. I can draw more than people, you know. How about stolen cars, weapons, stray cats?"

"Like, consult for us more often?"

"I was thinking something like a full-time job, maybe? Can you get me ten minutes with the chief?"

"Yeah, I don't know."

"Okay, just five minutes. In my downtime, I could help answer phones or file stuff or something, right?"

"I'm not sure we're even hiring, the chief keeps complaining about the budget, Ms. Krause."

"Adriana."

"Adriana." He repeated and she thought she caught a glimpse of a smile. His hand was resting near the envelope on the table; she put her hand on his.

"Please, Officer."

His fair cheeks blushed apple red. "Well, I guess it can't hurt to ask. Hang tight. I'll see if the chief is available."

13

"I'D LIKE to help you, Adriana. Really, I would. Me and your pop go way back, and you've always been talented," Chief Woodhull said from behind the biggest desk Adriana had ever seen. "But we don't really need a full-time sketch artist here."

"But I wouldn't be that. I wouldn't *just* be that. I can type; my mom taught me when I was young. I can file, answer phones, plan events. I worked two summers at City Hall. I can handle anything else you have for me. I learn fast and I *really* need a job."

The chief's office was so quiet and contained that Adriana could hear his wooden mantel clock. It looked grand on his bookcase, surrounded by framed photos, ticking away the day. She could also hear the slight groans of the leather chairs every time either of them shifted their weight. And she could hear Woodhull sigh as he grew impatient.

Woodhull hadn't aged as well as her father. His cheeks were pocked with acne scars and his weight pushed against his uniform at every seam. "I can't even remember the last time we had a sketch artist in here. Hinkley only called you in, without anyone else's consent, I might add, because of your drawing the other night."

He took a cigarette out of a little gold tin on his desk, probably not helping with the aging factors, then snapped the tin shut. She hadn't heard that sound in over ten years, but she could instantly place it: the poker games.

The chief used to sit in on her father's poker games every Sunday night. This was back when she was in grade school, but she clearly remembered the snack-littered table, the smoke from cigars, cigarettes, and pipes swirling around the kitchen table light, and Woodhull snapping that little gold tin open and shut a dozen times a night during those games.

Win big or lose big; just don't be a chicken shit, he would say while dealing. As the only girl allowed to attend those old boys' nights, she felt like an undercover spy. She paused; what she was about to say would either kill her chances or endear the chief to her.

"Win big or lose big..." she said. Woodhull looked up from his desk and exhaled a cloud of smoke and grinned.

"...just don't be a chicken shit. Words to live by."

He'd given her an opening, and she charged right in.

"Okay, then, how about a wager, Chief?"

It was her last play. Helping to catch the McDonald's mugger apparently hadn't impressed him as much as she'd hoped, and she didn't dare bring up the failed sketch she did for Laurie. All she had left was to entice the gambler in him.

Woodhull sat forward. "All right, I'm listening."

She knew she didn't have much of a poker face as a young girl. Maybe she could pull it off now by pretending she didn't care. What the heck, roll the dice...

"Okay, here's the deal: you describe your wife using only three words. Just three. And I will sketch her."

"Impossible."

"If you say so. But if I can make it happen, you find some regular work for me around here."

He grinned like he'd already won.

"But let's be clear. I have never met your wife, right?"

"Far as I know."

"Okay. And she never came to any of those poker nights, and I've never inked a tattoo for her, so...I can't possibly know what she looks like, right?"

"And that is exactly why it's impossible. So why bother trying?"

"Maybe I'm that good?" Now she pushed her luck. "And maybe that sketch of the McDonald's mugger was not just a fluke."

"Sweetheart, no one's that good."

Woodhull stared at her, appeared to weigh the odds on her wager, then said, "If I accept, and you can't draw her, what do I get?"

"Lunch, my treat, every day for a week. Anything you want from Cody's Diner." Adriana couldn't afford a lousy hamburger let alone a week of lunches, nor could she afford to back down.

He leaned back in his chair, took a long drag from his cigarette, then stubbed it out in an ashtray on his desk.

"All right, Addie, you've got a deal."

Woodhull hoisted himself out of his leather chair and walked to the office door. Adriana stood, confused, grabbed her bag and sketch materials, and followed him out to the middle of the bullpen.

"Hey! Listen up, guys." Woodhull waited for the half dozen officers to get quiet. "This here is Adriana, daughter of our distinguished mayor. She's a sketch artist who'd like to come work with us and we've made a little wager. She's going to draw a sketch of my wife from a description of just three words. If she can do it, she's got the job. And you guys are going to give her those three words. Most of you have seen Judy around here before, so..."

Adriana interrupted. "Wait, Chief. No, it doesn't work that way. That wasn't the deal." The cops all grinned. Ballsy little gambler girl shutting down the boss. "I need to know how *you* see her. I need you to picture your wife in *your* mind, then give me three words. Deal?"

"Yeah, okay. Come to think of it, I really don't want to hear what these guys think of my wife." Woodhull grinned and let a couple hecklers have their say. Then he paused for a moment and thought it over.

"Okay, here goes," he said. "Judy is...generous."

"Aw, ain't that sweet," one cop gushed.

"Caring."

An even bigger mocking sigh, this time from the ensemble.

"And *brunette*."

"That's a bullshit description." A couple officers booed. "C'mon, Chief, give the girl a fighting chance."

Adriana played the crowd. "It's okay, it's okay." She noticed a worried Hinkley in the bullpen, winked at him, then sat at an empty desk. She flipped open her sketch pad and quickly blocked out the rough predetermined proportions that all faces, *except one*, conform to. A hush filled the room as the officers moved closer to observe Adriana's mastery.

"Okay, Chief Woodhull, now's when I need you to picture your wife. Think of some fond memories and really, really try to see her face. It'll help me."

"I don't want to help you. I want a week of free lunches from Cody's."

The cops shut down that kind of talk with jibes. "You made the bet." "It's a telepathy kind of thing." "Arrest that man!"

Adriana didn't hear the laughter as she focused on the swoops and scoops her hand made while sketching. A chin, then a feminine mouth that morphed into a pleasant smile. The cops saw the ease she brought to her art and couldn't know that Addie was in a mental battle with images of the dead, rotting face that wanted to emerge here. It was as if pencil to paper ignited the phantom's obsessive need to inhabit her head, heart, and hands.

She trained her focus on the eyes. No, not black holes, not empty. But caring, generous eyes. The whole station seemed to melt away, a distant light at the far end of her conscious.

"Hey, Addie, you almost done?" Chief Woodhull's voice snapped her back into the room. He stood in front of her, trying to peek down at the drawing.

"Um, just another minute." Her throat was dry, and she cleared it. "Soon," she said with more confidence.

She added shading to the woman's cheeks, ears, and neckline, then set her pencil down. She stood and handed the sketch pad to the chief. He stared at it. At first impassive, then troubled, maybe even a little afraid. Adriana started to fidget. Then he looked up at his crew, shook his head at the wonder of it all, and smiled. "That's some kind of witchcraft, girl."

He held the sketch up for everyone to see. Guffaws, shouts, and a few whispers. "It looks just like her!" Applause followed.

"Okay, okay, I'm a man who honors his bets. Congratulations, Addie. I don't know how you did it, but it's...amazing. You're hired —*part-time* to start. And probationary, six months, like everyone else who starts here."

"Really?! Thank you so much. You won't regret it, Chief."

Elated, she gathered her supplies, barely able to contain herself.

"That's really an incredible gift you have. To see into someone's mind like that." Hinkley shuffled his feet, like a kid in awe of meeting a baseball star. "My aunt used to say she had a second sight, but I never saw any proof. Nothing like what you just did!"

Adriana blushed a little and put the sketch pad in her bag.

"Thanks for setting up the meeting, Officer Hinkley."

"Since you'll be working here, you should probably start calling me Rookie. Everyone else does." He chuckled.

Adriana smiled, zipped up her purse, and looked around, trying to imagine working here. A "straight" job that included her art, with people who had just expressed awe at her skill. So much better than inking flames and skulls on her goth friends. The judge would have to be on her side now, *right?*

"Hey, I was thinking," Hinkley said, "my shift ends soon. Do you maybe want to grab a drink, you know, to celebrate? It's on me, of course."

Excitement bubbled up in her, until she remembered Eric with Dylan. How long had it been since she left the house?

"But, you know, I don't want to..." Hinkley sounded like he was getting cold feet, and Adriana didn't want the thrill of this day to evaporate yet. Eric would just have to find a way to survive another hour or so with his son.

"That sounds like fun, actually," Adriana said. *Fun,* she thought. *What a concept.*

14

BRADLEY FELT OVERSHADOWED by his desk, so he rose and paced as he brainstormed with Lois King, who took notes.

"Maybe if you just speak to Card," he said.

Lois looked up from the leather-bound organizer unfolded in her lap. "Why me?"

"You hold an important position here."

She still looked unconvinced. "And say what?"

Bradley paced more aggressively, tossing out ideas. "He's young. He'll have his chance."

"But not this year?"

"Come on, Lois, a shopping mall? Draining the lake? It's nuts! Let his ideas churn and evolve as he learns more about Cellar."

"Yet his idea stirs the imagination. It's creative. And he's a good-looking guy."

The mayor could not believe what he was hearing. He stopped pacing in front of Lois, who sat on a sofa against the wall.

"Whose side are you on?"

"I'm saying…"

"Take one for the team."

"Me? Take a hit? Look, Ben is a newcomer, but other council

members like him. If I lean too heavy for you, I may offend the very members who I need to rally around other issues."

"Well, all right, but..."

"And I'm playing the opposition's point of view, challenging you."

His so-called ally was a bit too enamored with the opposition, he thought.

"Bradley, we can't take for granted that he's wrong and won't get any traction with voters. Frankly, I'm not so sure your promotion of the Bradley's KIDS program is holding sway."

"It's been working."

"For whom? I mean, I've got to ask... *There's a darkness in Cellar*'... Really? Is the average Joe Voter worried about that?"

"You don't think so? The big cities are overrun with violence. The kids out there are joining gangs, worshiping Satan and Alice Cooper, and God knows what else."

Bradley glanced over to the framed photos and newspaper clipping hanging on his office wall. *THE SAVIOR OF CELLAR*, one clipping read, the headline above a triumphant photo of Bradley up on stage at some rally. *Was that really a decade ago? How quickly the time flies. How quickly they all forget.*

Lois softened. "They worry about their kids, sure. But this isn't Cleveland. Listen, maybe we shift focus to outcomes, happier days?"

"I'm happy."

Lois gave him a doubtful look.

"Talk to him, Lois. Reason with him."

"For the team?"

"For the future."

THERE WERE ONLY three drinking places in Cellar. Gallagher's was the friendliest and tended toward a younger crowd, so that was where Matt steered Adriana. The place was packed, even for a Friday night, and he felt a tinge of regret as he carried two celebratory beers and a basket of fries toward their tall table. Two kids dressed in all black, both wearing thick eyeliner, were chatting with his date, if he dared call her that. Matt tried not to stare, but he hadn't seen a man wearing eyeliner before, outside of MTV. The couple frowned when Matt sat down at the table, their eyes slithered up and down his police uniform.

"This is Officer Hinkley." Adriana introduced him. "And this is Ian and Samantha. They're…uh, they know Dylan's dad."

"Just Matt is fine." He smiled, more at Adriana than her two friends.

"Matt, then," Adriana said, smiling back.

"Care to join us?" Matt gestured to the empty chairs around the table.

Ian said, "Thanks, but…"

"We should get going." Samantha grabbed one hot French fry and waved goodbye. She and Ian made their way to the pool tables in the back of the bar.

"What makes people dress that way?" Matt said.

"They're protesting, I suppose."

"Protesting what?"

"Life." After a beat, she laughed.

Matt chuckled and raised his glass. "I should have told you. I have something to celebrate too."

Adriana clinked his glass with hers. "Great. What are we toasting?"

"Six months on the force. Probation's over next week."

"Impressive. Congratulations! I guess that means you'll always have seniority over me."

Matt sipped, then confessed, "Only if I can last another six. I don't think anyone there likes me. Especially Kasich."

Adriana gave him an inquisitive look.

"Sometimes I think he's just hazing me for fun, but other times, I think he truly has it out for me. And… Well, do you believe in ghosts?"

Adriana choked on her drink and put a hand over her mouth to clear her throat. "Why do you ask?"

"That's how it feels in the office."

"Too many old dead people floating around?"

He grinned at her candor. "Well, I wouldn't put it quite like that, but...it's more like nobody wants to move forward on anything."

"Or can't."

"Yeah," he agreed. "But hey, you gave us quite a show today. How'd you learn to draw?"

"My mom, I think. She loved to paint. Beautiful landscapes and nature. I used to spend hours with her art books up in the attic. She had a great big easel my father put up there, along with all of her supplies." Adriana nursed her drink, taking a smaller, more careful sip. "But I guess I learned more from her books than from her. She vanished when I was a kid."

"Vanished?"

"I don't know. Left? Disappeared? I heard rumors when I got a little older, like that she ran away with a secret lover, or was locked up in some psych ward in Illinois. Ridiculous stuff. A few kids even told me their parents thought my father killed her."

Matt looked dumbfounded. "What? The mayor? Why would anybody think that?"

"Maybe somebody heard them arguing or something? Or they were lying. Kids are dicks to each other. I don't believe it, of course. I just think...maybe I was too much? Maybe I drove her away or something?"

"I'm sure that's not true."

Adriana went quiet and focused on her glass.

What was he supposed to say? *Shouldn't I be able to comfort her? Offer some profound words of reassurance or guidance? Something? Anything?*

"Anyway," she offered. "I don't think you'll have a problem lasting six more months on the job. Don't all you rookies want to make detective or something some day?"

"That's my dream job, actually. Cliché or not."

"Then you should go for it."

He beamed but felt like Adriana might not be finished thinking about her mother.

"That stuff about your dad, though…"

"Hey," she said, "isn't this supposed to be a celebration?"

Point taken. Matt smiled. "Another round?"

AFTER A FEW DRINKS, Adriana spent more and more time looking at the clock on the wall, so Matt walked her to her car. He didn't know how she handled the responsibilities of a kid at home at her age. He didn't think he could handle it, when even a simple night out at the bar required, at a minimum, prearranged childcare and keeping an eye on the time.

The sky was growing dark, and he was slightly concerned that his blood alcohol concentration might exceed the standards for driving under the influence. He admired how Adriana had conserved her intake. Another point in the responsibility column.

The veneer of light from the overhead lamps made Adriana look ghostly under her dark hair, wrapped in her black jacket. But not in a scary way. She shimmered, and he felt a longing to touch her.

She broke his reverie with a question. "Want to know a secret?"

"Absolutely."

She bit her lower lip and confessed. "Chief Woodhull has a photo of his wife, Judy, on the shelf right behind his desk. My, uh, sketch… matches it perfectly."

Matt threw back his head and laughed. "He'll never make detective."

"I know it was wrong, but I really needed to get this job. You have no idea. And I thought he might try to outplay me. I was right. Did you hear his bullshit description?"

As they stood at her battered car, Matt decided to tell her a secret. "I'm going to like seeing you every day at work."

Do ghosts blush? He thought he noticed a change in her complexion. Something shy. "But there's a dress code, you know."

Adriana laughed, then quickly kissed his cheek. Too stunned to say anything, he just stood there as she got into her car, started the engine, and eased out of the parking lot.

He smiled when she waved with long fingers, the same fingers that expressed themselves so freely and beautifully with pencils and pens. He watched her car disappear down the road.

Matt dug his keys out of his pocket, turned toward his own car— and was attacked.

"Hey! What the—!"

He flailed as his face whipped back and forth in reaction to a foe he could not see in the dark. Beaten and panicked, he called for help, his voice rising to shrieks that would have shamed him in any other situation. Then the torrent, the blurry assault, passed. Stunned, he looked around the parking lot and beyond in search of the culprit. Some drunk patron looking for a fight, maybe. Or those two ghouls Adriana knew. He remembered the way they looked at him in his uniform.

But there was nothing. No one. Just him, shaking in the moonlit parking lot.

15

THE BUMP in the road was so jarring that Adriana grimaced, thinking about the wear and tear on her car. She couldn't see it in the dark. Lisa had maneuvered the change in road surfaces so gracefully the other night as they turned onto their street. The thought of Lisa replaced Adriana's scowl with a smile. It was unlikely that her neighbor had been fantasizing about some man while she was behind the steering wheel.

Spending time with Matt had been delightful. Adriana felt appreciated, relaxed, and safe for the first time in days. When he teased that he should make her "walk the line" in the parking lot before allowing her to drive, she obliged by walking one of the white parking spot stripes end to end. No problem. Then she challenged him to do the same. He declined, and they'd laughed.

Her only misstep was bringing up her mom. But he didn't seem troubled with anything she'd said by the time she kissed her police escort good night.

She applied the brakes in her head. *Yeah, it was nice getting to know one of your co-workers before starting your new job. But that's all it was, okay?*

No, that's not all it was. She'd enjoyed the outing so much that she'd lost track of time. Eric would be pissed. *You said a few hours tops!* Yeah, yeah, yeah. She was already planning her defense out loud, forcefully, when her headlights illuminated a figure in the middle of the road.

She slammed on her brakes for real, and her heart skipped as she realized the little figure staring back at her was Dylan, crying and dragging his teddy bear down the road. She jammed the gear shift into park and leaped out, engine still running. When she crouched to embrace Dylan, his crying turned to sobs. "Mommy!"

"Honey, what's wrong? Why are you out here? Where's Daddy?"

She ran her hands down Dylan's body and looked him over to make sure he wasn't physically harmed in any way. He clung to her, his tears finally subsiding into quiet sniffles.

Over his shoulder Adriana could see the house, lit up in her car's headlights. The front door was open, and the living room was dark. "Dylan, baby, come on."

She kept him in her lap as she turned the car and crept up the driveway. She shut off the engine and heard loud music thumping from her home. As she stepped out of the car, Lisa approached, walking over from next door.

"Hey. I heard Dylan crying. Is everything okay?"

"I just got home and found him out in the middle of the road."

"Oh, my God."

"I left him with Eric, who is clearly doing a *fantastic* job of watching him."

They both glanced at the house, a little wary.

Lisa said, "Here, I'll take Dylan while you go find Daddy. Feel free to kick some you-know-what in there."

"Thanks." Adriana managed a weak smile as she headed toward the porch. "If he's passed out again, I'm going to kill him."

She stepped through the open front door to shrieking music, Killswitch Kevin's devil-may-care evening show, and inhaled an odd odor. *Is that piss or hash?* She passed through the tiny foyer into the living room, flipped on the overhead light, and found Eric exactly as she had imagined him—sprawled out on the sofa.

"Goddammit, Eric!"

Empty beer cans, a pile of cassettes, and a black leather pouch were strewn on the floor. She'd planned on looking for the leather pouch, where he stored his paraphernalia, to prove that he was bringing his shit into her house. Eric's sloppy habits had saved her the trouble.

Adriana couldn't play babysitter or mother to him anymore. She kicked his leg hard.

"Wake up! I can't believe you got high while I was gone, you fuck!"

Eric didn't move. Not even a burp or groan. He had to be really far gone.

"Come on, get your ass up and get out of my house!"

She kicked his leg again harder. Eric's body jostled on the couch and his mouth gaped open. Two lines of milky drool dripped from his bottom lip. She watched the cloudy substance spider down across his shirt and realized his chest wasn't moving. Terrified, she reached an unsteady hand to his nose and mouth. She jumped back. She'd felt nothing. No, she'd felt something worse than nothing: she'd felt the cold radiating from his skin.

No words would form. She was both hot and shivering with shock. Her legs almost gave out under her and she screamed.

"Help! Help!"

Lisa rushed in with Dylan in her arms.

"He's not breathing," Adriana said. "He's not breathing!"

"We need to call for an ambulance." Lisa handed Dylan to Adriana and made her way to the phone on the wall in the kitchen. As she waited for the other end of the line to pick up, she motioned for Adriana to turn off the radio, where Killswitch Kevin's voice was booming as he introduced the next song.

Adriana hit the power button on the receiver and the house fell silent. Dylan's eyes were wide and glassy from the turmoil. Adriana's shock was loosening and rapidly being replaced with outrage. With Dylan still in her arms, she returned to Eric and hissed, "You lousy bastard!"

Her cheeks burned with streaks of eyeliner as she began to sob and, with a fury she couldn't control, she kicked Eric again. His head jerked, his eyes popped open, and he stared at her in surprise. His mouth still oozed drool.

"Eric?" she said softly.

Lisa came up behind Adriana and gently pulled her arm.

"Wait! He's alive!"

"No, hon."

"But his eyes!"

"Come on. Let's wait outside for the medics."

16

THE ENTIRE STREET pulsed with red-and-blue emergency lights that strobed across lawns and smeared the faces of neighbors who stood on their porches or peered out windows. Adriana felt mauled by the intrusion of a hundred sets of eyes, her trauma displayed so publicly. Yet, by comparison, the impact of Eric's dead stare imploring her to bring him back to life was far worse.

"It certainly looks like an overdose." Chief Woodhull stood on the sidewalk with Adriana and Lisa, a short distance from the house. "But we'll do a full autopsy to make sure. Did you know he was using?"

"I saw the marks on his arm while I was inking his tattoo, but I wasn't sure if they were recent."

She went mute when EMTs rolled Eric's body down the driveway to the ambulance. She might have felt more embarrassed by the spectacle than grief-stricken. She was grateful for only one thing: Dylan had fallen asleep in her arms.

"So, you came home after the station?"

"Uh, and Gallagher's. I was celebrating the new job." She said this sheepishly and declined to mention Matt, Officer Hinkley, hoping it wouldn't come back to bite her. Or him.

"And you?" Woodhull asked Lisa.

"I was home. Annoyed with the loud music, but not really concerned until I heard Dylan crying. That's when I came outside."

"When Adriana showed up?"

"Right."

"Okay. If we have any other questions, we'll let you know. And your name, Mrs.?"

"Dr. Shah," Lisa said.

"Dr. Shah." Woodhull nodded and wrote in a small notebook, then looked to Adriana. His expression was much softer than it had been in his office that afternoon. "We're going to take just one more look around the house and then we'll get out of your way, okay?"

"Okay. Thank you," she said.

Woodhull gave her a nod and strode off toward the house.

Lisa put an arm around Adriana. "Do you want me to stick around?"

"No, it's okay. I just... I don't know how I'm going to be able go back in there. How am I ever going to sit on that couch again? And what about court in a few weeks? It's just so much."

"One thing at a time. This is tonight's thing. All that other stuff can wait," Lisa said.

Behind them, another automobile rolled to the curb and stopped. A heavy door slammed and was followed by the signature click-clack of stiff shoes on pavement.

"Adriana! Is everything all right?" Bradley shouted as he marched toward her.

"Dad, what are you doing here?"

"I heard the emergency call on my scanner. Is Dylan okay?"

"It's not us. It's Eric."

His jaw clenched. "Did he hurt you?"

"No. He... He's dead."

"What?"

"He overdosed." Her voice cracked when she continued. "I walked in and he was on the couch. Not moving."

Bradley pulled his daughter and grandson into a hug. It was so unexpected that she startled.

"It's okay," he said. "I'm here now."

The words didn't exactly warm Adriana, and she didn't return the hug. She just stood there like a lamppost until Bradley let her go. "Why don't we get you both back home and—"

"We can't go in until Chief Woodhull is done."

"I didn't mean here, I meant *our* home, on Pine Street."

"No."

"Addie—"

"I'm not going back there."

Lisa spoke up. "Uh, Mr. Krause? Hi. I live right next door. Adriana and Dylan are more than welcome to stay with us tonight if she doesn't want to be alone."

The mayor looked her up and down. "And you are?"

"I'm Lisa Shah. I moved in a few weeks ago. I was with Adriana when she found Eric."

"Ah. Well, Lisa, thank you for the offer, but I'd prefer…"

"Dad, Dylan and I will stay with Lisa tonight."

"Really?"

"Look, it's right next door, Dylan's going to need his PJs and some toys, and I'm exhausted." What she didn't mention was that she feared the memory trap of her old bedroom on Pine Street. Eric was everywhere. Secret trysts, photos from their time together, the silver crossbones necklace he'd given her for their one-month anniversary. And his mixtape. The one that included her special song, a melody she'd forgotten until just now and that she did not dare listen to.

"Dad, thank you for coming out, but I need to get Dylan ready for bed, and I'm sure Lisa would like to get some sleep too."

Bradley waved his hand and nodded, a gesture of consent.

"Okay. But if you change your mind, call me. I don't mind coming back over."

"Thanks."

"I love you," he said.

Before Adriana could respond, Bradley turned and marched toward the house, her house. It swarmed with officers, but Bradley went straight for Woodhull on the porch. Their body language spoke of tension and avoidance, and quiet sharp words were exchanged.

"What's that all about?" Lisa said, gesturing with the slightest tilt of her head.

"Who knows? I've never been able to figure those two out."

17

———

THE POUNDING OVERHEAD WOKE ADRIANA. She did not know where she was. The dark room was unfamiliar, and panic set in. She sat up. She was on Lisa's couch. Dylan was beside her, softly snoring on a pile of blankets that were illuminated by diagonal lines of sunlight that were just beginning to seep through the blinds.

That noise, though. It continued to thump from the room above her.

Lisa, in a flowing nightgown, hurried in from the kitchen. "Sorry. That kid and her music," she whispered as she hustled up the stairs.

Adriana stared at the living room ceiling. She recognized the tune, "Little Red Corvette" by Prince. The song had been reduced to a muffled bass rendition, and it took a moment for her to place the thumps in context.

Dylan started fussing with his blankets and rubbed at his eyes. Adriana reached across the end table and turned on a small lamp so Dylan could see he wasn't alone. She was thankful he had slept through the night. She wasn't sure how long he'd been alone with... Eric's corpse. Just thinking those words made her shiver...but Dylan hadn't seemed to have had any nightmares. Last night, anyway. Come to think of it, neither had she. The rest was very welcome.

Lisa's living room was clean and decorated in mostly soft pastels, the exact opposite of Adriana's home. Picture frames lined a powder blue curio cabinet, and the coffee table had ornate white doilies under large candleholders. Lisa was older than Adriana, but this felt like being at grandma's place.

A fluffy white cat ran into the room, got up onto the couch, and stopped next to Dylan. It cautiously sniffed him. The cat darted away as Dylan pushed off his covers. He followed the cat to a recliner on the opposite side of the room and reached to pet the white coat of fur, but the cat once again escaped, this time jumping to the upper reaches of the chair.

"Gentle with the kitty, honey. Not all of them like being petted."

The thumping music stopped abruptly. The house was still and so quiet, Adriana could hear the tick-tock of the grandfather clock in the hall. *No yelling or talking back?* Not what Adriana expected from a teenager whose mom had just shut off their music.

Then the staircase rumbled, and a girl quickly came into view, staring with curiosity at Adriana and Dylan. Her hair was dark with a dyed-bright-pink stripe, and the sleeves had been ripped off the band shirt she wore. This girl looked completely out of place in this house.

Adriana rose off the couch. "You must be Jennifer. Your mom's mentioned you a few times. I'm sorry it took so long for us to meet. I'm Adriana, and that's Dylan over there."

Jennifer didn't speak. She looked around the room, then up at Lisa, who came down the stairs behind her.

"It's okay," Lisa said. Then she turned to Adriana. "She's a bit shy with new people."

Jennifer stepped forward and offered her hand. Adriana smiled and reached out for a handshake.

"She's also deaf," Lisa said. "I know, I didn't mention it before. It's just…it's not the first thing people should know about her. Like, it's not all she is."

"But the music?" Adriana said.

"Oh, she loves her music. She has ninety percent hearing loss, but she can read the lyrics, she can watch the music videos, and she can feel the bass grooves and drums."

"Oh."

"Not the best way to wake up. Sorry about that. But the only decent thing her father left her were those gigantic speakers and the turntable. Sometimes I think he loved high-end equipment more than people."

Dylan shuffled to Adriana's side and hid behind her leg. He peeked out to watch Jennifer, who smiled and waved. She started signing.

"She says sorry for waking you up," Lisa said.

"Oh, please tell her it's no problem."

"You just did. Jenny has been reading lips for years now."

Jennifer and Lisa spoke with moving hands, then Jennifer said aloud, "Dylan?"

Surprised, Adriana looked to Lisa.

"I started teaching her lip reading at an early age because most hearing people will never learn sign language. I wanted her to be able to understand them. Now we're working on speech. She doesn't like to speak out loud often. She's insecure about being misunderstood."

Jennifer playfully swatted at her mom and a look of embarrassment crossed her face.

"She sounded fine when she said Dylan's name."

"She's better than she believes she is. But hey, that's true for most of us."

Jennifer said, "May I hold Dylan?"

"She used to babysit for our neighbors in Canton," Lisa said. "She loves kids."

"Sure." Adriana nodded a bit too much.

Jennifer knelt and played a round of peekaboo with Dylan, who giggled and loosened his grip on Adriana's leg. When Jennifer held out her hands, Dylan shyly walked to her.

"He tried to pet your cat earlier. Is that all right?" Adriana asked.

"Oh yeah, it's fine. Midnight can be skittish, but he loves the attention," Lisa said.

"Midnight?"

"Jenny thought it was funny. She'd always imagined having a black cat, like the witches in all those Halloween cartoons. So she already had the name picked out when we went to adopt. But he's the one she fell in love with."

"That's cute," Adriana said.

Jennifer took Dylan to the recliner where Midnight was now curled up on the seat cushion. She guided his little hand over the soft white fur. It touched Adriana to see him being cared for, especially after observing Eric's indifference. *Eric. Shit.* Her expression tightened.

"You okay?"

Adriana hesitated, then asked, "Could I leave Dylan with you for half an hour? I need to check on the house before I take him back. I'm sure there's some picking up to do after everything last night."

"Of course. Go. I have to change and head off to work in a bit or I'd offer to help. But don't worry, if you're not back by the time I leave, Jennifer is a very capable babysitter."

Adriana stooped next to Dylan and kissed the top of his head. He was so enthralled with his new friend that he barely responded.

———

THE WRECKAGE in Adriana's living room was worse than she had expected. Blankets, books, and other belongings had been tossed and bunched in corners. The coffee table had been dragged away from the couch and pushed near the kitchen. In the process, one leg had broken off, giving the table the look of a wooden avalanche. Only one couch cushion remained in place, and at first glance she couldn't tell where the others were hiding. She bent and picked up Dylan's sippy cup from the carpet. It was on its side, surrounded by a large purple Kool-Aid stain.

She managed to get the room mostly straightened up in just over twenty minutes while experiencing only one body-shaking crying fit that included a lot of shouting and cursing at Eric.

When she was done, she collapsed onto the one remaining couch cushion and wiped her eyes. That's when she noticed one of the lost cushions wedged behind her stereo.

She reached over the arm of the couch and pulled on the cushion. It stuck, but a second hard pull freed it, knocking the back panel of the stereo speaker ajar.

"Oh no. No no no." Had the police opened it when they searched her house? Had they taken her stuff?!

She pulled the speaker away from the wall. Six metal fasteners usually held the thing together. She'd had these speakers for years and used the back cavity as a lockbox to stash anything she wanted to keep from Bradley's prying eyes back in high school. She'd shown Eric, wanting to impress him with how clever the hiding spot had been all those years ago. Now she used it to hide valuables in case the house was ever robbed.

She exhaled in relief. Inside the cabinet she found a ziplock bag that contained the gold ring her mother had left behind, a few other keepsakes, and $127 in cash: her entire lifesavings. And it looked like Eric had remembered the hiding place. A fresh bag of weed and a bank envelope from Burnham Credit Union lay next to her stuff.

She untucked the flap from the envelope and unearthed hundreds of dollars in twenties.

What the hell, Eric?

Adriana turned the credit union envelope over. There was a phone number and the name *Robbie* written on the back in what looked like Eric's sloppy scrawl. How could the police not have found this stuff? Or maybe they had but didn't care. The guy on the couch had been dead, after all. Maybe Woodhull gave her a pass on the dope, knowing Bradley would be hurt if it came out?

Adriana didn't care about the drugs now but stared at the envelope for a long time. It was tempting: she could use the cash. But first she had to figure out why it was here. Eric didn't have any money. And he sure as hell didn't have a local credit union account. But she knew someone who did.

She shoved the envelope back into the speaker cabinet and replaced the back panel with the fasteners. Then she heard screaming outside. She ran to the door.

In Lisa's front yard, Jennifer chased a smiling Dylan in wide circles. He stopped just long enough for her to catch up to him, then shot off running again. Jennifer's hands were shaped like claws, and in a voice haunted by misshapen vowels, she roared a monstrous threat. Dylan squealed with delight.

18

THAT FOLLOWING MONDAY, Adriana began her first day of work at the Cellar Police Department by withholding evidence. She'd relocated the bank envelope from the speaker lockbox to her shoulder bag with the intention of showing it to her personal detective, Matt Hinkley. He'd kept the secret of Woodhull's wife's photo to himself, so she figured she could trust him with this too. And she welcomed his professional opinion, even if he'd only been on the job for six months. Either way, she had decided to keep the money she'd found. No one would blame her for wanting it to care for Dylan. It might be his only inheritance from Eric.

When she walked into the police station, Officer Packer welcomed her at the front desk and showed her to her workspace. Her office was in Conference Room B, the same room she sat in a few days ago to draw for Laurie. Her desk was an old wooden table in the corner of the room and a banged-up file cabinet stood in for desk drawers. The makeshift drawers were stocked with some paper and office pens, hardly suitable for serious drawing, but she'd wait until she'd been there a little longer before requesting anything more professional. The space was quiet when she shut the door, and it was out of the way of the bullpen traffic. For a moment, she sat in a reverie and marveled at how fulfilling it was to have her own office, her own creative space.

Then she heard a knock at the door. She swiveled in her chair and Chief Woodhull peeked in.

"Adriana, we didn't expect you to come into work so soon," he said.

"I'm okay. Kind of. And I think work will take my mind off things."

"Yeah, I hear you. Me too. Well, since you're here, I do have a project for you. If you're feeling up to it?"

"Of course."

Woodhull pulled a chair from the conference room table and sat close to Addie's desk.

"Our Annual Police Fundraiser is coming up. It's a small carnival stocked by some of the small businesses around town and the Friends of the Force. All of the proceeds benefit the local union."

"I remember the carnival; my father took me when I was younger."

"A lot of stuff for families to have fun with there, yeah. And it's good community outreach. Anyway, the last few years we've just posted an ad in the paper. Pretty boring. This year I was thinking maybe you could draw up some fliers or posters to hang around town."

"I can do that."

"Doesn't have to be anything grand, just something that'll get the information out there."

"Time, place, date."

"Yeah, that sort of thing. But maybe with a little pop, maybe a smiling police dog or, I don't know, you're the artist."

"That's why you hired me. I'll have some options on your desk before I leave."

"Sounds good." Woodhull jotted down the pertinent information in his notebook and left the sheet on Adriana's rough desk. He rose, replaced his chair at the table, then stopped by the door, considering. "If you need anything, just let me know."

The words were professional, but the tone was fatherly.

She smiled, then turned and took a few sheets of paper from the file cabinet, which squeaked and clunked when she closed it. Maybe she could ask to upgrade that after she got some better pens. *Don't get ahead of yourself.*

Memories from the old fundraisers swirled in her head. She usually had fun despite Bradley never wandering too far from the food tables. A few local restaurants set up tents in the center of the grounds with a surrounding circle of kid games, small rides, and other curiosities. Some years they even managed to have live music. Those were the best years. Adriana would dance with her friends while Bradley was busy shaking hands and kissing babies—and eating.

Not all her memories were pleasant, though. One year she eagerly waited in line to hop on a miniature Wild West train ride. Watching it take its curvy trip around the grounds, with one rising portion that simulated going over a bridge, she felt her excitement peak. But when it came time for her to board, she balked and couldn't move forward. The other kids tried to shove her onto the passenger car, eager to get on the ride, but something made her feel sick at the thought.

She moved out of line and let the other kids skip ahead of her. She went to go find her father when screams stopped her in her tracks. She turned as the train tumbled off the tracks at the bridge and bodies spilled out like marbles. Panicked parents called for help as they rushed to rescue their kids. Some had severe cuts, one had a concussion, and two had broken bones. Young Adriana did not approach the accident scene. In the unseasonably warm night air, she was frozen with guilt. Why hadn't she warned everybody? Would they have believed her if she'd spoken up?

She refocused and got to work. After an hour, Adriana had four different designs for the Annual Police Fundraiser and was ready to show them to Woodhull.

As she approached his office, with walls made of almost floor-to-ceiling windows so he could keep an eye on the whole station, she could see the bookshelves behind his desk and felt a twinge of guilt from the trick she'd pulled to get hired. She shook it off, though, and chose instead to reward herself for being enterprising: the judge had asked for only one thing—employment. Done deal. And only a week into the thirty days he had given her. *That* she was proud of. She was also really proud of the mock-ups she'd created.

"Addie, didn't expect you to finish so soon."

"I was inspired. Have four options for you. And a question."

"Okay, shoot."

"If I find anything around the house, I mean, something of Eric's, should I bring it in?"

"Absolutely. Why?"

She shrugged and performed the role of Overwhelmed Ex-Girlfriend. "I'm cleaning out all his stuff and..."

"What'd you find?"

She felt her face flush. *Go straight to jail, and stay there, Little Miss Artist-in-Residence.*

"Oh, God, the place was such a mess." So far, she had not lied, technically.

"Please, no lawsuit." Woodhull held up his hands. "We were only doing our job."

She was happy for the joke, it allowed her to loosen up. "Yeah. I know. But...I'm just trying to make sense of it all."

"Of course. That's why I mentioned earlier if you need—" He looked past her, distracted by something in the bullpen. "Sorry, Addie. Excuse me a moment."

Woodhull walked away quickly. Adriana watched his exchange with Kasich, who seemed unhappy about something, but that was par for the course since she'd met him. With her eyes on the dynamic duo, she inched toward Woodhull's desk and picked up the phone. She heard the operator answer, "Yes, Chief." She coughed and lowered her voice.

"Uh, yes, Officer Hinkley, please."

The next voice she heard was Matt's.

"Hinkley here."

Woodhull, still jawing with the sergeant, swung an arm toward his office, and Adriana tensed. She spit out, "Meet me at the pay phones, detective."

The hallway with the pay phone was alive with ricocheting sounds and sharp ears, so when she saw Hinkley waiting, she walked right past him and out the station's front doors.

The great outdoors felt liberating. Climbing sun, street noise, and busy people coming and going.

"What's up, Ms. Krause?"

"Back to Ms. Krause, are we?"

He whispered, "I'm trying to make this professional."

"It is," she said.

Surreptitious, almost paranoid, she pulled the credit union envelope from her pocket, then hesitated. Was she implicating Matt by showing him this? He must have read it on her face because he asked, "What? *What?*"

"You need to keep this a secret."

"Keep what a secret?"

She passed him the envelope.

"I found it when I was cleaning up. Eric must have hidden it, and it was full of cash."

"So?"

He's right, she thought. *What's the big deal?* "Well... I'm... See, Eric doesn't have an account at the credit union. But my father does."

"I'm still not following."

"Why would my father give Eric money? He hated Eric."

"Well, we don't know if that is what happened. The envelope is circumstantial evidence."

"And money."

"Correct."

Adriana wondered how she could clear up that matter. "Just help me understand my hunch. Why the hell would Dad give Eric money. If that's what happened?"

It only took a moment for Hinkley to suggest, "Tampering. Bribing?"

"Huh?"

He led her away from the busy entrance steps. "Maybe he was paying Eric to, you know, play for his team, mess things up for you in court."

Adriana reeled. "Yes!"

Matt took the envelope and examined it. "And who's this *Robbie* character?

"Eric's dealer, maybe? I think. I don't know for sure, but he mentioned meeting up with him at the Scarecrow."

Matt opened the envelope's flap. "Wow, that's a lot of money."

"I know!"

"So, if it's Bradley's money, and if—big *if*—it paid for the drugs Eric used that night, the mayor might be partially responsible for the OD. He'd be an accessory to the crime. Mr. Bradley's KIDS himself."

Adriana's head buzzed with excitement. "I'm going to tell the judge!"

Matt shook his head. "No, you're not."

"I'm not?

"No. That's the last step. The first step: find proof that the money in that envelope really did come from your dad."

19

"OKAY, BUDDY, LET'S ROLL."

Inside Burnham Credit Union, Adriana panicked when she couldn't find her mark. The new location was more spacious than the one her dad had dragged her to as a kid while he ran errands. Only after adjusting to the new remodeled floorplan did she spot the stout lady dressed in loud colors. The woman wore reading glasses on the end of her nose, and even from a distance, Adriana could swear she smelled the woman's fragrance. She followed it until she was close enough to speak.

"Hello, Mrs. Menendez."

The woman first looked at Dylan, who squirmed in his mother's arms. Then her eyes sharpened, and her mouth curved into a smile.

"Adriana! Is that you?! Sit, sit! How can I help you and your little fella today?"

"It's a little embarrassing, Mrs...."

"Oh, we're both grown-ups now. Call me Doris. What's the problem?"

"Well, a lot has happened recently."

"I heard the news. I'm so sorry."

"Thank you. Yeah, it's... But we'll pull out of it. The reason I'm here, before everything happened, Dad gave me some cash, you know, to help out."

"Uh-huh."

"He just handed me the envelope. I thanked him, but I never counted it."

To prove her story with a little show-and-tell, Adriana pulled out Eric's bank envelope while keeping her thumb over the name *Robbie*.

"Spiffy design, huh? Everything has upgraded since the move."

"Yeah, it, wow, looks very slick. But here's the thing. Dad has been so great, I just want to pay back every single dollar. Except…"

"You don't know the total?"

"Exactly, and it sounds so, I don't know, crude to have to ask."

Doris nodded, but didn't take the bait. Her brow furrowed, and Adriana averted her eyes. She noticed a tiny statue of Jesus Christ near a daily planner on the desk.

"I know it's a lot to ask, Doris. But I've been praying for so many small miracles these last few days, I just thought…is it possible you could maybe help me out with this one?"

Doris crossed herself and whispered, "I shouldn't be doing this, but I was a single mom once. It's tough. And mixing family and money. Double tough."

"Thank you for understanding."

"Withdrawals aren't my department. They moved me up to lines of credit, but you sit tight, Addie. Let me see what I can do."

As Doris rose and walked toward the row of tellers, Adriana looked the other way and blew out a sigh of relief. Then, after pretending to admire the new carpeting and artwork on the walls, she stole a glance and saw Doris conferring with a dubious manager. The man was considerably taller than Doris and stern. His gray hair and droopy shoulders seemed out of step with the sleek new remodel. When he looked toward her, Adriana shifted her attention to Dylan, who was reaching for the toy Christ.

Doris returned to the desk looking a little ruffled. "I'm tired of bosses. Aren't you, Addie?"

Adriana grimaced, adjusted Dylan on her lap, and expected disappointing news. Then Doris slid a small receipt slip across the desk.

"Mr. Mayor was in just a few days ago. Does that amount seem about right, Addie?"

"Yes. And... And it's more than I thought. Thank you so much, Doris."

"Such a generous man. You're a lucky girl."

20

"This is highly inappropriate."

Tom Galton leaned forward in the red Naugahyde booth, whispering, hissing at the mayor, even though Cody's Diner was nearly empty: the lunch rush had ended and dinner was still a few hours away. He showed no awareness of the song playing on the diner's jukebox, Pat Benatar's "Hit Me with Your Best Shot."

Bradley smiled. "Mr. Galton, we're just two guys talking over a couple burgers, nothing inappropriate about that." He dabbed at a bit of ketchup on the side of his mouth with a napkin.

"You know very well that I am advising Councilman Card on his mayoral run. Now, I'll eat your free burger, but I'm not going to give you any dirt or whatever it is you might be looking for."

Tom Galton was a tall, nervous man. He chewed quick, he swallowed quick, he spoke quick. Nothing about him, no gesture or opinion, took its time. He was almost completely bald, and he drew attention to it by obsessively finger-combing the few wisps of hair he had left. He married right out of college, divorced, and remarried less than a year later. These were the details Bradley found easy to memorize about his city co-workers.

"I'm not looking for anything, Mr. Galton. I'm just treating an old pal to a good meal," Bradley said.

"Uh-huh."

"The truth is, Tom, I'm not the one who should be looking for dirt."

"What's that supposed to mean?" Tom said. "Card hasn't done anything. I vetted him for weeks—no, no, I'm not having this conversation with you. I don't need to look for any dirt because there isn't any to find, which means there isn't any to bury. Or hide. Or shovel. Or whatever you do with dirt."

Tom's eyes darted around the quiet diner as if he were behind enemy lines and every booth, coffee mug, and silverware set was a threat.

"Not Card," Bradley said.

"Then who? You? Is there something you want me to find about *you*, Mr. Mayor? Some fake scandal you planted, maybe? So I'll go running to the press, blabbing my mouth, trying to make you look bad? But oops, sorry, everyone, that juicy secret was completely unfounded, and I'm left with egg on my face? No thanks."

Bradley wiped his hands, balling and staining a few paper napkins with grease from his lunch. He grabbed a briefcase from beside him on the seat, set it on the table, popped both locks, and took out a file folder.

"What's that? I'm not looking at that."

"They're pictures."

"Not interested," Tom said.

"You should be."

Tom stopped moving at a hummingbird's pace for a moment and sat back in the booth. He stared at Bradley. Bradley could see him turning it all over, calculating all possible outcomes of looking at the photos or getting up and leaving.

"All right," he said slowly. "Show me the photos."

Bradley handed Galton the folder, then revisited his food.

Tom flipped through the pages inside. Blurry clouds of static and dark swirls. Grainy parking-lot surveillance photos. "What the heck are these?"

"Those are ultrasounds." Bradley looked up from his burger to see Galton's confusion. "Your *wife's* ultrasounds. And the other photos at the back? Your wife leaving Planned Parenthood, where she aborted that precious little baby."

"Bullshit!"

"Now, what you and your wife do with your unborn baby is none of my business—"

"Stop. That is not my wife," Tom said.

"But given that Card is playing the family values ticket and wants to drag my child into the spotlight on morning radio..."

"Stop. That is not—"

"Well, then, I only think it's fair and in the public's best interest to know Card's chief adviser and his wife are..."

"That's not Sharon!" Tom shouted, then pulled himself back when kitchen staff looked over. "We haven't been trying for kids. We haven't even been, been..."

"Fucking, Tom? I figured, because..." Bradley peeked at the damning photo still in his briefcase: Galton's wife, in heat, straddling another man. "And I'm sure your wife didn't intend to get pregnant by her...lover."

"Bullshit!" Tom said again. "Sharon is not—"

Bradley played his trump card. He took the last picture form his briefcase and placed it on top of the rest.

Tom Galton looked like he imploded. He could barely speak. "She... What... What do you want?"

Now it was Bradley's turn to whisper. "Run *my* campaign. Start today."

"What?" Tom looked up from the photo. "Why? You haven't needed a campaign adviser in more than a decade. And now you're blackmailing me to get one?" Tom's voice found the power it had lost a moment ago. "Me? A former city employee who served your first shitty little administration straight out of college, back when we were driving around campaigning in your old Buick and you were gripping podiums to make it through."

Their waitress appeared, startling Tom with one word. "Check?"

Tom stood abruptly and emptied his wallet on the linoleum tabletop. Bradley tried to cool him down. "Keep your money. I'll pick up the—"

Tom moved in close, a nervous, thin man finally able to express his inner ferocity.

"Are you really this small, Mr. Mayor? Go ahead. Send your smut to the newspaper and radio stations. Rip my guts out at City Hall if you want. Then take your shitty campaign and go to hell."

He spun to leave, but Bradley grabbed his arm.

"Come on, Tom. Sit down and talk with me. You're the best in the business, the best in a hundred-mile radius. Card is fortunate."

"Fuck off."

"Tom."

"Let go!"

Bradley held on tight. He could not believe what was happening. He'd always had the upper hand. Intimidation was a skill he'd honed over the years, and now he felt cut by the sharp blade of his own knife. What was he thinking, trying to blackmail Tom? This wasn't some kid from the streets, this man had brains and connections. This was a bad hand he should have folded from the start.

"Tom, I'm sorry." He let go and handed Tom the file of ultrasound images and photos. "Take these and destroy them. I don't have copies."

"No." Tom threw the folder back at Bradley. "I'll destroy you. Card is going to win. He's going to kick your ass."

Galton stormed out of the diner as a waitress wrote the dinner specials on a blackboard near the entrance. She didn't notice that Bradley had begun to hyperventilate.

21

THE VOICE WAS faint at first, but it was singing "Hit the Road Jack," a song Matt rather liked. Until he recognized the crooner. Sgt. Kasich had a tilted grin on his face. He carried a thick stack of posters and a staple gun. He arrived at Matt's desk like a rogue rainstorm at a picnic.

"Hit the road, Jack," Kasich said. "You got three hours to plaster the town with these. The chief chose you specifically for the job, so don't dillydally." Kasich plopped down the stack of photocopied posters.

Matt inspected one of the posters and his heart fluttered. This was by Adriana. Only she could draw those shapes and block lettering so gracefully. She made simple lines and crosshatch shading look joyous, like they might leap right off the page.

"Annual Police Fundraiser. Food and games... Sounds fun!" Matt said.

Kasich stared at him, probably waiting for a joke or smart-ass comment. When he didn't get one, he growled, "You come see me when you get back, Hinkster. I'll be waiting."

It was a relief to be out of the station. No Kasich. No cold cases. And most importantly, *no Kasich*. Matt laughed to himself.

The sun was shining on ground still damp from the morning rain. Matt loped through the Cellar business district and stapled the posters to every telephone pole or community board he could find. He also stopped in open businesses and asked to place a poster in the window. He enjoyed the interaction with the store owners and their customers. Everyone seemed happy to see a grinning young cop, and the poster drew a few compliments, which he hoped to share with Adriana.

As he walked about town, he realized this is what it would feel like to run for mayor. A candidate must show up, shake hands, and engage. Mayor Matt Hinkley. He tried it on for size and then shook his head at the thought. *Detective* Matt Hinkley. That was what he was shooting for. That title felt like the right set of clothes, tailored to his true ambitions.

In the shoe repair shop, barber shop, and hardware store, Matt didn't just chitchat, he decided to behave as if he'd already earned his detective badge. He inquired about any suspicious behavior, neighborhood troubles, or how the police could best help the business district. This chore, which Kasich probably saw as more hazing, was turning out to be one of the better days since he'd joined the Cellar Police Department. At last, he was doing something: meeting the people he served. His grin grew to a smile, until he stepped out of the realty office and saw a young man with a large black marker defacing one of the posters he'd just hung.

"Hey!" Matt shouted. The offender looked up, startled, and bolted across the street. Matt took off close behind him. The kid's puffy jacket flapped out behind him as he ran. He was fast. He darted down the alley behind the hardware store. Matt slowed and rounded the corner, then picked up speed, but the alley was empty.

He jogged halfway down the corridor, looking behind dumpsters and in doorway nooks, but the kid was nowhere to be found. He'd vanished.

Matt walked back to the defaced poster slightly out of breath from the chase. He tore it from the phone pole. It was scrawled with graffiti and the mayor's face, smiling confidently under the "Featured Speakers!" banner, had been transformed into the face of a devil. Thick black horns poked out of his dark hair, and a pointed tail slithered up from somewhere out of frame. The black markings really soured Adriana's gorgeous work. Matt stared at it, more curious than annoyed. *Who still does this kind of a stuff? A punk*, he thought. But a quick punk.

On his way back to the station, he had to replace a dozen other posters that had all been desecrated with the devil face. *Is Adriana's dad really that bad? That evil?* Matt wondered. *Nah. This town loves its mayor.* Matt didn't like tearing down all his hard work, but he definitely didn't want people to see the ruined posters.

———

Councilman Benjamin Card entered the City Hall elevator in a rush and pushed *P1*. There was a police fundraiser poster taped above the buttons. He was pleased that the poster advertised "Featured Speakers!" until he saw "Mayor Bradley Krause... and others!" *Come on, I'm still just* the other?

The elevator doors opened to the concrete echo of the building's parking structure. He walked to his red BMW M5, a luxury he adored every time he slid into the leather interior. He heard the click-clack of a woman's high heels behind him.

"Hello, Ben."

He turned to find Lois King approaching.

"You're not stalking me, are you, Chairwoman? I keep hearing you want to talk to me."

"We don't get much time to chat at the council meetings. So I thought we'd..."

"Chat. In a parking lot, as I rush to my car?"

Lois smiled and shrugged in a friendly way. "You know, Bradley felt a little ambushed at the radio station."

"Oh?"

"A heads-up might have been—"

"Collegial?"

"The word 'etiquette' comes to mind."

Ben unlocked his car and placed his briefcase in the front seat. "Oh, I see. I forgot to ask permission."

"Come on, Ben."

"Come on *what*, Lois? Bradley's iron grip on city government can make it hard for a man to breathe, let alone be gracious."

"Ah, so that's why you decided to run for mayor. More oxygen?"

"Deesha and I had plenty of job offers. We could have gone anywhere. But my dear wife wanted to come back to her hometown."

"That's noble."

"We'll see."

"But you still haven't answered my question. Why challenge Bradley this year?"

There were so many ways Ben could answer this question, and Tom had prepared him for all of them, but the honest answer was tangled in personal history, family obligations, and love. He thought about dodging the chairwoman, then rejected that. *It's campaign time. Tell the people, each one of them, who you are and what you believe.*

"Lois... Years ago, there was this young Black kid. He was taunted and harassed while wandering around Silver Lake. Not just a one-off thing; it happened daily. The kid wasn't doing anything wrong, just out enjoying nature. This was before the woods got as overgrown as they are now, back when families would still spend an afternoon at the lake there."

"And so now you're pitching a new shopping mall to, what? Help clean up the area?"

Ben ignored the question and went on. "He loved the lake but started to fear for his safety, always being hassled, so he started sneaking out there at night, when nobody was around. He just couldn't get enough of, you know, that kind of open-air freedom. He couldn't let himself be deprived of that."

As he spoke, the characters in his story came to life for him, as they always had, from the first time he'd heard Deesha tell it. He could hear distant echoes of the kid's dad warning him about sneaking out at night.

Ben could tell that Lois was listening attentively, and he warmed to her for not hurrying him along.

"But one night the kid went out and never came back."

"What do you mean?" she said.

"Disappeared."

Lois asked, "And that's Bradley's fault?"

"If not him personally, it's the fault of men like him. Men in power who decide which streets get protected and which folks are left to defend for themselves. How often do Chief Woodhull's squad cars patrol the forgotten Black neighborhoods near the lake? How often do we get carnivals and community cookouts that far out from City Hall?"

Tires screeched, and a Ford Bronco whipped around the corner. Ben pulled Lois to safety between the parking spaces as the Bronco sped past them. The growling truck disappeared from view and its engine noises faded.

"Ben... I... Thank you."

"You're welcome." Card took a step back toward his vehicle. "Regardless of what the mayor may think, I only want to help. But I can't do that with Bradley behind the desk. It's time for a change, Lois. That's why I'm running. And that's all you need to report back."

22

ASCENSION CATHOLIC CHURCH sprawled across two city blocks and resembled a cross between a high school and a medieval fortress. The main chapel, the oldest part of the building, was built from solid dark redwood planks and loomed over the low storefronts that lined the flanking streets. Adriana shivered as she and Dylan approached its tall, heavy doors. The place made her feel like she was living in the 1600s, when she likely would have been accused of witchery and burned at the stake for her talents, rather than given a job.

It felt bittersweet that she was saying goodbye to Eric in the massive, intimidating complex where they had first met and then soon desecrated as a young couple during one gloriously boring sermon.

The church was gigantic, and its leaders kept expanding. Adriana carried Dylan into the main chapel. Two wide hallways had been added on either side after Father Martin's arrival over a decade ago. Not only did he lead his flock of worshippers, but the priest had also championed massive renovations. The hallway connected the altar with offices, conference rooms, and restrooms, and included speakers built into the ceiling so that anyone in those far reaches of the building could hear a live broadcast of the Sunday sermon, even if nature called. Or other human needs.

Adriana recalled the east wing's library of Jesus-friendly books that held her attention when she got tired of Sunday school lectures. A smaller library for the kids was in the basement, another area haunted by naughty memories of Eric.

There were plenty of spaces for receptions and community meetings of all kinds, which made Adriana wonder if the church leaders had hoped Catholics would dominate City Hall and all the other public buildings that were meant to bring Cellarites together. The church also hosted a Korean congregation in a secondary chapel, hoping to draw in the city's growing Asian population. Lisa and Jennifer had mentioned attending a few times. Despite the large Fellowship Hall, Eric's parents had decided to have the post-funeral reception at their home—a place that was at least as unfriendly as this fortress of God.

The organ rumbled its Gothic moan. Wide-eyed Dylan, holding Adriana's hand, gushed, "Oooooh." Some of the elderly mourners who had filled the front pews gave him stern looks. If that weren't reason enough to turn and run, a few pews behind Eric's family sat a group of his mooching friends, who waved sad, pale hands.

The vaulted ceiling may have inspired other Catholic parishioners, but it made Adriana feel tiny and insignificant. She saw Eric's casket for the first time and was jolted by an intense memory—

Teens in Bible class. Adriana, the summer between her junior and senior high school years, bored, listless. A tall, thin nun with burning eyes. In the doorframe, Eric, a gangly eighteen-year-old, appears escorted by his rigid parents. True Catholics who will not tolerate their son's sneers. A family tussle, a little movie framed by the entrance. The show ends when Dad firmly leads Eric into the room. Eric's eyes immediately find Adriana. He grins. A wolf has found his lamb.

Adriana felt Father Martin, a silver eminence, touch her arm and whisper, "We saved a seat for you in the first pew, dear."

She eyed Eric's parents. As if on cue, his mother turned and glared at her. Not even a smile for Dylan as Adriana lifted him into her arms.

"I can't, Father. Too close."

"It's painful, I know."

She sat down in the pew beside her, about a dozen back from Eric's family.

"This is where Eric and I first met."

"Is that so? Your origin story, then." Father Martin gave her a subtle grin and made his way down the aisle to greet other mourners.

More memories forced their way to the surface—

A dark library. Adriana pinned against a bookshelf of Christian literature. Eric's lips on her neck, kissing and talking at the same time.

"Hey, Addie, do you know what Father Martin and a Christmas tree have in common?"

Her body hot with need, she can barely find an answer. "N-n-no."

"Their balls are just for decoration."

She suppresses a squeal and grabs his crotch as they make out.

Dylan squirmed and called out, "Papa!" snapping Adriana back to consciousness.

She looked over her shoulder. Bradley had entered the church. Without his usual grandeur, he waved to his grandson and put a quiet finger to his lips.

"You'll visit Papa later, okay?" she said.

Father Martin had finished his rounds and now appeared before the congregation, though Adriana's mind was too flushed to hear a word he said. Instead, her eyes went to the mural behind him of the Madonna holding Baby Jesus. Slowly the saintly faces morphed into those of her and Dylan. This was Dylan's first time stepping inside the church, but so much of his story was written here.

Church bathroom ceiling speakers broadcast Father Martin's Sunday sermon, muffled by raw teen sex echoing in a marble stall deep in the lady's restroom. Adriana, shirt pulled off and hanging from the doorknob, skirt hiked up, sweating. Moans spill out of tight lips. Eric thrusting, fast and hard, a beast gorging at the Eucharist. Climax speeding toward her like a landslide—but her pleasure turns horrid as a premonition burns her eyes. She shrieks as—the church organ thunders overhead, and Eric finishes in a trembling release.

Father Martin's sermon painted Eric's life in the brightest light possible, no doubt inspired by a donation from his parents, and somehow fooled a few mourners to tears. Eric's mother bowed her head, heavy with grief, and Adriana immediately felt guilty for her thoughts. It was true, she would never really know the woman, despite making the effort after Dylan was born, but that didn't mean she had to think the worst of her.

As the sermon came to its conclusion, Adriana heard a different sound. After playing hard to get for weeks, she'd surrendered when Eric arrived at one of those old Wednesday Bible classes with a mixtape he'd made just for her. Most of the songs were dubbed from his record collection, but the final song was an original recording he made with his acoustic guitar. He had covered the Barry Manilow song "Mandy," but he'd worked her nickname into the famous chorus, singing "Oh, Addie," instead. Forever after, his pet name for her stuck. Even if the relationship hadn't.

Three years later, during her freshman and only year at Ohio State, Adriana saw Eric again. He was there because a friend wanted to buy some weed. After a few beers they picked up where they had left off in the basement of Ascension, and nine months later, Dylan was born.

"WILL you be pulling out of the race, sir? To spend time with your family?"

Adriana was stuck in the church foyer with other mourners when she heard the question. Although the congregation had thinned, there was a traffic jam as another crowd flocked around Ascension's stone entrance steps.

"What's going on?" she asked the woman in front of her.

"Not sure, dear. Looks like the police and a few local news vans. They've got their cameras set up and everything."

It was difficult to push through while holding Dylan, but once outside, Adriana discovered her father holding court on the stone church stairs.

What the fuck?

The mayor stepped up to a microphone and addressed the audience. "Thank you for your questions and your concerns at this very difficult time. No, I will not withdraw from the race. Instead, now more than ever, I am committed to making Cellar a better place and leading every resident into a brighter future."

A few mourners clapped quietly but unenthusiastically. This was a funeral after all, and it had not concluded: everyone still had to make their way to the cemetery for the burial.

Bradley continued his stump speech.

"This tragic death proves that we still have a lot of work to do. I will clean up our streets once and for all," he boomed. "I vow that I will do everything in my power so that we never again have to attend another funeral like this one. No one else will fall victim to the drugs I once helped eradicate with my after-school program, Bradley's KIDS. We did it before. We can do it again!"

This time the applause was a bit more robust and Adriana understood the gambit: the crowd was not dressed for church and likely had not attended the service. They had probably been herded in by the reelection volunteers. They were attempting to blend respect for the dead with the high spirits of a political rally.

Bradley scanned the audience, hungrily soaking up the attention, as though he'd been deprived of glory for too long. As his gaze swept through the mourners, he locked eyes with Adriana, and she hoped, even prayed, that he could read minds. If so, he would hear her fury.

How dare you use Eric's death like this! Did you really plan all of this? Call the reporters and invite them here? For a funeral? Fuck you, Mr. Mayor!

Adriana turned to rush down the stairs and into the relative quiet of her car. But she couldn't avoid Eric's mom and dad, huddled with their circle of sympathetic parishioners, so she reluctantly approached.

"Hi. I just wanted to say—"

The group glared. In unison, the men and women shook their heads. Eric's mom spoke.

"Go away. Our Eric was a good boy until he met you ghouls. Please leave," she said.

"Okay, you don't like me. But don't you want to get to know his son?"

"*Your* bastard child, you mean?" Eric's father said. "We don't want you here. Either of you!" He scowled at Dylan in Adriana's arms.

Her mind on fire, Adriana made her way to the parking lot as Bradley's speech blasted through the public address system set up in the grass.

"Papa! I want to see Papa!" Dylan said as she held him in one arm and dug in her purse for the car keys with the other.

"Later, honey."

She fastened him into the booster seat and shut the door. She wiped at her eyes and hated herself for letting Eric's family get to her, for letting her father's rally get to her.

The funeral procession would be stalled for another half hour at the rate Bradley was speaking, so she granted herself a few moments of calm in the car before she would be expected to breathe the same air as the "Savior of Cellar."

Tree branches danced in the sun above, scattering shadows across her dashboard. She watched the shifting shapes, hoping they would distract her from her misery. Maybe they did for a moment, but they could not stop the tears from coming.

She started the car and turned on the radio. She was greeted with Barry Manilow crooning "Mandy." Incredulous, she all but smashed the off button and cursed, "Fuck you, Eric!"

23

_____

DYLAN RUSHED in and out of a swath of afternoon sunlight as Jennifer chased him through the yard, playing the monster just like when they first met. She'd upgraded the intensity of her threat by teasing her clawed hands gently down Dylan's back, which made his giggles louder and nearly delirious.

Lisa watched from her back patio, smiling at the way children play, how they can make scary stuff into great fun. Adriana sat beside her, quiet since she'd gotten back from the burial.

"I imagine today was really difficult for you. I'm sorry," Lisa said.

"Fuck him."

"Pardon?"

"Eric. I wanted to shout it at the cemetery just as his casket was lowered into that big dark hole. *Selfish jerk!*"

"You have every right to be upset."

"That's what's weird, though. I know I'm mad, but I'm not sure I'm upset?" Adriana took a sip of her drink. "It makes no sense. I know he's gone, but a part of me feels the same as when he moved to Cleveland and never called. Only this time he's in a grave. Gone for good. Shouldn't it feel different? Shouldn't I feel, I don't know, something more?"

Lisa waited, sensing Addie had more to say. Dylan squealed again. Lisa noted with pride how Jennifer gauged her monster act on the trust she had developed with the little boy. If she pushed too hard, she might truly scare him. But if she held back, her prey would become bored.

When Adriana spoke, Lisa, the good doctor, turned in her chair to listen.

"But there's other stuff too."

"Like what?" Lisa asked.

"My mind, it's... So, ever since I was a kid, things would explode in my head and..."

"What do you mean?"

"I'd see things. I'd suddenly *know* things."

"Suddenly? You mean, like, all at once?"

"Yeah. Like, in church, I was sitting there and remembered the first time Eric and I had sex."

"That is memorable."

"Not the sex. I mean, *yeah*, the sex. But what I remembered was...just before I, you know...had an orgasm," Adriana nearly whispered, "I got really scared."

"Why? Was he hurting you?"

"No, no. I freaked out because I saw...*everything*. I saw us in the bathroom fucking. I saw me pregnant. I saw a baby. I saw Eric using for the first time."

Lisa hesitated, then asked, "And this all flashed in your head?"

"No. Yes, but it was *real*. I saw it like it was happening right then and there, all of it, in that shitty little church bathroom stall. And I saw Eric *dead*. It scared the hell out of me."

The women turned toward the children, who were now sitting on the grass playing a version of patty-cake. Jennifer held out her palm and encouraged Dylan to tap it with his palm while she taught him the nursery rhyme.

When Lisa glanced back at Adriana, she was crying.

"It's okay. Just feel your feelings. Go on." Lisa reached over and touched her arm.

Adriana smiled despite her tears. "She's so good with him. You know, in just a few days, Jenny has given Dylan more than Eric ever did."

"And Jenny's talking more. It's like she's not embarrassed with him. I think they're good for each other."

"Yeah."

They both sat there watching for a moment, taking in the calm backyard, despite the chaos of the outside world.

Lisa wanted to get back to these head explosions. "But these things you...witnessed...with Eric?"

"It's not only with Eric. It's happened all my life. They hurt when they happen. Like the most intense migraine. Like my brain is splitting in half. It's the reason I was pulled out of school, I couldn't focus, I was angry all the time. I get visions like that when I'm drawing too, just never as intense, or dark. It's usually whatever the client wants me to tattoo for them, you know?"

Lisa didn't, but she nodded.

"The only other time it's that intense, that...exhausting, is with the nightmares."

Those Lisa did know about.

"Every night I'm afraid to go to sleep," Adriana said. "And sometimes I think it's all just a dream and it can't hurt me and I'm just going crazy, but then I remember that poor woman at City Hall, the one attacked in the bathroom. The way she described it, the flooding water, the blur of a distorted face... I don't know. I feel like as long as I know she maybe saw it too, then I'm not crazy? Sometimes I just want to scream, *Tell me what you want!* But all that mangled face can do is hiss at me."

Lisa had experience with nightmares. Three patients within the last few years had exhibited similar recurring dreams that tormented them long after they were out of bed.

"Sit tight," Lisa said, and went inside through the back door.

ADRIANA LEANED FORWARD in her chair. She'd never told anyone about her visions before, her second sight, as Matt had called it, not in such a matter-of-fact tone like that. She shouldn't have shared so much. Lisa probably went inside to call the asylum, or worse, Bradley.

She inhaled the warm spring air and considered the visions, Mr. Mayor's campaign speech, the funeral, Eric's awful parents. She had to let it all go. She exhaled and let the breeze whisk away her worries. *Why couldn't life always be this calm?*

The screen door opened and Lisa returned with a handful of small packets.

"Adriana, you need some time for yourself. Let Jennifer babysit. The price is right. In fact, I should pay you because Jenny is getting a lot out of this too."

That made Adriana smile. For so long it had just been her and Dylan, and she loved him with all her heart, found value in every interaction, but to think, someone else was now also finding value in her "rad little dude."

Lisa continued. "I can't prescribe meds without formal sessions that would allow me to get a medical history and for us to go deeper, you know, explore the root causes of what's happening to you. But I get samples now and then. Maybe these'll help you sleep?"

Adriana felt a surge of gratitude and excitement as she accepted the blister pack. She turned the pack over and over in her hand. She wasn't sure she remembered what restful sleep felt like.

24

"WHERE YOU GOING, *ROOKIE?*"

Matt had almost made it through the station's door. Almost made it to his car. Almost made it back home to grab a quick nap before tonight's patrol. He wanted to be sharp. It would be his first solo patrol, with no one looking over his shoulder or breathing down his neck. He'd gotten a taste of that freedom yesterday while hanging the fundraiser posters, and he wanted more of it.

But he'd been a second too late. He turned to face Kasich.

"I caught midnight patrol, Sarge. Going home for a quick—"

"You can nap in the cruiser tonight," Kasich said, checking the wall clock. With one stubby finger, he gestured, *Follow me.*

The Cellar Police Station basement was musty and dark. Matt had only ventured down here twice since his first day tour, but both times he expected to see serpents slithering across the damp floor or rats scurrying behind the boxed refuse of administrative history.

Passing under the single buzzing ceiling light, Matt and the sarge threw elongated shadows across the walls, making it feel like others had joined their expedition to the bowels of the station.

"What are we doing down here?" Matt asked.

"Just c'mon."

Kasich led him to a heavy door against the back wall. It creaked and shed rust as it was pulled open. Inside was a small room with no windows. It was pitch-black. Kasich flicked on an inadequate ceiling lamp that revealed a tomb of ancient dusty files and boxes.

"This here is your next special assignment," Kasich announced. "Chief says we've got to start destroying old files. Anything misdemeanor and below gets shredded by that massive machine over there. Felony cases get refiled into these new file boxes here, helps to deter the mold. Anything more than a decade old is fair game. Get rid of it to make room for new stuff."

"That I'll be tossing out ten years from now."

"Hey, if you don't like it, Burger King is hiring."

"What about the cold cases you've had me working all this week?"

"You can't walk and chew gum at the same time? Work the cold cases for a few hours like you did today. Then come down here and work these."

Matt sighed and stepped into the archive, face-first into a spiderweb that stuck to his eyebrows. "Gross."

Kasich's laugh was not friendly. "Last rookie we sent down here never came back."

Matt wiped the spiderweb off his face and onto a nearby box. The box was soft and spongy with age.

This is bullshit. "This isn't police work," Matt said.

Kasich moved close enough for Matt to smell his stale breath, even over the musty air of the basement archive.

"Hey, kid—"

"I'm not a kid. I want to be—"

"Sherlock Holmes. Yeah, I know. Says so on your application. But it takes years to learn the intricacies of it."

"Then teach me something. That's all I'm asking for."

Kasich moved even closer.

"This. *This* is what I got to teach you. It's not all action-movie stunts and *Dirty Harry* one-liners, kid. When you've been working the beat, working the cases for thirty years, answering stupid calls and taking crap from *the citizens*...yeah, then you come tell me about what is and isn't *police work*."

Murder flashed in Matt's head. *Could I crush his skull when he turns to go, then hide the body down here? I don't think it'd ever be found...*

"You got time before patrol, Rookie. Better get started."

Kasich made his way back to civilization. Matt assessed the musty boxes of records. The smell burned his nostrils and nearly made him vomit.

He took a box off the shelf, set it on the floor, and crouched to flip through the case files. Most were dated from the early seventies, but there were a few cases from the late sixties mixed in. Infractions and felony cases were filed next to each other.

"No rhyme or reason," Matt said to the empty room. "Perfect."

He glanced at a few of the personal information forms, thinking he might recognize a name or address, but these people and crimes belonged to a past Cellar; families and businesses he was too young to remember, some happening before he was even born. He slid one of the case files back into the box and then froze. He'd heard a whimper from the far corner of the room.

He peered down the aisle of shelves. "Hello?"

A second cry, shallow and small, sent a shiver up his spine. *Was it a bat?* He wasn't sure what bats sounded like. *Was it a family of bats? A whole cloud of bats ready to blanket the entire room?* Every pore pricked when he heard movement, sudden and clumsy, in the depths of the archives.

"I—I—I'm Officer Matt Hinkley."

He took a step toward the back corner. "Do you need—?"

Then the sound was behind him. He spun around fast and was accosted.

"Hey!"

He swatted at an invisible force that pecked at his face, circled his head, then swerved between his legs and came straight up his belly and chest.

Matt couldn't see anything as he spun and fought off whatever creature lived down here.

He begged for help—"Kasich! Sargent Kasich!"—and was ashamed of his fear and desperation. He caught a glimpse of light, the open door, the way out. He moved toward it but tripped over the file box and flew against a wall of heavy tattered boxes. He landed on his back on the concrete floor, kicking and punching the empty air.

Silence.

Matt listened for movement. His eyes darted around the dim room. After almost a full minute of stillness, he rose and brushed off his uniform. He glanced through the open door. No one had heard him. No one came rushing to his aide.

One of the boxes he'd crashed into had burst its seams. Case files had exploded across the cold floor. Matt kneeled and started cleaning up the folders. A name on a file caught his eye. He opened the case file and began to read, his heart fluttering with each flip of a page.

"What the hell...?" He didn't know what had attacked him, didn't know how he was ever going to sort through all the old records down here, but as he sat reading, he knew one thing for certain: he would disobey his orders. It may only be a simple missing-person complaint from over a decade ago, but he would not destroy *this* file.

25

ADRIANA STRUGGLED with the blister pack of pills in front of the sink in her bathroom. She broke one out of its plastic bubble and washed it down with a Dixie cup of water.

"Sweet dreams," she said to her reflection, hoping tonight she would finally be able to sleep peacefully.

A hyperactive MTV video flickered in the living room. Adriana curled up on the couch to wait for the pill to take effect. She made it through a handful of videos before her arms felt heavy. Still, she resisted going to bed: she was afraid of the dream that waited for her. When she could not keep her eyes open any longer for the metal bands on Headbangers Ball, she turned off the television and padded down the dark hallway to bed. The digital clock on her nightstand read one-fifteen a.m. Two blinks later, it was one-thirty a.m.

She rolled onto her back and stared at the bedroom ceiling. She wondered if the pills would work on the first night or if she'd have to make this some sort of routine, build up a resistance to the nightmares. Rather than counting sheep, she ran the numbers in her head and believed her free supply would last about ten days. She could stretch that to almost two weeks if she skipped every third day. To get more she'd have to officially become Lisa's patient. She didn't know how expensive therapy sessions were, but she probably couldn't afford them. Then her mind began to jabber.

What would sessions with Lisa be like? Would we work on figuring out the dream or just talk about my childhood and parents like in the movies? Would she know if I kept something from her? It probably doesn't matter. The pills probably won't—

Then she was underwater again.

The familiar ripples of moonlight danced on the water's surface above her, the strange darkness of the lake floor was below her. She spun to swim down as she had every night before, but there was no pulse from the deep reaches of the lake. Nothing calling her down tonight. Adriana waited, suspended in the water, listening for the sound, any sound, but it never came.

She looked to the lake's surface above. She'd never dared to swim up before. The draw of the lakebed pulse had always been so strong. *But you're strong now too.* She kicked her feet furiously to propel herself upward.

At first, she didn't think she was making any progress. The moonlight overhead wasn't getting any closer. Maybe it wasn't just the arm that wanted to keep her down here, then; maybe it was the whole goddamn lake.

She was about to give up when, with one final kick, she broke through the lake's surface, gasping. The bitter night air triggered a coughing fit. Her throat and nose burned and her lungs emptied, then ballooned in shock. She was breathing for the first time in this dreamworld.

After she got her breathing under control, she glanced around the surface of the empty lake. It was dark, the surrounding shore lit only by a faint purple in the sky, but Adriana saw the hint of a tree line and beach to her left. She dropped her head underwater to make sure the rotting thing hadn't followed her up. She couldn't see much in the dark water, but it looked like she was alone. She swam for shore.

The beach was more dirt than sand, quickly giving way to grass and woods that seemed to go on forever. Adriana crawled from the water and remained crouched on the shoreline, just out of the reach of a giant oak tree that had split in half. The large V of gnarled branches and a few dead leaves extended into the byzantium sky. It was a shade of purple she'd never seen while awake.

She listened. The water lapped gently at the shore, hundreds of branches creaked under the weight of the breeze, nearby frogs croaked at the moon, and there was a faint chiming. Adriana didn't expect to find anything pleasant in this nightmare world, but the distant bell chimed continuously, monotone and somewhat soothing. But there was no dark pulse. Nothing from the bottom of the lake.

She looked for landmarks, anything that would help her determine where she was, but she couldn't see past the tree line. Scanning the shore, Adriana just barely made out the shape of a white rectangle in the distance. She thought it might be a small cabin or utility shed.

She stood and felt the coarse dirt and sand grind into the bottoms of her bare feet. As she walked the outline of the lake, she stumbled a few times on slippery sludge. Her legs were pins and needles as if all blood had drained from them.

Despite the ground she was covering, the faint chimes sounded no louder or quieter; no closer or farther away. But she was gaining on the white structure. A few more wobbly steps and it began to take shape. It was the back of a billboard, a sign. Adriana picked up speed, hoping the sign might give her some clue as to where she was.

The sign must have been here for quite some time because the paint on its back and posts was peeling. She stepped around it to find "Welcome to Easton Mill Lake." *Easton Mill Lake?* She didn't know the name.

Nailed below the sign was a smaller wooden plaque. Although its paint was also peeling, she saw a faded smiling trout wearing a fisherman's hat. Under the fish was the slogan "A Day on the Lake Restores the Soul."

"Easton Mill Lake," she said again. Maybe she didn't know the name, but the place *did* have a name. Things with names were less scary. This wasn't Lake Nightmare or Dead Man's Lake, it was just...Easton Mill Lake. If only the sign had included a helpful "You Are Here" map of the area. Or even a city name listed under the welcome message. She could be anywhere.

Adriana reached out to touch the sign, half expecting to move through it, as if it, or she, were some kind of ghost. Or maybe it'd poof right out of existence. Or grow its own rotting arms and grab ahold of her. Dreams could be strange like that. But her fingers landed on the hard, painted surface. It looked like rough wood but felt smooth as glass. She couldn't reconcile the texture with the sign's appearance, yet touching something man-made helped ground her. The thing at the bottom of the lake might only be a figment of her imagination. Nothing could live underground, festering like that. But she could push against this sign and it stood its ground. It was solid. She smacked her palm against the sign as hard as she could, just to make sure, something, anything, to mark this moment of discovery.

Then the sign answered with a loud, blaring honk. It was the antithesis of the soothing distant chime. It was harsh and immediate. It was close. Adriana startled and yanked her hand away. The sign honked louder, so she hit it again in some reactionary self-defense. It scared the wits out of her and she didn't know what else to do. As it blared louder and louder, she screamed at it, demanding that it stop. *It might wake him up. Might let him know where I am.* And when it wouldn't stop, she picked up a large rock from the ground and pounded the sign with it, once, twice, and then it shattered, and she was awake.

Adriana was standing in the street in front of her house. Her left hand clutched a rock from the road, and her arm poked through the frame where the back side window of her car used to be. Shards of glass were scattered on the back seat and the road below. Her arm was warm with rivers of blood. And she had a headache from the car alarm that blared its Morse code–like honk for help.

Neighbors' porch lights popped on. There were distant voices. Adriana stopped screaming, dropped the rock, then looked up and down her street, and saw Lisa exit her house, calling, "Adriana, what happened?"

All she could do was whimper.

Lisa ran over, carefully pulled Adriana's arm from the car window frame, and got a close-up look at the cuts. "Oh, my God."

Adriana snapped out of her deep dream state. "What's going— Why am I bleeding?"

"You're okay. But we need to get inside. We need to clean your arm. You might need stitches."

"But the alarm!"

"It's okay. I'll get your car keys and shut it off. Come inside."

THE BATHROOM SINK was covered in pink watery splashes of blood. A spool of gauze sat next to the blister pack of pills Adriana had struggled with earlier. The sink was a mess, but her arm was clean. Her wounds were a maze of surface cuts that would, thankfully, not warrant a trip to the OVUC.

"The cuts are ugly, but I don't think anything's broken," Lisa said as she wrapped Adriana's arm with the gauze. "We'll want to change this bandage in the morning, though."

"I don't know what happened I just…"

Someone knocked heavily on the front door. Adriana and Lisa stepped out to the living room, which was aglow with pulsing red-and-blue emergency lights from a police vehicle.

Lisa said, "One of the neighbors must have called it in."

"Shit!"

Adriana composed herself, then slowly opened her door. She was relieved to see Matt standing on her porch.

"Hey, is everything all right? We got a bunch of calls about a disturbance. What happened to your car?"

Adriana lifted her arm. "I guess I broke in?" She saw the horror on his face. "I'm okay. It's just a few cuts and probably a ton of bruising."

She stepped back to let Matt in.

"I don't understand..." Matt cut himself off when he saw Lisa.

"This is my neighbor, Lisa," Adriana said, shutting the front door.

"Hello. I'm Officer Hinkley."

Lisa smiled. Adriana had already told her all about Matt's charms.

"So, what happened?" he asked again.

"I think it's somnambulism," Lisa said. "Sleepwalking, brought on by some sleeping pills I gave her."

Matt's eyes traveled from Lisa to the living room windows and the car out front. "That's one hell of a sleepwalk."

"It was definitely a more violent episode than most. I'll want to read up on it a bit more, but most cases I remember hearing about were fairly benign."

"You're sure the pills caused this?" Adriana asked. She sat down on the couch. She was exhausted despite the excitement, and her throbbing arm felt sweaty under the gauze bandages.

"I can't be certain, but it is a potential side effect, yes. I didn't mention it because it's so rare. And most cases involve little more than a person sitting up in bed, sometimes undressing, or maybe cleaning the bathroom. Most people don't smash out their car windows."

"Are you sure your arm isn't broken? Do you want me to call medical assistance and have them take a look?" Matt was being so objective and professional, but all Adriana wanted was for him to put his arms around her, comfort her.

"No. No, I'm fine."

He started writing in his notebook. "Okay. There's no ticket or fine. After all, it's your own car. But I do have to file a report. There were multiple complaints called in and because of the damage. You'll need paperwork for insurance purposes."

Adriana flashed on her dad and wondered if he was still up. If so, he would have heard about this on his radio scanner and would likely show up at any moment.

"*Great.* Maybe this time when Killswitch Kevin reads the blurb in the paper they'll include a photo of me looking like a zombie in a nightgown."

Her sleepwear had a short hemline that was unraveling. Matt's eyes quickly darted away.

"Right, well," he said, "at least your little boy wasn't here for this."

Dylan. Where was Dylan? Had he slept through all of this? Even if he had, her neighbors hadn't. And any one of them could be calling Child Protective Services right now. Bradley was worried she couldn't provide well enough for Dylan, but after tonight's little public display, everyone might be worried she'd harm him too.

"Mommy?"

They all turned to find Dylan standing in the hall, dragging a blanket behind him.

"I'm hungry," he said.

Adriana turned back to Matt. "Thanks for taking the call, really, but is it okay if we finish this tomorrow?" Her eyes were pleading. *Not in front of Dylan.*

He flipped his notebook closed. "Sure, not a problem."

26

BRADLEY LOCKED HIS FRONT DOOR, then spotted his newspaper close to the road. That paperboy had a weak arm. *Couldn't the little twerp at least try to— No, this morning is supposed to be about relaxing, about letting go of the stress.* He inhaled the cool early-morning air. A new day, a reinvigorating day.

He crossed the dew-soaked lawn, tucked the newspaper under his arm, then headed to his truck. He already felt lighter. After this last week, he needed a day to himself. Most people in his position would see Eric's funeral as a speed bump in the road to reelection, but Bradley had managed to turn it in his favor. His speech had received tepid reactions at first, but by the end, supporters and mourners alike were applauding on cue.

He tossed the newspaper on the front passenger seat next to his fishing gear and a cooler as he climbed into his truck. *A day on the lake restores the soul,* he thought. He started his truck, cranked up the heater, and set off for his favorite fishing spot.

A few miles out of town, he turned off the two-lane blacktop of Route 7 and onto a woodsy road that offered glimpses of a light fog creeping off the shoreline of Silver Lake.

He parked the truck and sat for a moment, enjoying the view, pleased that he'd decided to take a morning off in the middle of the week. He needed the peace of a fishing trip to clear his mind.

He hopped out of the truck and strode to the passenger door, pulled it open, and jumped back as his newspaper tumbled to the gravel parking area. He grabbed his tackle box and kneeled to pick up the paper but stopped. The front-page headline read:

Mayor's Daughter Vandalizes Car

It loomed above a photo of the shattered window. Disbelief was followed by rage: he heaved his cooler against the trunk of a thick tree.

"Goddamn you, Galton!"

———

TOM GALTON AND HIS WIFE, Sharon, were both asleep when the bedside phone rang. His eyes shot open. She didn't stir. Not her problem. They had both become used to the endless calls pouring in since he signed on to Card's campaign.

Galton rubbed the sleep from his eyes with the sleeve of his nightshirt as he blindly reached for the telephone.

"Hello?"

"So, this is how it's going to be, eh, Tommy boy?"

Galton raised himself up on an elbow. "What? Who is this?" He didn't recognize the growling voice.

"Don't fuck with me, Galton." Oh, now he knew it.

"Bradley?"

"You and Card trash my family? Then I'll trash yours. Sharon and her stud—tomorrow's front page! Two can play this game. And I. Can. Play. It. Better!"

Each word was accompanied by a furious, rhythmic hammering. Galton was now sitting upright on the edge of his bed.

"Bradley, I don't know what you're—"

The line went dead.

Galton hung up the phone. "Well, fuck you too."

Sharon rolled over. "What's Bradley's problem?"

Galton stood and grabbed his slacks from the dresser. He had no idea what set Bradley off this morning, but he was very aware of the shitstorm the mayor could rain down on him and Sharon.

"We need to talk...honey."

―――――――――

BRADLEY LOOKED up from the shattered pay-phone receiver. He abused phones to make his point all the time, but they'd never exploded in his hand like that before. He dropped the bungle of wires and plastic. They hung lifeless against the Route 7 mini-mart's brick wall. The gas station was the closest phone to the lake and Bradley's rage wouldn't let him make it all the way back home before bursting out.

He marched back to his truck, waving off the owner of the mini-mart as he poked his head out to investigate the commotion.

Climbing back into the truck's cab, Bradley glanced over at the newspaper's front page again. This wasn't a small blurb in the police blotter; this was a front-page headline. And it reeked of Tom Galton. Bradley knew the way Galton operated. Hell, Galton had helped write Bradley's playbook for years.

The photo showed a lot of destruction, but thankfully they didn't get a picture of Adriana out in the street. Considering it, Bradley wondered if the story was even true or if Galton had made up the whole thing. Wouldn't be too difficult to hire someone to smash up her car, then feed the local reporters some garbage about seeing Adriana do it herself. Hell, Bradley knew hiring witnesses was easy and cheap. But would Card have allowed that? Maybe it was true.

And if it is, just what the fuck is wrong with that kid now? Bradley started the truck, shut off the goddamned heat, and peeled out of the gas station's parking lot to find out.

27

ADRIANA STOOD in the gravel parking lot and watched Wills, a man at least a decade older than her father, carefully rub a wrinkled hand across the surface of the rear door frame on her car. Bradley stood, arms folded, also observing.

"Can't believe little Adriana's driving now," Wills said, his eyes now paying more attention to her body than the car's. "You weren't even big enough to ride in the front seat last time I saw you at one of your daddy's poker games."

"Yeah, that was a long time ago." Adriana looked away. Wills eventually returned his attention to the car.

"There's no damage to the frame, so should be a simple replacement. Insurance would cover most of it."

Bradley spoke up. "Better if I pay out of pocket."

Bradley to the rescue, as always. Adriana hadn't asked for his help, but when he pulled up unannounced at her house that morning, he already knew all about the car window. She told him it was an accident and didn't offer any more information. He was uncharacteristically quiet, he just told her to follow him out here to Wills Auto Body shop, near the middle of nowhere. Adriana wasn't even sure they were still in Cellar town limits, let alone the county.

"Your call, Mr. Mayor. But I got to order the glass. It'll take a couple days. You need a loaner meanwhile?" Wills pointed to a classic 1951 Ford Bonus-Built truck parked in his garage. The garage was a cavern of shadows, but a few dust-caked windows let in shafts of sunlight, enough to make out the three bays, the loaner Ford, and the mountains of junk inside. Adriana saw mismatched stacks of tires, various workbenches covered in rags, and disassembled motor parts. Above the workbenches hung various hooks, chains, and other rusted old tools that made the shop look as if it might double as a torture dungeon after hours.

Adriana grimaced and felt a chill crawl its way up her spine. She was scared of her nightmares at the lake, *Easton Mill Lake*, she reminded herself now that she knew the name, but at least she wasn't being tormented by some sadistic mechanic.

Bradley glanced at the massive loaner. "That'll work. But hey..." He pulled Wills aside and slipped him some cash. Adriana couldn't hear the rest of their conversation, but she knew Mr. Mayor was asking for some kind of special treatment. Whatever, she had a bigger concern: How was she going to drive that boat of a truck?

Wills nodded in agreement to whatever Bradley had been pitching and then headed inside the garage. Bradley marched back to Adriana and started in on the riot act that she had been spared earlier. "So, the paper says you're on pills now?"

Adriana sighed. *Fucking police blotter.* "As I recall, you take pills too, Dad. How's that working out?"

"I have a prescription. You don't. You can't just take whatever you want, consequences be damned. That's crazy, Addie."

"Yeah, right. You try to steal my kid and I'm the crazy one."

Bradley grabbed Adriana and the pain in her bandaged arm flared. She pulled her arm free, but he still got in her face to continue his lecture. If he hadn't, Adriana might have seen the long lens of a camera poking out of the minivan parked on the opposite side of the two-lane blacktop. She might have stopped the sequence of events that were captured in black-and-white: Bradley grabbing his daughter. Adriana pushing back. Bared teeth in a struggle that ended in a standoff. But no, she couldn't see past the rage in Bradley's eyes, and by the time the skirmish deescalated, the camera lens was hidden back inside the minivan.

"One more time I save your ass, but no thanks from you. Just like your mother!"

"I didn't ask for any of this. I can get my own window fixed. Instead, I have to leave Dylan with the sitter early, skip breakfast, and follow you out here to your buddy's garage? And I'm still the bad guy? No wonder mom took off; there's no pleasing you."

"Oh, yes. Because your lives were so terrible with me. A beautiful home. All the time in the world for her painting and your drawing. Financial security. My—"

"Oh right, money. It's always about money. Thanks for all the help, Dad. I mean it. Thanks for paying for my half a semester of college before Dylan came along."

"Lot of good that…"

"Thanks for the break on rent, and for not letting me forget it, even for a second."

"Well, it's…"

"And thanks for funding Eric's overdose with all that cash you gave him. Yeah, I know you two talked after court. What were you even thinking?!"

That stopped Bradley cold. He blinked. He stammered. "I—I don't know what you're talking about. And neither will the judge."

"Oh? Maybe I'll suggest the judge take a look at your credit union transactions—"

He stepped close again and growled. "Why are you always such a bitch?"

"Just like my mother, right?"

The moment the words were out of her mouth, she feared she'd gone too far. She braced for a slap across the face. It didn't come. Bradley sighed and turned. He muttered something under his breath as he headed back to his truck.

Was it over? She hadn't planned on confronting Bradley about the money he'd given Eric until she was certain. Certain what it was for, certain she could use it to hurt him in court, and certain it wouldn't backfire on her.

Bradley's truck roared to life and he tore out of the auto body shop's parking lot, nearly taking out a stack of bald tires. Adriana sank against her car. The adrenaline that had flooded her system was retreating and the pain in her arm came flooding back to replace it. The revelation did not get him to back down completely, but it had at least gotten him to back off for now.

ADRIANA OPENED the squeaky door of the loaner truck and climbed up behind the oversized wheel. She stared at the dashboard to orient herself. *Stupid old truck.* She'd be lucky if it didn't fall to pieces on her way back into—

"Hey, Adriana." She startled. Wills poked his head in the open passenger-side window. He chuckled as she recovered from the scare. "Sorry, sweetie. Just wanted you to know this here was my daddy's truck. You be good to her, okay?"

"Of course." Adriana placated the old man with a smile.

"If you get stopped or anything, proof of insurance is in the glove box. But..." He reached through the window, pounded the dashboard, and the glove box popped open. A cloud of dust puffed from the glove box as registration papers and old maps rained down onto the floorboard. "Just a tap will get you in."

"Thanks."

His eyes lingered on her again. "You know, most of you goth freaks look too scary with all that makeup on, but you look good."

He winked, then mercifully stepped back from the truck.

Adriana waited until Wills had turned and started for the garage before visibly shivering.

She set her bag on the seat next to her, then reached over and picked up the items that had fallen out of the glove box. The registration papers were faded but legible, the insurance cards expired a few years ago, but the old Shell Oil maps were interesting.

She unfolded the first map and spread it across the spacious front seat. Not an easy task one-handed. She reminded herself that her arm wasn't broken, wasn't useless, but she wanted to heal quickly and was trying to use it as little as possible.

The interior creases of the map had worn through to rips here and there, but she could still see that all roads led to a lake in the center.

Easton Mill Lake.

Only, it wasn't. And she should have known better. She'd lived in Cellar her entire life and hadn't heard of an Easton Mill Lake. At this map's center was Bear Lake, a name she was only sort of familiar with. Adriana glanced around the map's edges and saw this particular one was for the next county over.

She started refolding the worn map, but then decided to scan the other lakes on it first. If Easton Mill Lake wasn't in Cellar, maybe it was nearby? Her eyes jumped across the map. Lake Springwood. Mud Lake. Horseshoe Lake. All a bust.

When she finished with the first map, she moved on to the second. This one covered the county to the north, but after a thorough scan, no luck with this map either. Adriana hastily folded and stowed it back in the glove compartment. She fished the last map from the truck's floorboards and saw this was the one for Cellar.

Her shoulders sloped in a moment of defeat, but she decided to look it over anyway. She moved her finger across the creased surface, locating familiar intersections and landmarks. She checked the lakes one by one and then stopped with her finger on...Easton Mill Lake.

No, this is wrong. She knew this lake. It was called Silver Lake. She'd driven past it dozens of times. She knew kids in school who lived near the lake. It was not the lake from her nightmares, not Easton Mill Lake. It was just Silver Lake.

She shoved the heavy door open and rushed to the cluttered service counter in the garage. Later she would realize how dangerous it was, going into the shop alone, especially after the way

Wills had looked at her, but at the moment, nothing mattered more than those three little words on the map. *Easton Mill Lake.*

Wills was rinsing a plastic bucket out with a hose when Adriana interrupted him. "Mr. Wills, this map. It says Easton Mill Lake here."

He stopped, took a while before turning to look at her, then smiled. "My daddy loved his maps. Always setting off on adventures. There's probably half a dozen of them rotting in there."

"But it's Silver Lake, right? This map is wrong?"

"It's Silver Lake now. Wasn't always called that."

"It's a real place?!"

"Of course, girly, ain't you ever been swimming or fishing out there?" Wills dropped the hose into his bucket and stood upright. "Why all the excitement about a lake?"

"I just— Do you know when the name changed?"

Wills rubbed his forehead and left a dark watery mark. "Your daddy would know."

"Yeah, like I want to talk to him right now."

"Well, he's the guy who changed it. Mr. Mayor, after he got elected. Some big talk about a subdivision. A new Cellar! This was a while ago, though."

"What happened to the subdivision?"

"I don't know. Something bad in the water, maybe? I don't recall."

Something bad in the water—like a putrid face with a rotting arm that wants nothing more than to hold you under until you're stuck decomposing with it?

"The water was polluted, you mean?"

"Sewage. Maybe lead. Or rusty auto body parts." He cracked up at the very insinuation of dumping old parts in the lake.

By the time he was finished laughing, Adriana was waving her thanks and already heading back to the—*her*—truck. This whole time, she'd been living just a few miles from Lake Nightmare, and it was time to pay it a visit in the daylight.

28

Once Adriana left Wills Auto Body shop, the posted speed limit ticked up to fifty-five miles per hour. But the ancient Ford rattled and shook at those speeds, so she slowed down considerably. She kept her eye on the loaner's rearview mirror, planning to wave tailgaters past, but on this morning, she had Route 7 to herself.

Adriana wasn't sure what she'd find at the former Easton Mill Lake. The face wouldn't be there, of course. *Or would it? Are you so sure it's not waiting for you?* But what about the sign? It would probably be painted over by now with a "Welcome to Silver Lake" message. And the smiling trout? If it was weathered and faded back when the lake still had its original name, it would have disintegrated by now.

There was still an hour until her shift started, so even while traveling at the slower speed, Adriana calculated she'd have enough time to check out the lake and return to town without being late to work.

She looked down at the map, now propped against the steering wheel, and almost missed the lake entrance. The turnoff was overgrown and flowering with early spring buds.

The heavy truck rolled slowly on a crunchy gravel path through the trees and to a small parking lot. She stopped, surveyed the area, then cut the engine. A worn rope sectioned off the parking lot from the grassy expanse around the lake, tied on one end to a wooden post and on the other to a rusty garbage can. A swarm of buzzing insects hovered above the trash. The lake was large enough to accommodate individual fishing boats, but the few tied up along the shore looked like they hadn't been used in years.

She got out of the truck and walked through the scattered trees and high grass to the edge of the water. Her eyes traced the shoreline and found a short wooden dock that jutted out over the water before crumbling, its last few planks broken from time and rot.

Had she seen the dock in her dream? She couldn't remember. The dream had been pushed out by the screaming pain she woke up with in the middle of the road, arm through her car's back window. Surely the sign would be here, though. But there wasn't a welcome sign anywhere she could see. Nothing on this side of the lake, anyway.

The morning sun was burning bright and hot so most of the surrounding area and woods disappeared in harsh shadows under the budding trees. Maybe the sign was hiding in those shadows too.

Adriana knelt and splashed the lake water with her fingers. It was ice cold, as if completely ignoring the sun's heat. She pushed up her sleeve and held her hand over the cold water. Her fingers trembled. She wanted to reach in, wanted to know there was no reason to be afraid, but her hand resisted. *You're being a baby.* With a sharp inhale, she lowered her hand beneath the surface and stretched as far forward as her arm would allow. Her fingers disappeared in the murky water.

Wills had said the water might have been polluted, *something bad in the water*, but that wasn't her concern. She could handle some old plastic bags or bottles. But could she handle dead, rotting fingers brushing hers? She quickly pulled her arm out.

She wiped her hand on her jeans and picked up a small rock from the ground between her shoes. She launched it as far as she could out into the lake. It vanished with a blip in the calm water.

She waited, but the rock didn't appear to disrupt anything, no fish nor demon on the lake floor. It was just gone.

A few walking trails slashed through the dense forest, allowing access to other areas of the lake. Adriana chose one, not sure if she was hoping or fearing that she'd find the sign from her nightmare. The twisty path was a tunnel of leaves and branches, until the foliage thinned out and she could see a small paved parking lot beside the main road. She must have found the secondary lot when she drove in. This paved lot was probably where visitors were supposed to access the lake grounds.

The lot was empty except for a single vehicle parked in the dark shade of a large tree near a white structure. Her heart skipped—the sign? But she realized it was a public restroom as she stepped out into the clearing. The restroom door opened, and a short man strolled out into the sunny lot. Adriana ducked back behind the tree line and squinted. *Dad?!*

Bradley walked into the shade of the tree and nearly disappeared against his truck. He dried his hands on his pants, then checked his watch. *What the hell is he doing here of all places? He storms out of Wills Auto Body to come...here?*

Adriana startled when another man, younger, closer to her age than Bradley's, stepped out of the woods smoking a cigarette. *And where'd he come from?* Adriana didn't see a second car. The stranger brushed some debris from his puffy jacket and walked toward her father. Bradley looked around, and she hunched a little lower into the brush. He pushed away from his truck and took a couple steps toward the stranger.

The two men talked, but they were too far from her hiding place for her to hear anything. Bradley handed him something, but again, she was too far to see what it was. There was another problem: she was running out of time and would be late for work if she stayed to figure out what this meeting was all about. *Politics? Sex? Another cash drop?*

After a futile attempt to move closer, Adriana gave up. She quietly trotted back to the beach and found the small gravel parking area where her loaner Ford stood waiting. The engine started up on the first try but a bit too loudly, she thought. She eased back out of the makeshift parking area onto the main highway and drove back to Cellar fast, the Bonus-Built shaking almost as much as her the whole way.

BRADLEY PULLED a newspaper clipping out of his pocket, handed it to the young man, and pointed to a photo in the article.

"Robbie, listen to me. Come on, pay attention."

"Yes, sir."

"Look at this. Do you recognize any of these faces?"

Robbie brushed his dark hair from his face and glanced at the photo.

"I don't think so."

"Look again. Slowly. Carefully."

"Yeah, I see it, but I don't think I know any of 'em." Robbie dropped his cigarette to the ground. He stepped forward to crush it, momentarily lost his balance, then righted himself and stamped out the glowing butt.

Robbie was among the first class to complete the Bradley's KIDS program. Bradley's idea for the initiative came to him while he was still a councilman serving under Father Hen, *Mayor* Henderson, after a series of heroin overdoses were front page news. The program got Bradley's name out there among the voters, and he guessed it did some good for the town too.

Robbie, just thirteen at the time, and his older brother, Shawn, were arrested while trying to rob the Mobile station on Burnham. Both were using and in need of cash for another fix. Shawn had a switchblade and got a year in jail. Robbie was the unarmed lookout, so his punishment was community service and a golden ticket into Bradley's KIDS.

Two years later Shawn was dead, the victim of a hit-and-run accident by a drunk driver. Bradley mourned the loss of "a troubled youth who'd beaten his addiction while serving time" in the papers and at his speeches. Robbie didn't deal with his grief quite as well. He suffered a stroke from a heroin overdose the night after his brother's funeral. He lost most of the mobility in his left side. Bradley's KIDS may have been well intended, but the program didn't always take.

"Those three gentleman," Bradley said, pointing at the newspaper photo again, "are Benjamin Card and his campaign team, his advisers."

"Uh-huh." Robbie nodded, like he suddenly understood the theory of relativity.

"Okay, and I'm just curious if…maybe…you've sold to or bought from any of them?"

Robbie took the newspaper clipping and brought it close to his right eye. His fingers crumpled the edges as he tilted the paper into the sun for a better view, the article now just inches from his face.

"Nope, I don't know 'em, Mr. Bradley."

"Maybe you just don't remember," Bradley said, reaching for the picture. "Maybe a bump would refresh your memory?"

Robbie held the picture tight.

Bradley pulled a twenty-dollar bill from his money clip. Robbie's eyes were glued to the cash. "You can have it," Bradley said, waving the bill. "When you say you've sold to someone in that picture."

"Who? Which one?"

"I don't give a shit which one. I just need one of them. I need you to remember. You want to remember, right, Robbie?"

"I got to write it down, Mr. Bradley, so I don't forget again." He fished a small spiral notepad and a nub of a pencil from his frayed winter jacket.

He marked up the page in symbols and small pictorials, more hieroglyphic than alphabetic. Bradley couldn't make sense of the markings, and as far as he knew, no one else could either. Except Robbie. *Small blessing*, Bradley thought. Let him take as many notes as he wanted.

"So, I sold to one of them? Man, it must have been a while ago because I don't recollect that. Does he just want me to get him some weed or something else?" Robbie asked, all business, his nubby pencil poised.

"You're not... Never mind. Look at the picture again."

Robbie's face went slack. "Which picture?"

Bradley inhaled sharply. He wasn't going to get anywhere with this right now. He handed the cash over, glancing around the empty lake.

"I can't talk to you when you're like this, Robbie. Next time show up with your head right."

"But..."

He turned and got back into his vehicle. Robbie stood in the parking lot looking at the twenty-dollar bill by holding it up against his right eye.

Bradley's tires screeched out of the parking spot, breaking Robbie's fixation on the money. The vehicle left a stinky white plume of exhaust smoke and fumes.

Robbie leaned forward and spit on the ground to get the exhaust taste out of his mouth. He pushed the twenty and his notepad into his pocket and dropped the newspaper photo. He watched it flutter and dance on the breeze in the parking lot for a moment, then shook his head, picked it up, and folded it into his jacket pocket.

Bradley pulled around a bend in the path leading away from the lake and stopped at the side of the road once he was obscured by an outcrop of trees. He watched Robbie walk back across the parking lot. With an extra twenty in his pocket, it wouldn't be long before Robbie called it quits for the day and shot up. Robbie didn't go overboard anymore, not like before. Just a little to even him out, to dull the headaches and the memories... If he still had any. Only then could Bradley actually talk to him. Robbie was a lot more malleable once he got his fix.

29

THE WAR ROOM for Benjamin Card's mayoral campaign was a previously unused conference room in his family law office. It was too small, lacked proper air circulation, and suited the Cellar councilman just fine.

His shirt sleeves turned up at his wrists, Card sifted through an assortment of black-and-white photos. His wife, Deesha, leaned close enough that Card felt the heat of her cheek next to his. She made quiet sounds that rated each photo as intriguing, unimportant, or out of bounds.

Galton tried to wait patiently, but since his meeting with the photographer he'd hired to follow Mayor Krause, Galton was near bursting with excitement. It hadn't taken long for Bradley to step out of line and give him some ammunition of his own. If Bradley was going to hold Galton and Card responsible for his bad press, they may as well lean into it.

"What do you think, Ben?"

"I don't know, Tom."

"What's not to know? Lois told you to back off. Bradley threatened me this morning. We're not attacking. We're defending. We need to show that we mean business."

"Yeah, that part I get. But then what? I'm not sure I like the escalation. It's too much risk for not enough reward. Families fight, and we don't even know what this fight was about. It's not enough to take him out of the race. It's not even enough to pull a significant number of votes over to our camp."

"What's he going to do? You're clean. Deesha's clean. I'm clean. And my wife is so far removed from all this that what Bradley does have won't hurt you. I say bring it on. He's the one who should be worried, not us. His little blackmail stunt at Cody's tells me he's scared. Now, I don't know of what yet. But we'll keep digging. In fact, I'd like to get over to the Cellar PD before they shred any more old records. Take the temperature over there. Word around City Hall is they're spring-cleaning old case files...at Bradley's personal request."

Deesha turned from the surveillance photos and straightened. "When did that start?"

"Maggie Woodhull mentioned it when I filed Ben's election papers," Galton said. "We were chatting about her day. She said she'd been putting off sending in the request. Said something about her brother being a little raw over the recent budget cuts. I didn't think much about it then. But now? I think the mayor might be trying to hide something."

Deesha shot her husband a worried look.

Ben read her face. "What do you think, hon?"

"File an injunction to stop the file cleanse until after the election," she said.

"I meant the photos. They don't paint Bradley in the best light. But I don't know."

Deesha smiled. "I understand your hesitation. But do you want to win? Or are you happy remaining Cellar's most prominent, *and gorgeous*, token Black man?"

Her words were a dagger to his heart. The big city law firms he worked at after college made it clear he wasn't on the partner track. Incompetent graduates with lower seniority moved up faster than he did at every review. After a few years, he accepted that he was only hired because it looked good having his face in the brochure.

He was tired of always working twice as hard to get half as far. He was also tired of playing nice. His charm and manners at the city council meetings didn't stop Lois from tracking him down in the parking garage. Didn't stop Lois from delivering the mayor's message.

Ben looked up at Galton. "Okay," he said. "Let's run with these. But next time, his daughter is off-limits."

30

ADRIANA STEPPED inside the Cellar Public Library and wiped a few strands of wet hair from her face. The lake had been a bust, until her father had shown up and met with that strange man. She needed to know more about Easton Mill Lake than some old gas station map could tell her. It hadn't been raining when she left work, but a sudden shower on the last block had soaked her. The tall limestone vestibule felt breezy and gave her a chill.

Walking through the second set of large wooden doors, Adriana looked around the library. She hadn't been here since researching homework papers in middle school, and while sizable, it was smaller than she remembered, but wasn't everything as you got older?

Laurie Kaplan appeared from behind the information desk, looking surprised to see Adriana.

"What are you doing here?" Laurie said in her hushed library voice. "I told you at the station, I don't remember anything more about that night. And I'd rather not talk about this at work."

"Oh, no. I understand," Adriana said. It took her a moment to place Laurie's face. She was the woman who was attacked in the

City Hall bathroom. The only other person to have maybe seen the Face. "I'm here about something else. Maybe you can help me?"

"I doubt it, Ms. Krause. I wasn't much help at the station."

"It's nothing for the police. This is for me. I need everything you have on Silver Lake, just outside of town," Adriana said, digging the old map from her bag. "It used to be called Easton Mill Lake."

ADRIANA SAT at a small desk against the back wall, legs scrunched under her chair, staring at a dark microfilm machine. To her left was a separate area set up for younger readers with picture books, toys, and puzzles. She should bring Dylan in and sign him up for a card. He could borrow all the puzzles and Hot Wheels he wanted. That is, if she still had custody of him a month from now. *No, don't even go there.*

Laurie brought over a few canisters of microfilm in a small plastic tote.

"We don't have much filed under Easton Mill Lake, but the name Easton Milling Company showed up a bit in older articles. I also checked on Silver Lake, and that had a few more recent results, including three within the last week."

Laurie set down a few issues of the *Cellar Courant* beside the microfilm boxes. She threaded the first roll, showing Adriana the process.

"Thank you," Adriana said, testing the navigation wheel on the microfilm machine.

"You're welcome. If you need anything else, you can come find me. I'm here for a few more hours."

Adriana nodded and picked up the top print edition of the Courant as Laurie walked back to the front desk. The Courant's cover story featured Bradley standing tall and proud outside of Ascension, the day of Eric's funeral, promising to once again rid Cellar of the "drug problems infecting our young and disenfranchised." Disregard the fact Eric didn't even live in Cellar anymore and was far too old for the Bradley's KIDS program. *What a terrible fucking name, anyway. I'm Bradley's one and only kid and he never seemed too concerned about me.*

Adriana shivered. Her shirt was still damp from the rain outside and the air in the library was cool, but she wasn't sure that was the reason.

Below the fold Adriana found the headline and story concerning Silver Lake.

Councilman Card Sees Bright Future at Silver Lake

She read on. The article detailed Card's plans, if elected mayor, to drain Silver Lake and build a sprawling shopping complex on the underdeveloped, town-owned land, like those found in larger cities like Cleveland and Columbus. He promised more revenue flowing into Cellar thanks to weekend shoppers visiting from nearby towns, easing taxes, and providing the opportunity to upgrade utilities. Not to mention, more work opportunities for Cellar residents.

She set that issue aside and flipped through the other few print copies. More of the same. Councilman Card and his mall, with only Bradley and his business-as-usual politics standing in the way. None of this was helpful.

Adriana turned back to the microfilm machine and twisted the large gray knob under the monitor. The machine whirled up and newsprint filled the display. Spinning through the first roll of film, Adriana found photos of the lake surrounded by large mounds of rubble and debris.

Easton Milling Co. Now Bankrupt
    by Sandy Dieker
    Cellar's largest employer for the past fifty-four years, the Easton Milling Company, closed its doors last Friday. Demolition of two small machine shops commenced immediately, with the larger factory building set to hit the commercial real estate market next week. The surrounding lake and land, which is leased from the Cellar municipality, will be

returned to the town with the possibility of being leased to the new owner of the factory.

Turn to page A3 for more details.

Scrolling through a few more articles about the Easton Milling Company's bankruptcy, Adriana found nothing about the lake's name change. Most focused on the mill shutting down, the effects on the workers, the pensions lost, the numerous consequences for Cellar. So much fallout from one company shutting its doors. *No wonder Bradley had run unopposed until now. Who would want to take on that mess?*

Adriana reached the end of another canister and rubbed her eyes; the mostly sleepless nights had long taken their toll. She hadn't dared to try the sleeping pills again and had accepted that life would be lived one dizzying caffeine buzz to the next if she couldn't figure out what wanted to keep her at the bottom of that damn lake. She hoped Councilman Card got his way and they would end up draining it; then she could see what was really down there.

The third roll of microfilm was more of the same, until she landed on an article about a hiring fair. This was years before the bankruptcy and included a few photos of booths set up on the lawn around the lake. There was a small stage for presentations, a picnic area for family members, a few tables covered in informational brochures and applications—and the sign! It was out of focus and grainy, but Adriana could make it out in the background, "Welcome to Easton Mill Lake." The happy trout in the fishing hat hung there too.

Her thudding pulse jumped up to her ears. A small part of her was relieved to discover she wasn't losing her mind, and this was, in fact, a real place. But the rest of her felt ice cold. Lake Nightmare was, in fact, a real place.

She spun the navigation jog wheel again, loading up the next article. More—she needed more. *Why her? Why this lake?*

She was almost through the box of microfilm canisters and still no answers, nothing. Not even silly clichés, like the lake being the dumping area for some long forgotten serial killer or the ancient burial ground for tribes run off their land. Nothing that would explain the rotting arm in her dreams. Nothing about the man with his face nearly split open.

She held her hand on the fast-forward knob and sped through the rest of the film roll. At the end there was a moment of drag and then the monitor showed bright white as the film snapped off the roll.

Adriana's eyes burned from focusing on the monitor for so long. She leaned forward and put her head on her arm. She just needed to close her eyes for a minute. She'd spent hours at work earlier turning it all over in her head. Dreaming of a lake that hadn't existed for over a decade. A lake she just happened to discover this morning, where she ran into her father meeting with a strange man. She couldn't see how the pieces fit together. She couldn't understand...

And then she was underwater again.

31

THERE WAS a pulse from the bottom of the lake.

She swam toward it. There'd be no strolling the shores of Easton Mill Lake this time. The Face was calling for her.

The water was cold, but she barely noticed. She was distracted by the realization that her arm bandages didn't follow her into the dream world. She ran her fingers over the skin that, earlier today, was cut and scabbed and healing. It was now smooth and clean, but the pain was still there. She surged down again and continued her swim to the dark below.

As she hit the lake floor, her feet sunk into the algae and silt. She kicked up a bit of mud and tensed, preparing for the arm: for its explosion from the ground, its frantic searching, its death grip once it found her.

But the ground was still. She dragged her fingers through the sand and dirt. There was no buried hand, no buried arm, no Face, nothing. The thing was playing some weird game. Why did it will her down here if it didn't want her? What *did* it want, then?

In answer, the ground pulsed again. Adriana lifted her hand from the muck. Something was down there, beneath the lake floor.

Another pulse.

Then a third.

And then the lake floor erupted. First the front grill and fender of a car emerged from the ground, then it exploded upward into the water, unleashed from the muck, and plowed into her.

Her chest took the brunt of the hit. The collision would have knocked the air out of her if she had been breathing. Thin lines of blood swirled up from her chest in the dark water around her. She kicked her legs and regained her footing on the lake floor.

What the hell?! She spun in the water, searching for the car. But the water was still again. The car had vanished as quickly as it had appeared.

Adriana started to check her wounds. Her hips felt dislocated, as if the bottom half of her body had been turned ninety degrees. And one of her ribs had splintered and cut through her shirt. Dark blood bloomed around her chest.

The trails of blood started lazy and slow, then surged around her. She looked up just in time to see the car attack again. The front grill met her head-on with a muted explosion.

Her face hit the library table, her body and arms spun out of control, and the microfilm canisters flew in every direction. She fell, wide-eyed, onto the carpeted library floor.

She screamed and shoved her arm outward in a belated attempt to shield herself from the underwater car collision. She had landed on her bandaged arm and it lit up in pain.

When no car followed her out of the dream, when she registered that she was on dry carpet and was breathing again, she quickly pawed at her stomach, chest, and face. No broken bones protruding, no gashes splitting her open, no dark clouds of blood. Nothing but a cut on her forehead from the fall off her chair.

Laurie rushed to Adriana's side. "What happened? Are you okay?"

"I think so," she said and looked around the room. Library patrons were frozen in shock, peering over at the commotion. One woman picked up her child and walked away from the fray, as though Adriana might be radioactive.

"Do you want me to call someone?" Laurie asked. "One of your police friends or maybe an ambulance?"

"No," Adriana said, getting up. "I just nodded off for a moment and, well, ended up on the floor."

"That scream. My Lord, I thought someone was being murdered back here."

"Sorry. I didn't mean to…"

"It's okay. Come with me back to the desk. We can get you something for that cut on your head."

Adriana collected her bag. She heard a few murmurs but couldn't make out what was being said. Her ears felt clogged. *With water? No, but maybe the last bit of adrenaline she had to give today.* Her whole head felt like it was still swimming.

She reached down to pick up one of the microfilm canisters that had fallen and lost her balance again. Laurie caught her.

"It's okay. Leave them. I'll get them," Laurie said, glancing around at all the staring eyes. "Let's get you mended."

32

MATT PULLED into the parking lot for his morning shift just as the sun crept over the police station and the streetlights blinked off. He locked his cruiser and took a sip of coffee from his thermos, then a gulp. He wasn't used to working odd hours, but he didn't have any seniority and was stuck with whatever shift he was assigned. Even if that meant an early shift after a late-night patrol.

Adriana's loaner truck was parked three spaces down, hours before she would normally be scheduled. *Looks like I'm not the only one stuck with changing shifts.*

"Morning, Packer." Matt greeted the front desk cop with a nod and tip of his thermos. Ty Packer was one of few officers closer to Matt in age, and Matt had hoped when he started that they might become friends, maybe even partners.

"Stuff it, Rookie." But Packer was already entrenched with the older officers. Matt had felt a moment of glee when Packer was put on front desk duty, a few-weeks' punishment after a suspension from some infraction Matt wasn't privy to.

The light was on in the conference room that had become Adriana's makeshift office. He walked over and poked his head in. "Burning the early-morning oil, I see..." But the space was empty.

No sign of Adriana. Her magic bag of art materials was not plopped on the desk. Not even a hoodie hanging from the back of her chair.

Matt called to a few officers hovering around the microwave, "Have you guys seen Adriana this morning?"

"Nope, haven't seen her."

"Your girlfriend gone missing?"

That familiar voice. Matt turned and found Sgt. Kasich sporting the crooked sneer he had perfected over the years. *Had Kasich ever enjoyed his work? His life?*

"Morning, Sergeant. I noticed Addie's vehicle in the parking lot. She's usually not here this early."

"Maybe she went out after work, had one too many, took a cab home," one of the officers said.

"Or maybe she got lucky," Kasich said just loud enough for Matt to hear.

"Yeah," Matt said, and faked a chuckle that he wished had been a fist to an easy target: Kasich's round face.

Back at his desk, Matt put his service revolver in the top drawer, filled his favorite mug with coffee from the thermos, threw away the pen that had started to dry out yesterday and took a new one from the thin box next to his phone.

But something troubled him. *Instinct.* He glanced back at Adriana's empty office. He reached for the phone to call her, then just as quickly set the receiver back in its cradle. *Don't suffocate her; she's fine.* He comforted himself by imagining her at home in her own bed, *alone,* safe and sound, sleeping deeply.

Matt passed the morning idly working on the cold case files Kasich had assigned him. When he couldn't bear the boredom any longer, he rose, stretched, and walked toward the front desk. He glanced back out at the parking lot and saw Adriana's truck still parked, unmoved. From behind him, Packer put down his newspaper and said, "Cover the desk for me, Rookie. I've got to get in my morning break."

"Sure," Matt said, still surveying the parking lot.

"I heard there's donuts in the break room. Got my heart set on a glazed."

Matt settled in behind the welcome desk. He mentally started filling in the crossword puzzle Packer hadn't finished. 17 Down: *Four legs, no arms, but gets a lot of writing done. Desk*, of course. The clue may as well have been *Behind which Matt will waste away most of his life.* The welcome window was about as exciting as customer service at a department store. Hardly any traffic, just the occasional Cellar citizen needing to pay a parking ticket, report graffiti or a stolen bicycle. The only bright spot was the occasional housewife who dropped off some home-baked goods to say thanks for serving and protecting.

He sat up when he heard the service bell jangle. The large entrance doors opened and a skinny kid with furtive eyes walked in. Matt recognized him. This was the kid who drew the devil faces on Adriana's posters. The kid, young man, Matt now saw, that he couldn't catch the day he'd been hanging them up.

"Hi. May I help you?" Matt hid his eagerness.

"Uh. Yeah." The man held up one of the torn down posters, this one unmarked with graffiti. *Evidence.* Matt thought of citing him right then and there. "Got to buy, I mean, uh, want to buy a ticket. For the fundraiser?"

"Ah. Did you rip down that poster as a reminder then?"

"Huh?"

"Nothing. Sorry. One ticket coming up. I can't wait for the fundraiser this Saturday. I love the dunk tank."

Matt reached for the booklet of tickets on the desk as the young man pulled out a wad of cash. His bankroll didn't square up with his old puffy jacket and torn jeans.

"How much for the ticket?"

"Just one?" Matt asked.

"Uh, yeah. I mean, do you need more than one? To get in?"

Buying time, Matt delayed his answer. Instead, he grabbed a pen and paper from the desk drawer. "No, just one. Can I get a name?"

"You need my name?"

"In case you win the raffle drawing." Matt prayed Packer would extend his break. He was lying about the raffle to get this guy's name and he wasn't sure Packer would play along. In fact, he was sure Packer would blow the whole gambit.

"Oh. Okay. Yeah. Uh, Robbie."

Matt's face lit up as he remembered the credit union envelope where Eric had scrawled *Robbie. This can't be the same guy, can it?*

Hoping Robbie hadn't noticed his reaction, Matt feigned ignorance, spelling the name. "R-O-B-B-Y?"

"No, man, just I-E at the end."

Gotcha! Maybe. Matt hesitated, then took the gamble: "Too bad about Eric, huh?"

"Yeah, man. He was…" Robbie stopped, then started again. "Huh? Who?"

"Eric. Weren't you guys friends? Thought I saw you at the funeral."

Robbie stammered. "Wh-what? Funeral? I wasn't at no—I thought you said Erin."

"Oh. Sorry again. My mistake. Street address? Phone number?"

Robbie took a step back. Even his stammering speech came to a halt. Only his eyes moved, like a frightened, trapped animal. "That's okay, I don't need no raffle. How much for just the ticket in?"

Matt had no choice but to tear a ticket from the perforated booklet. Robbie grabbed it, shoved some cash across the desk, and turned to go.

"Hey, you've got change."

"That's cool. Keep it." Robbie pushed through the entrance doors.

Matt made his way around the desk to follow, hoping to see a car and license plate.

"Hey, Rookie. What are you doing up here? Where are those files I gave you?"

"Huh?" He turned. Kasich again.

"We got deadlines around here, Hinkster. And what about the

archives downstairs? I should have had a progress report, like, *yesterday.*"

"Yes, sir." His commanding officer likely heard the twinge of mockery in his voice, but Matt was saved from a confrontation when the station's doors opened again. Two figures, almost glowing in the backlit morning sun, entered.

Councilman Card and his wife, Deesha, stepped into the foyer. Deesha was draped in a long maroon coat and Card stood tall in a dark suit and silver tie, giving him the appearance of a high-priced city lawyer Matt had seen on TV. It took him a moment to reconcile them here in the police station. Matt felt like he was meeting a celebrity couple.

"Morning, Officer. We have an appointment with Chief Woodhull," Card said.

"Ah, okay. Let me show you to his office," Matt said.

"Thank you."

Matt skirted past Kasich, who eyed the couple with an uneasy face. Most days he wore a *Re-Elect Bradley Krause* pin. He must have forgotten it, today of all days.

"It's just this way," Matt said. "Congratulations on your campaign, by the way, Councilman."

WOODHULL FELT CRAMPED in his own office. After offering seats to his gleaming guests, he instinctually reached for this little gold cigarette case. He anticipated some political grab-assing before being asked for some favor or another. That's always how these requested meetings went with Bradley. And Woodhull would play nice for now. If Card happened to beat Bradley come election time, Card would be setting the police budget and other amenities. Better to keep him happy, if possible. Fortunately, Card was a busy man and he got right to it.

"Thanks for the time, Chief Woodhull. We'll be brief."

Deesha added, "Just two concerns, really."

"Right. First, I wanted to mention that I don't support cuts to the police budget. This is not the time to give crime a chance to grow in Cellar," Card said.

The chief stopped fidgeting with his cigarette case and perked up. "I'm with you on that." He let out a short chuckle. He wasn't sure what this morning's meeting was going to be about, but he was not expecting support from his oldest friend's newest rival.

Woodhull held up the little gold cigarette case. "Care for a smoke?"

"No, thank you," Card said.

Deesha shook her head and pushed on. "The budget dictates how many patrolmen you're able to hire, yes? And we all need protection at some level. I have family here, and their neighborhood... Well..."

"I hear you." Woodhull nodded, fully understanding which neighborhoods she was referring to, and also quite sure he wouldn't be adding more patrols to those hoods anytime soon. Those neighborhoods on the edge of town didn't contribute as much to the city's coffers, so it didn't make sense to spend more on patrolling them. It wasn't about race; it was about economics, Woodhull told himself.

"Second..." Card paused, with a look of concern. "Are you... Rather, is the department prioritizing shredding old police files now because of concerns over having the funds to do so if the present administration wins reelection?"

Woodhull liked Card's implication and feared it. How many people in Cellar even knew old files were periodically destroyed? And of those few who did, how many knew the mayor specifically requested this batch be handled *now*? Deesha leaned in, eager to hear his answer, and Woodhull realized Card and his wife were sharper than Bradley gave them credit for. *And that will definitely bite Bradley in the ass, but some of those teeth marks will end up on me as well.*

Woodhull sighed. His smile was gone.

"Well, you know, it's just routine. Every department in Cellar is instructed to do a little spring cleaning each year, Councilman. Any rumors of budget cuts or this task or that task jumping the line are just that: rumors."

MAGGIE WOODHULL BROUGHT her second cup of coffee to the front counter of the city's administration office as soon as her copy of the Cellar Courant arrived. As always, she would check the classifieds and other sections to make sure all city business had been properly posted, and she would look for news items that might pertain to her department.

She also hungered for a juicy headline now and then. She spilled coffee down her chin when she noticed the morning's lead story.

"Jesus...!"

Bradley's KID: Wicked Witch?

A sequence of black-and-white photos that had the grainy raw power of a documentary or television exposé featured Bradley —*click, click, click*—accosting Adriana at that dilapidated auto shop outside of town. Adriana fought back, but the thick mascara and black fingernail polish gave her the look of a ghoul who might cast a nasty spell on her father.

Moments later Maggie entered the mayor's office and tossed the paper on his desk.

"What the heck, Bradley? Are you trying to lose?"

Bradley grabbed the paper, smiling. "What do you—"

His smile faded as he looked over the story. He quickly flipped to the inner page where the piece continued with more damaging photos, and then all but tore open the other sections of the newspaper.

"Where the hell is the other story!"

"What other story? You mean there's more of this stuff?"

"They didn't publish *my* story! *My* photos!"

"You have photos of this argument, too?"

"No, I have photos of Tom Galton's Jesus-freak wife sneaking in and out of Planned Parenthood for an abortion. I have photos of Sharon riding some twenty-year-old kid while Tom's out of the house. And they didn't run a single photo!"

"That's private. That's not a news story; that's a hit piece."

"Oh, that's not news but *this* is?" Bradley shook the paper at her.

"I agree, this isn't either. But anything the mayor does is going to attract attention. You know that. And you usually use it to your advantage." Maggie gently took the newspaper from Bradley's fists. "This might not have been the best time for you to fight Adriana in court. But it certainly is not the time to fight her in the streets. I don't know what's going on with you lately, but"—Maggie was speaking with more conviction than she had ever mustered before —"if you want to stay here, stay in office, you better figure it out."

33

MATT JOTTED in his police-issued note pad; he was drawing himself a treasure map. After showing Councilman Card and Deesha to Woodhull's office, he made his way downstairs to the tomb of mildewed records. Over the last week, he'd curated a small box of records he had no intention of destroying. Not because of the crimes themselves, but because of the parties involved. He hid the box in the middle of the shelves, trying to make it look as if the box had been there with the rest of the files for the last decade. The crude map was so he could find them again as the soft decaying box blended in a little too well with the others.

Satisfied that his cache was hidden well, he walked to the opposite end of the storage room. This area was closer to the entrance and the light bleeding in from the other half of the basement made it easier to work. These files, near the door, would be the focus of today's report to Kasich, which was intended only to keep the department in the dark about his own research.

As he boxed up files destined for the shredder, he was aware of his heightened fear. Not a fear of being caught rescuing certain files, he was almost certain Kasich wasn't reading his reports, but his fear that whatever had assaulted him down here before would return.

He could defend himself—ninetieth percentile in his class at the academy, but only if he could see the dangers coming. Another surprise attack might send him into flailing panic again and that troubled him. Did he have the guts to make it to detective? The file in his hands trembled. He dropped it into the discard box, threw on the lid in frustration, and headed back to safety upstairs.

As expected, after typing and delivering his report, replete with case numbers and other insignificant administrative data, Kasich only skimmed it before tossing it aside. "And what about those cold cases on your desk? *Yesterday* for those too."

"Yes, sir," Matt said, but this time he did not sour it with sarcasm. He walked toward his desk feeling defeated. He picked up his coffee and sipped while looking out the window. Everyone outside was hustling through their day with so much purpose, while he was inside writing monotonous reports that would never be read. Perhaps Kasich knew Matt was destined for the desk and that's why he kept giving him all this busy work. Perhaps Kasich knew he wasn't brave enough for real danger, or even a dark storage room.

He let go of all those thoughts when he saw Adriana out in the parking lot unlocking the bulky Ford truck. He set his coffee down, looked back toward the bullpen, making sure he hadn't picked up a large tail named Al Kasich, then made his way outside.

"Hey, Addie, is everything okay?" Matt asked as he approached.

She put her shoulder bag down on the driver's seat. "Yeah, why?"

"This morning I noticed the truck. You left it here overnight?" He didn't want to sound like he was prying, but she turned and he saw the cut on her forehead. "Wh-what happened there? Were you sleepwalking again?"

"No, not exactly."

"You mean you *were*—?"

"No, no." She looked exhausted. "I just hit my head. You'll think it's silly."

"Why would I think that?" She didn't answer. "You know you can talk to me, right?"

She tossed her jacket into the truck. "Okay. I'll tell you *if* you hop in and buy me breakfast. I took the bus this morning and haven't eaten yet."

AS SHE DROVE with Matt in the passenger seat, Adriana considered whether or not to let someone else know about the dreams, about Lake Nightmare, and about finding her dad at the real-world lake on the very same morning she decided to drive out there. She'd told Lisa about the dreams, but that was the first time she'd ever spoken about them out loud. Lisa had tried to help, the sleeping pills did knock her out, but had the terrible side effect of smashing one's car window. Still, if she hadn't talked to Lisa and gotten the pills, she might not have ever discovered that the lake was a real place. A real place in Cellar County, no less.

As she pulled into the parking lot at Cody's Diner, she decided she would lay it all out. Put her cards on the table, as they say. She had trusted Matt with Eric's hidden envelope, and he hadn't snitched on her, he had even helped her investigate and plan her con at the credit union. Maybe he could help with this too.

Over a plate of pancakes and bacon, she told Matt everything. He listened, quietly and intently. Adriana didn't know if when she finished, he'd laugh it all off as some harmless bad dreams or want to arrest that thing at the bottom of the lake himself, but she couldn't believe how good it felt to stop hiding it, to stop living with it all on her alone, to let someone else in.

"After that nightmare yesterday, Laurie had to bandage my forehead at the library's information desk. Everyone was staring. I would say it was embarrassing, but honestly I was so frightened I don't think I had time to register anything else."

Matt reached across the small booth's table and put his hand on hers. Adriana flinched and almost pulled away. It was unexpected yet comforting.

"So you spent the night at urgent care?"

"No, I took the bus home. I was too afraid to drive. Like the dream was a premonition or something. Like I'd have an accident while driving home. Crazy, I know."

"Not so crazy."

Adriana felt the tension in her shoulders release. Last night, lying in bed, she'd made up six different stories about why she'd left the truck at the police station just in case someone noticed. Matt had noticed, of course, because he was good at his job. But that wasn't the only reason. *He also noticed because he likes me.*

Matt said, "Next time? Don't take the bus. Call me."

"Thanks. And I will. No way can the squad car smell worse than the bus."

"You'd be surprised with some of the people we have to deal with. Speaking of which, guess who I met this morning." Matt looked eager, like he had a secret of his own to share.

Adriana couldn't guess. "Who?"

Matt leaned in closer and lowered his voice. "Robbie. From the envelope." He sat back, beaming. "I think so, anyway. His name was spelled the same, and he knew Eric when I mentioned him, then pretended not to."

"What was he arrested for?"

"Huh? Oh, he wasn't. Walked right in the front door on his own. Wanted to buy a ticket to the police fundraiser. I tried to get his address or phone number, but I think I scared him and he bolted. I went to follow him, but Kasich got in the way."

"Damn."

"Yeah."

She picked at a piece of toast on her plate. "I wonder why he wants a ticket to the fundraiser. I can't imagine he wants to support you guys, given his chosen profession and all."

"I don't know, but you two have something in common: he's not much of a fan of your father. He's the one I saw defacing your fundraiser posters. I didn't know it until I saw him again this morning. He walked in wearing the same old puffy jacket he had on the day I chased him."

"Puffy jacket?"

"Yeah, old winter coat, bright blue, falling apart at the seams."

"Holy shit! Then that's who my father was meeting out at the lake."

"What?"

"The stranger out at the lake had the same jacket. Robbie's jacket. There's no way it's just a coincidence that—"

The waitress swept into view. "Can I take that plate for you?"

Adriana wasn't finished eating, but she nodded anyway, then looked back at Matt. He was deep in thought, working out the many puzzles in his head. He had this cute little look on his face anytime he concentrated. She saw it sometimes at the station when he thought no one was looking. She allowed herself a brief smile. If she hadn't taken this job just to keep Dylan from Bradley, if her dreams weren't trying to kill her, if she hadn't recently buried her ex, this would've been a pretty good morning.

34

ON HER DRIVE home from work, Adriana kept wanting to pull over, get out of the Ford, and catch the bus again. The incident at the library and its impact had made her paranoid and insecure behind the wheel. She'd admitted to Matt that it was ridiculous to see the dream as a warning, yet she couldn't shake it from her psyche.

When she finally made it home and parked along the curb, she felt a wave of relief. She was eager to see Dylan. She walked across the lawn to Lisa's and smiled when she heard little footsteps running to the door after she rang the bell.

"Mommy!" Dylan yelled as the front door swung open. His hugs lit up her days, no matter how tired she was from her mostly sleepless nights.

As she entered Lisa's cozy home, Jennifer waved to her from the recliner where she sat with one of Dylan's Little Golden books. Midnight, Jennifer's cat, was sprawled out on the back of the recliner just behind her head.

"Hey. Is your mom home?"

Jennifer pointed upstairs and said, "Afternoon nap. She has late patients tonight."

Adriana sometimes forgot Jennifer was deaf. She spoke more

often than Adriana guessed a person who was deaf would and almost never had a problem reading Adriana's lips. Their short conversations when she dropped off and picked up Dylan never suffered for it.

"You are home early?" Jennifer asked, enunciating slowly.

"Yeah. I haven't been sleeping well. Chief ordered me to go home when he saw me dozing. Maybe I should ask your mom for some napping tips."

Jennifer laughed, then got up and started picking up the toys Dylan had left in his wake. His Ghostbusters figures were picnicking on the couch next to a bowl of Cheerios, and he had turned Jennifer's biology book into a parking lot for his Hot Wheels. Adriana recalled that Lisa had said she homeschooled Jennifer following some incidents at her last school. It must be hard to make friends after moving to a new town, even before you're separated into different classrooms with special teachers. And Adriana knew how isolating that was. She had been pulled out of regular classes before finally being homeschooled herself. How would anyone expect someone like Jennifer maneuver through an environment like that? Adriana remembered the cliques in her school and how even she had sometimes made fun of other kids for the smallest differences. Studying at home may have its benefits, but Adriana also remembered it being extremely lonely.

"Hey, Jenny." Adriana touched her arm to get her attention. "Would you like to have a sleepover tonight while your mom's at work?"

"A sleepover?" Jennifer looked confused.

"Yeah, that's when friends hang out, play records, eat a lot, we could order a pizza!"

"Sleepover." Jennifer smiled. "That sounds fun."

Adriana heard a radio alarm begin buzzing upstairs. "I think your mom is up. I'll ask her if it's okay."

LISA WAS in her robe pouring coffee into a mug as Jennifer banged around upstairs packing her sleepover bag when Adriana said, "The nightmares are getting worse."

"Yeah, the car-window thing was scary."

"It's not just that." Adriana told Lisa about her dream at the library, forgetting that the cut on her forehead told its own story.

Lisa sat at her kitchen table and sipped. "Your drawings never included a car, so this is new, right?"

"Right."

"Have you tried drawing the face again?"

"Yeah, I tried a few times after throwing the first one away. Maybe it was a dumb thing to do, but it scared Dylan so much. Only, now I can't quite seem to remember it. It's just a blur, which is so weird because faces are, like, *my thing*."

"And you haven't seen it in the dream again?"

"Nope, just the once. For years it was just the arm. Every time. And now it's park signs from before I was born and giant cars driving up from the bottom of the lake."

"I've treated people with nightmares and sleeping disorders in the past, but nothing like this."

"Sleeping disorder?" Adriana asked.

"It's just a general term for not being able to sleep through the night." Lisa stirred her coffee and was quiet for a moment. Then her face lit up. "Maybe you could try sleeping with a drawing pad tonight. If it wants to be seen, maybe subconsciously knowing the drawing pad is there will invite it back."

"Never thought I'd be inviting that thing anywhere."

"Well, if it's going to keep you awake at night anyway, treat it like any other problem: confront it. Maybe that will help you see it again, to draw it again."

"So lay out the welcome mat?"

"Yeah. Stop letting it taunt you. You start taunting it."

Adriana pulled her loudspeakers away from her living room walls and placed them on either side of the couch. She flipped through her records and selected a few with great drummers or songs with prominent bass lines. She didn't have any Prince, one of Jennifer's favorites, but she did have a lot of Bon Jovi, Whitesnake, and, even though she wouldn't let anyone else see them, Madonna's first three albums.

The television flickered, but with the sound turned down. Adriana hadn't purchased a closed-captioning box but thought the screen visuals would be a nice distraction if the conversation lagged. She wasn't sure what she and Jennifer would do. Adriana hadn't been to or hosted a sleepover in probably ten years, unless you counted the occasional friends who passed out drunk at the end of a tattooing session.

She set out a few bowls of snacks on her coffee table, which was an old trunk covered in a small decorative sheet. Dylan bounced over to the coffee table, removed the pacifier from his mouth and started sucking on a pretzel stick. The doorbell rang.

"Jenny's here." Adriana announced to Dylan, who promptly ran for the door.

Two hours later, the snack bowls were empty. Adriana and Jennifer took turns picking songs to play. Jennifer sat on the couch leaning against the loudspeaker, smiling. Adriana sat on the floor stationed at the turntable. For the first time she really appreciated the various instruments and layers of each song. It was a different experience when you were focused on listening and nothing else.

Adriana felt bad she had to turn off the music when it came time to put Dylan to bed, so she turned on MTV, still with the volume down, because she remembered Lisa mentioning Jennifer enjoyed watching music videos. But while munching the last slice of pizza, Jennifer ignored the TV and kept glancing at Adriana's shoulder.

"What?" Adriana asked.

"Is that a tattoo?"

"Oh." The ink from a shoulder tattoo stretched up out of the neckline of Adriana's T-shirt. She pulled down the collar so Jennifer could see more of the design, a dolphin with numbers down its back, like stripes. The numbers read *3 24 85.*

Mesmerized by the design, Jennifer asked, "What do the numbers mean?"

"Dylan's birthday. I've always liked dolphins, and the name Dylan means 'born near the sea.' Someday, maybe we'll live near a beach or maybe the coast."

"Oh, that sounds nice."

Adriana added, "I'm tired of being surrounded by cornfields."

No, what she meant to say was that she was tired of being boxed in by Bradley. A flash of the idyllic life filled up her senses—salty beach air stinging her nose as Dylan played in the sand, the sound of a thousand evergreens swaying in a cool breeze while the two of them walked through the woods—then the pending custody hearing whacked her. How could her father think that tearing them apart was the right thing to do?

Jennifer said, "Have you always wanted to get out of here? Like, before Dylan was born?"

"Yeah, for as long as I can remember, actually," Adriana said. "Have you thought about where you want to live when you get older?"

"No. We've moved around so much already. I was actually born here in Cellar."

"Really?"

"Yeah. Mom moved us away when I was young, though, so I don't remember living here before."

"Which place has been your favorite to live so far?"

"Indiana. Which was a lot of corn like here. But there was this beautiful tree in our neighbor's backyard. Its leaves were red almost all year round, and I had a perfect view of it out of my bedroom window. It was like a tent covering their entire yard."

Adriana closed her eyes and could see the tree perfectly, as if she'd traveled through time and space to stand in Jennifer's old bedroom, looking out the window. A veil of peace fell over her, the same feeling Jennifer must have felt in that room.

"Would you like a tattoo of that tree?" Adriana asked.

Jennifer bounced up on to her knees on the couch. "I'd love that!"

"It would be temporary, of course. But I have some body paints I could use. They wash off in just a few days."

"Do you need me to describe it to you?"

"Nope, it's all up here already," Adriana said, smiling and pointing to her head. It was a welcome change from the rotting skulls and flaming hearts her usual clientele requested.

After some digging around in her bedroom closet, Adriana found the body paints and set to work. Jennifer laid on the couch and Adriana sat on the floor. She painted the windowsill on the side of Jennifer's calf. She worked slow, lining every branch and every leaf, as if she were inking someone permanently. At first the cool paints tickled Jennifer a little, but after they warmed up, she relaxed and laid still.

When Adriana finished, Jennifer sat up and admired her new temporary tattoo. She was so excited that she signed without speaking. Adriana laughed.

Jennifer looked up. "Oh, sorry. It's amazing! Thank you. I love it."

"Come back when you're eighteen and we'll make it permanent if you want."

Jennifer nodded as she looked back down at her leg. Adriana grabbed bedding she'd stacked next to the TV. "It's getting late. I should let you get to sleep."

She made the couch comfy, then handed Jennifer the TV remote and turned out the overhead light.

"Thanks for inviting me over," Jennifer said.

In her bedroom, Adriana shoved her body paints back in the closet, sat down on her bed, and wrapped her comforter around her. The house felt different with another young adult in it. Safer, maybe. Would she be able to sleep at all tonight? She wanted to. She needed to. She'd dozed off at work today for Christ's sake, and she could not jeopardize this gig. A bath might help. They always did. And she so rarely had the time to take for herself.

Adriana grabbed a change of clothes, then noticed the blister pack of pills Lisa had given her lying on top of her dresser. Through the doorway she saw the flicker of light from the living room television. Jennifer was probably still awake, and Adriana rationalized that Jennifer wouldn't let her leave and punch out any more car windows. So she popped a sleeping pill and then, *what the hell*, popped two more.

In the bathroom, she lit a candle, filled the tub, and then stepped into the warm water. The pills had taken a while to kick in the first time. She'd stayed up and watched an entire hour-long episode of Headbangers Ball. So she'd enjoy the bath, relax, and then curl up in bed with her drawing pad. Lisa had been right. It was time to lay out the welcome mat.

35

THE BATHROOM WAS HUMID. A thin layer of steam rose from the tub and Adriana's body. Drops of moisture trickled down the tiled walls that gleamed with candlelight. She sat forward in the bath and turned on the faucet again to add a touch more warmth. She felt the heat spread up from her lower legs before shutting the water off and leaning back in full, luxurious recline.

The buzz of filaments in the bulbs above her bathroom mirror were the only distraction, so she focused on the water gently lapping against the side of the tub, so like the night sounds of the lake. As her mind began to clear, her heavy arm slid off the outer edge of the tub and she knew the pills were kicking in faster than they had the last time. Maybe taking three wasn't the best idea she'd ever had.

She sucked in a deep breath and slid under the water, escaping the annoying buzz of the lights, and let the warmth soothe her. A spa night for Mom.

Then a single pulse disrupted the water and every muscle in her body tensed.

She squeezed her eyes shut hard. *No. Not yet. I'm not ready. I don't even have my drawing pad with me.*

When she couldn't bear it any longer, knowing the dark lake floor was waiting for her, she opened her eyes.

Nothing. It was calm. No muddy lake floor, no algae or rusty automobile parts, and no thrusting arm. Looking up, she didn't see moonlight, the purple skies, or clawing trees. She saw the bathroom ceiling, wobbling and swaying through the lens of bathwater.

She was relieved to be alone. She hadn't fallen asleep. Sleep was the welcome mat to her tormentor, the face that only existed at the bottom of Easton Mill Lake. And because she was still awake, she still had time to grab her drawing pad.

She came up for air.

And she screamed.

The Face glared at her from the foot of the tub. It rose from the water and towered over her, opening its blackened mouth and screeching.

"EEHHHHHHHDDDDD!"

Its rotting arms shot out of the water and grabbed her shoulders, shaking her as it repeated its horrific cry. "EEHHHHHHHDDDDD!"

She rocked side to side in the tub and tried to kick the foul thing away, one quick foot to the chest. Another kick to the head. But her foot sunk into the rotting skin and disappeared into the thing, somewhere beyond reality. Then the face lunged at her again, demanding something she could not understand. She kicked wildly, trying to get free from his hold on her.

"Get off! GET OFF!" she screamed, her hands slapping and clawing the tiled wall, desperate to get some traction.

A bolt of pain jumped through her foot and up her leg: a tile shattered under one of her kicks and cut the bottom of her foot.

The face hissed louder—"EEHHHHHHHDDDDD!"—as if struggling to say more, but limited by the rotting muscles and tissues of its jaw, the mouth dangling from only one hinge. It dug its sharp fingernails into Adriana's shoulder, above her dolphin tattoo, and she felt blood spurt from torn flesh. She lashed out and screamed—

At Jennifer. Jennifer was there, terrified, holding on to Adriana's shoulders.

"Adriana! Adriana, what's wrong? What's wrong?!"

Waves of bathwater splashed over the sides of the tub, soaking Jennifer's pajamas.

Adriana started to understand she was no longer in danger but struggled to calm herself. "What's happening?"

"I heard you kicking, or I felt it. The thudding vibrations were so heavy through the wall, I thought you might have fallen."

Jennifer got Adriana a towel.

"Thank you." Adriana said and got out of the water, wrapping herself in the towel. She spun and pulled the drain from the tub. She wanted that cursed water gone. "He was here."

Jennifer looked around the small bathroom. "Who?"

"I—I—"

"*Who* was here?"

"I don't know." Adriana sat on the closed toilet seat, trembling but now clear-headed.

"You're bleeding," Jennifer said.

Adriana saw real blood—not an imaginary sensation—dripping down from her shoulder. And a bloody footprint walked from the tub to the toilet and was now pooling under her left foot. Her whole body trembled.

"Here." Jennifer unfolded a second towel and draped it over Adriana.

"Thank you. One more favor?"

"Anything."

"In my bedroom there's a sketch pad and some pencils on my bed. Could you bring them to me?"

Jennifer applied Mickey Mouse Band-Aids to Adriana's shoulder as Adriana feverishly marked up the paper until that ugly, malformed face emerged. The face she'd seen at the bottom of the lake a few weeks ago. The face that had scared Dylan more than court that morning, and, if she was being honest, her too. The face that had skipped over the welcome mat and joined her in the tub.

36

ADRIANA WHISKED batter in a mixing bowl with some difficulty. The cuts and bruising she'd sustained after putting her arm through her car window were healing, but the awkward motion stirred up new pain. Her injuries from last night weren't helping either. Her shoulder should be fine soon, just a few scratches from that *thing*, or from Jennifer, she couldn't be sure, but the cut on the bottom of her left foot was deep and she had to put most of her weight on her right side this morning. *Act normal. Be normal*, she thought as she stood in the kitchen making breakfast.

She had finally seen the Face again, a little closer than she had wanted to get, but now she had a new drawing. A drawing she could maybe match to mug shots or missing persons or whatever kind of records the police had. She'd seen all the cold cases piling up on Matt's desk. They must have a treasure trove of files somewhere.

"I love waffles!" Dylan told Jennifer. He stood on a chair by the counter watching his mom mix the batter.

Jennifer sat at the kitchen table. Neither of them had mentioned last night's bathtub incident. Would Jennifer say something to her mother about it, or should Adriana preemptively call and tell Lisa herself? She wanted to break the silence.

"Do you like waffles, Jenny?"

"I love waffles!" she answered, teasing Dylan with a smile.

Adriana poured the batter into her waffle iron, trying hard to focus on cooking and trying not to think about the wailing screech that thing made—*EEEHHHHHHHDD*—when it was in the tub with her last night. Then the doorbell rang.

"Ding-dong," Dylan mimicked, and hopped off his chair to answer the front door. Adriana set down the spatula and followed him. He opened the front door and stood staring up at Matt, in full uniform, who was holding two coffees from Cody's Diner.

Adriana nearly recoiled in embarrassment in her bare feet and an old bathrobe. "Matt." She quickly pulled the robe around her like a straitjacket.

"Hi. Uh, sorry, I should have called. Did you forget?"

Forget what? Adriana searched her brain for any plans or an early work shift, but last night's encounter had scared away any semblance of a schedule.

"The police union fundraiser?" Matt offered. He looked hopeful and not at all hurt that she had, in fact, forgotten. "When I asked you last week, you agreed..."

"Right, that's today?"

"Yeah, but it's okay. I can head up there on my own if you—"

"No, no, I want to go. I do. I just forgot."

"Okay. I was..." He stopped and sniffed the air. "Is something burning?"

"Oh shit!"

MATT HADN'T EXPECTED a homemade breakfast, and he had to admit that warm food, even a bit burned, was far better than what he would have thrown together in his apartment.

"Breakfast isn't going to make us late, is it?" Adriana asked as she cleared the table.

"No, we have a little time. It was delicious. Thank you." Matt smiled. He felt a little guilty that Adriana fled to her bedroom after saving the waffles and returned in a blouse and jeans. *Does she really want to go or is this a pity date?* He'd tried not to stare when the robe had slipped off her pale shoulder, exposing an innocent tattoo and Band-Aids. He wasn't staring, he told himself, the colorful Band-Aids had just caught his eye. *More injuries?*

Dylan played on the floor with his toys. Every couple of minutes he would bring a different toy into the kitchen to show Matt. First it was a Hot Wheels tractor, then a book about the Poky Little Puppy. Each time Matt would examine the item with genuine curiosity and ask Dylan questions. "What do you grow on your farm?" "Which games does the Poky Little Puppy like to play?" Each time Dylan shrugged and mumbled, "I don't know," before running off. Matt never really thought about being a dad before. He wondered how he'd do at it, especially if he had to do it alone, like Adriana.

"I have to go," Jennifer said from the hallway.

"It was nice meeting you, Jenny," Matt said.

"You too!"

Adriana rose from her chair to hug Jennifer. "Tell your mom that tat is…"

"Temporary! I will."

Matt overheard Adriana thank Jennifer for her help last night. "And tell your mom I'll call her later, okay? To explain." *Explain what?* He leaned over in his chair to catch a glimpse of them. Jennifer gazed up at Adriana with concern and maybe even a little fear. Matt took note of the unspoken exchange, then turned his attention back to Dylan.

Adriana returned to the kitchen, lost in thought, it seemed, and began to rinse the dishes. Matt moved to the sink and grabbed a towel.

"Sorry if I spoiled your time with Jenny. Are you sure she doesn't want to join us at the festival?"

"No. She said she had some chores to do today. And you're fine. Stop apologizing."

"She's really good at reading lips. I had no idea that was a real thing. You see it in movies, but that was a first for me in real life."

"Yeah, Lisa told me she's worked really hard at it."

As they finished the dishes, Matt glanced at his watch.

"Sorry," Adriana said. "I know you're supposed to be on duty at the fundraiser. Let me get Dylan changed, and then we'll be ready to go."

Whatever was pulling at Adriana, he hoped she'd feel comfortable sharing it with him soon. He knew about her father, about the dreams, and the lake, but this seemed like something bigger. He hoped Dylan would have fun at the festival and that, in turn, would cheer Adriana up.

37

MATT PULLED his cruiser into the open grassy field near the fairgrounds. Adriana sat up front holding Dylan in her lap. Kasich stood guard in the makeshift parking lot near the entrance. Matt had never seen him in his civilian clothes before: Bermuda shorts and a Hawaiian shirt that tented his belly. Kasich waved over Matt's patrol car as they pulled in.

"Did you finally make an arrest, Rookie? Oh, Ms. Krause, that's you," Kasich joked.

Adriana leaned toward Matt's open window. "Nice to see you too, Sergeant."

Kasich directed them to a section reserved for on-duty vehicles, and Matt parked the cruiser.

The grassy fairgrounds were already crowded with vehicles and people. In the distance, a live rock band was running through their playlist of sixties rock covers on the bandshell stage, and a small crowd had gathered to listen and dance. Kiddie rides, food stalls, and games were spread out in the open spaces and welcoming everyone at the entrance was a ticket booth. Matt stepped up and bought a ridiculously long perforated roll of coupons for rides and raffles, then tore off a generous portion for Adriana.

"Thank you," she said.

Their eyes met, until a passing couple caught Adriana's attention. Councilman Card and Deesha strolled by, mingling, shaking hands, and calling out names. They seemed at ease and moved through the crowd natural as fish in a pond.

"Sorry, Addie," Matt said. "I forgot about the speeches. Card goes first. Your dad won't be on until later."

"Thanks for the heads-up. I'll be fine, so long as I don't have to stand and cheer."

A joyous crowd erupted in laughter and applause, and Dylan looked to see what was going on. Matt pointed to a "Dunk the Officer" banner strung between two trees. "You see what they're shouting about? That's called a dunk tank. Want to watch me go under?"

"Yes!" Dylan squealed.

Adriana asked, "Really?"

"Yeah, Kasich put me on the schedule. *Twice.*"

"Well, isn't he thoughtful."

"At least we have a nice day for it. I was worried it'd be cold and rainy, but I won't mind a dunk or two in this sun."

As they walked closer, the crowd cheered again as an older officer splashed into one of two glass tanks. He was a showman: underwater, he opened his eyes and waved at the onlookers.

Matt was a born people-watcher who found the mass of Cellarites amusing. A tall woman with one of those new Fuji disposable cameras bumped into everybody, including a tree, as her eyes were obscured by the camera, snapping one shot after another. Two teenagers raced like jets through the throng toward the bumper cars.

"Can we play dunker now?" Dylan asked.

Matt laughed and crouched again to talk to Dylan. "Okay, here's how it works. For one ticket you get three balls. You or your mom throw them at that target there. If you miss, nothing happens. But if you hit the target, I get dunked. Okay?"

"Yeah!"

Matt whispered to Adriana, "I bet that water's going to be cold."

"All for a good cause," she said and nodded toward the Friends of the Force banner.

Matt showed his badge to the man running the game. The guy checked Matt off a list on his clipboard and handed him a baseball cap branded with the union's insignia and a pullover T-shirt that said "Cellar Police" in large block letters.

He climbed the steps to the seat above the tank and dipped his hand into the water to gauge the temperature. For the audience, he made a show of hugging himself, "Brrrrr," and he heard Dylan laugh.

"Okay, everybody, let 'er rip!"

Adriana handed over a few tickets and got a basket of balls from the game's operator. She launched the first softball, and it was way off target. She laughed off her embarrassment and then picked up Dylan so he could shoot. Dylan threw and his ball plunked down on the grass and rolled a short distance. He fussed, but the crowd applauded, and the man running the event encouraged him. "Oh, so close."

From his perch, Matt watched the spectacle of one missed pitch after another, then grimaced when the public address system whined with feedback. The feedback was cut and a woman's voice blared out across the fairgrounds.

"Hello, everybody. I'm Lois King, Chairwoman of the Cellar City Council. Isn't this a glorious day?"

The audience whooped and clapped. Lois added, "And welcome to another election year!"

Matt heard a softball thwap against the dunk bucket structure. Another miss. Adriana, grinning broadly, wound up for another throw as Lois—*thwap*—carried on.

"Our first speaker has made a name for himself in business, politics, and by marrying the former Deesha Lynn Robinson, our very own homegirl. Please welcome the Honorable Councilman Benjamin Card!"

The rock band kicked into James Brown's "I Feel Good" as Card ran across the small stage, waving and smiling. He took the microphone from Lois and shouted, "Hello, Cellar!" His enthusiasm was infectious to almost everyone. Everyone except one guy, Matt noticed, who was moving toward the stage.

The man reached into his jacket and pulled out—*a gun?*—a photograph. Matt released the tension in his shoulders. Maybe he was jumping at shadows because he'd never worked such a large event, or maybe he felt guilty getting stuck playing Dunk the Officer instead of patrolling, but seeing things that weren't there wasn't going to help.

Adriana handed over another strip of tickets for more ammunition, then rubbed a ball in her hands and cocked her arm with a wicked grin.

But Matt's attention quickly turned back to the odd man in front of the bandshell. The man searched another pocket and pulled out an object that glimmered in the sun.

Card was on a roll, all but singing his campaign bullet points to cheering fans.

Matt only saw a glint, a tiny silver blip in the crowd, but every ounce of his gut told him it was a gun. Aimed at Card. Frantically, he called out and waved his arms at Adriana, "Don't, don't, don't!" as he heard a bang. Adriana's ball hit its target and Matt plunged into cold water.

38

ADRIANA HEARD a few loud cracks from the bandshell stage. She looked to Matt, submerged in the Dunk the Officer tank, his eyes wide and his hand jabbing at the glass, warning her. Then came the screaming. As Matt pushed off from the bottom of the tank and flung his body over its edge, she was trampled by a herd of people who were ducking and surging in one direction and then the next.

"Dylan!" She spun, searching for her boy, when she heard Matt shouting, "Over here, Addie!" He crouched in front of Dylan, fending off bodies as they pushed and shoved and ricocheted off the glass tank.

"Were those gunshots?" she asked.

"Yes. Three, I think."

"Did you see if anyone was hurt?"

"I don't know. Everything happened just as I was going under. I need to get up there and help." Matt stood, but Adriana grabbed his arm.

"Don't leave us." She knew he was on duty, knew he should go, but she was terrified.

He hesitated. Then nodded. "Stay close to me."

Adriana carried Dylan and followed Matt through the mayhem.

The screaming was terrifying, but the scene in front of the band-shell was worse. Two bloody bodies were sprawled on the lawn, including Benjamin Card, who'd apparently fallen off the stage after being shot.

"Go there." Matt pointed to the corner of the stage. "Stay there."

He ran to Card, whose head was resting in Deesha's lap.

"He's dying. My husband is—!"

Adriana pulled Dylan tight against her. He was crying and she tried to calm herself so she could soothe him.

Matt stripped off his Cellar Police T-shirt and pressed it against Card's bloody belly.

"Councilman Card, can you hear me? Can you speak?"

Card was nonresponsive. Matt took the radio from his belt.

"I need all medical personnel to the bandshell. Multiple gunshot victims including Councilman Card. Get me an ambulance. And where the hell is everyone?! Officers report!"

He instructed Deesha to hold the T-shirt firmly against the wound. He stumbled over to the next victim. The man laid face-down in the grass next to a woman frozen in shock. Matt turned him over and saw it was Tom Galton. He recognized Card's campaign manager from the pictures in the newspaper. He assumed the woman was Galton's wife. There was a lot of blood, but Galton was conscious.

"Mr. Galton, I'm a police officer. My name's Matt. Have you've been hit?"

Galton, holding his wounded arm, tried to point somewhere behind Matt.

"I'm fine. Just my arm." Galton took in sharp, short breaths. "You have to stop him. That way... He went around...those restrooms. Toward town center."

Matt stood and surveyed the porta-potties.

"Okay. Okay. Help is coming."

Galton nodded. Matt rushed toward the restrooms and collided with Kasich, whose bulky panic made him grab at the rookie for balance. Kasich's Hawaiian shirt was bathed in sweat.

"What the hell's going on?!"

"Active shooter. At least two victims, maybe more."

"A shooter? What the hell are we—?"

"Shut down the exits," Matt shouted. "Don't let anybody out of the parking lot."

"But how am I supposed to—?"

Matt grabbed Kasich and shook him. "Do it now. He might still be here!"

He maneuvered past Kasich and rounded the restrooms. The guy was gone. He thought of Adriana and Dylan. He'd left them unprotected and cursed himself for it.

He looked around as he jogged back to the stage. He saw frightened people scattering in all directions, crashing through brush and temporary fencing. They were all climbing over each other toward a safety he was not sure existed anymore.

39

WOODHULL TOOK in the chaos as he arrived at the fairgrounds. His high blood pressure pinched at his temples with each beat of his pulse. *How could this happen here in Cellar?*

It only took his officers a few minutes to lock down the area. He was proud of his team for that. And only a few minutes later, emergency services got two ambulances on scene. Not bad, but sometimes that was a few minutes too long, Woodhull knew.

Benjamin Card held on, though. He was unconscious, so it was touch and go, and he couldn't answer any questions. Did he see the shooter? Had he received any threats? But the man was strong or stubborn or both. Card was loaded up on the first ambulance and rushed off to Ohio Valley Urgent Care. Card might eventually be transported to a larger hospital, but the nearest was more than two hours away and Woodhull knew immediate help was usually better than delayed expert care.

He had a moment to question Tom Galton though, the only other shooting victim. He was fully conscious, but with an arm that would likely need surgery. He hadn't seen anything and wasn't aware of any threats, at least none against Card. Before Woodhull could dig any deeper, Galton was loaded up on the second ambulance also en route to the OVUC.

With both victims now cleared from the scene, Woodhull joined Kasich near the bandshell steps. *"Jesus,"* he said. "And Bradley wants to cut our budget. Good job locking this place down, Al." He patted Kasich on the back.

"Uh, thanks, Chief. I was helping out at the entrance when I heard the shots but got here as quick as I could. I guess I ain't retired yet."

"And what about Hinkley? Did he see anything?"

Kasich paused. "Well..."

"Don't cover for him, Al. If he's not gonna cut it, I need to know."

"He was swimming in the dunk tank when it happened."

"What?"

"A couple of the off-duty guys signed up to help the Friends of the Force."

"But Hinkley wasn't off duty!" Woodhull barked. "Where's he now?"

Kasich pointed toward a picnic bench near some of the food booths where Matt, Adriana, and Dylan were hunkered down.

"Okay. Al, I want you to take the lead here. I'm taking the rookie and most of the other officers back to the station. I've called for a few vans to move all the witnesses back to the station so we can question them. It's going to be a shit show there for a while. If you learn anything new here, contact me and *only* me. Yeah?"

"Okay, Chief."

"Help get these folks ready for the move, all right?"

He felt confident leaving the scene with Kasich in charge but fought the urge to scold his rookie as he approached the picnic tables.

"Hinkley, you're soaking wet!"

Matt stood, dripping. "Yes, sir."

"What they hell were you doing playing games when you should have been patrolling? I swear, ever since I hired Adriana, it seems like you two think it's always playtime. Don't think I haven't seen you both running off in the middle of your shifts or joking in the breakroom long after."

"Sorry, Chief, you're right, I should have been—"

"Kasich made him do it." Adriana interrupted.

"*Made* him?"

"He signed me up," Matt said. "I didn't know about it until today. Just a little hazing, sir."

"All right, all right." Woodhull didn't have time for this but felt his confidence in Kasich momentarily waver. "Follow me back to the station. I want you to hover near all the interviews and grab what details you can. I need a *face*, Addie. I need a goddamned face so we can track down this nut before he hurts anyone else. Can I trust you two to get some work done?"

BACK IN HIS OFFICE, Woodhull stood with the phone receiver pressed to his ear and looked out at the bullpen. He couldn't remember the last time it was filled like this. Every witness they could wrangle from the fairgrounds was brought in and his officers were trying like hell to piece together what had just happened.

Woodhull watched Adriana move around the station. She had that weird look on her face that happened whenever her brain was locked in to some other universe. He could forgive a lot of the slacking off if she could come through for them today.

"Of course, sir," Woodhull said into the phone receiver propped in the crook of his shoulder. The FBI, the *fucking* FBI, were already on their way down to Cellar. If his heart rate hadn't dropped to normal before this call, it certainly wasn't going to after it. Some liaison officer was going over protocol with Woodhull before their men arrived. Her tiny voice from miles away, dictating Woodhull's next moves. *Attempted assassination... Jurisdiction over the scene... Full interrogation...* He consciously tried to take long, slow breaths. This was all more than he ever guessed he'd have to deal with in Cellar.

MATT DRIED off in the station's locker room and dressed in his spare uniform. It was difficult to button up his shirt, his hands were shaking so bad, but it was nice to be in fresh clothes. He felt like a child after having been dunked and then berated for it. But now he could get back to work. He joined everyone else out in the bullpen as witnesses continued to flood the station. It seemed like every officer was brought in for this.

Matt was a witness of sort too, and he was still emotionally raw from the adrenaline that had coursed through his body after the shots were fired. As he replayed those moments in his mind, he was discovering that memory played tricks with sight, sound, and accuracy. He could remember seeing the glint, but couldn't remember seeing how the suspect was dressed, how tall, nor how old he was. Just that flash and then the chaos. He recalled hearing three bursts, not four, as most of the other witnesses had reported.

He wondered why accounts of crimes and other incidents didn't always line up. Now he knew. Most people's memories were terrible, distorted through emotions and a million unrelated thoughts and filters.

He still hoped to make a great detective someday. But on this day, he knew he was a lousy witness.

Matt followed Adriana as she listened to interviews. She did not have a credential that allowed her to write official reports, but that was okay, because Matt knew her gift wasn't with forms or files. She had probably absorbed more already in her own way than all of the officers conducting the interviews combined. Adriana's instincts, and what his aunt used to call second sight, would be a huge asset today as Matt's peers weren't used to working in this kind of chaos. Everyone spoke over each other, every phone was lit up, lines for the few bathroom stalls stretched into public areas, and there were a hoard of kids lying across benches or running laps around desks. Dylan sat quietly, his eyes wide. Matt wondered if he had his mother's gift for seeing beyond the ordinary.

Adriana continued to make the rounds as Matt left her and walked back to his desk. He didn't speak the same wavelengths Adriana did, so he wouldn't be able to learn any new information without actually talking to the people who were there. He grabbed an intake form from his top desk drawer and took the next witness waiting to give a statement.

Over the next few hours, more than two dozen people from the fundraiser gave him their statements. Most didn't see anything helpful, as their attention was turned to the stage. Everyone heard the shots and saw Tom Galton stumble and fall, and only then realized Benjamin Card had gone silent as he crumpled from the bandshell stage. That's when they all ran.

The station slowly emptied out as statements were taken, contact information was given, and people were sent on their way. Matt realized it was a little weird wishing for more busy, purposeful days like this, but he liked being productive, liked fitting pieces of information together and the sense of accomplishment that followed. If only people didn't have to get hurt for this to happen.

He called and gestured to the next person in line, an elderly woman who appeared annoyed by the long wait, and she sat in the chair beside his desk.

"Hi, I'm Officer Hinkley. Could I see your driver's license or state ID please?"

"Sure, but I don't know how that's going to help you catch him."

Matt explained that it was the easiest way to gather contact information.

"Right, but while we're sittin' in here worried about forms and silly statements, the murderer is getting away!"

"Last I heard, Councilman Card is still alive, ma'am. But do you know who we're looking for?"

"Yes! I saw that man shoot Mr. Card. That's what I've been trying to tell the officer in the hallway for close to an hour now. He just kept telling me to wait my turn!"

"I'm very sorry, ma'am. But I'm here and listening now. You know who shot Councilman Card? Can you tell me his name?"

"Oh, heck, I don't know that."

"Okay. Did you see where he came from or where he ran off to?"

"I kept him in my sight for a minute, but that crowd pushed and shoved, and I lost him."

So you don't know who shot Card or where he went, Matt thought. *Yet another dead end.*

"Okay..." he tried. "Do you remember what the guy looked like?"

"Oh yes, he was so angry. I only saw him for a moment, but, well, I don't think I'll ever forget that face."

"You can describe him, then?"

"Yes. I just said I remembered what he looked like, didn't I?"

Matt hopped out of his chair and looked to the Chief's office. Woodhull was still on the phone, but, scanning the bullpen, he managed to find Adriana. He stammered. "Uh... Could you...wait here for a minute?"

"Been here close to ninety minutes already. What's one more? Just gives the killer another sixty seconds to get away."

40

ADRIANA TENSED. She was back in the conference room, sketch pad on her lap, and anxious about her second chance at a facial sketch. The first one with Laurie hadn't gone well. It wasn't a disaster, and Adriana had still managed to land the gig, but this time there would be no bluffing, no third chance.

The woman sitting across from her introduced herself as Patty Lynn. Matt warned that she was a bit "prickly," but that she had seen the whole thing and could describe the shooter. Adriana pulled the sketch pad close. She was relieved the station had almost emptied now, and she was able to reclaim her makeshift office. No one else had claimed to see the shooter's face.

"He stunk," Patty Lynn said. "Like a dead cat. That's probably what grabbed my attention, that smell, and why I got a good look at him."

Adriana nodded as she kept her eyes focused on Patty Lynn, even as her pencil began to swerve around the page of her sketchbook, laying down the template of a face.

"He had on a coat. It was failing at the seams, little tuffs of padding sticking out everywhere. It was a mess. Not sure why he'd be wearing that old thing on such a lovely day."

Adriana drew hints of a jacket collar and left it at that.

"His eyes looked so tired, droopy," Patty added. "And his nose was plump for such a skinny face, like the kind of guy who's hungry but never eats?"

Matt asked, "How old do you think he is?"

"Oh, gosh, he had no age. He looked young and old, depending on the angle."

Matt pushed, "Angle? What do you mean?"

"He was constantly moving, all jittery and hyper. So I'd see a patch of him, a flash and then another, and like I said, it was a warm one out today, but the way he shivered, I'd swear he was freezing."

Adriana kept drawing. Faint lines appeared on the sketch pad, the rough idea of a face. Then Patty Lynn mentioned that the guy seemed to have one long eyebrow, not two distinct brows. She grasped at any detail that was offered. She knew Woodhull needed something good and when she glanced at Dylan, waiting in the bullpen, she felt a shiver run up her back: she needed to keep her job to keep her boy.

Her pencil jumped and skittered across the page and Hinkley sat forward when he noticed the flurry of action. She blackened the eyes, making them sunken sockets, and scratched a crescent, indicating a chin. The overhead light burned bright, but the room went dark for Adriana as she disappeared into the zone that shut out all other noises. Slightly parted lips emerged as the mouth cavity was shaded.

Then Adriana began to struggle. Frustrated, she rotated the sketch pad, putting the image at an angle, as though it were the face of a man lying on his side. She tossed her pencil and grabbed another as the first had dulled and dug back into the page. Moments later, her scratches and scrawls became an actual face.

Adriana stopped, confident she'd captured everything as Patty Lynn had described. Only, when she glanced up, finally letting the light of the room back in and looked at her sketch, a wave of recognition surged up her chest and wrapped around her throat. She began to tremble, then screeched—"Nooo!"—and hurled her sketch pad against the wall.

Staring back up at her from the pad wasn't the face Patty Lynn had described. It was the Face that had attacked her in her bathtub.

"What's wrong?" Patty Lynn asked. She picked up the sketch pad and saw the drawing. "What in good gravy is that?! I wait over an hour for *this*? Can't you people get anything right?"

41

ADRIANA'S SCREAM rung out through the station. Everyone startled. A few officers drew their weapons. Woodhull rushed from his office, through the bullpen, and barged into the conference room, his eyes set on Hinkley. "Everything all right in here?"

Matt looked up from the sketch pad. Adriana was out of her chair and pacing, both hands pushed against her temples. It looked like her head was about to explode.

Woodhull grabbed the pad of paper. "Whaddya got?"

He grimaced. The sketch was of some horror movie ghoul, some sort of phantom who would appear out of thin air and then vanish into the shadows. He tossed the drawing pad on the conference table.

"What the hell is this, Ms. Krause?"

She grabbed the drawing and forced her gummed-up eraser back and forth over the face, obscuring the monster. First the mouth disappeared in a smear, then the jaw that looked like it was hanging on one hinge. She dug so hard into the paper she nearly gouged a hole in the middle. When she stopped the eraser was dark and muddy with graphite.

This is what you get for laying down the welcome mat. What's wrong with you? She silently berated herself. She had transformed Patty Lynn's description of the would-be assassin into a pulp-fiction kind of horror show. Her heart sank.

Woodhull called for an officer in the bullpen and told him to escort Patty Lynn to a seat where she could wait. "Thank you for your help, ma'am," he said.

She did not go gently. "What kind of nuthouse are you running around here?"

Woodhull took a deep breath and then turned back to Adriana.

"Why did you erase the only sketch we have?"

"You thought *that* was going to help you find the shooter? Really?"

"It's a scary sketch, Addie." Matt tried to cool her down. "We're all a little bit in shock about what happened today."

"Shock?" Woodhull said. "We're police officers, Hinkley, we keep our cool in a crisis. And you, Ms. Krause, are supposed to be our crime sketch artist, who, it turns out, can't even draw a face!"

"I'm afraid," Adriana admitted.

"I've got an eyewitness to the biggest crime Cellar has ever seen, and I can't get a drawing of that suspect because you're *afraid*? Afraid of what?"

"This thing, this face. I've never *not* been in control of what I was drawing. And I swear, when I was listening to her description, I was drawing the face she saw. Only, when I looked down, it was this… It's haunting me. It has been for years, but it wasn't until—"

"It's a drawing, Ms. Krause. It can't hurt you!" Woodhull tore the smeared page from the drawing pad, then handed the pad back to her. "Get a fresh start with this woman and try again. I need a sketch of whatever she saw."

"No."

"No?" he repeated.

Hinkley spoke up. "Chief, maybe we should—"

"No maybes. No nightmares or ghosts. Just give me a goddamn

drawing with eyes, ears, and a nose!" Woodhull seethed, then shut his eyes and started practicing some breathing exercise. He lowered his voice and softened his tone.

"Look, I know you've been going through a rough patch, Addie. I'm not saying things are good right now. But we have a job to do. We don't know if Card's going to pull through. And even if he does, we have to catch this asshole before he hurts someone else."

Adriana's eyes welled up.

"I'm asking...*Ms. Krause...*" Woodhull stared her down. "Will you, *pretty please*, do your job and get me a sketch I can use!"

"Chief—"

"Get the fuck out of this room, Hinkley!"

Matt opened his mouth to respond, then shut it, nodded, and left the room.

Woodhull turned back to Adriana.

"I'm under a lot of pressure here, Addie. People don't get shot in Cellar. And then in one afternoon we hit the Daily Double. And to make it worse, one of them is a mayoral candidate who's fighting for his life at the oh-vuck. I got Feds, the *FBI*, on their way down to our quiet little town, and when they get here, I can't hand them some abstract drawing of your nightmares."

"I understand, but—"

"But what?"

Adriana stared at the sketch. To others it was a giant smudge, a nothing drawing. Yet as she stared, the smudged face felt like it might fly off the paper and attack her, like it had when she'd tried to relax in her bathtub. There was only one thing missing.

EEHHHHHHDD!!

"No," she whimpered. "I can't, Chief."

Woodhull exhaled hard. "Okay. You're fired."

"I'll file reports. I'll—I'll... I need a job to keep Dylan!"

"It's very simple around here. Do the job you've been given, the one you begged for, or get out! Police work isn't for everyone, Addie. Open a tattoo shop. Draw ugly things all day long there. Here, we need suspects, accurate drawings of *human* suspects."

His gaze was stern. She got the message. She grabbed her bag from the chair and left the room. She moved fast, picking up Dylan and heading for the exit before Matt could stop her, before Woodhull could make her feel any worse, and before she completely broke down sobbing.

42

ADRIANA SAT on the city bus holding Dylan in her lap. *Fired.* She almost couldn't believe it. Without the job the judge would surely grant Bradley custody, it was the one thing he'd asked her to do before the follow-up hearing.

Dylan crawled off her lap and into the empty seat beside her to look out the window. They were riding away from the station and toward home. Matt had driven them to the fundraiser that morning so she didn't have her loaner at the station. A fact that escaped her until she was out in the parking lot searching through tears to find the big dumb truck.

Mercifully, the next bus arrived only ten minutes later. She felt embarrassed standing at the stop outside the station, her failure looming behind her.

If you've invited someone in...into your head, what was the best way to get them out? Adriana didn't know. All she knew was, she couldn't let this thing live in there any longer than she already had. It was like a song stuck in her head, repeating itself over and over. So she was going to do the only thing she could think of to get rid of it: she was going to draw it again. Exorcise the thing from her head onto the paper and let it live there. She pulled her sketch pad out of her shoulder bag, flipped to a fresh sheet, and started drawing the Face again. Deliberately this time.

She angled the sketch pad away from Dylan to keep the monstrous face from his view, even though he was fixated on the shops and people rushing by outside the bus window.

Adriana sketched frantically. She didn't even have to try this time, the Face burst forth from her pencil like it had been waiting for this opportunity. She finished the sketch, took in the same horror she'd seen there back at the station, then flipped to a new page and started again.

"Papa!" Dylan said, and pointed out the window.

Adriana looked up but didn't see her father anywhere.

"No, honey, Papa's at work today." Probably buried in work and phone calls after the shooting. Now that she considered it, *Was it odd Bradley hadn't shown up to the police station? Hadn't he inserted himself into all the action? Was it weird he wasn't at the fundraiser?* Matt told her he was supposed to speak after Card. But maybe Bradley wasn't supposed to go on until hours later. She didn't know the actual schedule, and as she finished a second sketch of the Face, she decided she didn't care.

She flipped to a fresh page and started a third drawing. Her pencil flowed across the sketch pad. The Face still came easy. So easy, in fact, she was sure she'd empty it all out of her head soon, maybe even before the bus got them home.

BRADLEY KRAUSE HAD NOT PREPARED a speech for the fundraiser because he knew he wouldn't need it. Instead, he had run a series of errands around town, with his police radio scanner humming low the whole time. He'd stopped at the hardware store. Picked up a few things at the bait shop. And he'd done some light grocery shopping at Glendale's, where he could slowly browse the aisles and chat with other shoppers. He didn't have a shopping list with him because it didn't matter. His goal was merely to be seen around town.

Yet as the day dragged on, he felt a low-grade anxiety creep into his body. He wanted it all to be over with so he could move into the next phase of action: the great man leading his city through a tragedy. *The Savior of Cellar.* He'd show strength in the news interviews, confer with law enforcement, then help his people grieve.

He'd studied the careers of other leaders, men and women who had made their mark by stepping up and responding bravely to extraordinary circumstances. He would be remembered for how he handled the Benjamin Card tragedy. His legacy would be set. He warmed at the thought of it.

Not that such thoughts didn't also make his stomach churn. He would not be reacting. He would be an actor in a play he had instigated. There would be surprises, he assumed, especially because the tool he had employed for these purposes was rather blunt. But those bumps in the road would be okay, beneficial, even, because then he wouldn't be feigning surprise, he'd only have to wait for details and then act naturally. How hard could that be? Shock. Concern. Courage.

He was putting his bag of groceries in the passenger seat when he almost spilled the entire haul. His police scanner fired up, squawking like he'd never heard.

"Man down, man down. Shots fired!"

Bradley got in behind the steering wheel and fiddled with the knobs on his radio. Code words and numbers spewed into his truck cab, voices filled with anxiety and panic. The dispatcher didn't know who had been shot, not yet, but he did. Or did he? He wasn't watching a television broadcast. He'd have to wait for the evening news. How could he know who had taken a bullet? Maybe some foolish, but noble men had wrestled for control of the gun and an innocent bystander got hit. Maybe, maybe, maybe.

He sat in his truck, listening for details, and debated how long to wait before contacting the dispatchers and Chief Woodhull, who would surely already be rushing to the scene. He started the engine. He would drive home, keep listening, and wait for a call from the police. That was the proper protocol. The mayor must be kept informed about all important events…

He didn't have to go far before his CB radio prompted him. When he responded, he heard Woodhull. The chief was all business.

"Don't come to the fundraiser grounds. I repeat, do not come to the fundraiser, Brad. Your speech has been canceled."

"Why? What happened?"

"Shooting. I'm told Ben Card was the target."

"God, no!" Bradley hoped his voice sounded sincere.

"Where are you?"

"Downtown. I've been running errands all morning."

"Get back to your residence. I'll send a couple officers to keep guard."

"Why, Woody?"

"Brad, we don't know who did this or why. We need to keep you safe until we have more information. It looks like it's going to be a long fuckin' week."

Bradley could hear sirens not too far off. It was all happening. Curtains up. The play had begun.

43

BRADLEY PULLED into his driveway and was pleased that Woodhull's sentries had not yet made it to his gates. He hauled his bag of groceries into his dark home and set his keys on the kitchen counter, remembering to keep the receipt with date and time of purchase in a safe place. He unpacked a few of the groceries...

Then heard a creak upstairs.

He froze. Was it normal settling, his weight shifting the old bones of the house? Or was someone up there? Woodhull's officers wouldn't have let themselves in. He stood still, listening. He should be alone in the large house, but maybe others were going off script. Maybe others had hatched their own plans? Plans against *him*.

Bradley moved cautiously to the hallway closet, where one of his hunting rifles was stored. He told himself the sounds upstairs were likely a rodent. Nevertheless, he undid the safety latch on the firearm so that he'd be ready to blow a squirrel or any other vermin to high heaven.

His first step on the stairs creaked and it sounded like thunder. *Jesus*, he thought. *Keep the noise down.*

To avoid further groans, he took a wide stance and placed his feet on the far end of each step as he slowly ascended. He looked silly, but not as silly as this intruder, this *rodent*, would look when Bradley got the surprise drop on him.

On the top step he paused, leaned forward, and looked up and down the hallway. He heard a scrape, or rattle, a sound he couldn't define, come from the guest bedroom. *Aha!*

The door to the room was slightly ajar. Another muffled rattle confirmed that something was inside the room. He girded himself for action, slowly poked the barrel of his rifle through the opening, took a deep, quiet breath, and then—

A dark shadow charged out of the room and slammed against him. His rifle exploded once, then twice, and then was pulled from his hands as he fell back and cracked his head against the opposite wall. Bradley grabbed his skull and howled. He looked up at what had attacked him. His pain turned to fury.

"What the hell are you doing here?"

Robbie rushed over to Bradley. "I'm sorry, I'm sorry. I didn't know it was you. I thought maybe the cops had found me."

"Help me up."

Robbie obliged. "I—I—I didn't know where to go, man. Holy shit. Cops are everywhere."

"So you came here? You idiot! Did anyone see you? The police are on their way here right now to keep me safe from you."

"What?"

"Get the hell out before anybody sees you!" He started, then stopped. It was broad daylight, a junkie in lousy clothes would be spotted in this neighborhood. *Be smart about this, Brad. Bad optics. And you may still need him.*

"I'm not leaving." Robbie's face twisted up in anger. "You can't just shoo me away. You had me kill someone! I ain't been a saint before, but murder, man? The gun was so loud. I didn't think it'd be that loud. I couldn't hear anything after. And the blood... Devil man! You're the fucking devil! Why the hell did you—"

Bradley shoved Robbie against the wall, rattling the thin man and shutting him up. Bradley held him there as his mind churned.

"Shut up and listen. You've got to keep your head down until we can get you out of town. Everyone's on high alert right now. We've got to be smart. Can you be smart?"

He thought about placing Robbie in the basement, but his police protection might want to search down there for intruders. He could keep them away from the second floor by saying he'd already cleared it. But how could he keep this kid from muttering and fucking up? How could he keep him quiet? *The needle.* He'd keep quiet if he were doped up and asleep.

"You got your junk with you, Robbie?"

44

WOODHULL RECEIVED a call from Ohio Valley Urgent Care that Tom Galton was out of surgery, stabilized, and would be up to speaking with him. It was a small victory, but he'd take it while they waited for Card to pull through his coma.

No new leads came in after the fiasco with Adriana's drawing. The mayor was under protection: three rotating officers now perched outside his home, which was one more than Woodhull wanted to spare, but until they knew more, he had to assume his old friend was a target too. The station was at twice the capacity it would have been any other week, and everyone was still so buried in their work, no one noticed when the Chief finally slipped out.

Woodhull moved through the wide OVUC halls in full uniform, wishing he still kept a change of civvies in his car, like the good old days. He wanted a break from all the official-duty noise, the Feds breathing down his neck, the press conferences and reporters he'd have to deal with in the coming days—all of it.

"Hey, Tom."

Galton looked up from his hospital bed as Woodhull entered the room. Despite the pain killers he'd been given, Card's campaign manager didn't look relaxed. He had that same frenzied, anxious energy that the Chief remembered from his City Hall days working for the mayor.

"Not more questions, I hope," Galton said. "I just told the FBI agents everything, twice."

Shit, they got the call before I did? Am I being pushed out of this case already?

"Just wanted to check in on you. How's the arm?"

Galton's left bicep was wrapped in thick layers of bandages and his elbow and lower arm were elevated on a row of pillows.

"Well, as the saying goes, I'll live. One bullet removed, but it crushed a bone. And there's nerve damage. I'll need some rehab once they let me out of here."

"There goes your golf game."

"What golf game?"

Both men chuckled.

"I wanted to get back home tonight," Galton said. "But they want to keep me for observation. Anything to run up the insurance bill."

"You know it. But may as well take the time to rest and heal. It'll be your first vacation this decade."

"Right, only had to get shot to get a few days off."

Woodhull sat down next to Galton's bed. "Tom, I've been wondering…"

"Ah, so it is more interrogation."

"No. It's just, hell, politics has never made much sense to me."

"You could have fooled me," Galton said.

"What I mean is, I don't get all the calculations that go into these things. But if you could help me understand, that might help me figure out why someone would want to kill Card. Card doesn't strike me as a fool. I don't think he would have gone into this whole race blind. So what makes him think he can beat Bradley, a guy who's been in office so long it feels like he was born there?"

"You don't jump in because there's a trend or the numbers look good. You jump in because you have a mission. All great leaders do. Some of those missions benefit the people. But most don't."

"So Card is on a mission?"

"More like..." Galton hesitated. He turned his head and stared out the window at the dark parking lot. "It's more like Deesha's on a mission."

"How do you mean?"

"Deesha grew up in Cellar. You know? Like most of us, she has family here. Unlike us, her family hasn't exactly prospered under the current or past leadership."

"So this is some Black-versus-white thing?"

"No, I don't think so."

"Then what it is?"

"Opportunity, for everyone."

The answer sounded vague to Woodhull, a nice bumper sticker slogan maybe, but not a real message.

"Did you know they visited me last week?"

"I was his campaign manager, remember?"

"Was?"

"I don't see a future for him now." Galton looked pained by his own words. "Even if he pulls through..."

"Was it your idea that they come in to talk with me?"

"No. They insisted when they found out records were being destroyed. But I would have set up a meeting between you all eventually. We were just moving into that phase of the campaign. Card had talks with a few others already, including Lois King. Or, more accurately, Lois had a talk with him."

"What do you mean?"

Galton didn't hide his disdain. "*Lois*... What is her function, exactly? City Council chairwoman? More like Bradley Krause's lapdog. I know you and Bradley are close, but at least you know how to use your brain independent of the man. Lois? She was only sent to relay a message."

"What kind of message?"

"Drop out of the race. Wait your turn, *boy*..."

Typically shrewd, Woodhull thought. Bradley keeps his hands clean, his mouth shut, and could deny everything if someone accused him of sending a messenger.

"At least Lois didn't threaten anyone," Galton said.

"Threaten?"

"Yeah, she could teach Mr. Mayor a few things about tact. I get it, we're competitors. But really, coercing me with—"

"Bradley put pressure on you?"

"That guy'll do anything to win. He had photos of my wife. He threatened to expose them if I didn't leave Card and join *his* campaign."

"He was blackmailing you?" Woodhull saw a different side of Galton. His normal state of anxiety morphed into a contained fury.

"It was a family values ploy. Hurt me so that he could damage Card."

Sounds like Bradley was afraid. "Do you think Card could have won?"

"I wouldn't have joined his team if I didn't think he had a fighting chance. Mission, remember? It's all about the mission. Even if Ben didn't win, he and Deesha had a platform. It's not my story to tell. But look at how many people came out to hear them speak today. They have some tough questions waiting for the mayor. And for their police chief, too." Galton chuckled, as if realizing none of it mattered now. "Get enough people asking those questions and you eventually get change. Even with Bradley still lounging behind the mayor's desk."

"Honey?" A soft voice spoke from the open doorway.

Woodhull turned to see Sharon Galton. "I got the clothes and papers from the house you asked for."

Woodhull stood. "Get better, Tom. Thanks for the chat."

"Just get the son of a bitch who did this, okay?"

Woodhull nodded.

On his way out, Woodhull passed by Councilman Card's room and ignored Officer Hinkley on duty at the door. The Rookie was on his shit list and a little door duty would get him out of the chief's sight for a while. He thought hard about his meeting with the Cards. They seemed unnaturally concerned with the archives that were set to be destroyed. *Agenda. Mission. Damn right*, he thought.

45

"So soon?"

Maggie Woodhull stood behind her office counter and looked up from the press release Bradley had just handed her. She set it down next to her morning coffee.

"It has to be done, Mags. I need you to post this so the public knows city government is still functioning despite the tragedy."

"I don't know, Brad. It seems so rushed. It's only been three days since…"

"Look, Mags, I agree. But I'm calling the special council meeting more for reassurance than procedure, though we do need to fill Ben's chair."

Bradley glanced back at the officers who'd followed him from his home this morning to his office at City Hall. *Babysitters.* At least they were keeping their distance while he tried to get some work done. *He* knew he wasn't in any danger. Maybe if he could get Woodhull alone later, he could talk him into pulling his detail.

When he turned back to Maggie, he could almost see the words *So soon?* gather again in her mouth, but she didn't speak. Instead, looking at the notice, she shook her head. He leaned in over the counter and placed his hand over hers.

"I know a lot of people are scared right now. There's some maniac with a gun running free on our streets. Those people need to know *we're* not scared. We're going to keep showing up and fighting for them. They need to see us working."

"Okay."

"Thank you." Bradley stood straight again. "I know it seems rushed, but we have to find an interim replacement. Our town can't shut down for just one man, we can't have any deadlocked votes or..."

Bradley stopped when he heard footfalls echoing in the hall behind him. He turned and flushed with embarrassment when he saw Deesha Card. He was sure she had heard his remark and her presence disarmed him. She wasn't tall, yet her dark blue pantsuit with matching hat gave her a sense of authority.

"Mayor Krause," she nodded. "I appreciate the flowers your office sent."

"Deesha, no problem. We're all pulling for your husband. I know the police are doing everything they can to find the lunatic who did this."

"I'm sure Woodhull is doing his best...when he's not stuck in a booth at Cody's."

Maggie protested. "My brother works his butt off for this town."

"It's okay, Mags," Bradley said. "I don't think Mrs. Card meant to speak ill of your brother. This is a difficult time. But it's true that I've approved unlimited overtime for our police force, and nobody should be taking long lunch breaks. They'll get to the bottom of this."

He caught Deesha glancing at his detail, three officers standing around not doing much more than shifting their weight from side to side.

"Thanks, Mr. Mayor."

He nodded to Deesha and excused himself. He had work to do and didn't care to spend the rest of his morning reassuring his opponent's wife.

Maggie composed herself, then asked, "How may I help you, Deesha?"

Before Bradley turned the corner down the hall to his office, he glanced back to see Deesha take a small packet of papers from a fancy leather satchel and present them to Maggie. Bradley found it curious that she was here on business while her husband lay in the OVUC fighting for his life. He would definitely have to get Maggie to tell him what that was all about.

———

JENNIFER SAT in the backyard shade, leaning against the fence. Dylan ran across the grass trying to get a kite off the ground.

She enjoyed her time babysitting Dylan but had never had Dylan alone for this long before. He'd stayed the night, and it was already lunchtime without a word from Adriana next door. Jennifer glanced over at Adriana's house. It looked normal enough from the outside, but something about the inside still scared her. She couldn't erase Adriana's face, the look of terror, from that night in the bathtub.

Would she go back if invited for another sleepover? She pulled up her pant leg, the grass tickling her calf, and admired the temporary tattoo she'd gotten that night. It was fading and some of the branches of the tree had flaked off. But the trunk of the tree was still there, and a scattering of the red leaves. *Yeah*, she decided, she would spend the night again. Bathtub terrors or not, she really enjoyed her time with Adriana. Maybe she'd even suggest another sleepover when Adriana came to pick up…

Dylan? Where's Dylan?

Jennifer scrambled to her feet and scanned the backyard. She spotted his kite lying in the grass near the garage, the spool of string half-unwound and bunched in small piles.

"Dylan?"

She couldn't see him. He could be hurt, could be crying somewhere nearby and she wouldn't be able to hear him. He could have been taken, could have been screaming for her while she was looking at her dumb leg. He could... *Breathe*, she told herself.

She ran to his kite and picked it up. Some of the loose string wound around the side of the garage. She jogged over to the path that led around the garage and out to the alley. She hoped he was... He wasn't. The path was empty.

Her heart was thudding. *I lost him. I can't believe I lost him.*

She looked back at Adriana's house. Both yards were fenced in with high picket boards. He wouldn't have been able to climb it. Maybe he went inside? The back door and screen door were both closed. Mom was at work. There was no way Jennifer could reach her. Adriana needed some time alone after being fired. Jennifer knew she wasn't supposed to bother her. But this was an emergency, right? She couldn't imagine having to say she'd lost Dylan out loud. The words hurt just to think. He'd been there one moment and then just...gone. Poof. *Like the thing in Adriana's bathtub.*

Crossing the yard, Jennifer set the kite back on the grass. It would be hard to tell Adriana, yes, but the sooner she could get an adult to help, the sooner they could find Dylan.

She rounded the corner of the back porch to cross the driveway, heading toward Adriana's house when—

Something grabbed her leg. She startled and jumped back. An arm protruded from the under the porch. A child's arm. Dylan crawled out from his hiding place and rolled on the ground laughing himself silly. She imagined him making the same roaring noises she did when she chased him around the yard.

Jennifer crouched and scooped him up, pulling him into a hug.

"You scared me!" she said.

Dylan shook with laughter but embraced her in a tight hug.

"Your mother would have killed me. Don't do that again."

She felt her pulse coming down and let go of Dylan. He sprinted back to his kite, picked up the scattered string, and resumed his attempts at getting it into the sky. She watched it flop and spin and drag behind him. As much as she enjoyed her time with Dylan, she hoped Adriana would be rested enough to take him back soon.

46

"First time I've ever been to one of these," Lois confessed to Bradley as they walked from their offices to the main chambers for the special city council meeting.

Everyone else, including Lois, might echo Maggie's thoughts. *So soon?* But Bradley didn't care. He had his own script and he was sticking to it. "It's not so different from any other session, really, just unexpected."

"Well, I hope it's my last. Terrible to think about what would have happened if the gunman had decided to come to your speech instead of Card's. Why does this have to be an open session? You're not worried about him being here in the crowd?"

Bradley's biggest worry was his police escort. He hated having the shadows. "Lois, don't worry about the shooter. Jones can handle our security, and he's got help this week." Bradley motioned to his police detail. "And if there is a concern, Chief Woodhull will inform us. We run the city, remember?"

The chairwoman did not look convinced. "Run the city? Really? I thought I was running the fundraiser until I heard gunshots."

The main chamber was unexpectedly sparsely filled. Apparently, the community shared Lois's fear. Bradley recognized some of the faces in the crowd and nodded or waved to a few. But he could name only two of the people in attendance: Steve "Gonzo" Talley was a Cellar fixture who had not missed a single meeting in a decade and always took copious notes from which he created a homestyle newsletter that he shared with anyone who'd read it, typographical errors and all.

The other was Deesha Card. *Her again.*

The low turnout seemed to put Lois at ease. "I guess we'll be okay. Unless Gonzo is packing heat," she smirked.

Bradley didn't respond. His mind was spinning as he recalled his clumsy moment with Deesha earlier. He'd forgotten to circle back and ask Maggie what Deesha had dropped off. *What is she up to?* Paranoia had set a fire in Bradley's head.

Lois called the meeting to order. Then Bradley took over. "Thank you, Chairwoman King. As everyone here in attendance now knows, our charter demands that we must schedule a special election to fill Councilman Card's seat until, God willing, he is able to return. After perusing our city schedule, I've selected three possible dates that would work for this."

"Mayor Krause!"

A voice from the audience interrupted Bradley. He set down his notes and rubbed the back of his neck. It felt warmer than usual in the chambers today. The fire in his head was spreading. *Damn meds,* he thought. He swiveled and when he saw who had called out, his face drained of all its color.

Tom Galton approached the city council table in a wheelchair pushed by his wife Sharon. They must have arrived after Bradley scanned the room. Galton was as pale as Bradley, and what was left of his thin hair was pasted to his sweaty forehead. The man was a pitiable sight and would have garnered a lot of sympathy, had their audience been any larger. Then a camera flash exploded, and Bradley was reminded that he'd invited the local newspaper to send its photographer to capture his moment of leadership. *Damn.*

Galton continued. "I have a proposal of my own, Mr. Mayor."

Bradley hesitated. Were public statements allowed at these meetings? Surely there was a procedure for... The fire was now a raging inferno, and he couldn't recall.

"Okay," he managed. "You may present it."

"Thank you. Forgive me if I don't stand."

The other politicians in attendance gave a few polite chuckles. But not Bradley. Bradley was confused as to how this man was even allowed out of the hospital. *So soon? Too soon.*

"Rather than a special election, I nominate Mrs. Deesha Robinson-Card to temporarily fill her husband's seat on the council. She's familiar with most of his workload already, she serves as a partner in her husband's law firm, and she understands our city codes."

Bradley shifted in his seat. He had guessed Deesha was the reason Card decided to run for mayor. Fine, let them have their fun losing. But he couldn't allow *this*. She would be the first person on the council in years with enough brains to challenge him.

Lois spoke up, and Bradley was grateful. He needed a moment to find his breath. "Tom, while your suggestion may be valid..."

"There is precedent in Cellar politics. I've brought copies of the research and discourse so that each council member can quickly get up to speed on this matter." That silenced Lois and allowed Galton to continue. "Also, there is still time for Deesha to file her intentions to replace Benjamin in his run for mayor. *Correction.* Sorry, I meant to say..."

Galton looked like he might pass out. Sharon wiped his sweaty brow with a handkerchief, and Bradley could barely contain his contempt for their showy grab for pity.

"Thank you, Darling," Galton mewed before sucking it up and finishing. "As I was saying, there is plenty of time for Deesha or anyone else in town, for that matter, to file for candidacy if she wishes to seek the office of mayor."

"I doubt that, Tom!" Bradley blurted out. "The registration deadline was weeks ago."

"Actually," Tom countered, "the law states that if a candidate must drop out due to illness, injury, or death, new candidates may file within one week of..."

Bradley couldn't hear the rest of Galton's statement. His fever was rising. And he already knew Tom was right. Tom had been an excellent adviser during his first administration precisely because he had an uncanny grasp of finicky details. Bradley was just hoping no one else at the table had known about the provision.

"Lois," he boomed, suddenly unable to keep control of his voice and annoyance. "Your thoughts, please."

Lois shrugged. It seemed she didn't have a clue, and neither did any of the other members. When Bradley took a furtive glance at the scattered audience, their faces going in and out of focus, he saw someone standing. *Focus!* He saw Deesha standing.

"I am Deesha Robinson-Card, the rightful interim council appointee and mayoral candidate for the city of Cellar, Ohio."

Lois hammered the gavel. "Deesha, please, you're out of order."

"No, Lois. I'm out of patience. My husband may go to his grave without one shred of evidence or assurance that his killer will be found."

"Making demands and accusations, I mean, there are procedures, paperwork, and..." Lois sputtered.

"Be assured that I filed all relevant documents with city administrator Maggie Woodhull just this morning."

Bradley felt a river of fever sweat cascade down his back. *Deesha will win in a landslide. She's smart. Well liked. Gorgeous. And she'd win the sympathy vote.* He dug in his suit pocket for those tiny white pills that kept his blood pressure and arrhythmia under control. He found the bottle, popped the top off, and poured into his hand, but the bottle was empty.

"Fucking meds!"

Lois drew back in shock. Bradley's cursing didn't stop. He swore at the little reminder note he had stuck to his fridge at home. Then he shouted at the mustard-colored Frigidaire, which he never so much as glanced at before leaving the house. "Why didn't you remind me of the note!" he shouted to the open air.

Bradley's heart raced as he fingered the pill bottle, thinking he could scrape one last little fucker from the round bottom, and then he no longer saw ceiling or floor, nor could he discern if he were alive or dead, because he teetered, tottered, and then collapsed into an endless dark tunnel.

47

THE NEW OVUC intensive care unit was barely a year old and glistened in the afternoon sunlight, yet it turned Deesha Card's blood cold. She would have felt no worse standing alone in an arctic tundra. Could these shiny new digital machines save her husband? They looked so lifeless. So uncaring.

Benjamin looked like he was enjoying a deep, restful sleep except for the *drip, drip, drip* of intravenous intubations, an oxygen mask, and the soft thumping of the monitors.

"Ben, you missed quite the show." Her voice was soft because the door to the room was always left open, and nurses were not far away. She wasn't sure he could hear her at any volume but hoped he could. "But it's done, Ben. I did it. I thought maybe it was too soon. Like I'm giving up on you or... You know what I mean. But Bradley, that monster, was already moving to fill your seat. He got so worked up, he fainted, right there in the meeting."

Deesha took a moment to relish Bradley's overreaction. Then her smile faded.

"I know it's all my fault. We should have moved on, made a new life for ourselves somewhere else. I know that's what you wanted. To have me all to yourself, not sharing me with my obsessions. But I had to come back. I just couldn't...turn my back. I need answers. I—"

A nurse walked by the open door and hollered down the hall. It startled Deesha and the officer posted outside the room. She was grateful for the round-the-clock protection, even if she sometimes thought it was a waste of resources. *In the event of what? Some lunatic blasting his way into the deepest reaches of the oh-vuck? When that officer could be out there actively looking for the madman?* Her quick temper sometimes shamed her, like when she took that cheap shot at Woodhull in Maggie's office. Woody wasn't really her target. Her anger was born from all the neglect of the past, and all the reasons she had for doubting that anyone from her old neighborhood deserved the care afforded dignitaries of the Ohio valley.

"Ben, you embraced my mission. You came here for me. You loved me. Now look what happened."

She reached out to touch his face, then was startled by a voice...

"Mrs. Card?"

She pulled back and looked up.

"Sorry to bother you. I just wanted to offer my condolences. You probably don't remember me, but I'm Officer Hinkley. I met you and your husband at the station last week and I was the first officer to arrive..." Hinkley stood in the open doorway. "Sorry again. Councilman Card seems like a strong man. I'm sure he'll pull through. I'm praying for it, in fact."

"It's appreciated, Officer. I don't suppose you've heard any updates around the station?"

"Not about the shooting, no, ma'am. The FBI arrived and are working the case with Chief Woodhull. They didn't really keep me in the loop. I did find...um..."

Deesha was eager. "Yes?"

"Uh, it's nothing, ma'am. Nothing that can't wait. Sorry to bother you. My shift here is ending and I just wanted to say again that I'm really pulling for Mr. Card."

"Thank you," she said. Officer Hinkley nodded and stepped out as another uniformed officer took over his post at the door.

Deesha turned back to her husband. "You've done so much for me, Ben. But now I'm going to do something for you. I'm going to end all this. I'm going to bring it all out in the open; let the whole town see. And I just pray that somehow, wherever you are, you'll know that your Deesha, your *girl*, had the guts to continue."

She took his hand and held it to her cheek. Maybe he could feel the warm tears there, maybe he couldn't. She liked to believe he did.

48

ADRIANA'S PENCIL scratched and jumped all over the page of her sketchpad. As soon as she finished one drawing, she'd turn to a clean page and start another, never breaking her concentration. She was so in tune with the drawings that she barely heard the banging or the muffled voice.

"Adriana?"

Maybe the sound was coming from the thick pad of paper, or from beyond the dark place she had entered with every drawing. She needed to get it out. What started on the bus ride home from the station had continued almost nonstop over the last few days. But she was getting somewhere. She knew she was. She also knew her time was limited; life would have to once again take over. Mommy responsibilities. Food. Clean clothes...

"Come on, Addie. I know you're in there. And I get it if you're pissed at Woodhull or all of us at the station, but I need to talk to you. Answer your phone. Open the door!"

The banging was much louder this time, desperate.

"This is official business, Addie. I'm here as a police officer. But a friend, too, so..."

The pounding on the door finally came into focus. Adriana

dropped her pencil and looked around her living room. She made her way to the front door and unlocked the dead bolt. Matt stood on her porch in full uniform.

"Addie...?"

She saw the confused look he gave her, and then remembered she hadn't bathed or put on clean clothes, and her dark hair was sticking to the corners of her mouth.

She gave the screen door a soft shove, inviting him to do the rest, then walked back to the couch and let her pencil fly across the white pages again.

Matt cautiously stepped inside. Adriana hadn't turned on any lights and the curtains were drawn, so the only light in the room was the narrow shaft that reached through the open door. Enough for him to see the sheets of paper on the floor surrounding the couch, and what looked like a stack of new sketchbooks waiting patiently for Adriana's magic touch.

"Addie, what's going on?"

She didn't look up. "Why are you here?"

"I just finished a shift at the oh-vuck and I've been worried about you. Are you okay?"

"No, not really. I'm kinda freaked out, actually."

"Yeah, I can imagine. I know losing the job was tough, but Woodhull, maybe he'll come to his senses and give you another shot after all this? He's just overwhelmed."

"So am I. Sorry, I don't really have time for small talk. What do you want?"

She hated the way she sounded, but conversation dragged her away from her sketches. Talk was not only cheap; it was useless. She needed this thing out of her, this Face.

"I hadn't heard from you since you left the station."

"Left? Hah! I was thrown out, no thanks to you."

"Hey, I tried. Woodhull threw me out too, remember?"

Adriana dropped her gaze back to the sketch pad. Matt had tried sticking up for her and might have put his job on the line in doing so.

"Where's Dylan?" he asked.

"Lisa and Jenny agreed to take him after I told them what happened at the station. I need a little time to process it all."

"And are you? Processing?"

Adriana looked up from her sketch but kept drawing.

"Can you just stop for a minute? I also came by to deliver some news. It's your father..."

This startled her. She set her pencil down. *He's dead*, she thought. The maniac shot him too. The first serial murderer in Cellar history. Dad is gone.

Or maybe he's the one behind her getting fired. *Get rid of her, Chief. Can't have her earning her own way if I still want to control her.* Or maybe he's the one who shot Card. *Can you imagine Mayor Krause doing hard time?*

She finally said, "What? What about him?"

"He collapsed at a city council meeting this morning."

"Is he alive?"

"Yes. He's going to be fine. They got him to the oh-vuck and the nurse I spoke to said he should be out tomorrow. They want to keep him a night for observation, that's all. It was stress, blood pressure issues, and some problem with his meds?"

"His heart meds?"

"Yeah. An officer tried calling to notify you. But I guess you don't have an answering machine."

"Oh, yeah, right. One more expense."

"I'm just saying, you're the next of kin, so I'm officially notifying you. My name is Officer Hinkley. Remember me?"

She looked up at him and her glare softened.

"I could drive you up there if you want to go see him."

She didn't respond but her head was spinning as she imagined her father in a hospital bed, resting, pinned down by intravenous needles.

"Addie, did you hear me?" Matt said.

"Yes."

"I know it's been a tough week."

A tough week? she thought. *More like a tough decade. Dad's fall is just icing on top of a multi-tiered fucked-up life.* Then another idea popped into her head: Would the court still think Mr. Mayor was stable enough to take custody of Dylan? How was Dylan safer with a man who collapses at work because of a weak heart? Or one that might be in some assassin's crosshairs?

Matt repeated, "I'll drive you if…"

"Maybe I can still win."

"Huh?"

"Bradley never shows any sign of weakness. This is going to hurt him. With Card in a hospital bed, my father looked strong, but now he's flat on his back too. Maybe he'll back off and it won't matter that Woodhull fired me. Court's not until next week, and…"

Matt pulled at her sketch pad. She let it go and watched his face twist.

"You're drawing that face again?" he said, tossing the sketch pad onto the couch. "Why?"

She looked from him to the drawing. A minute ago, it seemed like the most important thing in the world. But now?

"I don't know."

Three little words, but they broke the dam. Everything she'd been trying to suppress, everything she'd been trying to hold back, trying to clear the way for the Face to drain out of her came flooding now.

Matt pulled her close and slid his arms around her as she heaved deep sobs. He might have been okay holding her there for hours if she'd let him, but she pulled herself free and forced herself to regain control. She didn't have time for any of this. She looked back at her sketch of the Face.

"Don't look at that," Matt said.

"I can't stop looking at it."

"Throw it away or put it in a drawer or something."

"No, I need to keep going."

"No. You don't. You can just stop."

"Not yet."

"What's the big deal with this thing, anyway?"

"The thing that's haunted me for most of my life finally has a face and you ask what the big deal is?"

"I didn't mean... I just... It isn't real."

"Not real? What about when it attacked you down in the file room? What about Laurie? It attacked her at City Hall! Do you remember the sketch I did for her? It wasn't helpful because all she could remember was a blur of a face. Maybe this face." She picked up the sketch pad, but Matt took it from her.

"Addie, I wasn't attacked in the records room, okay? I told you it felt like an attack, yeah, but the more I thought about it, it was dark, I didn't know the layout yet, and I ended up scaring myself and tripping over one of the boxes on the floor. That's all. As for Laurie, no, she didn't see who attacked her in the City Hall bathroom, but we caught the guy last week. It was some ex-boyfriend that had been stalking her for a while."

"What? Why didn't you tell me?"

"I didn't know you'd given her case a second thought. You never mentioned it. She called us to report some noises outside her bedroom window. She thought she was being silly, but when Kasich and I got there, we caught the guy in her yard. He confessed to being in the City Hall bathroom that night, and three other incidences we didn't even know about. There's no monster, no ghost, and no ghoul out there attacking anyone. You're safe."

Adriana felt dizzy. She'd been holding on to Laurie's experience as proof she wasn't losing her mind, proof that this thing existed outside of her. Because if just one other person had seen it, then it was something that *could* be seen, something that could be *caught*.

Adriana took one wavering step and Matt reached out to catch her. She righted herself, then walked off down the hall to her bedroom.

"Addie?"

Matt didn't immediately give chase. Maybe he was confused. Was he a cop or a boyfriend? Adriana didn't care; she needed to be alone.

In the bedroom, she looked around at the mess and tried not to break down again. *What am I doing? Laurie didn't see him? Matt didn't feel him? Maybe I am just making it all up.*

A soft knock on the bedroom door.

"Addie? I'm sorry. Can we talk?"

She stood frozen. How was she going to explain what he'd see when she opened the door?

"Okay," she said. If she really were crazy, she'd have to let people in to help. She could start with the mess in her bedroom, and if he could handle that, maybe he could help her handle everything else. "But don't freak out."

He promised, and she opened the door. As he stepped into her bedroom, she could see he was about to break his promise. First his eyes went to the dresser where she had stored her drawings from two days ago, dozens of them. Then the nightstand where she'd stacked the drawings she did on the bus. Then he saw the bed blanketed with yesterday's sketches—dozens of them, and they were all the same. The Face, the Face, the Face, the—

"What the hell, Addie?"

In her embarrassment, she began to collect the sketches, making neat little piles, as if that would make it better. But Matt had already grabbed handfuls of the sketches and apparently could not make sense of any of it.

"I know. I know. I told you, I can't stop."

"You keep saying that. What do you mean you can't stop?"

"I thought, after the station, that maybe if I drew it a few times, I could get it out of my system, you know? Only, when I close my eyes, even just for a minute, this is still all I see. And I can't control my hand or let it rest. It just starts, almost on its own now!"

"I—I... So you've been locked up in here drawing the same face, over and over, for days? Addie. You have to talk to someone about this."

"I am. I'm talking to you now."

"I mean like a professional."

"I was too ashamed to tell Lisa when I took Dylan over. I thought it'd only be a few hours, a day at most. But now every sketch feels different to me somehow, even if they're all the same. The drawings, the patterns, the routine... I feel like they're helping me understand something. I just don't know what that something is yet. And now maybe I never will."

"Adriana, you've got to get... You've got to get back to something that's..."

"Normal?"

"Yes! If not for you, then for Dylan's sake."

"*Everything* I do is for him. Including this. If I can't get this thing out, I can't work. If I can't work, I can't protect him. And these"— she snatched the handful of drawings from Matt—"are the only thing I know to do right now."

She flung the sketches at the wall and turned her back to Matt as the pages fluttered to the floor around her.

"Go," she said.

"Let me help."

"Just go. Please."

"We can figure this out together—"

"GET OUT!"

Adriana slumped to the floor, drained.

"Addie..." He took a step toward her. She put her face into her hands.

Behind her, she heard Matt walk slowly back down the hall, through the living room, and out the front door. She wiped her eyes, then began collecting up the sketches from the floor around her. She stacked them again, hating the weight of the pages in her hands. These meaningless yet completely obsessive drawings.

When the floor was cleared, she got up and sat on the bed with her stack of drawings. She thumbed through them. Face, Face, Face, Fa—

Wait.

She tidied up the edges of the stack, and then thumbed through them again. Face, Face, Face... It was the Face in every drawing, she knew that, but the drawings weren't exactly the same, like she initially thought. Each one was almost imperceptibly different from the previous one. Not in technique or the angles of the lines, but in the subject itself.

She moved to the other side of her bed and grabbed the stack of drawings from her nightstand. She thumbed through these. Face, Face, Fa— *Holy shit!*

Each drawing was the same face yes, but when flipping through the sketches, one right after the other, the Face...moved.

Small movements. Like frames of a movie. *I've been drawing a goddamn flipbook!* The eyes didn't move. The nose didn't move. But the mouth, the lips, *they moved!*

The Face—through the hundreds of sketches she'd made—was speaking to her.

49

LISA WOKE to the sound of her doorbell; she'd dozed off on the couch while Dylan took his nap in her home office. She jolted at the frantic pounding on the front door. Although she was an effective therapist, she had her own emotional triggers. Loud bursts or sudden movements threw her back to life with her former husband. The man who responded to every interaction like a malfunctioning land mine, apply the slightest amount of pressure and you never knew if he'd lie dormant or explode without warning.

"Lisa! It's Adriana!"

Lisa moved to the door, fearing another episode with a nightmare. But when she opened the door, she was surprised to find Adriana excited and smiling.

"Addie, you scared the hell out of me. Come on in."

"I'm sorry, sorry. But I need Jenny's help."

"For what? Is everything okay?"

"I'll find out shortly."

Lisa retrieved Jennifer from upstairs and the three of them sat on the couch.

"Lisa, does Jenny know what a flipbook is?"

Jennifer answered for herself. "No."

"Okay." To demonstrate, Adriana took a thick stack of drawings from her shoulder bag and slowly flipped through them, just as she had done in her bedroom. Face, Face, Face, Fa— "Do you see how the image seems to move, Jenny?"

"Yes!"

Although Jennifer seemed enthusiastic, Lisa didn't like the imagery. "Why are you showing these to her? They're frightening."

"You're right. I should have warned you. But Jenny was there when I was attacked in the bathtub. And this…"

"This is the face you keep seeing? Your nightmare?" Lisa said.

"Yes."

"It's creepy. Why are you so excited about it?"

"When it was in the bathtub with me, it was shaking me and, I think, trying to tell me something."

"Well, sure, we all think our dreams have meaning. But Jennifer's not a therapist."

"No, no. I don't mean on a spiritual level. I mean it was literally trying to speak to me. And she reads lips, right? All I want Jenny to do is watch the changes in the face's mouth. I thought all my drawings were the same. But they're not—not exactly. Turns out, they move. They speak!"

"I just… I don't want Jenny to adopt your nightmares."

Jennifer didn't look afraid. "I'll try," she said.

The three sat close. Adriana started flipping the pages again, and they all watched as the mangled mouth moved again and again.

Jennifer gave her head a quick shake. "This is hard. It's not like reading real lips."

Adriana reassured her as she continued to flip through the pages. "It's okay. Take your time. It might not be saying anything. It could just be my sloppy drawing or my eyes playing tricks. But if it *is* trying to communicate…"

"A name? Maybe?" Jennifer said.

Adriana encouraged her to go on. "What name?"

"Eh-ehh…" Jennifer slowly sounded out what she saw. Lisa knew it was difficult for her daughter. They had worked so hard on finding her voice, and at the beginning, every new word seemed to stall her out for days. Right now, she was seeing that early concentration and determination on Jennifer's face again.

"Ehhhhd..."

"That's the sound I've heard in my dreams," Adriana said. "But I don't know what it means?"

"Ed-Edward? Maybe. Flip them again."

Adriana obliged. She thumbed the edge of the stack again, and again the Face came to life, silently speaking from the pages.

"Yes! It's saying Edward. I'm almost certain."

"Edward?"

Jennifer nodded.

"I..." Adriana paused and looked defeated. "I don't know anyone named Edward."

She looked to Lisa, who shook her head.

"Sorry, I don't either."

Adriana reluctantly set the stack of drawings down.

"No, keep going," Jennifer said. "There's more."

HINKLEY PULLED off his uniform and hung it in his locker. During his overnight shift standing guard outside Card's room at the OVUC, he kept wishing he were working the case instead. But after his fight with Adriana, he was drained and looking forward to clocking out so he could get some rest. Maybe walking out on Adriana, alone in that house with all those drawings, wasn't the best decision, but she'd been pretty adamant about him leaving. *Should I have told her about Laurie's stalker earlier? Would that have made any difference?*

Walking into the bullpen, Hinkley heard the phone ringing on his desk. He reminded himself he was off duty and continued walking straight until Kasich got up and answered it.

"Cellar Police. Kasich here." Kasich looked disapprovingly at him from across the room. "I hope you got something on the shooting.

We really don't have time for much else. This ain't a dating service we're running here."

Adriana. Shit. Matt hurried across the open space to take the phone from Kasich.

"Rook, it's your girlfriend. She's got something for you." The Sargent handed him the phone receiver. "Make it quick."

Matt almost hung up without saying anything. She had just thrown him out. Had been mean about it. Had turned into a completely different person over the last few days. The warm, gifted artist he was getting to know, getting to like a lot, had become someone cold and jaded. *This better be the apology of a lifetime.*

He put the phone to his ear. "Addie?"

"I've got a name."

"What?"

"A name for the Face. I know his name."

She sounded like she had finally cracked; she was worse off than he'd thought. Dreams were one thing, but making up an entire identity for this boogeyman…

"Okay," he sighed. "What's his name?"

"Edward Robinson. I don't know who that is, Lisa doesn't either, but that's what the Face has been trying to tell me over and over again: his name! Edward Robinson."

Matt couldn't speak.

He knew the name.

"Matt? Hello?"

He knew the name, but there's no way she could.

"Matt? Are you still there? Look, I'm sorry about before at the house. I was an asshole and you were only trying to help. This thing has just taken over my life, and I don't have room for much else right now. But if we can find this Mr. Robinson and, I don't know, get him to stop doing whatever he's doing, then maybe I can get back to something that resembles normal, like you said."

He pulled a small notepad from his desk drawer and flipped to the map he'd drawn of the basement records room. The map marked the location of the files that had caught his eye, the one he had hidden and refused to destroy.

"Matt, I'm really..."

"Stay there," he said. "I'm coming over."

———

WOODHULL GLANCED up at the movement outside his office door. Hinkley had come up from the basement archives and moved quickly past his desk. He spotted an old case file tucked under the rookie's arm. Hinkley works cold cases all the time, so that's not a big deal, but Woodhull watched Hinkley side-step the front desk and walk right out of the station with the old file.

The chief bolted from his chair and jogged out of his office toward the station's entrance doors. He stopped halfway across the bullpen as he saw Hinkley's car peel out of the station's parking lot.

"Dammit."

50

MATT TOOK a sip of the tea Lisa had offered; he'd planned to be home in bed by now after his long overnight shift. Adriana was clutching her drawings after showing him the flipbook. He still wasn't sure he believed it, or that Jennifer could read lips from a bunch of sketches, but there was no other way they should know the name Edward Robinson.

Lisa turned on the overhead light. The midmorning sky had grown dark with rain clouds. She joined them at the kitchen table.

"So, Kasich assigned me to the cleanup effort down in the records room. Any closed or cold case records more than ten years old are to be shredded. But while going through the boxes, I found this." He held up the file he'd taken from the station. "I took a quick glance in it that first day and then put it aside so I could revisit it later. But that was before everything this past week. I haven't had a chance to dig any deeper yet."

He pushed the old file to the center of the kitchen table so both Adriana and Lisa could see the name under the case number: *Edward Robinson*.

"Holy shit." Adriana reached for the file. "Who is he?"

"He *was* Deesha Card's little brother."

Adriana picked up the file. It was thin.

"Deesha's brother? I didn't even know Deesha had a brother," she said.

"Neither did I until I found this. If I hadn't been following Card's campaign in the paper, I doubt I would even know her maiden name, but she hyphenates: Robinson-Card."

"So he has a record? What did he do?"

"He vanished. It's a missing-person case."

Adriana opened the folder and Matt pointed to the relevant case notes. "Deesha was only fourteen years old when she filed the report. It says she came back to the station a few times looking for updates, but it doesn't look like they worked the case very hard. Eventually she stopped coming in, or they stopped updating the file if she did."

Adriana looked like she was trying to process everything. Matt gave her a moment, then pointed again.

"And I just saw this on the way over. Look at his last known whereabouts."

"No fucking way! Easton Mill Lake? *My* lake?"

"Yeah. Apparently, he enjoyed hanging out there. In the report, Deesha said a few boys had harassed him out there after school, chasing him into the nearby woods, taunting him. At the time he disappeared, he was only going out to the lake at night, against their father's wishes. Then he snuck out one night and never returned."

"You think the boys messing with him, what, killed him?"

"I don't know. They never found a body. Maybe he ran away? Maybe he was kidnapped?"

"Or maybe he's been lying at the bottom of Easton Mill Lake for twenty years." Adriana said, setting down the file. "Poor Deesha! That's horrifying."

The kitchen was quiet except for the scant pattering of rain outside as they all tried to absorb the idea.

"And this whole time," Adriana said, "I thought he was attacking me. Trying to hold me under in those nightmares. Do you think… maybe he was only trying to tell me his name?"

"I don't know." Matt broke eye contact. He'd known about her nightmares but had no idea that what she was dreaming might have been an actual crime, a real person. The way she talked about them… He should have paid better attention, should have helped her investigate more.

"Addie, did you maybe know him or Deesha when you were younger?"

"No. I don't think so, anyway. The first time I heard Card's name was when Killswitch Kevin said it on the radio, the morning he announced my arrest to the entire town. And I didn't know his wife's name until way after that."

Adriana glanced again at the file. Matt saw she was upset, but not like earlier. She looked heartbroken. "I mean, I was only a toddler when this case was opened. But to think, this whole time he's been reaching out and I've been trying to run from him. If only I'd listened sooner."

"Hey," Lisa said. "Do not blame yourself. You're listening now, and that's more than anyone else was doing. Matt said the original officers didn't even work the case, and it was fresh for them back then."

"Almost twenty years ago," he said. "There were two intake officers. The first is a name I don't recognize, so he's no longer on the force, at least not in Cellar. The second was Sargent Woodhull. Before he was the chief."

"My biggest fan," Adriana said. "I don't suppose we can just walk into his office and tell him I dreamed up some possible new evidence in a twenty-year-old cold case?"

"A twenty-year-old cold case I was ordered to destroy."

"So what, then?"

"I think maybe we talk to Deesha first."

51

BRADLEY STOOD under the Ohio Valley Urgent Care entrance awning. He tucked a blister pack of pills into his pants pocket. It had started to rain and his ride was late. He was annoyed with last night's stay for several reasons. It made him look weak when he needed to take charge. Even though he'd come to in the ambulance, they refused to turn around and take him back to the city council meeting. It was like he was being held captive. The barrage of tests and questions from the medical staff felt invasive. And it took them all morning to ready his discharge papers.

But all that would fade in a day or two. The thing that really jabbed at him would linger: his only child did not pay him a visit or even call during his stay.

His ride finally pulled up to the curb.

"I don't recall 'chauffeur' being part of my job description," Woodhull said. "Why didn't your lady friend pick you up?"

Bradley got into the passenger seat and rubbed his damp hands in front of the car's heater. "You wanna keep your voice down about all that. She's working." Bradley looked around. "Only one car? Where's the backup? And please, no whining about the budget. The tap's wide open right now."

"I figured we could handle ourselves." Woodhull said and pulled out of the OVUC parking lot.

Their drive down the highway was quiet. Not that Bradley minded much; all Woodhull knew how to do lately was complain. The quiet was nice for a change. But then Woodhull missed the turn for Bradley's neighborhood.

"Uh, something on your mind, Chief? You just blew past our turn."

"Too much. Lots of questions being asked. First Black man in Cellar to campaign for mayor is shot, his wife decides to risk her life by replacing him... And I heard you took quite the meeting at Cody's Diner."

"With who?"

"Tom Galton. You two had a little squabble there?"

Bradley laughed, but it felt forced. "If I made a list of all the squabbles I've had over lunch..."

"It had something to do with unflattering images of Tom's wife and Card's campaign? Blackmail, Bradley? Really? I thought you knew to be more careful than that."

A little bird must be whispering in Woodhull's ear, Bradley thought. *But so what? The paper didn't run the photos anyway. No harm, no foul. Carry on, Woody. Whaddya got?*

The police cruiser meandered around the outskirts of town as the two men continued to talk, occasionally throwing elbows or verbally one-upping each other. Their relationship had always felt more like an arm wrestle than a hug.

Woodhull took a turn that led the men out of town and past Wills Auto Body shop. Bradley unrolled his window a crack to get some air, ignoring the rain drops that flew in. "Doctors told me to get some rest today. Maybe a nap. Not sure where we're going..." That was a lie; Bradley knew where Woodhull was heading, he just wasn't sure why. "But will you get me home before dinner, Chief?"

Woodhull didn't answer, but he did pick up speed until he was rounding curves on the two-lane blacktop at a velocity that ramped up Bradley's nerves, especially in this weather. He said nothing and soon felt the cruiser slow down. Fifty yards later, Woodhull eased the car off the pavement and onto the gravel.

As the engine idled, the chief stared across the road at a large oak surrounded by underbrush. The rain was starting to pick up and soon the dark pavement turned inky black.

"Brad, why am I suddenly answering questions about the records you want destroyed? And why now? We haven't given a second thought to anything buried down there for decades. Suddenly it's at the top of your list."

"Who's asking questions?"

"Card and his wife showed up just before the fundraiser. I told them it was all routine, nothing to worry about. Not sure that was enough for them. Next thing I know, Card's laid out, Tom's next to him with a clipped wing, and you're raving at thin air in a public forum before fainting. I mean, Jesus, Brad, right in front of your own city council and the goddamn newspaper photographer! Are you completely losing it?"

Bradley didn't answer; he only looked out at the rain splashing across the surface of the nearby lake, the birds flying from tree to tree looking for shelter, the windshield wipers wiping the slate clean before the window filled up with rain again, anything but looking at that goddamned oak tree.

"Look, not to add to your stress or anything," Woodhull continued, "but the rookie I had down in that basement shredding files, the one who's sweet on Adriana, he took a file from the archives before hurrying out of the station this morning."

"Was it—?"

"I didn't see which one. And it happened too fast for me to stop him. It might be nothing, but it might... I'm not sure what he thinks he knows, but I would bet he took it straight to Adriana. Those two have been inseparable for weeks now."

"Goddamn it." Bradley fumbled for the blister pack of pills he'd gotten from the OVUC. "I'll figure out how to get it back."

Woodhull shifted the car back into gear. "I can protect you from some crazy gunman. I have the manpower to do that. But if someone found out about that night, I can't protect you from that, Mr. Mayor."

52

ADRIANA AND MATT talked through the case file until the burnout of Matt's overnight shift set in and he crashed on her couch. He slept right through breakfast this morning. Dylan finally woke him up by crawling up and over his legs while Adriana was in the bathroom.

Before Matt had even finished his bowl of cereal, Adriana jumped back into yesterday's discussion. "Okay, so a little boy went missing. Deesha's brother. We've got Woodhull on the intake form, but almost no investigation. Does that sound right to you?"

"I don't want to make excuses for him, because it's inexcusable, but things were different back then. Little Black kid goes missing from the neighborhood out by the lake, in 1967, an all-white police force probably isn't going to look very hard."

"You really think things were that twisted back then?"

"A lot of things are still that twisted today. I was excited about Card's run for mayor, but I'd heard a lot of people say he didn't have a chance, simply because of the color of his skin."

"That's so fucked up." She looked at Dylan, who was distracted with his own breakfast, and tried to push away the imagined anxiety of discovering him missing and then the rage of those in charge refusing to help.

Matt nodded as he shoveled a spoonful of Cheerios into his mouth.

"But I still don't get what any of that has to do with me. Why haunt, I mean, you know what I mean, why *reach out* to me?"

"Maybe your ability to see into other people's heads, your second sight, drawing from intuition or seeing through someone else's eyes. That's powerful. And if he's trying to get a message out, you happen to be one of the few who can receive it. Or maybe you two did share some experience or knew each other and you were just so young you don't remember. I still think we should ask Deesha if she'd speak with us."

"Won't that get you in trouble?" After being fired, Adriana was all too aware that Matt was still the newest cop on the force and had no seniority.

"How can they fault me if I help solve a crime?"

She was struck by his comment. "Crime? How do we know there was a—"

The doorbell startled them.

"Door!" Dylan hopped off his chair and ran to the living room.

"What would I say to her? To Deesha," Adriana asked. "It feels... disrespectful? Silly? To tell her I'm dreaming about her missing brother."

"I hear you. But...what else do we have?"

"The drawings," Adriana said.

"But you wouldn't show those to her, would you? Even if you thought she might recognize him, they're pretty dark and might upset...?"

Adriana remembering the doorbell. "Dylan?"

No answer. She got up and made her way to the door. Matt followed.

The living room was empty. The front door was wide open.

They found Dylan in the front yard, surrounded by several police officers.

"What the hell? That's my kid! What's going on?"

A woman broke off from the group of officers and approached the house.

"Are you Adriana Krause?"

"Yes. Who are you?"

"I'm Rebecca Gill, an officer from Child Protection Services. We have a court order signed by Judge Reilly to take Dylan into custody."

"What?! I don't understand. Why?"

"We also have a warrant to search the premises for—"

"You're not taking my kid!"

Rebecca nodded to the officers. Adriana lunged for Dylan, but firm hands grabbed her and held her back. Dylan was put into the seat of a police cruiser. Matt hurried over.

"Officer Packer, I don't get it," he said.

"Court order, bud. We're just here to assist."

"But why are—"

Packer waved him off and got into the car. "Not your fight, Rookie."

"Mommy!" Dylan cried.

Adriana struggled to shake free of the officers, but it was no use. The patrol car slowly pulled away from the curb and disappeared down the street.

"Dylan! I'll come for you! Mommy will—"

"Ms. Krause, please calm down." Rebecca tried handing her the court order again. Adriana, her hands still restrained by the officers, kicked at the paper.

The officers wrestled her to the ground.

"Hey!" Matt yelled.

Adriana laid on her stomach with two officers retraining her. She sobbed with her entire body, her face caking with dirt as it clung to her wet cheeks. It felt like time had stopped, the world had stopped. Dylan was gone.

"ADDIE, PLEASE." Matt lay on the ground next to her.

She had stopped shaking, but fresh tears continued to wet her flushed cheeks.

"I know this is bad, Addie, but we can and we will fight it. But not with these officers, they can't bring Dylan back. We have to save the fight for where it matters. I will help you figure this out, I promise."

She squeezed her eyes shut. Matt was right but that didn't make it any easier to not want to lash out and rage against these officers, her co-workers just days ago, for taking her son. She let out a soft whimper as she nodded her head. The officers cautiously let her go and she got to her feet.

Adriana wiped the caked-on dirt from her face, then took a step toward Matt. He pulled her into a hug.

"Ms. Krause," Rebecca said, "I need to do a sweep of the house for my report. Would you like to be present for that?"

Adriana nodded again, and she and Matt followed Rebecca into the house.

The CPS officer ignored Dylan's room and the bathroom, opting for Adriana's bedroom first. Rebecca scanned the tops of the dresser and nightstand, sorted through a few piles of clothes, and then made her way to the kitchen. In the kitchen she found the stack of the Face sketches on the counter. She stopped and flipped through the first few.

"Those are just some of my drawings." Adriana noticed she and Matt had left Edward's file open on the table. *Oh shit.* "Uhh, I have more drawings in a portfolio under my bed. I could show you those if you want to follow me back to the..."

"Not interested, Ms. Krause."

Rebecca set them aside, turned, and stopped. Adriana saw what she saw—the file. Rebecca eagerly scooped up the file, glanced at the contents, and handed it to an accompanying officer.

"That's not..." Matt started, then stopped when Rebecca put up her hand.

"I'll be taking it back with me."

Adriana took Matt's hand. She couldn't believe a little slip of paper gave this woman the power to come into her home, to take whatever she pleased, to take her child. "Why is this happening?"

"You have an ongoing court dispute, am I right?"

"Yeah, but—"

"The custody request was originally filed by Bradley Krause, as I understand it."

"My father."

"And he has the right to express further concerns if he believes the conditions in the child's home have worsened."

"So my dad did this?"

"My job is to follow the court order to protect this child. You should speak to your lawyer about any other concerns you may have."

Matt stepped in front of Adriana, who felt ready to attack. "Ma'am, how can we appeal this action?"

"I assume you both know where the courthouse is. Try there." Rebecca tore off a copy of the court order, set it on the kitchen counter, and then showed herself out.

53

SHE WANTED to be underwater again. Adriana didn't know what to do without Dylan. He wasn't just next door with Lisa and Jennifer. He wasn't in his room taking a nap. He was taken, gone. Alcohol helped a little, but after a few hours of crying and drinking, she was down to the last couple stray cans of beer in her refrigerator.

"Where are you when I need you, Eric?" Her sarcasm was harsh.

Matt had first tried to help her get ahold of anyone at CPS, the courthouse, or City Hall who could help. But that all proved to be a dead end. That's when the drinking started. So next he tried to deter the drinking. That didn't last long; Adriana was determined to numb the pain.

Now, while Matt was in the shower, she unscrewed the panel behind the stereo speaker and grabbed Eric's last will and testament: the small stash of marijuana he had left behind.

She opened the ziplock bag and inhaled an aroma she'd never much liked, then wondered if she could cook it in the box of brownie mix she had bought for Dylan. *The directions said, what? Add water and an egg, whisk...then sprinkle in the weed?* Hell, it was worth a try.

Hypocrite. She had blamed Eric's drug use many times for their situation; now she was conspiring to get high because the beer was running out? *Yes, I'm a hypocrite, I am also in deep shit with no help in sight.*

Except Matt. A cop. *Would he arrest me when he gets out of the shower?*

Two hours later her head spun as if it were circling the moon. After not feeling anything right away, she had binged on the brownies. Matt declined but was done trying to dissuade her. She could see, even through the drunken spinning haze, that he knew how hard being separated from Dylan was for her.

After he cleaned up the beer cans and what remained of the brownies, Matt helped Adriana to her room. She crawled into bed.

"I'll be right out there on the couch if you need me."

"No. Come sleep here." She pawed at the pillow next to her. Matt looked around the room. Now that the drawings were cleaned up, the space was quite inviting. The curtains danced in a cool breeze from outside, her dresser was covered in soft underwear and bright tank tops. Then he saw one of Dylan's Little Golden books on the floor and the reality of the day set in again.

"Not tonight," he said, pulling the sheets up around her.

"Okay," she whispered, somewhere between waking and sleep.

The shadow of a man, *Matt, Matt the man*...loomed over her, tucking her in, and her last thought before dropping into dreamland was about whether she was going to overdose. *Like Eric. Will we meet in heaven or in an opium den somewhere in the afterlife?*

Her body felt heavy. She sank through her mattress and the floor of the room. *Another night at the bottom of Lake Nightmare.* The icy water was a shock to her system. But when she looked down in the dark lake, there was no bottom in sight. Nothing but endless inky water. Frantically, she kicked her legs and swam toward what she hoped was the surface.

When she broke through, the cold air clawed at her face. She dipped below the surface momentarily, partly to get away from that cold, but mostly to double-check the lake really was bottomless tonight. No pulse, no muck, no Edward. She bobbed back up and inhaled the sharp air.

"Fuck!" Her voice echoed around the trees and then back to her, colder and thinner. She hadn't taken the pills. She hadn't brought her sketch pad to bed with her. She was here alone, unprepared, and not by choice.

Then she realized she was not alone.

She gasped and took in half a mouthful of water. A man stood a couple hundred feet down the shoreline. The man didn't turn, didn't move, didn't seem to hear her.

She swam the short distance to the shore. Her head was crystal clear here in the dreamworld. No fog. No dizziness. No spinning world.

She kept her focus on the man. *Edward?* Whoever it was, he had an ax. It looked like he was chopping firewood. *Maybe for heat? Do ghosts get cold?* His back was to her and she couldn't see his face.

She pulled herself out of the water and her soaked shirt froze stiff. *Had it been this cold last time?* She couldn't remember.

"Hello?" she called out. "Edward?" The man didn't turn, he just silently continued his work. The distant monotone chiming, the oddest windchimes she'd heard last time filled the otherwise sound-less night. It was difficult to see in the faint purple light of the dreamworld.

No one had ever joined her in her dreams before. No relatives trying to connect from the other side. No friends in a strange class-room or in her dreamworld bed. No one, other than the Face at the bottom of the lake.

She wandered down the shoreline. As she got closer to the man, she noticed the Easton Mill Lake welcome sign was gone. No more happy trout. No more soul-restoring days on the lake. Just darkness. And a man. With an ax.

He brought the ax down on the chopping block. Adriana expected the dense thud of splintering wood. Instead, the hit sounded wet and soft, like mud thrown at a tree.

"Hello?" She repeated.

But he ignored her, lifting his ax again and taking another swing. Another wet hit.

She inched her way closer.

"Edward?"

The man turned. Not to her, but to a dark pile nearby to grab another piece for the chopping block. As he turned, Adriana recognized the man.

Bradley picked up another piece from the pile and slung it up onto the chopping block. It landed with a grunt. A human grunt. This was not a pile of firewood; this was Eric's torso. His chest, his head, sprawled out on the tree stump chopping block. His arms had been hacked off and stringy muscle tangled in the ripped sleeves of his flannel shirt. Yet his chest heaved. He was struggling but somehow still breathing.

Bradley lifted the ax over his head again and brought it down deep into the broken torso, causing Eric to scream and throw his head back against the flattened stump.

Adriana froze. She didn't run. She didn't scream. She just stood there.

She wanted to help Eric. She had been so pissed at him and felt so guilty at the same time for dragging him back to Cellar. She wanted to stop her father. But he had an ax. She had nothing.

Bradley yanked it out of Eric and a lump of his intestines spilled onto the shore. Wispy trails of steam curled off the warm guts. He raised the ax again.

"Stop!" she'd found her voice. At the shrill sound of her scream, Eric opened his eyes.

"Addie!" He beamed at her. "Addie, save—!"

Bradley's ax came down hard on Eric's chest again. Milky-white blood splashed and sputtered out of his chest. A gash that had split open his midsection ran up and over the side of his neck, coating his shirt in a thin wet puddle of the pearly blood.

"Addie, the kid! Save the ki—"

Another ax swing split Eric's chest in two. A mist of the white blood rushed past her, frozen and stinging her face. Half his rib cage and everything inside of it rolled off the chopping block like a monstrous tumbleweed.

Bradley reached down and repositioned Eric's head on the center of the chopping block stump.

Adriana rushed Bradley and tried to push him back, but his girth was planted firm, immovable. He raised the ax, intent on delivering one final chop.

"Save the kid!" Eric's head yelled.

She couldn't move Bradley, so she reached for Eric's head to save him from another assault. But the ax came down on her outstretched arm; the cold blade carved a large slice out of her forearm and did not stop until it caught in the crook of her elbow.

The pain overloaded every nerve ending and was more brilliant than anything she had ever felt. She tried to hold the pieces of her arm together, to cover and soothe the pain, but found her other hand wrapped up in thick, bloody layers of...

Her bedsheets.

Adriana's eyes opened. She was awake in her own bed, but the pain continued to ring out and up her arm.

She couldn't move. She was pinned down by the shadow of a man sprawled on top of her. He held a needle near the crook of her arm and glared at her through a cheap black ski mask. She thrashed to escape, the needle scored the inside of her arm, the overriding pain struck again. She was able to free one leg and used it to kick the man in his stomach. He lost his breath and teetered back enough for her to launch another kick that sent him falling off the bed and onto the floor.

But the man had stuck her deep. The needle throbbed in her arm. She yanked it out with a deafening scream and threw the syringe across the room.

Disoriented and angry, the man staggered to his feet near the foot of the bed. Adriana launched herself from the mattress, grabbed him, and they crashed against the dresser. Her nails dug into his face as she kneed him in the stomach. He howled and drug her down to the floor with him.

"Adriana!" Matt burst into the bedroom and almost tripped over her while she wrestled with the man on the floor.

"Matt! He attacked me. He—!"

The man threw a punch that slammed into the side of her face, knocking her sideways and off him. Matt grabbed for the man, caught the collar of his shirt in one hand and the black ski mask in his other. The man yanked free, shirt collar tearing and the ski mask peeling back from his bloodied face. Before Matt could catch his balance and lunge again, the man scrambled toward the open bedroom window and threw himself out. Matt got to his feet and started for the window when Adriana called, "Matt, no, save the kid. Save the—!"

"What? What kid? Dylan isn't here."

"What?"

"Rebecca from CPS and the officers, remember? They took him earlier."

The room went blurry before she could understand what he was saying. Out of the dreamworld and...*the bad guy...out the window... gone...I'm fine...* She expected her nerves to calm. Instead, they flared. Her head screeched, her muscles tightened, and she was on the verge of collapsing.

"Addie," Matt said. "What the hell happened here?"

"He had a needle. I think he injected me...with something. It was...the man...from the lake."

"Edward?"

Adriana's responses came slow and in waves. "The other man. The..."

"Addie. Addie! Stay with me."

Matt inspected her arm and found smeared blood a small puncture wound that had widened to a tear.

"I'm taking you to the oh-vuck, Addie."

"But I took...the needle from him..."

"I don't care. We don't know what he—"

"I took the needle...and I threw it." Her head lolled and her body weakened with every word.

Matt glanced around the messy floor. He found it and handed it to her. She managed to focus her eyes just long enough to glimpse the syringe.

"Oh...this looks like heroin." She felt the panic somewhere deep inside her. But heard her soft, dreamlike voice floating around the room.

"How would—how would you know?"

"Eric."

Matt wasted no time with more questions. "Let's go, Addie."

She tried to agree but trailed off and lost her balance. Matt scooped her up into his arms and began moving through the house.

"We've got to get you checked out." Matt carried her through the front door and out to his cruiser.

"I'll be okay... I'll be okay," she said, and then she went limp in his arms.

54

ROBBIE STUMBLED THROUGH BACKYARDS, bushes, and through two alleys before stopping to make sure no one had followed him out through the bedroom window.

He cut across a small field and started heading down one of the empty roads. This far off the main drag he didn't have to worry about avoiding streetlights, but it was hard to see the ground under his feet. He stumbled more than once on rocks that peppered the asphalt.

That should have been an easy job. He didn't even need to use the key Bradley gave him; the stupid bitch had left her window open. But somehow he had fucked it up again, after promising the Devil Man that he wouldn't.

Robbie didn't know why Mayor Krause wanted to pump his own daughter with that stuff, it was too much, especially for someone who didn't use, but Bradley promised it'd be the last thing he'd ever have to do. Just get in, do it, and get out without being seen. He'd only done one of those things, maybe two? He wasn't sure how much he was able to get in her before she woke up.

Robbie walked past a roadside billboard for the local Radio Shack, he recognized the sign. That meant two blocks more to the meeting place. The mayor had told him a driver would be waiting. He knew the intersection well, and he hadn't and wouldn't mess up this part of the plan. He'd hop in that car and tell the driver to get him the hell out of Cellar. Not back to the Devil Man's house, not back to the alley where he flopped most nights. No way he'd go back there. He'd be out of town and out of state in a few hours. The mayor would never find him. The cops would never find him. None of his problems would find him.

"I'm done with that shit, man!" He said it out loud, which felt good. He told it to the trees and the dark sky and basked in the way it felt. The freedom, the weight lifted, getting out from under Devil Man's big ugly thumb. Ever since those days in the Bradley's KIDS program, he'd been told to do *this* and told to do *that*. Little stuff at first. Then medium stuff. Then Card. And Adriana.

He heard an engine rumble to life and then a silhouette of a car appeared in the distance, its headlights off. That must be his ride. He wasn't sure who Bradley had sent to pick him up, but it was probably another one of the guys from the KIDS program. The engine of the dark car revved and then the vehicle started rolling forward.

Robbie moved toward the car and waved to see if the driver would wave back. Nothing. As he squinted to get a better look at the guy behind the wheel, the headlights popped on, blinding him. He shielded his face and called out but couldn't hear his own voice over the roar of the engine.

The car came at him, fast. The shiny chrome grill bit into his legs, chewed up his thighs, and swallowed him underneath the speeding wheels.

THE DASHBOARD LIGHTS illuminated Wills's grizzly, unshaven face. The old mechanic put the car in reverse and sped backward, thumping over Robbie again. He stopped and the headlights flooded the road ahead. Empty gray asphalt stretched on, uninterrupted save for Robbie's mangled, bloodied body lying across the lane lines in the road.

Satisfied that his job was done, Wills pulled off the road to head back home. He turned on the radio. Dionne Warwick, one of his favorites, sang "That's What Friends Are For." He hummed a bit, then reached for his CB mic.

"It's done."

55

"Does she have any allergies?"

The OVUC doctor asked Matt all kinds of questions as he began a battery of tests to determine Adriana's condition.

"I'm not sure. I don't think so."

"Is she on any prescription medication?"

What about the sleeping pills? Would those matter now, and if they did, would that get Lisa in trouble?

"None that I'm aware of. Is she going to be okay? She stopped responding almost immediately. She was out for the whole ride here."

"Are you family?"

"No, I'm…just a friend." He realized that while they had grown close recently, he hadn't really known Adriana all that long.

The doctor sighed. "She's going through a massive chemical and physical trauma. We can pull her out of this, but she's going to be here a few days. I can't give you any more information than that without authorization from her or her family. I'm sorry, you're going to have to wait out there."

Matt was escorted from the exam room by one of the nurses.

After a few hours of treatment, Adriana was finally assigned a room and Matt was allowed to see her. He followed the nurse and an orderly pushing her gurney. He overheard them say that the doctors suspected more than one substance had contributed to her nearly overdosing. As they lifted her into a hospital bed and adjusted the IV and monitoring devices, he lingered.

When the nurse finished, she pulled a chair close to Adriana's bed and motioned to it. "I'll be by about once an hour to check on her. The doctors prescribed a sedative to help Ms. Krause relax, so she'll be sleeping for a while. But you're welcome to wait here now."

Matt thanked her as she left the room, then collapsed in the chair. This whole night, the whole day, didn't make sense to him. First CPS showing up out of nowhere. He knew Adriana had worried it was a possibility, but she hadn't had any public episodes recently. And why did CPS take Edward's missing-person report? Then the attack. Why her, why heroin, and—*well, that was what happened to Eric just weeks ago. It looked like an overdose, and the Chief was there himself because of Adriana's relationship to the mayor. Was Eric murdered?*

"Matt?" Adriana whispered.

"Addie!" This was the first time he'd seen her open her eyes since they'd left the house. "How do you feel?"

"Matt. You have to get me out of here," she said in a soft, hollow voice.

"No, it's okay. You're okay. You're safe and you need to rest."

She slowly shook her head. "The man. He's the man... He met my dad at the lake. Robbie."

"*Robbie* was the guy in the house tonight?"

"Yes. I caught a glimpse of his face when you pulled at his mask."

"What would he be doing at...?" Matt let his mind run through the facts. "Okay, so this Robbie guy was defacing those posters of your dad for a reason. Turning Bradley into the devil. Maybe he bought a ticket to the fundraiser to hurt your father. You said it before: Why would a junkie want to support the police union? But then Card got shot and the place cleared out. He couldn't get to your dad at the fundraiser, so he came here to go after you?"

"I don't think he was there to hurt Bradley. I think he was there because of Bradley. My father gave money to Eric, then Robbie. What was he paying for?"

Matt shook his head. "No. I know you don't get along with your dad. But I can't believe Mayor Krause would—"

"I believe it. Which is why I need you to get me the hell out of here before he gets here and has me locked up or worse. *Please,* Matt." She begged.

"I can't just..."

"That nurse won't be back around again for another hour. If we're going to go, we have to go now. I can't be trapped here all night and doped up. You need to get me out of here."

Matt leaned and peeked out the door. Two night nurses were chatting at the end of the hall. The orderly was nowhere to be seen. He turned and saw Adriana pulling herself up and out of bed. She stumbled and almost fell face-first onto the floor. He caught her shoulder and lifted her up to a seated position on the bed.

"Please," Adriana said softly. Then her head dropped, and she was out. The sedative must be working its magic.

Had he ignored the clues about Mayor Krause because he was smitten with the man's daughter? Or were there just too many secrets in Cellar for him to know at this point? He didn't have answers, but he knew this much: he wanted to protect Adriana. And if she wasn't safe at home, and wasn't safe here, then he'd take her somewhere else.

He pinched the IV tube and slid the needle out of her arm. Her eyes fluttered opened for a moment, but she made no sound. He got her up to a standing position. Her weight pulled him to one side, but he was able to get her a few steps before she collapsed into his chair and her eyes closed.

"Addie, I need you to keep going. I need you to keep your eyes open. If you want to get out of here, I need your help."

She gripped his arm and lurched forward out of the chair. He put his jacket around her to conceal her hospital gown. He checked to make sure the hallway was still clear. They pushed on and out of the room. There was an exit at the end of the hall opposite the nurses' station, convenient for keeping away from the hospital staff, but he'd parked his police cruiser on the other side of the building.

They moved through the hallway quietly but awkwardly. Even if Adriana hadn't been sedated, she'd already been through so much and he knew her body was at its limit. He was sure they'd be caught. After what felt like an eternity, they burst through the exit doors and were hit with the cold night air.

Adriana shivered in her hospital gown, even under Matt's jacket. He hoped the chill would at least help keep her semiconscious. They made their way around the brick exterior walls of the OVUC. They rounded a corner and saw the parking lot stretch out before them. He paused to catch his breath, then they began shuffling toward his police cruiser. Each step seemed more difficult than the last for Adriana.

Then a man popped out of a nearby car.

"Shit," Matt whispered. He paused and strained to hold Adriana up without any forward momentum assisting him. Her hospital gown flowed out below his police jacket and only covered her bare legs down to the knee.

The man stopped with a look of concern.

"Date gone bad?" the man asked.

The guy had an OVUC name tag but wasn't wearing scrubs. His uniform suggested he was a custodian. *Hopefully he won't ask too many questions.* But the man stepped forward, a good citizen, and said, "Miss, are you all right?"

"Sir." Matt clumsily reached for his police badge and raised it. "Please stand back. Police business."

"But she looks like she needs a doctor."

"She's seen a doc. Now we need her for questioning at the—"

A siren screamed and Matt nearly dropped Adriana. He expected glaring searchlights and shouting voices. Then an ambulance sped by, and he used the surprise to muscle Adriana toward his car without ceremony. When he opened the passenger door and glanced back, the man was gone. Maybe he had run indoors to report what he had seen or had brushed it off and gone in to start his shift. Either way, Matt knew time was short. He helped Adriana into the passenger seat and buckled her in. He got in behind the wheel.

Adriana's head lolled toward him, and she murmured, "417... Pine Street."

"Where's that?" he asked, confused.

"My dad's house. Dylan. He probably has Dylan by now."

Her head rolled in the opposite direction. She leaned against the door, then passed out.

Matt stared out the windshield and clicked on his police radio. His shift had started an hour ago and on any other night he'd be hoping for a call right about now. He didn't feel good abandoning his duty to help Adriana. And he didn't know if the dispatchers had been trying to get a hold of him. He just prayed that this late-night shift would be as uneventful as most of the others.

He put the cruiser in gear. *What the hell are we going to do when we get to the mayor's house? Should I call for backup? Backup for what?*

56

ADRIANA HEARD Matt put the car into gear. Through her closed eyelids she perceived the glow of overhead parking lot lights before everything faded to full darkness as they moved away from the OVUC.

The police radio squawked and scratched at the air, but it was faint, and she felt far, far away from it all as the sheen of twinkling stars and moon beams tickled her sleepy eyes. Then a bump in the road and a fast turn of the car startled her and she awakened in the back seat, disoriented. She looked out of the car window at the dark. Everything was rushing past in a blur.

"Matt?"

No answer. Adriana sat up and saw she was no longer in the police cruiser. She was sitting in the back seat of her father's 1965 Buick Riviera, and she wasn't alone. A young girl was asleep beside her on the seat. Her father was up front, driving and listening to the squawk of his CB radio.

"Where are we?" Adriana asked.

Bradley did not answer.

Adriana looked at the young girl again. "Where's Dylan?"

Bradley acted like he didn't even hear her. *That asshole.* Furious, she kicked the back of his seat to force a reaction, but her foot disappeared into the fabric. She pulled her foot out of the void, rubbed it in disbelief, then looked up to the rearview mirror. She saw Bradley behind the steering wheel in the reflection. Her father's face looked twenty years younger.

She turned to the little girl and saw a pink-and-purple butterfly barrette in her hair. Adriana had a barrette just like that when she was—

Bradley slowed the car, turned, and then accelerated again as they passed the Easton Milling Company's factory, which meant they would soon be looping around the lake. *Her* lake. The road dipped and the car bounced hard. The young girl stirred and mewed in her sleep. Bradley looked over his shoulder into the back seat. He looked right through Adriana as their eyes met. He was checking on the child.

Adriana was thrown forward. A collision. A horrible crumpling sound that was short and decisive and heavy. The car had hit something. A rapid knocking tumbled over the hood, up the windshield, and then off the passenger side of the car.

Bradley cried out, slammed on the brakes, and gripped the steering wheel as the car turned sharply, skidded, and veered off the road. They finally came to a stop with a second collision, the front bumper twisted around a wide oak tree. He pushed open the driver-side door and examined the car. Adriana exited the car, moving right through the side panel just like her foot kicked clean through the seat and stood beside him. The cracked windshield and dented hood were illuminated by the bright glow of the moonlight.

"What the hell—" Bradley looked back at the road, once again looking right through Adriana. She followed his gaze and saw the pavement sprayed in the red of his rear taillights. They stepped toward the road, their eyes following the reach of illumination, until they both saw it and froze.

The body of a young boy lay crumpled on the road, his arms and legs splayed and twisted at unnatural angles.

"Oh God!" Bradley howled, his body trembling from the shock. "Oh no."

Bradley stopped, turned, and walked right through Adriana as he jogged back to the car. He grabbed his CB radio transmitter. Stretching the cord to full tension, he sat in the brush next to the car.

Why isn't he calling for help? Adriana wondered. *What is he doing?!*

She realized he was crying.

"Why? Why, why, why?"

Bradley wiped his face and cleared his throat. He clicked the radio transmitter and spoke with the steady control and command she'd always heard growing up.

"Woody. It's me. I need you, fast."

As her father sat on the ground waiting for a response, he couldn't see what she saw. The young girl, Adriana at three years old, was staring out the rear window at the body on the road.

"Adriana. Addie!"

Adriana woke up in the front seat of the police cruiser. Matt was gently shaking her shoulder.

She opened her eyes. Her head was heavy and buzzing.

"We're almost there," Matt said.

She tried to understand. The ache she felt now was the worst in a long life of migraines. The sedative made her thoughts move thick and slow. "Save the kid..."

"Dylan?"

"The kid. Save..." Her eyes closed again.

57

"Can you meet me here?"

"I'll be there in fifteen." The reply was riddled with static, but Adriana heard it clearly. She was back in the Buick.

Woodhull's voice. Right! He called for help! Bradley did the right thing. Good. She looked over in the back seat at young Adriana, whose little body was coiled in a ball, feigning sleep since Bradley had gotten back into the car. His leg was shaking as he stared through the rearview mirror at the boy's body on the road.

Help is coming, Adriana thought. *Just hold on.* Her body drifted through the passenger door and she emerged standing in the road. Everything was bathed in red brake lights and nothing moved. She wasn't sure if the Easton Milling Company had already gone bust by that night, but even if they were still in business, no one would be out here this late.

A few minutes later, two beams of white light cut through the night and blinded her. There were no sirens. *Where's the ambulance? Where are the EMTs?*

A police cruiser slowed to a stop close to the body strewn on the pavement. The car door opened and Sargent Woodhull, twenty years younger than the man who was now called Chief, got out and surveyed the accident scene. He took a deep breath then looked at Bradley.

"The kid came out of nowhere, Woody. I was just—"

Woodhull held up his hand. "Let me take a look."

He walked right past the boy. Instead, he inspected every inch of Bradley's car.

"Any other cars pass you out here? Anyone at all see you?"

"No." Bradley shook his head.

"Why aren't you helping?" Adriana yelled in a voice they couldn't hear.

When he came to the back window, Woodhull saw little Adriana. "Did she wake up?"

"I don't think so. She hasn't moved."

"She didn't see anything? Okay."

Adriana realized this wasn't the dreamworld. This was a memory: her younger self saw the boy through the back window and heard Woodhull through the open car door. Everything felt like the dreamworld, though. The air was cold, the frogs were a wall of sound surrounding them, the giant split oak tree...

Through the open car door, she heard the dashboard chiming—quiet wind chimes—the sound she'd heard in her dreams as she walked around the lake. The Buick's red brake lights combining with the blue flashing lightbar on top of Woodhull's cruiser created the purple moonlight she'd seen.

Woodhull finally walked over to the body. He crouched down and searched the boy's pockets. He pulled out a few coins, a rubber band, and a Cellar Public Library membership card.

"Edward Robinson," Woodhull read off the card. "He's a Cellar kid."

"Fuck," Bradley said.

Fuck, indeed, Adriana thought. *This was the start of it all. The nightmares, the arm, the Face. Edward.* She wanted so much to help him here and now, to save him. But she knew it was too late. He was gone.

Bradley moved close to Woodhull. In a whisper he asked, "Can you make this go away?"

"I wouldn't be out here messing around if I couldn't, but Bradley... This is big."

Woodhull stood and hiked up his duty belt. His gear jangled loud enough to quiet the crickets and frogs for a moment. The two men stared hard at each other in the silence.

"Police chief," Bradley said. "Just a few years from now. That sound good to you, Woody?"

"Careful, Brad, you're not mayor yet."

"And I won't ever be if this doesn't go away. No one will care that it was an accident."

Woodhull seemed to digest the offer. How do you calculate the complications, the cost, the weight of a lie this big?

The radio from the police cruiser broke the silence. "B and E on Radford. Your ETA, repeat, your ETA, Officer Woodhull?"

The voice was familiar. It took another raspy broadcast before Adriana recognized the dispatcher's voice: Maggie Woodhull.

He ignored the radio and looked at Bradley. "It's not just a title I want."

"Name it."

"I run my own shop. I'll cooperate with City Hall, but I won't be bullied."

"Me? A bully?" Bradley said. The police radio wheezed and cackled. Then Bradley nodded. "Okay. I get it. No interference."

One more interruption from Maggie over the radio about the B and E, then Woodhull took charge.

"All right, get your little girl out of here and get home. Do not stop anywhere. You do not want people seeing the front end of your car. Rinse it off and tarp it up when you get home. We'll figure out what to do with it later."

"Okay. I might know someone who can help with that." Bradley started trembling again. Maybe it was just the cold night, but Adriana hoped there was still some good in him back then that rebelled, physically, against what he was doing.

"Okay," Woodhull said. "Do as I say, keep your cool, and just keep doing what you're doing and no one will find out."

"All the work… I can't fuck this up now. All the people who have helped with the campaign. Not now… The polls open in three days. This town is finally going to get the mayor they deserve. I want them to love me, Woody."

"They will. Now go home. Save the stump speeches for the—"

If it hadn't been so quiet that night, they might not have heard it. But the wind died down, the frogs and crickets hushed, and an unnatural quiet blanketed the air around them until the boy groaned.

ADRIANA DRIFTED in and out of consciousness as Matt kept the speed of the police cruiser steady and smooth. Through the fog of sleep, she caught a glimpse of the sign for Pine Street flash by. The sight of it troubled her. She felt sick as her mind pulsated between realities, then and now.

"No. Stop. This is the wrong way," she said.

Matt slowed the car.

"But you said we needed to find the car."

"It's not here."

"Then where?" Matt looked around the neighborhood and Adriana could tell he was growing more anxious every time she came back from the hallucination, or time travel, or whatever the hell it was. But she was working with new information each time.

A few weeks ago, when she broke out her car window, the night she learned the name of the lake, Bradley took her car in to Wills Auto Body. That gave her reason to think he would've done the same in the past.

"Turn around," she said. "Head out on Route 7 toward the lake."

"There's nothing out there."

"Yes, there's…"

He hit the cruiser's turn signal to pull off Pine Street. "Addie, I'm supposed to be patrolling on the east side. How will I know where...?"

She didn't hear the end of Matt's question; she was out again.

BRADLEY AND WOODHULL stood white as ghosts above the boy. He moaned again.

"Fuck, the kid's alive," Woodhull said. He reached for the radio on his belt, but Bradley caught his hand.

"Don't."

"What do you mean?"

"Alive or dead, the result is the same for me if this hits the papers tomorrow. Make it go away, Woody. Like you promised."

"I'm a cop, not a—!"

Bradley let go of the radio, dropped his hand to the duty belt, and grabbed Woodhull's Glock 17. Before Adriana could process what had happened, before Woodhull could stop him, Bradley fired three shots into the boy.

Woodhull jumped back; his hand instinctually went to his now-empty holster.

"Brad! What the fuck?"

"No!" Adriana screamed.

Bradley stood, the gun audibly shaking in his hand.

The police radio spit static, and then Maggie's voice said, "Woody! Come back."

Bradley yelped, startled by the noise, and dropped the gun in the road.

"Respond now, Woody," the distorted radio voice said. "Don't make me send Jerry out there after you."

Woodhull rushed to the vehicle and reached for the mic. "Woody here. All clear. I repeat, all clear. Send Jerry on that B and E."

Maggie signed off. "Copy that."

Bradley picked up the gun, moved to the police cruiser, and handed over the Glock.

"Get rid of the body...*Chief.*"

Adriana stood near the two men, observing Woodhull as he awakened to the dark depth of Bradley's ambition. Her father walked back to his car. He got in, started the engine, and backed away from the old oak. He drove away without looking back. Woodhull's headlights revealed Bradley's bumper sticker, now dotted in blood: *Krause for Mayor.*

58

ONE LARGE BLINDING streetlight illuminated the junk heap that was otherwise known as Wills Auto Body. Matt passed it as he sped down Route 7 and traveled another mile before he realized the auto emporium was the only thing this far out of town.

After a U-turn, he crept along the dark shoulder of the road and stopped before entering the spotlighted lot. He was convinced that life as he knew it was over. Recovering his standing in the Cellar Police Department would never happen after being delinquent all night. And he might face criminal charges for aiding, no, commandeering Adriana's escape from the OVUC. Why was he risking so much for her?

Matt leaned over and nudged Adriana awake. Frightened, she lashed out.

"Addie. Addie! Stop! You're okay. You're okay."

She relaxed back into the passenger seat and looked around. "Where are we?"

"That's what I want to know. You told me to drive out here instead of your dad's place." He pointed down the road to the auto shop sign, rusty and tortured by a single dirty yellow light.

"We have to find the Buick," she said.

"What's so special about this car?"

"It's the car that hit Edward."

"What? When?"

"Twenty years ago. I don't know why I'm suddenly remembering it or... seeing it, reliving it. I don't know, but it all makes sense."

"Maybe to you. Somebody hit this kid? Edward? That's why he's missing?"

She nodded.

"With your father's Buick?"

She nodded again. "Back then it was brand new. I don't remember the car, or I didn't. Not until my dream at the library when it tried to run me down underwater. But I'd seen it in a few photos growing up. And I remember now, when I would have trouble falling asleep, dad used to drive me around, let me lie and sleep in the back seat. That's what he was doing that night. The night Edward snuck out to the lake. These dark roads would have been a great way to lull a toddler to sleep. And they're usually empty at this time of night."

"But not that night?"

She shook her head. "I woke up in the back seat because of the thump. Something slammed into the car and tumbled up over the roof, landing in the road behind us. When my dad wasn't looking, I glanced out the back window." Adriana took a shaky breath. "The boy was just lying in the middle of the road. He wasn't moving."

Matt reeled. He reached for his radio.

"What are you doing?"

"Radioing Woodhull. We've got to go pick up your father. We should have gone there like we planned—"

"We can't."

"Why?"

"Bradley radioed Woodhull that night and..."

Adriana shared what she remembered. Woodhull agreeing to help Bradley. Edward trying to speak. Bradley silencing him.

"You keep telling me without any evidence; there's nothing we can do. That's why finding this car is so important. And my bet is

Wills either chopped it up or hid it for him. Is maybe still hiding it for him."

Matt turned away from her and looked at the auto shop, the run-down oasis in a sea of black wilderness. If this was going to be the end of his career, he decided he would go out with a bang. "Okay, let's go."

THEY PEERED into the windows of the auto shop garage. A car was on the lift, but it wasn't the old Buick. Adriana's car was parked in the next stall, her rear window replaced with a brand-new pane. The third stall was empty.

"What's in back?" she asked. Matt eyed the tall, dark clapboard house on the property next to the shop. Seeing no signs of life, he hurried Adriana into the relative dark of the side yard.

Behind the garage he was stopped by a gate and a chain-link fence. Inside the gated area were rusted auto parts, tires without treads, and barrels of old engine oil. There was one vehicle in plain view, but it was an old truck on cinder blocks.

"There's not much here, Addie. Maybe we ought to try your father's?"

"What's behind those trees?" She pointed.

Matt followed her gaze to a grove of fruitless trees surrounding a low tin structure with a slanted roof. She unlatched the gate and was halfway to the tree line before he decided to follow. He'd already broken her out of the OVUC, neglected his shift, and used his cruiser for personal business tonight. *Why not add trespassing?*

He slowed when he saw the tin shed's double doors were padlocked.

Adriana shrugged. "Do you have anything that could break the lock?"

"We're not doing that."

But he did want a look inside. He circled the building hoping for a window. No luck, but there was a corner in the back where the rusted tin had begun to curl away from the frame. He pulled at it, careful not to slice open his hands, but it didn't want to give. He looked around for something to pry the tin back enough for them to fit through. He told himself this wasn't as bad as cutting the lock; they weren't breaking and entering, only *prying* and entering.

He grabbed a small gnarled branch from the ground and shimmied it into the opening. The metal gave away easily, though a few rivets busted as the wall tore away. Matt bent down and peered into the newly opened corner. It was too dark to see anything inside.

"All right, we should be able to slide through here. Just be careful, this stuff looks like it'll give you dozens of diseases." On his hands and knees, he crawled in through the opening.

Inside, he got to his feet. The dark was flat and unyielding. He kept waiting for his eyes to adjust.

"I can't see anything," Adriana complained. He could hear her crawling in behind him.

Then she screamed.

She flailed and hit the side of the tin shed hard.

"Addie?!"

The screaming stopped. "Ewww, eww, eww. A rat walked right over my hand."

He bent down and felt for her arm, then helped her up. "Let's hope that scream didn't wake the neighbors." He hated that he sounded like he was scolding her.

"What neighbors?" she said. "Creepy old Wills decided to set up shop in the middle of nowhere."

Matt kept his hands in front of him and took small steps forward. If the inside of this shed was anything like the yard, there'd be a hundred tripping hazards in the small space. His fingers smacked against loose canvas covering a hard edge.

"There's something here. Don't—" Too late: she walked right into him with a startled yelp. Her breath was warm on his neck.

"Sorry." She took a step back.

"It's okay." He slid his hand across the canvas. It glided along a horizontal surface, then swooped up at an angle until he found another higher horizontal plane.

"I... I think it's a car," he said.

"Wait, really?"

"Reach out. Do you feel my hand?"

"Yes."

"Good. And the car? Follow it around to the other side. Maybe it's unlocked."

He heard her slowly move around the dark shed as he began peeling back the loose canvas covering the vehicle. A sharp metallic ping sounded from the other side of the car.

"Adriana, are you okay?"

"Yeah, I think I found—"

A harsh light exploded in his eyes. He pulled away until his vision adjusted. When he turned back, Adriana was smiling and holding a caged construction lamp. The high-wattage light bulb revealed an automobile half-covered in old tarps and sheets of plastic.

Adriana grabbed at the ragged coverings and yanked the heavy, stubborn tarp until it slid to the floor. The chrome branding behind the front set of tires sparkled in the lamplight: *Riviera*.

"Holy shit, this is it!" she said.

"Maybe," Matt cautioned. Adriana wasn't listening; she was already examining the front grill of the car.

"Look at this!" She crawled under the car and reached for something.

"Let's not get ahead of ourselves. It's just an old car in a shed. We're not even sure it runs."

"Not only does it run," she said, scooting back out from under the car with something in her hand, "it was out earlier tonight."

59

THE OLD TWO-STORY family house adjacent to the auto shop looked abandoned from the outside, with its rotted clapboard siding and failing gables and gutters. It had not been painted in decades, most of the windows were boarded over, and the front door was tagged with a paper "Do Not Enter" sign from the Fire Department. Not that the sign mattered. The door was impossible to pass through anyway because it was nailed shut.

But the house was not uninhabited. A ragged curtain in the only functional upper-level window was pulled aside as Matt and Adriana walked onto the auto shop property and began peering through its garage windows.

Wills was unperturbed as he watched the couple round the corner of the main building and head toward the back of the property. He picked up the phone on a bedside table and dialed. It rang for a while, but finally the other party picked up.

"It's two in the morning. Who the hell is this?"

"Do you know where your children are, Mr. Mayor?"

"Wills?"

"Yes, sir, just sitting here watching your kid trespassing on my property."

"What the hell is Addie doing out there? She should be…"

"Does she always slink around at night in a hospital gown?"

"Are you sure it's Adriana?"

"Yes, sir. And she's got a cop with her. Anybody you know? It sure ain't Woody."

Wills waited for Bradley to respond, but his mind sawed through the possibilities. Had the mayor set him up? Had he sent the cops here? Wills had done his job: he'd run down that junkie and then backed up to make sure. He always did as he was told and did it well. But he'd never ended up with cops on his land before tonight.

"Why would they come to your place?"

Wills didn't know how or why they'd come to his shop, but from his high perch he could see them head toward the tin shack.

"Maybe they're in the market for a used car. A Buick Riviera, perhaps?"

"Wait, what?! That car was chopped and shopped years ago. You said it would disappear."

Wills grinned and chuckled. "And it did disappear. Until you called for another favor."

"You were paid to get rid of it. We had a deal!"

"My daddy always said contracts was made to be broken. I decided a little insurance might be nice in case you or your uniformed pig ever decided to put some pressure on the family business. Looks like that was a good idea, 'cause now I've got cops snoopin' around my place at two in the morning."

The line was quiet, so Wills stayed quiet. He had held his hand for decades but was now playing it. He knew what he was holding, and he wasn't bluffing.

Finally, Bradley folded.

"What do you want, Wills?"

60

BRADLEY HUNG UP THE PHONE, his mind spinning like a daisy wheel. Robbie was gone, good riddance, but he had obviously fucked things up again. Adriana was out walking around, which meant there'd be no girl-gone-wrong newspaper headline about an overdose and hospitalization. Yet she was traipsing around in a hospital gown? That might be enough to justify taking custody of Dylan.

But why is Adriana and her rookie boy toy out at Wills's place? Were they looking for the Buick? How would they even know to look when Bradley himself had just found out the damned thing was still around?

"Everything okay, Brad?"

The woman's voice soothed him in ways he had not expected. After years of being the bachelor mayor of Cellar, he had begun to fantasize about finishing his historic run of leadership by sharing his success with a First Lady next term, and maybe the term after that. The town would appreciate that kind of stability. No more rumors of his dalliances with call girls in Cleveland or the nonsensical whispers that he'd somehow disposed of Adriana's mother.

"I'm sorry," he said. They usually spent their time together at her house. "You might have to get used to late-night interruptions.

There's always someone in town who wants something from their dutiful mayor."

"I understand."

Rebecca Gill was quickly becoming his favorite person. None of the nagging of his ex-wife. None of the flightiness of Maggie and her dozens of hobbies. Rebecca had a tough job and she did it well. *Without bitching about it*, he thought.

He couldn't let Wills fuck this up for him. Things had been going well, and once he got legal custody of Dylan, things would be perfect. He knew Rebecca wanted children, and her work with Child Protective Services only reinforced that desire each day, but he knew the custody battle was the only chance they had for a child.

It was a sensitive topic that they'd explored briefly when she told him that she could not have children. She said it like a full-disclosure document: "Take me as I am, or don't." He knew some men would be disappointed, but Bradley always tried to see solutions, not problems. What if the man in her life could bring a child to the relationship?

"Rebecca, these next few weeks are going to be rough. The campaign, Card's condition, Deesha's decision...and now Dylan."

He'd been fighting for weeks for the boy. If that's what it took to win over Rebecca, and more voters, then he'd do whatever it took to get the kid.

"I'll take what comes," she said. "I know you're devoted to Dylan, and that means a lot to me. He was living in the wrong home. It was brave of you to take action, but it was the right thing to do."

Bradley liked that Rebecca had made her work with CPS a mission. If she couldn't have her own children, she could foster better lives for the endangered boys and girls who had no parent to truly count on.

He smiled and moved in to kiss her just as the phone rang again.

61

ADRIANA FOLLOWED Matt through the woods that encased Wills Auto Body. She couldn't wait to get back to the police station. They confirmed the Buick Riviera was indeed an actual chrome and steel car and not some dreamworld hallucination, but she wasn't sure what the next step was. Maybe Matt needed to fill out an arrest warrant? Or log the evidence they'd found? Or gather a few officers for backup or something? Either way, this was one lie her father wouldn't wiggle his way out of.

"Why can't we just walk back the way we came?" she asked, shielding her eyes from a wayward branch.

"Because now I know this is all real, which makes that car just about the most dangerous piece of evidence in Cellar. Your father's not going to leave something like that unguarded. We probably already gave ourselves away walking in through the front door. That was foolish. I won't make that mistake again."

"So you think this is enough to bring Bradley down?"

"Maybe. But I still think we should talk to Deesha first. I'd rather not rely on lip readings from sketches. A firsthand positive identification would be..."

Adriana bumped into Matt. "Why'd you stop?"

He made a shushing gesture and crouched down. She followed his lead. From the darkness of their hiding place, she heard the police radio of a second cruiser pierce the rural calm with static and urgency.

Another squad car was parked near theirs. They watched an officer walk around Matt's cruiser and peer in through the windows. Adriana quietly asked if Matt recognized the officer.

"Might be Packer. He was part of the squad that came to your place with the CPS lady. He's only been on the force for about five years, but he's already gunning for the chief's office. I should go down there and talk to him. You stay here and stay hidden, okay?"

Packer was on alert when Matt broke through the tree line, so he made a show of not looking like a threat. With his hands momentarily splayed, he said, "Hinkley here. How can I help you, Officer Packer?"

"Where the hell've you been, man?" Packer was well built and stood a head taller than Matt. His physical presence gave him a natural authority.

"What do you mean?"

"No response for hours. The dispatcher's been trying to contact you. She was afraid maybe you had an accident or something."

"No. I was investigating…"

"Investigating?"

"A guy flagged me down. Said he suspected a B and E."

"What guy?"

"It was a false alarm. He went home and left me to find my way back to the road."

Packer looked skeptical. "Have you had your six-month review yet, Rookie?"

"Coming up soon."

"Just so you know, this kind of jack-assin' around doesn't look good. And some guy from the hospital called in suspicious behavior over at the OVUC. Something about a false police ID. You know anything about that?"

"My badge is right here," Matt offered. "Just as real as yours."

"Uh-huh. They've got a missing patient, too. A young woman."

"Oh yeah?"

"Yeah." Packer looked Matt up and down, then returned to his squad car and radioed back to base. Adriana could only hear portions of his back-and-forth with dispatch, but it seemed like ordinary shop talk until Packer spun around toward Matt.

Oh no. Matt's in trouble! Someone reported us leaving the oh-vuck, or breaking into Wills's place.

"What is it?" Matt said.

"Crazy night. A body was found on the other side of town. They think maybe vehicular manslaughter, hit-and-run."

Hit-and-run? Like Edward. Adriana tucked herself farther into the bushes as Packer seemed on high alert.

"Oh my. In Cellar?" Matt asked for a location, and Adriana recognized the street name. It was only a few blocks from her home.

"I'm heading over there now. Better not let Woody see you in that uniform, Rook. Looks like you've been hunting skunk."

"Just doing my job."

"Maybe. See ya." Packer flipped on his light bar and drove off into the dim light of dawn.

Adriana waited in the tree line to make sure the other officer wasn't going to circle back. Then she got to her feet and joined Matt on the edge of the road.

The sky was starting to brighten after the long night. Adriana reached into her pocket and pulled the evidence they'd found while examining the Buick: shreds of polyester fabric stuck to the engine mount.

Now, with a bit more light, she showed it to Matt again. "I'm sure it's the same color."

"Yeah? I mean, it fits. Robbie's jacket was bright blue, just like this. And these shreds obviously haven't been with the car very long or they'd be oily and, you know."

"So Robbie's body was found? He's the victim?"

"Packer didn't have a name yet. But I think so. One less loose end," Matt said. He looked at his cruiser, then took Adriana's arm. "Come on."

"Where?"

"You need some clothes, and I could use a clean change as well. I want to get back to your place before your entire neighborhood is swarming with officers."

62

IN THE MORNING light it was easy to see how the tin hut had been breached. Woodhull crouched and pulled on the rusty material that had been peeled away for entry. Bradley stood back, worrying he might dirty his slacks. Wills also hung back, but only because he had already peered into the rupture after Adriana and Matt snuck away in the dark.

"Trespassing, breaking, and entering. It's reason enough to suspend the rookie. Maybe let him go permanently," Woodhull said.

"That's not really the headline here, Woody," Bradley said. "I want to know *why*. Why did they come here? And how did they even know to look for the car? It was supposed to be destroyed decades ago."

Both men turned to Wills, who innocently raised his eyebrows. "Why are you looking at me?"

Woodhull pressed for answers. "You must have told her something, Wills."

The mechanic shrugged. "Told her what? I didn't mention the Buick at all when she took the loaner. But yeah, I kept the car instead of stripping it. It just seemed a shame to waste such a sweet ride."

Bradley growled, "We had a deal. If you had kept your word, there wouldn't have been anything for them to find."

Again, Wills showed no concern. "All they know is I got an old Buick. Is there a law against that?"

"There's a law against blackmail, Wills."

"And running over little kids," Wills said. "Pretty sure there's a law about that, too, Mr. Mayor."

Bradley grabbed at Wills's denim overalls, but Woodhull stepped in before a real scuffle got started.

"Hey! *Hey!* We've all got a finger in this pie! Now listen, Wills, if you're trying to flip on us, that's not going to work. You get me?"

"All I know is the girly took the loaner, but before she drove off, she had all kinds of questions about the lake, the old name and everything. Like she'd already been thinking about it."

"Addie might remember the car," Woodhull said. "I know she was only a baby then, but if she remembers anything about that night, it might have stuck with her. And she might be looking for answers. Maybe even go to Deesha."

Bradley pointed sharply at Wills. "All he had to do was chop up the car and—"

"We're past that, Brad!" Woodhull barked. "We've got a new problem here! When was the last time you drove this thing, Wills?"

Wills exchanged a look with Bradley before offering a careful answer. "Last night. Can't let a car just sit around. Took it out to the highway to kick out the carbon."

Bradley took over. "Make him do his job, Woody. Chop it up and get it out of here! If he'd done that...!"

"We'd still have a problem," Woodhull said. "Somebody shot Ben Card. And I'm pretty sure it wasn't Wills."

Bradley composed himself, then asked, "You got a suspect?"

"Wills, we'll meet you in your shop. Give us ten," the chief said.

THEY STOOD at the open doors of the tin hut looking in on the Riviera. The grill was damaged, the bumper still warped from that old giant oak tree, and the hood showed the kind of wrinkles that are consistent with a collision. Wills hadn't done anything to make the vehicle pretty. That was the point they suspected: Why destroy evidence when he could use it to protect himself from the mayor?

"You just had to drag Addie into court."

"I can give that little boy a future."

"You can't fix what you did that night. Not by doting on Dylan."

"Fuck that. 'What I did'... I gave you a career. 'Police chief' sounded pretty good back then, didn't it?"

"You don't own me. I've earned my respect in this town."

"For what? Demanding better lunch specials at Cody's Diner?"

Woodhull grabbed the mayor. Bradley fought back. They grunted and tussled, then fell against the front of the car.

"All right, stop, stop!" Bradley backed off. "What the hell are we going to do?"

"You're the politician. Cut a deal. Give Addie something she wants, and she'll stop whatever the hell it is she's trying to do."

"She's trying to destroy me."

"Well, that's because you kidnapped her child!"

Bradley waved a dismissive hand before brushing some of the car's dirt off his slacks. "You didn't answer my question."

Woodhull looked confused.

"Do you have a suspect?"

It took too long for the chief to answer. It raised the tension. Bradley asked again. "Do you—?"

"Bradley's KIDS. Nice idea. Show the mayor cares, the mayor's involved." Woodhull stepped out of the tin hut, then turned back. "One of the teachers who volunteered at the program kept tabs on the ones that didn't stay clean. She wasn't at the fundraiser. She was shopping nearby when a young man running full tilt exploded out of an alley and nearly knocked her down. He stopped to try to help, out of his fucking mind. Thinking that she recognized him, she said,

'Robbie?' and he freaked out even more. She tried to calm him down, but he just started shouting. You know what he said?"

"How would I know, Woody?"

"He said, 'The devil! He's the devil!' She came into the station last night, realizing maybe she had seen Card's shooter. Had she, Brad?"

Bradley tried laughing at the implication. He was good at that kind of thing, at making an adversary feel foolish. This time it didn't work. Only a whoosh of sound spilled out of his mouth, and he seemed to have trouble keeping his mask of a grin.

Woodhull looked toward the auto shop and lowered his voice. "And now he's lying dead on the other side of town. So what's your plan this time?"

63

MAGGIE WOODHULL STOOD in her office desperately trying to hold back a wave of tears and only somewhat succeeding. City Hall had been a flustering whirlwind of action this morning. First the overnight hit-and-run had everyone talking, then Bradley arrived like a hurricane, storming in several times with sharp orders that were neither customary nor friendly. She could handle her business when work needed to be done, but this was personal: he'd told her to lie on an official form.

Postings about any open meetings were regulated by state statutes, and she knew exactly how to handle them. The public needed time to take note of the schedule and make plans to attend. That was law, and Bradley knew it. So it hurt that he told her to backdate a notice for a hearing concerning Deesha's mayoral campaign filing. He knew the position that put her in. But the thing that destroyed her was how effortlessly he'd done it. Like it wasn't a big deal. Like it was just expected. She would have to...

Lois King marched into Maggie's office. Maggie did her best to compose herself. Lois only ever stopped by for a little girl talk. She thought maybe that would help take her mind off this filing thing.

She was wrong.

"Maggie, the press conference will begin at eleven thirty a.m. sharp."

Maggie knew nothing about this. "What press conference?"

"I know it's last minute, but Mayor Krause and Chief Woodhull have important breakthroughs in the Card shooting to announce. We need an all-points bulletin, pronto, and though we don't have much lead time, Cleveland, Columbus, Dayton, and Toledo press should all be notified and given a chance to cover the event. And we've got to get the Killswitch wackos on board to broadcast live so that other press outfits can at replay that feed if they can't get here to set up their own."

"What are they going to say?"

"That's not really something you need to know to send out the bulletin, is it?"

"I'll need to prep the news crews on what to expect."

Lois could be cold, but Maggie had never seen this type of severity before. Perhaps she was just following orders. If so, Maggie didn't like Bradley's commands any better coming from Lois than she did from the man himself.

"An update on the Benjamin Card shooting is all we need to say for now. I'll have more for you later." Lois spun and disappeared out the door, click-clacking down the limestone corridors of City Hall. Maggie set aside the backdated file, which was still missing her signature, and got to work on this new bulletin.

KASICH WATCHED as the chief marched into the mostly empty bullpen. Half the officers on duty were out at the hit-and-run scene. Most weren't even working it; they were just observing. Kasich was happy to stay and hold down the fort. The chief passed by Kasich and gave the sergeant a head thrust that said, *Follow me.* Kasich stood, and his gut told him something bad was going down. Had he fucked up? Maybe the Rookie?

Nah, he thought. *Chief and I are cool. I was only doing my job. Not my fault if the kid goes AWOL and steals a patrol vehicle.*

He didn't hustle over to the chief's office but wished he had when he saw Woodhull waiting impatiently, hand on the door-frame. Kasich took a seat in front of the large desk as the door shut behind him.

"Al..." Woodhull said. "Where the hell is your rookie?"

It was about Hinkley. *That pain in the ass.* "Gosh, I..."

"I mean, where did we go wrong with this kid? He disappears in the middle of the night, and no dispatch check-ins."

"I honestly don't know, Chief. He hasn't been easy. Has his own ideas about stuff. I mean, you can't fix stupid."

The chief didn't seem satisfied with Kasich's answer.

"And what about the archives, Al? The basement full of soiled files and reports that should have been dumped by now. Are we on track with all of that?"

"As far as I'm aware."

"See, I think that's the problem: there's a lot you're not aware of. Was Hinkley given proper supervision? Did you ever spend any time with him down there? Making sure everything was, you know, moving along?"

"I gave him the flight plan. But I'm not going to stand there and hold his hand."

"You know he stole a file from down there? Walked right out the front door with it."

"I didn't—I... No."

Woodhull sat back, and Kasich noted that he was now avoiding his eyes. Maybe he was assessing more than the Rookie situation. Maybe he knew that his veteran sergeant had checked out about four years ago and enjoyed his relaxing desk.

"Would he contact you for any reason?" Woodhull asked. "Like off hours, wanting to build a relationship, asking for help, tips, whatever."

"Well...not exactly."

"In other words, no, he *never* reached out? Weren't you going to take him under your wing?"

Kasich thought now that maybe the twerp rookie deserved a little better. But it wasn't like anyone had taken him under their wing decades ago when he started out. Everyone has to learn the job for themselves along the way.

The phone rang and broke the silence.

"Woodhull here… Hold on." Woodhull pressed the phone against his chest. "I need to take this. Thanks, Al. We'll catch up later. But if you hear from him…"

"10-4, Chief."

FINALLY, a little good luck, Woodhull thought as Packer's report came down the phone line. He'd remember this one when it came time for promotions. Guess his time-out on the front desk really did the kid some good: Packer, on his own initiative, had called the chief to share his weird run-in with the rookie. Stumbling out of the woods in a rural area. His uniform soiled.

"You drove off after your conversation with Hinkley?" Woodhull asked to clarify.

"Yes, sir."

"Any buildings or signposts out that way?"

"Yes, sir. There's an auto shop down the road."

"Oh, right, I think I know the place. Did Hinkley follow you out of the area?"

"I watched in the rearview, sir. He just stood there on the side of the road."

"And you didn't circle back?"

"No, sir. Maybe I should have. Sorry."

"No, no, Officer. Good job. We've got enough men at the scene. I need you to break off and circle Adriana Krause's neighborhood."

"The sketch girl?"

"Yeah, she's been working a special case with Hinkley, but, uh, we've lost touch. Can you head over that way?"

"Yes, sir. Do you want me to radio in if I find them?"

"No, no. If his car's there, surveil but remain unseen. I'll notify dispatch that I've reassigned you. I just need a call if you see any movement. Am I clear, Officer?"

"Yes, sir."

"I'll remember this, Packer. Thank you."

"My pleasure, sir."

64

ADRIANA SAT at her kitchen table flipping through the Yellow Pages. The house was eerily quiet without Dylan, but she tried to push that thought away. Bradley had used CPS to take him prematurely, and that could have been the end of it. Except she had evidence now. Her nightmares finally made sense. And this would all be over soon if she and Matt could just get to someone who would listen. Someone like Deesha.

Adriana found the listing for Card's law offices and tore the page from the phone book.

"Did you find it?" Matt stepped into the kitchen. Adriana had found a pair of Eric's jeans and one of his old Metallica T-shirts for Matt after changing out of her hospital gown and into some real clothes. She stifled a smile, noting the contrast of the heavy metal shirt against his fair skin.

"Yeah, got it right here." She stood and closed the Yellow Pages.

"Great," he said. "Now we just have to sneak past the officers at the hit-and-run site again, pray that Deesha will talk to us, and somehow convince her we've solved the twenty-year-old case of her missing brother. All without being arrested for basically stealing a police car and breaking you out of the oh-vuck last night."

"Piece of cake," she agreed.

Matt set his dirty uniform on a kitchen chair. "Are...are you sure you're up for this? Going up against your father, I mean. It's one thing to be worked up and talk a big game, it's another to openly accuse the most powerful man in town of murder. Especially when the chief of police helped him cover it up."

"If you're worried about your job, you don't have to—"

"No. No, I'm worried about you." Matt reached out and took her hands. "Losing your job, losing Dylan, and almost losing your mind to those drawings..."

"I am. Up for this, I mean. He killed that little boy. I can't let him get away with that. *We* can't let him get away with that."

Would she have discovered the flipbook had Matt not come over and tried talking her back from the edge? Would she have ever heard the message that Edward was screaming at her through the page, through her drawings? Would she have been able to fight off Robbie's attack alone?

"And thank you," she said, "for being here. For believing me even when I wasn't sure I believed myself. For everything."

She leaned forward and kissed him. It was something she'd wanted to for a long time. She didn't want to overthink it. She didn't want to walk off to war having not done it. And she didn't want to stop.

Matt's pale complexion turned apple red. It was a good, long, needed kiss. A kiss that ended in two astonished smiles.

"That was..." Adriana started.

"Yeah."

"Sorry. It's all been so overwhelming," she said.

"No, it's okay. It's better than okay." He cleared his throat and regained his composure. "But I agree, everything has been over-whelming. So let's just...take it one step at a time."

"Okay." *Does he want to move slower? Did I just fuck everything up?*

Matt took the torn phone book page from Adriana. "First, we get to Deesha. Having her on our side will help immensely. And she deserves to know about Edward."

Oh, he meant one step at a time in the case. "Right. Then?"

"Then we figure out how best to deal with your father."

BRADLEY'S HAND trembled as he looked at his watch. One hour from now he would face the television news crews, mostly the invited local and state reporters, but there had also been queries from national news feeds. City Hall employees set up his lectern and microphone, and even a rubber mat so he wouldn't slip on the limestone floor. He knew exactly what he would say, and he was fully prepared to narrow the scope of questions so that he didn't stumble and incriminate himself.

Regardless, as he smiled and nodded to his employees, his mind drifted to the doctor's appointment he had scheduled last week. After removing a blood pressure cuff from Bradley's upper arm, the doctor looked grim.

"Not good, Brad. Not good," he'd said.

"It's the meds. They don't work like they used to."

"I can't up the dosage without damaging your kidneys, Bradley."

The mayor cringed, then said, "Can't you give me something else? I mean, I'm in the middle of a mess."

"A war?" The doctor tapped his own temple. "Offer stands: I can set you up with an excellent psychologist in Cleveland. No one in Cellar would know."

"I'm just tense…"

The doctor cut him off by moving to his desk, shaking his head. "Come on, Brad. The panic attacks started years ago. When will you face your demons, whatever the heck they are, and get on with life?"

Bradley didn't like the word "demons." He looked at his longtime physician and shook his head. "Don't have time for the headshrinkers right now. Maybe after reelection."

Against his better judgment, the doctor scratched out a prescription. "Last time, friend. This is the last time I do this for you."

Before leaving the City Hall lobby, the mayor fingered his bottle of meds, then strode back to his office, where his mood improved. "Dylan! How did you get here?"

The boy was sitting in the mayor's swivel chair, holding his Hot Wheels truck. "Auntie Becky brought me."

"Of course she did."

"When's Mommy coming?"

"Oh, I don't think she'll be here today, buddy. You're going to be spending a lot of time with Papa and Aunt Becky, okay?"

Rebecca smiled, moved toward Bradley, and discreetly let her fingers touch his. "Are you as nervous as I am about this press conference?"

"They're never easy, but I'll be fine. We'll focus on Card. I doubt anyone will even bring up…"

They both cast a glance at Dylan then dared a quick kiss.

Maggie Woodhull entered. "I've got a list of more media requests and—" She stopped when she saw Rebecca standing so close to the mayor. "Oh, sorry, I should have knocked."

"No, come on in, Maggie. What do you have?"

With her eyes on Rebecca, Maggie handed Bradley the printed sheet.

"Thank you. Anything else?" he asked.

She paused, then shook her head before turning to leave.

"Hey, Mags. I had a good talk with Woody this morning. Like old times. Don't worry about us."

"Haven't lost any sleep over it."

"The police budget will work itself out."

"I'm sure it will."

He could see the tension in her face and hear it in her voice. He assumed he'd pulled away from Rebecca before his affections could be noticed. Maybe not. He flushed with mild anxiety. One more fire to douse and then it expanded when an image of Robbie flash-flooded his mind. By now, the coroner would have the kid's body on a gurney and an autopsy would begin. They no doubt would have bagged up that tattered old coat for evidence, and the key.

How could I have overlooked the key?

"There is one more thing I need you to do." The words replayed in Bradley's mind. "And you can't fuck it up. Understand?"

Robbie had nodded agreeably, but the mayor had not been convinced the kid was listening.

"Hey. We go way back. Right, Robbie?"

"Huh? Oh, yeah. Yeah, we do."

"And I've done a lot for you, haven't I?"

"But the thing I don't get…"

"You don't get it? What do you mean?"

"No, no, I'll do it. But what I'm saying is… I didn't think Addie was a user."

"She's *not* a user, Robbie. I thought I explained."

"Yeah, yeah, you did. Uh-huh, but what I'm saying is…"

"Just give her the junk. That's your job."

"I always liked Addie. But I only saw her when Eric was…you know? She never touched the stuff."

"Look. I know you think I'm the devil or whatever. But what I'm doing, what *we're* doing, is what's best for everyone involved. Adriana may hurt for a little while, but what you do tonight will help save the rest of her son's life. It might seem evil right now…"

Bradley had reached in his pocket, pulled out an object, and then offered it to Robbie. "Know what this is?"

"Yeah, yeah, man. It's a key."

"But not just any key. This is the key to Adriana's house. You let yourself in real quiet, then you pump her full of that shit and get out—get out fast, right?"

Robbie had taken the key and stared at the shiny silver surface.

"Robbie? You get me?"

"Yeah. Yes, sir."

Bradley shook free of the memory and now looked over at Dylan, who was on the floor racing his Hot Wheels over Rebecca's polished shoes. He hadn't told Robbie to ditch the key. When the coroner found the key in his pocket, would he question whose door it unlocked?

He made a mental note to tell Woodhull. Maybe he could get the key before it was logged into evidence.

"Rebecca," he said. "When it's time to get in front of the press, I want you to be there, behind me with Dylan. Lois and Chief Woodhull will be there, and one of my assistants will lead you all into place."

"Are you sure?"

"Never been more sure. Solidarity. The people who mean the most to me. Backing me up at this troubling time."

She smiled, but Bradley sensed she kept the bright lights dim in case Maggie barged in again.

65

"CALL FOR YOU. LINE TWO!"

Deesha didn't like when the secretary shouted. *Just transfer the call*, she thought. But the girl was still in training, and Deesha needed every volunteer she could get for the campaign. Taking on Bradley Krause... What was she thinking? It felt impossible anytime she gave it even a moment's thought.

She stepped away from her manager, Tom Galton, and answered the phone. "Deesha speaking."

The voice was a whisper. "The mayor's going to hold a press conference. About Ben. And I think..."

"Who is this?"

"I'm calling from City Hall."

"...Maggie?"

Rushed, tense, the woman's voice said, "Your name was not included on the contact sheet. Turn on local radio. Killswitch. Today at— I have to go."

"Maggie, don't hang up. What contact sheet? What's going on?" The phone was near silent; the background static was Deesha's only indication that the person at the other end of the line hadn't hung up.

"I don't know. I don't know anything anymore."

The phone line went dead.

"Tom, I just got the weirdest call." Deesha turned to see Matt and Adriana standing in her office doorway.

66

ADRIANA DIDN'T KNOW Tom Galton personally, and so far, she didn't like him. He kept sweeping his good hand through his wispy, oily hair, and his stare felt accusatory.

Deesha, on the other hand, appeared more confused than hostile by the unexpected visit. "This is somewhat unusual. We are the campaign that wants to replace your father."

"I'm not into politics," Adriana said. Matt sat next to her in front of Deesha's desk.

Galton said, "How is he?"

"Dad?"

"Yes."

"Um…" She paused. *Yes, how is Dad?* She had refused Matt's offer to drive her up to the OVUC after Bradley fainted at his meeting. They hadn't spoken in a while.

"He's fine," Matt answered.

"Yes, but he's not really the reason I'm here," Adriana said. "Mrs. Card, I came here because I didn't know who else to turn to."

Galton again: "Not your father?"

Matt sat up in his chair, maybe ready to defend her. She placed her hand over his. *My fight, not yours,* she thought.

"Mrs. Card..."

"Deesha. I'm not *that* much older than you."

Adriana managed a polite smile, but inside she was bursting to let everything out. "Deesha, I have something that may be difficult to see. I wonder if you...if you could identity a face that has been... haunting me."

Galton adjusted the sling on his bad arm. "We really are very busy today, Ms. Krause."

"I know, I know."

Matt jumped in. "All we ask is that you take a look at a sketch."

"Oh, come on. Deesha...?" Tom said.

"Tom, I want to hear them out. I know from the papers Adriana and her father don't see eye to eye on most things. And this officer here was assigned to protecting Ben for a bit after the shooting. We can give them a few moments of our time."

"I wasn't only the officer assigned to protective duty at the OVUC, I was also assigned—*ordered*—to review some old police records." Adriana could tell he wanted to sound professional, but the Metallica T-shirt really undercut his authority.

Galton sneered. "We know what they're doing over there. They're destroying old case files."

"Not yet," Matt said. "So far, I've ignored my orders. I held off destroying anything when I literally stumbled across a missing-person report you filed, Mrs. Card."

"Can we see it?" Galton asked.

"Unfortunately, it was confiscated shortly after I showed it to Adriana."

"So you have nothing?"

"We have this." Adriana's heart broke as Deesha's eyes glazed over with tears at the mere mention of the report. That was not expected. It was the sketches that Adriana thought would have an impact. Now she feared her crude portraits would crush her.

"Yes," Deesha said. "I lost my brother. Many years ago. He was just a boy."

"I'm so sorry," Adriana said. "But I don't think it was an accident that Matt found those files." Adriana pulled a folder full of pages out of her bag.

"I know how this is going to sound, but...I think your brother has been trying to...communicate with me." She laid the folder in front of Deesha, then braced herself.

Deesha looked hesitant, as if she thought she was being tricked. Finally, she opened the folder, then quickly closed it again.

Galton grabbed the file off the desk. "What the hell is this? Did Bradley put you up to this? You bring these photos into our office!"

"Wait, Tom!" Deesha said. "They're just sketches."

"They're trash. I know her dad. And I know what he's capable of!"

Galton flipped the folder open, clearly expecting something other than Adriana's sketches.

"Tom, let me look again."

Adriana watched as Deesha searched through the gruesome sketches. She took her time and finished with a deep sigh.

"The frown... That crease between the eyes." She rose from her chair and turned away from her visitors, still looking at the stack of sketches. "He was always so... How could a little boy be so serious?"

Softly, Adriana asked, "So it's him?"

Deesha turned to Adriana. There was a pleading in her eyes that made Adriana want to look away. "How did you... Where did you... What inspired these drawings?"

Adriana's head was so full of memories and fragments and fear that she could only say, "I draw crime sketches for the police."

"Oh, come on." Galton was still not convinced. "You just happened to have the impulse to create horrid portraits of Eddie?"

"No. I've seen him."

Deesha dropped the sketches on her desk. "Don't do this. Do not play with my—"

"I'm so sorry. But it's true. I saw my father kill him."

ADRIANA SLOWLY WALKED Deesha and Tom through that night all those years ago, out by the lake. The accident. Woodhull. The gun. And the nightmares that followed. She told them about Bradley using CPS to take Dylan and the attack in her bedroom to make it look like she had overdosed. She told them about the car out at Wills Auto Body, and Matt confirmed Robbie was now lying in the morgue.

She was stopped by a knock on the office door.

Deesha's volunteer secretary came in and scanned the room. "Sorry to interrupt, but Killswitch just announced the mayor would be on in a few minutes with an important update in Ben's case. He thinks they found the shooter!"

67

OFFICER PACKER WAITED in his cruiser. He wasn't enjoying his babysitting gig trailing Adriana and the Rookie all over town. He wouldn't waste valuable town resources like this when he was chief. At least the downtime gave him a moment to enjoy his breakfast. As he reached for the last lemon crème in his to-go bag, he opened the car door and leaned out before taking a bite. He didn't want sprinkles of crust and sugar to dapple his uniform. Despite the precautions, before he could take a second bite, Adriana and Hinkley burst out of the office-building entrance, ran to their vehicle, and backed up carelessly before speeding out of the parking area.

Packer cursed and tossed his treat into the bushes that lined the parking lot. He leaned back into his cruiser, clicked on the emergency lights, and let his siren whoop to clear motorists. Once he could see Adriana and Matt in the traffic, he turned off his lights and palmed his radio mic.

The dispatcher was already on alert for his transmissions, so there was no small talk or code words passing between them.

"I need Woodhull."

"Copy that, but he can't be reached."

"He asked for an update."

"I know. But he just rushed out to the press conference at City Hall. Told me to hold all calls, including yours."

"What press conference? Why is Woodhull giving speeches?"

"Not just the chief. The mayor, too. Regarding the shooting. No one here really knows, but if there's been a break in the case, they're keeping tight-lipped about it."

"10-4. Guess I'll hear the news soon. Looks like Adriana and Hinkley are heading there now."

Packer pulled off the main road and decided to take a shortcut to City Hall. He wanted to beat them to the party. He flipped on the car radio to catch whatever news he could before the presser and heard Killswitch babbling at his usual pace and place.

"We got you some breaking news, my Cellaritos. Well, it ain't exactly broke. But it's smokin'! The mayor himself, that guy at City Haul Your Butt to Reelection, has something he needs to tell us about the Benjamin Card shooting, the alleged shooter, and God knows what else. Let's go there *now* or *nevuh!*"

Packer hollered, "Bring it on!" He stomped the accelerator, whooped his siren, and flared his free-to-speed blue lights.

68

THE PRESS EVENT had already begun when Adriana and Matt squeezed into the lobby. Standing behind media and the others who had gathered in City Hall, Adriana shivered as her father suggested that recent events were the result of a grand conspiracy.

"We have reason to believe that more than one individual may have been involved," he said. "A man of his background and limited means would not know how to plan or carry out such a heinous act. Nor would he be sophisticated enough to suspect that the people who had lured him into this assassination attempt would then rub him out in what we believe was made to look like a late-night hit-and-run accident on a dark street. But this was not an accident. This was murder, and we will pursue it until we find the truth."

Cameras flashed, bodies shuffled, and there was a murmur among the crowd that Bradley allowed to rise then fall before continuing. Always the showman, her father.

"To that end, I will meet with city council this afternoon to allocate emergency funds to expand the police department's budget, and we will continue to cooperate with state and federal law enforcement. Now I'd like Police Chief Woodhull to speak and answer questions."

Adriana leered above the crowd as Bradley stepped back and joined Lois King and the Child Protection Services officer who had stolen her boy. She felt white heat scorch her heart when her father bent over and then lifted Dylan into his arms, in full view of the cameras and reporters.

"Dylan!" Her voice was loud enough to carry throughout the limestone halls.

She saw Bradley tense, briefly search the crowd with flashing eyes, and then pretend he had heard nothing. Even Woodhull startled when he heard her cry, but he too pushed forward.

"The alleged shooter, who nearly took Councilman Card's life, is a Cellar resident. His death and the surrounding circumstances are especially troubling for the mayor, because Robert 'Robbie' Brenner was one of the first young people to join Bradley's KIDS. The hope was to save the lives of young people like Robbie. Instead, at this time, we believe his past drug addiction was used to manipulate him with a promise of enrichment. Yeah, I'm talking money, and who knows what else."

A reporter shouted, "Has a weapon been found?"

"No. And please hold all questions until—"

Another reporter asked, "How many years was the suspect in the drug program? And have any other Bradley's KIDS lost their lives to—"

"Yes!"

Woodhull froze, a deer caught in the flashbulbs, as the sprawl of media and others turned to see who had answered the question.

Adriana stood. "Robbie was Eric's dealer. You all covered Eric's death a few weeks ago. That's two young men dead! And they both recently took money from Mayor Krause."

A roar of demanding questions filled the hall.

Reporters stood and moved toward Adriana for clarification, a statement, a photo, anything. The herd grew to a stampede, and the chaos tumbled into a riot. Lights and other equipment fell and shattered on the stone floors.

Adriana strained to see past the horde. Bradley handed Dylan to

Rebecca, pulled Lois under his arm, and then as a flock, they fled down the corridor toward the mayor's chambers. Woodhull was the only one who stood his ground.

"Stand down! That's an order! For the safety of others, stand down or I will declare this event over!"

No one listened and the chief turned from the podium and disappeared from Adriana's sight as people surged toward and around her. Matt began shoving reporters and cameramen to clear a path for them to escape. His voice thundered yet could not be heard above shouted questions and other arguments that broke out among those being crushed, pushed aside, or just plain ignored.

Adriana knew that it was impossible to get out of the lobby through the entrance but saw a slight opening in the crowd that would lead her deeper into the protection of City Hall. She went for it.

"Matt!"

She clutched his hand and tried to pull him along with her. They stalled until the sweep of several police officers intercepted her and, as though on wings, moved her through the crowd. One cop took charge.

"I'm Officer Packer. I'll get you out of here."

She lost her grip on Matt's hand. "Wait, Officer."

Packer turned and saw Hinkley drowning in the sea of reporters.

"Hey!" Packer shouted. "This man is a police officer! Back off. *Back off!*"

69

BRADLEY'S spacious office now felt far too small. Dylan huddled close to Rebecca and Lois, while Bradley flipped on his police scanner to listen to dispatch. The scanner noise covered up the muffled chaos of the reporters on the other side of the door. On an adjacent bookshelf, he was confronted by a framed, decade-old photo that showed him standing under a banner, "Bradley's KIDS Keeping Illegal Drugs out of Schools," with a group of teenagers. He did not need to look hard to notice Eric and Robbie.

A commanding voice took charge. Before this whole mess, that calming and leading voice would have been his own, but, rattled and overwhelmed, he was relieved when Woodhull took charge.

"This will be over soon, everybody. You're safe here. Let's all calm down."

Woodhull took a moment to pat the shoulder of each individual before he moved close to Bradley and whispered, "Keep your cool. Doesn't matter what she said. Proof. How is she going to prove any of it, huh? And to who? Between you and me, we run this town." A moment later, he added, "We'll make them an offer. A good one."

Bradley didn't find much comfort in Woodhull's plan. Not with how spectacularly their last plan imploded. That presser should have put everything to rest. Robbie fingered for Card's shooting, Wills set up to take the fall as the mastermind behind the attempted assassination, and, later, the shocking revelation that Wills took his own life in the front seat of the very car he had used to run over that poor missing kid two decades ago.

Bradley imagined the flies already starting to swarm Wills's body. He never had a chance to put up a fight. Woodhull snuck in through the back of the garage with Bradley's revolver, and that was the end of it. Good riddance. *Should have done his fucking job and vanished the car.*

His office door opened to the cacophony out in the hallway, and Officer Ty Packer escorted Adriana and Matt into the chambers.

Time stopped.

Internally, Bradley flung through a range of emotions. Rage. *How dare she accuse me?* Betrayal. *After everything I've done for her?* Relief. *At least it's only her and that idiot rookie cop. The last thing I need is the press snapping a photo of us all hiding in here.* And finally, confusion. *How much do they know, and how the hell do they know anything?*

The tense silence ended when Matt said, "Mayor Krause, we have reason to suspect your involvement in—"

"Stand down, officer," Woodhull said. "You are off duty as of an hour ago and of no help to us today, Rookie. Meet me in my office when you report in tomorrow so we can discuss your escapade last night and your future."

"Chief Woodhull, I have the right to speak."

"You should have come to me first, Hinkley."

"Is this really a scab you want to pick now, Addie?" Bradley took a step forward. He didn't like the feeling of his back being up against the wall, figuratively or literally.

Adriana didn't flinch. "You're a murderer."

"Why would you say such a thing? I gave you a life, Addie."

"You gave me a nightmare!"

Lois King trembled as she moved toward her mayor. "Bradley, what is this all about?"

Maggie snuck a glance at Rebecca, who looked on in disbelief as she listened to the father-daughter squabble. Then she turned her gaze to her brother. "Yeah, Woody. What's going on here? What were you guys going to say out there to the press?"

The chief looked at his sister, then scanned the room. Bradley also saw it: too many witnesses.

"Officer Packer."

"Yes, sir."

"Escort the women here to a quieter place. The conference room down the hall might be best."

Packer didn't move. "Uh, Chief. I'm just not sure escorting anyone through the crowd out there would be wise. They're hungry for flesh right now."

"I gave you an order, Ty."

Officer Packer looked like a man trying to process too much information.

"Go, Packer. And take the child, too."

"No way!" Adriana shouted. She made a move toward Dylan, but Rebecca put her arms around him in a protective stance.

"Get your hands off him!"

Woodhull boomed, "Packer!"

"You want your boy back, Addie?" Bradley asked. "A simple solution. Nobody gets hurt. I'll drop the court case."

He probably ended his and Rebecca's chances with that one little sentence. *Casualties of war*, he told himself.

"In exchange for what? Lying for you?"

"You go away with Dylan and never come back here to your 'nightmare.' Sounds like that's what you've wanted all along anyway."

Adriana looked over at Dylan as if pondering the offer. Bradley assumed she daydreamed about leaving Cellar all the time, running away to start a new life. He didn't understand it. He had given her everything and she had refused half of it and pissed away the other half. He didn't want to give up Dylan, which most likely meant giving up Rebecca, but if it was the only way to keep Adriana quiet, then it was one more sacrifice he'd have to make.

"Addie, you can't," Matt said.

She met Bradley's glare. "I could go to Killswitch. Tell him my story. Then I wouldn't need a *deal*."

"But what about your boyfriend, Addie?" Woodhull said as he moved through the room. He spoke softly to Hinkley. "Would a promotion help? A recommendation to the state detective unit? I'm buddies with the captain."

Rebecca handed Dylan to Lois, then moved across the office. "What am I hearing, Brad? Was this the plan all along? Is this why you convinced me to take Dylan now? And those police files you said she stole. She didn't, did she? *You* wanted those files. You used me?"

She wiped away a tear, and then slapped him hard across the face.

She turned to Adriana. "I'm very sorry for my actions. And I am officially returning custody of Dylan to you."

Lois put Dylan down, and he ran over to Adriana. She scooped him up into a long hug and covered his face in kisses. The office door opened and closed on the cacophony outside, and Rebecca was gone.

"Bradley?" Lois spoke up.

"I've made this city a better place," he insisted. "If it weren't for me—"

"Edward Robinson would still be alive," Adriana said. "And Card wouldn't be lying in the oh-vuck. I saw you with Robbie, Dad. I saw you hand him the money."

"Wild accusations with no shred of evidence."

"No? I found the cash you gave Eric right before he ended up dead. And Matt and I found the car out at—"

"Adriana!" Woodhull cut her off. "Addie, if you have evidence you've been holding back from the night Eric died, you should bring that in. In fact, this whole conversation should be happening at the station, where we can take your statements." Woodhull looked at Lois and Maggie. "You two should get back to work now. We'll clear this mess up. Officer Packer?"

Packer stood stationary again. Woodhull hiked up his duty belt as he crossed the room to the officer and pulled his radio free. "Am I going to have to call someone down here to escort you out? You want more time on the front desk? How about a month this time?"

"No, sir." Packer reluctantly assisted Lois and Maggie out of the room and closed the door behind him.

Woodhull locked the door, then turned and began *his* campaign to save one more Bradley Krause campaign.

"Worse things have happened, Hinkley. There is no evidence that Bradley had anything to do with it. In fact, there's no evidence of any crime at all! Sometimes kids just run away."

"What color jacket was Robbie wearing last night? We found shreds of fabric on the chassis of an old Buick Riviera being stored at Wills Auto Body on Route 7."

"More evidence? Great! Bring it in. We'll keep it safe for trial."

"Like you're keeping old case files safe, Chief?"

Woodhull didn't appeal to Matt or confer with Bradley. He pulled the Glock from his holster. "All right. Enough playing around. You're under arrest for the theft of records pertaining to—"

"Chief, Kasich ordered me to open cold cases."

Woodhull raised his gun. Matt struck the chief's arm to knock the gun away. Woodhull struggled to hold on to his weapon. A loud crack startled everyone in the room as it fired. A chunk of the floor came free where the bullet hit. Adriana shrieked and turned to protect Dylan with her own body. Woodhull swung back and caught Matt's brow with the butt of the gun.

Matt tumbled and splayed out on the office floor.

The door handle jiggled. There was a rapid knocking.

"Chief?" The words came muffled through the door. Officer Packer must have heard the gunshot. "Chief, is everything okay?!"

"We're fine!" Woodhull answered.

"No! Get help! Matt's—" Adriana yelled, but Woodhull grabbed her and covered her mouth. He pulled her away from Dylan. He screamed for his mom as she fought back. But Woodhull wrestled her to the floor.

"Woody!" Bradley's head was spinning. Packer had certainly heard the shot and most likely heard Dylan's screams; he'd bring more officers. Adriana and Woodhull tussled on the floor, but he was strong and able to subdue her. After a minute, she stopped struggling, her breathing ragged and panicked.

Bradley glanced around for an exit. Adriana wouldn't cooperate, not now, not with Matt lying knocked out on the floor and Dylan crying out of control. *What's the next move? How do we get out of this? How do I get out of this?* Bradley didn't know.

70

WOODHULL LET Adriana go after she stopped fighting him. She gulped in a deep breath and rolled onto her stomach. She pulled Dylan into her side and comforted him. She tried to reach Matt. Blood covered his face and pooled on the floor around his head, but he was still breathing. She tried to stand, but Woodhull pushed her down and pressed the barrel of his Glock to her forehead.

"It stops here, Addie."

"No, Woody!" Bradley took a step forward.

"Then what comes next, Mr. Mayor? You're the one who got us here. It's a clean case of self-defense. She comes here after a night of partying, multiple drugs in her system, and verbally attacks you on live TV. We try to talk some sense into her and she lunges at me with...a pair of scissors."

"Adriana, please," Bradley said. "There's a real simple solution to all of this: just take the deal. Take Dylan, get out of here, and forget all about that terrible accident. It was so long ago."

He hesitated, then continued. "I've had to live with it every day, but destroying me won't bring that kid back. Nothing will. I know. I've been punishing myself for two decades. I lost my marriage, my relationship with you, with my grandson... The only way to move forward is to give Dylan the best life we can, to make sure that he doesn't have to live his life under this shadow. That's all I've been trying to do. That's what we need to do."

"Or else?" she said. "You've got a gun to my head. That's not much of a negotiation."

"You didn't leave me any other choice. You never talk to me. You never let me see Dylan. You spy on me, following me out to the lake. You just keep picking and picking at every little thing. I run this town. You could have had a very easy life, but instead you rejected every olive branch I offered. So now, yes. We negotiate life or death. Because you're threatening my life, my legacy, everything I've built, everything I've worked for."

"A legacy built on lies."

"Oh, grow up. That doesn't erase the decades of good I've done for this town. For you. For Dylan. The house you live in, the food you eat, the clothes on Dylan's back. All because of me. And none of it was good enough. So fine. Take Dylan and leave. You talk about how much you struggle all the time; see what it's like to struggle without Dad's safety net. Without Dad's support. Without Dad's love."

"Love? Love! You don't—"

Woodhull swung and hit Adriana so fast that for a moment, she didn't know what happened. The pain rocked her head. She felt dizzy, and then the room went dark.

SOMEWHERE FAR AWAY SHE heard the muffled yells of her father fighting with Woodhull punctuated by Dylan's cries. She wanted to cradle Dylan close, to never let him go again. She wanted to take him away from all this chaos and violence.

She should accept Bradley's deal. She should forget all about the Buick Riviera, Edward's body lying on the pavement, the rotting arm jutting from the bottom of the lake, and the Face that attacked her in the bathtub. She should forget about Wills and his crooked grin and Robbie on top of her in her bed, and forget the faces of her new friends, Lisa and Jennifer. Jennifer, who had shown Dylan so much love and who had seen the lips move in those drawings. Jennifer, who had given the Face a name.

"Edward," Adriana whispered. Bradley wanted her to forget that face, too. "I will never forget your face."

A screech, a force as strong as a gale wind, shattered the dark veil over Adriana's vision as it swept into the office, toppling chairs, lamps, and sweeping clean the shelves of photos, books, and trophies.

Then the Face, a gaping wound of rage, shrieked toward Adriana before veering off and circling the room, entrapping everyone in the past and present as it screamed, "EEEHHHHHHH!"

The deafening sound rattled Woodhull, who dropped his weapon and covered his ears. Bradley dove for the Glock and managed to grasp it as the Face charged at him, laying siege, screeching with such force that the mayor's flesh contorted.

"Edward! Edward! EDWARD!" The Face pummeled Bradley with its name.

Bradley aimed the Glock at Edward and, like he did twenty years ago, fired three shots at the boy. The bullets passed through the phantom and scarred the wall behind it, just inches from where Woodhull stood.

Adriana blanketed Dylan with her body and crawled under her father's desk. Dylan's cries were drowned out in the chaos.

Woodhull ducked away from the bullet holes in the wall. "Brad! Stop! Jesus Christ. What the hell?!"

But Bradley couldn't hear anything except the damning cries of the spirit. It circled around the room, and Bradley's weapon followed. He fired wildly in all directions. Picture frames shattered, holes tore into the walls, Woodhull yelped, but Bradley continued to squeeze the trigger. The shots were thunderous in the small office. He continued, even after the clip was empty. *Click-click-click.*

Edward's spirit grew and loomed over the entire room.

"Say my name," the voice hissed.

"I don't know you!" Bradley bellowed.

Adriana startled as a heavy thump moved the desk. She turned to see Woodhull crumple to the floor, a splattering of blood and brains on the office wall behind him. One of Bradley's stray shots had found a mark after all.

"Say it!" Edward demanded. "Look at me and say it."

Bradley dropped to the floor and crawled over to Woodhull. He jostled at his old friend's duty belt and pulled a fresh clip out of its snap case. He reloaded the weapon and pointed it up at Edward's spirit. Edward's rotting muscles and tissues dangled above the mayor.

Bradley's aim wavered. He looked over and seemed to finally register Woodhull's body lying next to Matt's. The little bit of color that remained in his face was now gone and he began to weep. Instead of firing, he dropped his arm.

Through a deep chest-shaking sob, Bradley managed to cry out, "Edward!" He raised the gun again. "I'm sorry. I'm sorry," he whimpered. "I'm sorry."

Bradley put the barrel in his mouth. A loud boom filled the office.

Edward's shrieking quieted. Then another voice spoke.

"Drop the weapon! Police! Drop the fucking weapon!"

A team of officers swarmed the chambers, with Packer leading the charge. Officer Kasich entered on the run and slapped Bradley's hand away. The gun dropped, and Kasich kicked it out of reach.

Packer knelt next to Matt and checked his vitals. "Officer down! This man needs help now!"

"And the chief," another officer said.

Packer moved over to the chief's body and performed the same vitals check. He said nothing. It wouldn't take a coroner to see Woodhull had no chance.

"I didn't do it. I didn't do anything!" Bradley demanded. Two officers tackled him on the office floor and handcuffed him. Finally, justice. Not for her or the nightmare of a father she'd had to put up with, but for Edward.

Adriana crawled out from under Bradley's desk with Dylan. Edward's spirit was gone, but the room had filled with officers. Through the splintered office doorway, she saw Maggie and Lois out in the hallway. The two women looked rattled and concerned, but she was thankful they had both questioned Bradley near the end. The reporters had been barricaded back in the lobby entrance by several officers.

She turned Dylan's head away from Woodhull's bloodied body. She hoped it hurt Bradley to see what he'd done to his friend, to his town, to the people he was supposed to protect.

Two officers helped Matt up off the floor. His eyes were hazy, lost in a cold confusion, until he saw Adriana and smiled.

She held Dylan tight to her chest, shielding him from all of it. All this deceit, all this pain, and all this death. He was only a toddler, just as she had been when Edward was so savagely and unfairly killed. As she was escorted out of the room, she squeezed Dylan tighter and said, "Mommy's got you. I've always got you."

She prayed silently that as Dylan grew, his memories would be kinder to him than hers had been.

EPILOGUE

THE DAY BENJAMIN CARD was cleared to be discharged, the OVUC staff audibly cheered. He'd survived the worst of his battle and would enjoy a slow but full recovery.

Adriana was happy for him, of course, and for Deesha, who was by his side the morning they visited. Matt, handsome in his uniform despite the head wound. And Dylan, making sure to show everyone his new crayon set that he took everywhere.

Adriana was also settling into her new understanding of who she was. For too long she'd doubted the souls and spirits who visited her. And she doubted the impulses of her art, the way her pens and pencils would suddenly take over, as if they were connected to some other world. She held the connection. And she controlled the talent. A pen isn't talented without the human hand.

Card reached out to touch Deesha's arm, then turned and eyed Adriana and Matt.

"Thanks," he said. "Both of you. We're very grateful."

"Yes, and I hope you'll consider my offer, Adriana," Deesha added. "I could use someone loyal by my side. It'd be a great job opportunity for you and a huge help to me."

Deesha's first few weeks in office had been overshadowed in the papers. Headlines in the *Courant* covered every step Bradley took through the justice system. He'd confessed to the FBI and was awaiting trial. Adriana wasn't sure if it was the evidence she and Matt had uncovered, or seeing Edward in his office, or just sheer exhaustion. But he would stand trial, finally, for his crimes. After the confession, Edward's remains were recovered from Silver Lake.

Wills's body was discovered in the old Buick on his property. The FBI were confident they could tie the gun back to Bradley. He eventually copped to that, too.

Profiles also chronicled Chief Woodhull's death and his part in the coverup all those years ago. Kasich was promoted to interim chief, delaying his retirement for now, and Matt said he was mostly handling the position well.

"I have been considering your job offer, actually," Adriana said, "and working with the first woman to be elected mayor of Cellar would be a privilege. I accept. Though, it's going to take a lot of work to get this town back to normal."

Deesha started to smile, but her emotions took hold of her, and Adriana could tell she was trying hard not to cry. Deesha had told Adriana that she knew Edward's path to the lake, and each day he didn't return she walked in his steps in search of clues. She combed every inch of the two-lane country road until she found tire skids and a damaged tree. She had a feeling. She knew something had happened there. But she couldn't prove it.

"I still can't believe it's over," she said. "The way you and Eddie connected. And the way you and Matt connected the dots."

"You mean *Detective* Hinkley?"

Matt was still years out from being eligible to make detective, but Adriana had been teasing him ever since the day her father, now *former* mayor of Cellar, was marched out of City Hall in handcuffs by Officer Ty Packer. The video reels replayed on local, state, and even national news for days and now played in her head: emergency vehicle lights, TV cameras and photographers clamoring for a look at the fallen politician.

"Well," Matt mused, "better days ahead, right?"

Deesha could no longer hold back the tears. "I just wish Eddie were here."

Card comforted his wife as Adriana adjusted Dylan in her arms. She looked across the room to the doorway, where Edward stood. He was calm and finally looked at peace. Their eyes met and he smiled.

Then Dylan stopped fussing, smiled, and tried showing his new crayon set to the empty doorway.

ACKNOWLEDGMENTS

Thanks to my partner, Kristen Renee, for her time, patience, and suggestions as she listened to me work through nearly endless plot variations and character decisions.

Thanks to Mike Martin for his early guidance and wisdom, and Nicole Dieker for her early developmental edits. They both helped shape this story and ensured this project started down the right path. Thanks to Douglas Glenn Clark for his story consultations as I worked to finish this project.

Thanks to my family for their continued support of my various projects.

Thanks to Cassandra Dunn for her edits and suggestions along the way.

Thanks to Nancy LaFever for her final edits and for solidifying my voice on the page.

Thanks to Marinda Valenti for her proofreading edits.

Thanks to Christian Caldeira for his support and excitement for this project and so many others over the years.

Thanks to Ute Orgassa, Abigail Murphy, Catherine Lu, Erin Foster, and all other early readers for their time and suggestions.

Finally, thank you, dear reader, for letting my characters and the town of Cellar occupy a small space in your head. Hope you'll visit us again soon!

ABOUT THE AUTHOR

Alan Lastufka lives in Oregon. He writes horror, supernatural, and magical realism stories. His short fiction has been praised by *Writer's Digest*. The screenplay adaptation of his story, "The Fort," was an Official Selection at numerous film festivals.

Face the Night is his first novel.

When he's not writing, Alan enjoys walking through Oregon's beautiful woods with his partner, Kristen.

Connect with Alan Lastufka at alanlastufka.com for more of his work, including bonus materials and short stories.

BY ALAN LASTUFKA

NOVELS

Face the Night

SHORT STORIES

"The Fort"

"Another Small Gift"

CPSIA information can be obtained
at www.ICGtesting.com
Printed in the USA
LVHW091516110322
713250LV00023B/1139/J